THE 13TH REALITY

BOOK 1

THE JOURNAL OF CURIOUS LETTERS

JAMES DASHNER

ILLUSTRATED BY
BRYAN BEUS

ALADDIN

New York London Toronto Sydney

ALADDIN

An imprint of Simon & Schuster Children's Publishing Division

1230 Avenue of the Americas, New York, NY 10020

First Aladdin paperback edition December 2009

Text copyright © 2008 by James Dashner

Illustrations copyright © 2008 by Bryan Beus

Originally published in hardcover in 2008 by Deseret Book Company

All rights reserved, including the right of reproduction in whole or in part in any form.

ALADDIN is a trademark of Simon & Schuster, Inc., and related logo

is a registered trademark of Simon & Schuster, Inc.

For information about special discounts for bulk purchases, please contact

Simon & Schuster Special Sales at 1-866-506-1949 or business@simonandschuster.com.

The Simon & Schuster Speakers Bureau can bring authors to your live event. For more

information or to book an event contact the Simon & Schuster Speakers Bureau at

1-866-248-3049 or visit our website at www.simonspeakers.com.

The text of this book was set in Adobe Garamond.

Manufactured in the United States of America

1209 OFF

2 4 6 8 10 9 7 5 3

Dashner, James, 1972–

The Journal of Curious Letters / James Dashner.

p. cm. — (The 13th Reality ; v. 1)

Summary: Thirteen-year-old Atticus "Tick" Higginbottom begins receiving mysterious letters from around the world signed only "M.G.," and the clues contained therein lead him on a journey to the perilous 13th Reality and a confrontation with evil Mistress Jane.

ISBN 978-1-59038-831-0 (hc)

[1. Space and time—Fiction. 2. Letters—Fiction. 3. Family life—Washington (State)—Fiction. 4. Washington (State)—Fiction. 5. Science fiction.] I. Title.

PZ7.D2587Jou 2008   [Fic]—dc22   2007042579

ISBN 978-1-4169-9152-6 (pbk)

This book is dedicated to my wife, Lynette,

and to our mothers,

Linda Dashner and Patti Anderson.

Thank you for making my life so far

a wonderful thing to have lived.

CONTENTS

CONTENTS

CONTENTS

ACKNOWLEDGMENTS

I used to think this section was major lame. Why on earth, as a reader, would I give a flying tahooty about the people who helped the author? Well, I'm here to tell you that you should be very interested. Because without the awesome people I mention below, this book wouldn't be in your hands.

Before anyone else, I need to thank Chris Schoebinger and Lisa Mangum at Shadow Mountain. Despite being an author, I can't come up with words great enough to express how much they've changed my life. Fabulicious. Astoundendicularly whammy. Terrificaliwondershonks. (See, told ya.) Thank you, Chris and Lisa.

Thanks to my wife, Lynette. Always my first reader,

she's not afraid to tell me when something sounds like a two-year-old blurted it out while sitting on the potty.

Thanks to my sister, Sarah Kiesche, for keeping up my Web site during the Jimmy Fincher books and being my number one fan.

Thanks to my agent, Jenny Rappaport, for her work on my behalf.

Thanks to J. Scott Savage. His keen and almost eerie understanding of how to weave a good story has helped me greatly. And our regular lunches to "talk shop" have been invaluable. I do wish he'd use a little more deodorant, though.

Thanks to Annette Lyon, Heather Moore, Michele Holmes, Lu Ann Staheli, Lynda Keith, and Stephanni Hicken. These crazy ladies all read the manuscript and gave excellent feedback.

A huge thanks to the younger folks, whose advice was perhaps most relevant: Jacob Savage, Alyssa Holmes, and Daniel Lyon.

Thanks to Shirley Bahlmann (and her kids), Danyelle Ferguson, and Anne Bradshaw. Shirley is the only one besides my wife who has helped me with every book I've written.

Thanks to Crystal Hardman, Tony and Rachel Benjamin, Pam Anderton, and Julie Sasagawa. Eating at Jim's Restaurant will never be the same.

Thanks to Peter Jackson for making the *Lord of the Rings* movies.

Thanks to the dude who invented football.

Thanks to the many chickens that provided me with spicy buffalo wings over the years.

And last, but certainly not least, thanks to all the Jimmy Fincher fans. Without your loyal following, Atticus Higginbottom would have never been born.

PART 1
THE FIRE

CHAPTER
1

MASTER GEORGE AND MISTRESS JANE

Norbert Johnson had never met such strange people in all of his life, much less two on the same day—within the same *hour* even. Odd. Very odd indeed.

Norbert, with his scraggly gray hair and his rumpled gray pants and his wrinkly gray shirt, had worked at the post office in Macadamia, Alaska, for twenty-three years, seven months, twelve days, and—he looked at his watch—just a hair short of four hours. In those long, cold, lonesome years he'd met just about every type of human being you could imagine. Nice people and mean people. Ugly people and pretty people. Lawyers, doctors, accountants, cops. Crazies and convicts. Old

3

hags and young whippersnappers. Oh, and lots of celebrities, too.

Why, if you believed his highfalutin stories (which most people quit doing about twenty-three years, seven months, twelve days, and *three* hours ago), you'd think he'd met every movie and music star in America. Though exactly *why* these famous folks were up in Alaska dropping off mail was anybody's guess, so it may have been a slight exaggeration of the truth.

But today's visitors were different, and Norbert knew he'd have to convince the town that this time he was telling the truth and nothing but the truth. Something scary was afoot in Macadamia.

The first stranger, a man, entered the small, cramped post office at precisely 11:15 A.M., quickly shutting the door against the blustery wind and swirling snowflakes. In doing so, he almost dropped a cardboard box full of letters clutched in his white-knuckled hands.

He was a short, anxious-looking person, shuffling his feet and twitching his nose, with a balding red scalp and round spectacles perched on his ruddy, puffy face. He wore a regal black suit: all pinstripes and silk and gold cuff links.

When the man plopped the box of letters onto the post office counter with a loud flump, a cloud of dust billowed out; Norbert coughed for several seconds. Then, to top everything off, the stranger spoke with a heavy English accent like he'd just walked out of a Bill Shakespeare play.

"Good day, sir," he said, the faintest attempt at a smile creasing his face into something that looked like pain. "I do hope you would be so kind as to offer me some assistance in an important matter." He pulled a lace-edged handkerchief from within the dark recesses of his fancy suit and wiped his brow, beads of sweat having formed there despite the arctic temperatures outside. It was, after all, the middle of November.

"Yessir," Norbert answered, ready to fulfill his duty as Postal Worker Number Three. "Mighty glad to help."

The man pointed outside. "Simply dreadful, isn't it?"

Norbert looked through the frosted glass of the front door, but saw only the snow-swept streets and a few pedestrians bundled up and hurrying to get out of the cold. "What's dreadful, sir?"

The man huffed. "By the Wand, man, this place, this *place*!" He put away his hanky and folded his arms, exaggerating a shiver up and down his body. "How can you chaps stand it—the bitter cold, the short daylight, the biting wind?"

Norbert laughed. "I take it you're just a-visiting?"

"Visiting?" The sharply dressed man barked something between a laugh and a snort. "There'll be no vis- iting from me, my good man. The instant these letters are off, I'll be heading back to the ocean. The very *instant*, I assure you."

The ocean? Norbert eyed the man, a little offended by the stranger's dislike of the only town where Norbert had ever set foot. "Well, sir, how long you been here?"

"How long?" The man looked at his golden pocket watch. "How *long*? Approximately seven minutes, I'd say, and that's far too long already. I'm, er, eager to be on my way, if you don't mind." He scratched his flaky red scalp. "Which reminds me—is there a cemetery closer than the one down by the frozen riverside?"

"A cemetery?"

"Yes, yes, a cemetery. You know, where they bury poor chaps with unbeating hearts?" When Norbert only stared, the man sighed. "Oh, never mind."

Norbert remembered hearing the word *befuddled* once on television. He had never been quite sure what it meant, but something told him it explained exactly how he felt at that moment. He scratched his chin, squinting at the odd little man. "Sir, may I ask your name?"

"No, you may not, Mister Postman. But if you must call me something, you may call me Master George."

"Alrighty then," Norbert said, his tone wary. "Uh, Master George, you're a-telling me you just arrived here in Macadamia seven minutes ago?"

"That's right. Please—"

Norbert ignored him. "And you're a-telling me you

come all this way just to mail these here letters, and then you're a-going to up and leave again?"

"Egads, yes!" Master George squeezed his hands together and rocked back and forth on his heels. "That is, if you'd be so kind as to . . ." He motioned to the box of letters, raising his thin eyebrows.

Norbert shook his head. "Well, how'd you get here?"

"By . . . er, plane, if you must know. Now, really, why so many questions?"

"You got yourself your own plane?"

Master George slammed his hand against the counter. "Yes! Is this a post office or a trial by jury? Now, please, I'm in a great hurry!"

Norbert whistled through his teeth, not taking his eyes off Master George as he slid the box closer to him. Then, reluctantly, Norbert looked down, a little worried the stranger might disappear once they broke eye contact.

The box was filled to the rim with hundreds of envelopes, yellowed and crumpled like they'd been trampled by a herd of buffalo, the addresses scrawled across the wrinkly paper in messy blue ink. Each frumpy envelope also bore a unique stamp—some of which looked to be rare and worth serious money: an Amelia Earhart, a Yankee Stadium, a Wright Brothers.

Norbert looked back up at the man. "So, you flew

in your own plane to the middle of Alaska in the middle of November to deliver these letters . . . and then you're heading back home?"

"Yes, and I'll be sure to tell Scotland Yard that if they're in need of a detective to ring you straight away. Now, good sir, is there anything else I have to do? I want to make absolutely sure there will be no problem in the delivery of these letters."

Norbert shrugged, then shuffled through the stack of envelopes, verifying they all had stamps and proper addresses. The letters were destined to go everywhere from Maine to California, from France to South Africa. Japan. China. Mexico. They were headed all over the world. And by the looks of it, the man had estimated the required postage to perfection.

"Well, I'll have to weigh each one and type the location into the computer, but they look all right to me on first glance. You wantin' to stick around while I check them all?"

Master George slipped a fat wallet out of his jacket pocket. "Oh, I assure you the necessary postage is there, but I must be certain. Here." He pulled out several hundred-dollar bills and placed them on the counter. "If you find that additional postage is required, this should be more than sufficient to pay in full. Consider the rest as a tip for your valuable service."

Norbert swallowed the huge lump in his throat.

"Uh, sir, I can tell you right now it won't take nearly that much. Not even close."

"Well, then, I will return home feeling very satisfied indeed." He squinted at Norbert's name tag before tipping his head in a formal bow. "I bid you farewell, Norbert, and wish you the very best."

And with that, Master George slipped back out into the frigid air.

Norbert had a sneaking suspicion he'd never see the man again.

⁓

Norbert had just placed the box of odd letters on a shelf under the front desk when an even stranger character than the finely appareled English gentleman stepped into the quiet post office. When the woman walked in the door, Norbert's mouth dropped open.

She wore nothing but yellow—her floor-length dress, her heavy overcoat, her pointy-toed shoes, her tightly fitted gloves. She pushed back the hood of her coat, revealing a bald head that shone as bright as a chrome ball, a pair of horn-rimmed glasses perched on her steep ridge of a nose, and eyes the color of burning emeralds.

She looked like a lemon that had been turned into an evil sorceress; Norbert surprised himself when he chuckled out loud before she said a word. By the way her

eyes narrowed into green laser points, Norbert figured that wasn't the smartest thing he'd done in a while.

"Something funny, mailman?" she asked, her voice soft and seductive, yet somehow filled with a subtle hint of warning. Unlike Master George, she had no accent Norbert recognized—she could've been from any city in Alaska. Well, except for the fact that she looked like a walking banana.

After a long moment with no response, she continued, "You'll find that Mistress Jane doesn't react kindly to those who mock her."

"Um," Norbert stuttered. "Uh, who . . . who is Mistress Jane?" As soon as he said it, he knew he must sound like an idiot.

"Me, you blubbering fool. Are you daft?"

"No, ma'am, I can hear just fine."

"Not *deaf*, you moronic stack of soiled snow, daft—*daft*. Oh, never mind." She took a step closer, placing her gloved hands on the counter right in front of Norbert. Her eyes seemed to have tracking beams focused on his own, pulling his gaze into a trance. "Now listen to me, mailman, and listen to me well. Understand?"

Norbert tried to utter agreement, but managed only a small squeak. He nodded instead.

"Good." She straightened and folded her arms. "I'm looking for a little stuff-bucket of a man—red-faced, ugly, more annoying than a ravenous mouse in a cheese factory. I know he came here just minutes ago, but I *don't* know if I'm in the correct Reality. Have you seen him?"

Norbert called upon every ounce of willpower in his feeble little body to hold his face still, hiding all expression. He forced his eyes to focus on the Lemon Lady's bald head and to not let them wander to the box of letters on the shelf at his feet. He didn't have a single clue what was going on with these two strangers, but every instinct told him Master George equaled good, Mistress Jane equaled bald—he blinked—uh, *bad*.

What does she mean about being in the correct reality, *anyway?* Norbert marveled that two such interesting people could enter his tiny post office within a half hour of each other.

"Polar bear got your tongue—?" Mistress Jane asked with a sneer, glancing down at his name badge. "Norbie? Anybody in there?"

Norbert ignored his racing heart and simply said, "No."

"No what?" the yellow woman snapped. "No, you're not in there, or no, the man I'm looking for didn't come here?"

"Ma'am, you're my first customer of the day, and no, I've a-never seen any such person as you described in my life."

Mistress Jane frowned, held a finger up to her chin.

"Do you know what Mistress Jane does with liars, Norbie?"

"I'm not a-lying, ma'am," Norbert answered, trying his best to look calm. He didn't like fibbing to such a scary woman—and crossing his fingers under the counter wouldn't amount to a hill of beans if she found out—but somehow he just knew that if this evil lady wanted to stop Master George from doing whatever he was trying to do, then those letters needed to get in the mail, no matter what. And it was all up to Norbert Johnson.

The lady looked away as if lost in deep thought over what she should do next. "I know he's up to something," she whispered, barely audible and not really speaking to Norbert anymore. "But which Reality . . . I don't have time to look in them all . . ."

"Miss Jane?" Norbert asked. "May I—"

"It's *Mistress* Jane, you Alaskan ice head."

"Oh, uh, I'm awfully sorry—I just wanted to know if there's any postal service you'll be a-needing today."

The nasty woman looked at him for a long time, saying nothing. Finally, "If you're lying to me, I'll find out and I'll come back for you, *Norbie*." She reached into the pocket of her overcoat, fidgeting with something hidden and heavy. "And you won't like the consequences, I can promise you that."

"No, ma'am, I'm sure—"

Before he could finish his sentence, though, the last and by far *most* bizarre thing of the day occurred.

Mistress Jane disappeared.

She vanished—into thin air, as they say. *Poof,* like a magic trick. One second there, the next second gone.

Norbert stared at the empty space on the other side of the counter, knowing he needed a much stronger word than *befuddled* to explain how he felt now. Finally, shaking his head, he reached down and grabbed the box containing Master George's letters.

"These are going out *tonight*," he said, though no one was in the room to hear him.

CHAPTER
2

A VERY STRANGE LETTER

Atticus Higginbottom—nicknamed "Tick" since his first day of kindergarten—stood inside the darkness of his own locker, cramped and claustrophobic. He desperately wanted to unlatch the handle and step out, but he knew he had to wait five more minutes. The edict had been decreed by the Big Boss of Jackson Middle School in Deer Park, Washington. And what Billy "The Goat" Cooper commanded must be obeyed; Tick didn't dare do otherwise.

He peeked through the metal slats of the door, annoyed at how they slanted down so he could only see the dirty white tiles of the hallway. The bell ending the school day had rung ages ago and Tick knew that by now most of the students would be outside, waiting for their buses or already walking home. A few stragglers still roamed the hallways, though, and one of them stopped in front of Tick's jail cell, snickering.

"Hope you get out before suppertime, Icky Ticky Stinkbottom," the boy said. Then he kicked the locker, sending a terrible *bang* of rattled metal echoing through Tick's ears. "The Goat sent me to make sure you hadn't escaped yet—good thing you're still in there. I can see your beady little eyes." Another kick. "You're not *crying* are you? Careful, you might get snot on your Barf Scarf."

Tick squeezed his eyes shut, steeled himself to ignore the idiot. Eventually, the bullies always moved on if he just stayed silent. Talking back, on the other hand . . .

The boy laughed again, then walked away.

In fact, Tick was *not* crying and hadn't done so in a long time. Once he'd learned to accept his fate in life as the kid everyone liked to pick on, his life had become a whole lot easier. Although Tick's attitude seemed to annoy Billy to no end. *Maybe I should fake a cry next time,* Tick thought. *Make the Goat feel like a big bad king.*

When the hall had grown completely still and silent, Tick reached down and flicked the latch of the door. It swung open with a loud *pop* and slammed against the locker next to it. Tick stepped out and stretched his cramped legs and arms. He couldn't have cared less about Billy and his gang of dumb bullies right then— it was Friday, his mom and dad had bought him the latest gaming system for his thirteenth birthday, and the Thanksgiving holidays were just around the corner. He felt perfectly happy.

Glancing around to make sure no one had hung around to torture him some more, Tick adjusted the red-and-black striped scarf he always wore to hide the hideous purple blotch on his neck—an irregular, rusty-looking birthmark the size of a drink coaster. It was the one thing he hated most about his body, and no matter how much his parents tried to convince him to lose the scarf, he wore it every hour of every day—even in the summer, sweat soaking through in dark blotches. Now, with winter settling in with a vengeance, people had quit giving him strange looks about the security blanket wrapped around his neck. Well, except for the jerks who called it the Barf Scarf.

He set out down the hall, heading for the door clos-est to the street that led to his house; he lived within walking distance of the school, which was lucky for him because the buses were long gone. He rounded the corner and saw Mr. Chu, his science teacher, step out of the teacher's lounge, briefcase in hand.

"Well, if it isn't Mr. Higginbottom," the lanky man said, a huge smile on his face. "What are you still doing around here? Anxious for more homework?" His straight black hair fell almost to his shoulders. Tick knew his mom would say Mr. Chu needed a haircut, but Tick thought he looked cool.

Tick gave a quick laugh. "No, I think you gave us plenty—I'll be lucky to get half of it done by Monday."

"Hmmm," Mr. Chu replied. He reached out and swatted Tick on the back. "If I know you, it was done by the end of lunchtime today."

Tick swallowed, for some reason embarrassed to admit his teacher was exactly right. *So, I'm a nerd,* he thought. *One day it'll make me filthy dirty rotten rich.* Tick was grateful that at least he didn't really look the part of a brainy nerd. His brown hair wasn't greasy; he didn't wear glasses; he had a solid build. His only real blemish was the birthmark. And maybe the fact that he was as clumsy as a one-legged drunk. But, as his dad always said, he was no different from any other kid his age and would grow out of the clumsiness in a few years.

Whatever the reason, Tick just didn't get along with people his own age. He found it hard to talk to them, much less be friends. Though he did *want* friends. Badly. *Poor little me,* he thought.

"I'll take your lack of a smart-aleck response—and the fact you aren't holding any books—as proof I'm right," Mr. Chu said. "You're too smart for the seventh grade, Tick. We should really bump you up."

"Yeah, so I can get picked on even *more*? No, thanks."

Mr. Chu's face melted into a frown. He looked at the floor. "I hate what those kids do to you. If I could . . ."

"I know, Mr. Chu. You'd beat 'em up if it weren't for those pesky lawsuits." Tick felt relieved when a smile returned to his teacher's face.

"That's right, Tick. I'd put every one of those slackers in the hospital if I could get away with it. Bunch of no-good louses—that's what they are. In fifteen years, they'll all be calling you *boss*. Remember that, okay?"

"Yes, sir."

"Good. Why don't you run on home, then. I bet your mom's got some cookies in the oven. See you Monday."

"Okay. See ya, Mr. Chu." Tick waved, then hurried down the hall toward home.

He only tripped and fell once.

"I'm home!" Tick yelled as he shut the front door. His four-year-old sister, Kayla, was playing with her tea set in the front room, her curly blonde hair bouncing with every move. She sat right next to the piano, where their older sister Lisa banged out some horrific song that she'd surely blame on the piano being out of tune. Tick dropped his backpack on the floor and hung his coat on the wooden rack next to the door.

"What's up, Tiger?" his mom said as she shuffled into the hallway, pushing a string of brown hair behind her ear. The cheeks of her thin face were red from her efforts in the kitchen, small beads of sweat hanging on for dear life along her forehead. Lorena Higginbottom loved—absolutely *loved*—to cook and everyone in Deer Park knew it. "I just put some cookies in the oven."

Righto, Mr. Chu.

"Mom," Tick said, "people stopped calling each other 'Tiger' a long time before I was born. Why don't you just call me 'Tick'? Everyone else does."

His mom let out an exaggerated sigh. "That's the worst nickname I've ever heard. Do you even know what a tick *does*?"

"Yeah, it sucks your blood right before you squish it dead." Tick pressed his thumb against his pant leg, twisting it with a vicious scowl on his face. Kayla looked up from her tea set, giggling.

"Lovely," Mom said. "And you have no problem being named after such a creature?"

Tick shrugged. "Anything's better than Atticus. I'd rather be called . . . *Wilbur* than Atticus."

His mom laughed, even though he could tell she tried not to.

"When's Dad gonna be home?" Tick asked.

"The usual, I'd guess," Mom replied. "Why?"

"He owes me a rematch in Football 3000."

Mom threw her arms up in mock desperation. "Oh, well, in that case, I'll call and tell him it's an emergency and to get his tail right home."

Lisa stopped playing her music, much to Tick's relief, and, he suspected, to the relief of every ear within a quarter mile. She turned around on the piano bench to look at Tick, her perfect teeth shining in an evil grin. Wavy brown hair framed a slightly pudgy face, like she'd never quite escaped her baby fat. "Dad whipped you by five touchdowns last time," she said sweetly, folding her arms. "Why don't you give up, already?"

"Will do, once you give up beating that poor piano with a hatchet every day. Sounds like an armless gorilla is playing in there."

Instead of responding, Lisa stood up from the piano bench and walked over to Tick. She leaned forward and gave him a big kiss on the cheek. "I wuv you, wittle brother."

"I think I'm gonna be sick, Mom," Tick groaned, wiping his cheek. "Could you get me something to clean my face?"

Lisa folded her arms and shook her head, her eyes

set in a disapproving stare. "And to think I used to change your diaper."

Tick barked a fake laugh. "Uh, sis, you're two years older than me—pretty sure you never changed my diaper."

"I was very advanced for my age. Skilled beyond my years."

"Yeah, you're a regular Mozart—well, except for the whole music thing."

Mom put her hands on her hips. "You two are just about the silliest kids I've ever—" A loud buzz from the kitchen cut her off. "Ah, the cookies are done." She turned and scuttled off toward the kitchen.

Kayla screamed something unintelligible, then ran after her mom with a huge smile planted on her face, dropping tea cups all over the floor and hallway.

Tick looked at Lisa and shrugged. "At least she's not burning things." Kayla had been caught several times at the living room fireplace, laughing with glee as she destroyed important objects in the flames. Tick headed for the staircase. "I'll be back in a minute—gotta use the bathroom."

"Thanks for sharing *that* bit of exciting news," Lisa quipped as she followed Kayla toward the kitchen.

Tick had his hand on the banister when his mom called back for him. "Oh, I almost forgot. You got a letter in the mail today. It's on your bed."

"Ooh, maybe it's a *love* letter," Lisa said, blowing a kiss at Tick.

Tick ignored her and ran up the stairs.

⸺⸺⸺

The bed squeaked as Tick flopped down next to his pillow where a tattered yellow envelope rested, his full name—Atticus Higginbottom—and address scrawled across it in messy handwriting. The stamp was an old picture of the Eiffel Tower but the postmark smeared on top of it said, "Macadamia, Alaska." The upper left corner of the envelope had no return address. He picked up the envelope and flipped it over—nothing there either. Curious, he stared at the mysterious letter for a moment, racking his brain. Who could possibly have written him from the state of Alaska? No one came to mind.

He wedged his finger under the sealed flap on the back and ripped the envelope open. A simple rectangle of white cardstock that barely fit in the envelope held a long message on one side, typed by what appeared to be an old-fashioned typewriter. Baffled, Tick pulled the card out and began to read.

Dear Master Atticus,

    I am writing to you in hopes that you will have the courage of heart

23

and the strength of mind to help
me in a most dreadful time of need.
Things are literally splitting apart
at the seams, as it were, and I must
find those who can assist me in some
very serious matters.

Beginning today (the fifteenth of
November), I am sending out a sequence
of special messages and clues that
will lead you to an important,
albeit dangerous, destiny if you so
choose. No, dangerous may not be a
strong enough word. Indubitably and
despicably deadly—yes, that's better.

I will say nothing further. Oh,
except several more things. If ever
you want the madness to stop, you need
only to burn this letter. I'll know
when you do and shall immediately
cease and desist.

However, if this letter remains
intact for one week after you receive
it, I will know you have chosen to
help me, and you will begin receiving
the Twelve Clues.

Know this before you decide, my
friend: Many, many lives are at stake.

Many. And they depend entirely on
this choice that you must make. Will
you have the courage to choose the
difficult path?

Do be careful. Because of this
letter, very frightening things are
coming your way.

Most faithfully yours,
M.G.

P.S. I recognize that, like most
young people, you probably love
sweetened milk and peppermint sticks.
Unfortunately, I have neither the time
nor practical means to send you any
as a welcoming gift. Please do not
think me unkind. Good day.

Tick stared at the letter for ten minutes, reading
it over and over, wondering who could've played such
a trick. His sister Lisa? No—he couldn't see her using
words like "despicably" and "indubitably." His mom
or dad? Certainly not. What would be the point? Tick
had no true friends to speak of, so the only other option
was that it was a trick from the bullies at school. But
again, such an idea made no sense. Plus, how would

anyone he knew manage to get an Alaskan postmark on the envelope?

His dad did have an old aunt who lived up there somewhere, but Tick had never even met the lady as far as he could remember, and doubted she even knew he existed. Plus, Tick didn't think her initials were M.G.

A knock at the door snapped his attention away—his mom wondering why he hadn't come down for cookies. Tick mumbled something about not feeling well, which was far truer than he liked to admit.

It couldn't be for real. It had to be a scam or a joke. It *had* to be.

And yet, as the purple and orange glow of twilight faded into black darkness, Tick still lay on his bed, contemplating the letter, ignoring his growing hunger. He felt hypnotized by M.G.'s message. Eventually, no closer to understanding or believing, he fell asleep to the soft hum of the central heating.

But in his dreams, he kept seeing the same words over and over, like a buzzing neon sign on a haunted hotel:

Very frightening things are coming your way.

CHAPTER
3

A KID'S WORST NIGHTMARE

Tick woke up to the wonderful sound and smell of sizzling bacon, coupled with the uncomfortable sensation of sliding down a mountain. By the time he shook his head and burned the cobwebs of sleep away, he realized his dad had taken a seat on the edge of the bed, making the mattress lean considerably in that direction.

Tick tried not to smile. Edgar Higginbottom was a tad on the heavy side. Certainly with his pale skin, scraggly hair, and a nose the size of Rhode Island, he didn't qualify as the most handsome man on the planet, but whatever the big guy lacked in looks, he more than made up for in kindness and humor. Tick thought his dad was the coolest person on the planet.

"Morning, Professor," Dad said in his gravelly voice. Everyone in the family joked that Tick might be the smartest one living in the house, so his dad had taken to calling him *Professor* a long time ago. "Gee, I came home last night all ready to take you down in Football 3000 again, but you're up here dead to the world. I even brought a movie home for us to watch. You sick?"

"No, I just didn't feel that great last night." Tick rolled over, slyly pushing the envelope and mysterious letter farther under his pillow. Luckily, his dad hadn't seen it. Tick didn't know what he was going to do when his mom asked about it. In the brightness of the morning, it almost felt like the letter had been a dream or a prank after all, though he couldn't wait to read it again.

"Well, you look like three days of rough road if you want to know the truth," his dad said. "You sure you're okay?"

"Yeah, I'm fine. What time is it?"

"Ten-thirty."

Tick sat up in bed. "Serious?" He couldn't remember the last time he'd slept in so long. "It's really ten-thirty?"

"No."

"Oh." Tick fell back on the bed.

"It's ten-thirty-*six*," Dad said with his patented wink.

Tick groaned and pressed his hands over his eyes. It didn't seem like it should be a big deal, but for some reason it bothered him that the letter from Alaska had drained his brain so much that he'd slept for more than twelve hours.

"Son, what on earth is wrong with you?" Dad put his hand on Tick's shoulder and squeezed. "I'm pretty close to calling the Feds and telling them an alien's kidnapped my son and replaced him with a half-baked clone."

"Dad, you watch way too many sci-fi movies. I'm fine, I promise."

"It's been at least seven years since I've seen a movie without *you*, big guy."

"Good point." Tick looked over at his window, where a fresh batch of snow curtained the bottom edges. The sight made him shiver.

Dad stood and held out a hand. "Come on, it's not too late for breakfast. Mom made her famous puffed-oven-pancakes. Let's get down there before Kayla tries to throw them in the fireplace again."

Tick nodded and let his dad help him up, then followed him out of the room, the whole time thinking about the letter and wanting desperately to tell someone about it.

Not yet, he thought. *They might think I'm crazy.*

"So what was that letter all about?" his mom asked. The whole family sat at the kitchen table, little Kayla next to Tick, her hands already sticky after only one bite.

Tick's hand froze halfway on its journey to put the first chunk of puffy pancake, dripping with hot syrup, into his hungry mouth. He'd hoped his mom had somehow forgotten about the mystery letter; he'd failed to come up with a plan on what to say.

"Oh, it's nothing," he said, then stalled for time by popping the bite into his mouth and chewing. He lifted his glass of cold milk and took a long drink, his mind spinning for an answer. "You know that Pen Pal Web site I subscribed to a while back?"

"Oh, yeah!" Mom replied, lowering her own fork. "You never told us how that went—did you finally find someone?" The Pen Pal site took a bunch of data from kids all around the world and then matched them up as writing buddies with others kids their same age and with the same interests. A parent had to approve it, of course, and Tick's mom had done just that, giving the company all kinds of information and filling out a million forms. Maybe it wasn't too far of a stretch to think one of the pen pals might want to send a letter via regular mail instead of e-mail. It was Tick's only chance.

"Maybe," Tick mumbled through another huge bite. He stared at his plate, hoping she'd move on to grill one of his sisters about something else. She didn't.

"All the way from Alaska," she continued. "Is it a boy or a girl?"

"Uh . . . I don't know actually. Whoever it was just signed it M.G."

"Alaska, huh?" Dad said. "Hey, maybe your pen pal knows old Aunt Mabel up in Anchorage. Wouldn't that be something?"

"I highly doubt it," Mom answered. "That woman probably hasn't set foot out of her house in ten years."

Dad gave her a disapproving stare.

Lisa chimed in, her plate already empty. "Tick, how can you *not* know who it is? Didn't you have to give them your address?"

"We told you not to do that unless we checked it out first," Dad said, his brow creased in concern. "You know what the world's like these days. Is this from someone we've already approved?"

Tick suddenly lost every ounce of his appetite. "I don't know, Dad—yeah, I think so. It didn't say much. It was kind of dumb, actually." He wanted to tell them the truth, but something about the letter made him nervous, and he bit his tongue instead.

He forced the rest of his pancake down, anxiously waiting to see where the conversation went. For several moments the only sounds were the soft clanks of silverware against plates, drinks being put back on the table,

Kayla babbling about her favorite cartoon. Finally, his dad mentioned the big game between the Huskies and the Trojans, opening up the morning paper to read about it.

Relief washed through Tick. When he stood to take his dishes to the sink, his mom put her hand on his arm.

"Would you mind taking Kayla out to play in the snow? She's been asking for it all morning."

"Uh . . . sure," Tick replied, smiling at his sister even though his thoughts were a million miles away. "Come on, kid."

Late that night, after watching the movie Dad had brought home—a creepy sci-fi flick where the hero had to travel between dimensions to fight different versions of the same monster—Tick lay on his bed, alone, reading the letter once again. Night had fallen hours earlier and the darkness seemed to creep through the frosted window, devouring the faint light coming from his small bedside lamp. Everything lay in shadow, and Tick's mind ran wild imagining all the spooky things that could be hiding in the darkness.

Why are you even doing this? he asked himself. *This whole thing has to be a joke.*

But he couldn't stop himself. He read through the

words for the hundredth time. The same ones jumped out at him without fail.

> *Dreadful time of need.*
> *Indubitably and despicably deadly.*
> *Very frightening things are coming.*
> *Lives are at stake.*
> *Courage to choose the difficult path.*

Who would send him such a—

A noise from the other side of the room cut him out of his thoughts. He leaned on his elbow to look, a quick shiver running down his spine. It had sounded like the clank of metal against wood, followed by a quick burst of *whirring*—almost like the hum of a computer fan, but sharper, stronger—and it had only lasted a second or two before stopping.

What in the world . . .

He stared at the dark shadow that arrowed across the floor between his dresser and the closet. He reached for his lamp to point it at the spot, but froze when he heard the noise again—the same mechanical whirr, but this time followed by a series of soft thumps that pattered along the carpet toward him. He looked down from the lamp too late to see anything. Tick froze. It sounded like a small animal had just run across the room and under his bed.

Tick pulled his legs to his body with both arms, holding himself in a ball, squeezing. *What was it? A squirrel? A rat? What had that weird sound been?*

He closed his eyes, knowing he was acting like the biggest baby on the planet but not caring. Every kid's nightmare had just come true for him. Some . . . *thing* was under his bed. Probably something hideous. Something crouching, ready to spring at him as soon as he got the nerve to peek.

He waited, scared to open his eyes. Straining his ears, he heard nothing. A minute went by, then two. He hoped an ounce of courage would magically well up inside him from somewhere, but no such luck. He was thoroughly and completely creeped out.

A sudden image from an old movie popped in his head: a horrible, monstrous gremlin eating through the bottom of his bed, straight through to the mattress, biting and chewing and snarling. It was all Tick needed.

Moving faster than he'd thought possible, Tick jumped off the bed and sprinted for the door, ripping it open even as he heard the sound of small feet scampering across the carpet behind him. He bolted out of his room and quickly closed the door.

Something slammed into it from the other side with a loud clunk.

CHAPTER
4

EDGAR THE BRAVE

Five minutes later, Tick's dad stood next to him in front of the closed door to his room, robed and slippered, flashlight in hand. "Are you sure?" he asked, his voice still deep and rough from having woken up. "Did you see it?"

"No, but I heard it loud and clear." Tick shuddered at the memory.

"Was it a rat?"

"I don't know. It . . . It sounded like a machine or something." Tick winced, sure his dad would finally send him to an insane asylum—first his bizarre behavior at breakfast that morning, now this.

"A *machine*? Tick, what book were you reading

before you went to bed? Stephen King or something?"

"No."

"Was it the movie we watched?"

"No, Dad. I promise I didn't imagine it. The thing had to have been huge—more like a . . . a dog or something." Tick felt stupid and resolved to quit babbling.

"Well, I guess opening the door is all there is to it, then."

Tick looked up at his dad, whose face wore a scared, tense expression, and felt oddly relieved that his old man was just as spooked as he was. "Let's do it, Dad."

Dad smiled, flicking on the flashlight. The hallway light was on as well, but Tick thought you could never have too much light when searching for mechanical demons that ate through the bottom of a bed before gobbling up the child who slept on it.

Several seconds passed, the two of them staring down at the brass doorknob.

"Well?" Tick asked.

"Oh . . . yeah." Somewhat sheepish, Dad reached forward and twisted the handle, pushed, then pulled his hand back like he expected a troll to jump out and bite it off.

As the door swung open with a long, groaning creak that echoed through the house, a wave of light from the hallway spread over the carpet like a rising tide. Tick tensed, sure the strange something would dart at them the second it had a chance, scuttling across the floor like a possessed badger. But he saw nothing unusual.

Dad reached around the edge of the doorframe and turned on the bedroom light. In an instant, every last shadow in the room disappeared, bringing a completely different feel to everything.

Tick felt his fear go down a notch. Just a notch. "Maybe it went under the bed again."

Letting out a big sigh, Dad walked over and knelt down next to the bed, where a heavy quilt draped nearly to the floor, hiding the space underneath. "Listen, Tick, I'm not gonna lie to you—you've got me just as freaked out as you."

"Really?"

"Let's just say if something runs out at me, I'm going to scream like a little girl and run to your mom."

Tick laughed. "Me, too."

Dad quickly pulled up the quilt and beamed the flashlight under the bed, sweeping it back and forth like a sword of sunshine. Nothing but a few random books scattered across the dusty carpet. "Not under there," he said with relief. He leaned against the bed to push himself to his feet—no small effort for a man the size of Edgar Higginbottom.

"The closet?" Tick said, licking his dry lips.

"Yeah, the closet. Where every monster that's ever eaten a child dwells. Just great."

They edged across the room, which now seemed as wide as the Sahara Desert. Tick noticed his dad tiptoe-ing, which for some reason made him laugh, though it came out sounding like a panicked hyena cornered by three starving lions.

"What?" Dad asked, settling back down onto his heels.

"Nothing. Go for it." Tick gestured to the closet door, which stood ajar a couple of inches.

Dad reached out and flung it open, then took a quick step back. Nothing moved in the cluttered pile of dirty clothes, sports balls, Frisbees, and other junk. There didn't seem to be enough space for a mechanical dog-sized monster to hide.

Tick stepped forward and nudged a pile of clothes with his foot. No response. They spent the next ten minutes searching the room from top to bottom, their initial fear having almost completely melted away, but found nothing.

"It has to be here somewhere, Dad. I'm telling you, there's no way I imagined that thing. It scared me half to death."

"Don't worry, son, I believe you. But sometimes we wake from dreams and they seem very . . . *real*. You know?"

Tick wanted to argue, but he was smart enough to consider the possibility, even though it kind of made him want to kick his dad in the shins for suggesting it. Tick *had* been on the bed for a long time—maybe he'd fallen asleep without realizing it. But then the thing that clunked against the door . . . ?

No, he was convinced it'd been real. But why worry his poor dad any longer? He nodded. "Yeah, maybe."

"Come on," Dad said, flicking off the flashlight and putting his arm around Tick's shoulders. "You can sleep on the little couch in our bedroom. It'll be like old times when the branch outside your window used to give you the heebie-jeebies on a windy night. It's been years since we've had a sleepover."

Tick felt dumb and embarrassed, but he didn't hesitate, grabbing his pillow and blanket before following his dad out of the room. In the hallway, they shared a glance, then Dad shut Tick's bedroom door, pulling on the knob until they both heard the comforting click of the latch taking hold.

CHAPTER
5

A MOST UNWELCOME
PATCH OF SMOKE

The next Saturday afternoon, still in the bliss of Thanksgiving vacation and full from leftover turkey sandwiches, Tick sat in the front room, staring out the window at the falling snow. His family lived in a heavily wooded area and the east side of the state of Washington made for lots of snow in the wintertime. Many people in town grumbled about it, but Tick never did.

He loved the cold, he loved the snow, and he loved what came with it—Thanksgiving, then Christmas vacation, then the football play-offs, then the annual Jackson County Chess Tournament—where he'd won his age bracket three straight years. But even more than any of that, Tick loved the look of the cold white powder resting in soft clumps on the dozens of evergreen trees outside his house.

He heard a rumble coming down the street and saw the mailman's truck slugging through the thick snow with chained tires. Tick watched as it pulled up to their mailbox; he saw the mailman reach out and put a stack of letters inside. A flash of yellow in the bunch made Tick's heart jump-start to super speed. He leaned forward for a better view but it was too late. The truck lumbered away, sending twin sprays of snow shooting out behind the tires.

Tick jumped up from the couch and ran to the front door, where he quickly put on his coat and snow boots. The rest of his family seemed busy with their own thing so no one noticed his nervous reaction to seeing the golden piece of mail.

It had been a full week since receiving the letter from Alaska, and he'd thought seriously of burning it every single day. He knew the weird thing in his closet had to be related to the "very frightening things" he'd been warned about. It seemed so simple to throw the letter into the fire to make sure nothing else happened.

But the part of Tick that loved chess and brainteasers and science desperately wanted to see what the "Twelve Clues" were all about, so he hadn't burned the letter and the week had dragged on worse than the one right before Christmas.

And now, it looked like his choice *not* to burn the letter may have paid off.

He trudged his way through the few inches of snow to the mailbox. His dad had cleared everything with the blower earlier that morning, grumbling about how early winter had set in this year, but now Tick could barely tell he'd done anything at all. The storm was one of those that just kept on coming. The world lay bathed in white, a wintry wonderland that Tick knew would put even the scroogiest Scrooge in the holiday spirit.

He reached the brick mailbox and opened it up, pulling out the stack left moments earlier. He shuffled through the stack, taking each piece off the top and placing it on the bottom—a JC Penney catalog; power bill; an early Christmas card from Aunt Liz; junk mail; junk mail; junk mail.

And then there it was, the envelope, crinkled and golden, with Tick's name and address written messily in blue ink across the front; no return address; the stamp an exotic temple perched high on a mountain. As promised, his next message had arrived.

And this time it was postmarked from Kitami, Japan.

Tick couldn't believe his luck—no one had to know about this second letter. Something inside of him still itched to tell his parents, but he couldn't bring himself to do it. Not until he knew more, *understood* more. Not until he'd figured out the puzzle. With a crazy mix of excitement and panic, he locked the door to his room and sat on the bed, the yellow envelope in his sweaty hands.

He paused, considering the creepy thing from his closet one last time. He could still stop, burn both letters, and never look back.

Yeah, right.

Tick tore open the letter. He pulled out a single piece of the same white cardstock that had been used the first time, though this time it was only about half the size of the first one. As before, one side was blank while the other contained a typed message:

Mark your calendar. One week from the day before the day after the yesterday that comes three weeks before six months from six weeks from now minus forty-nine days plus five tomorrows and a next week, it will happen. A day that could very well change the course of your life as you know it.

I must say, I hope to see you there.

Scribbled directly below the last line were the initials "M.G." and a note that said "This is clue 1 of 12."

Tick sat back against the wall, his head swimming in confusion and awe.

He no longer doubted the messages represented a very serious matter—clues to something extremely important. He was sure the phrase in the first letter that said many lives were at stake wasn't a joke and it scared him. No matter the source, Tick knew he had to get to the bottom of it.

And he felt an overwhelming itch to figure out the first clue. He looked over at his calendar and started running through the words of the message, trying to mentally pinpoint the special day it referred to, but his mind kept spinning in too many directions for him to think straight. *Let's see . . . one week from today . . . six weeks before . . . six months . . . minus forty-nine days . . . ARGH!*

Shaking his head, Tick grabbed the first letter from M.G., folded it up with the second, then stuffed them both into the back pocket of his jeans and ran downstairs. It was time to get serious. First things first.

"Mom, I'm running over to the library!" he yelled as he quickly put on his coat and gloves. He was out the door before she could respond.

By the time Tick left his neighborhood, the snow had let up, the air around him brightening as the sun fought its way through the thinning clouds.

Deer Park was a small town and since the city center was only a couple of miles from Tick's house, he walked there all the time. And, being a bookworm and study bug, the library often ended up as Tick's destination of choice. Especially when he wanted to use the Internet. His family had it at home, but it wasn't as fast as at the library, and Kayla always seemed to want to play her Winnie the Pooh game the second he sat down at the computer, bugging him until he gave in.

He crossed over the town square where, during the summer, a huge fountain usually sprayed. Now the square lay as a flat expanse of whiteness, countless footsteps in the snow crisscrossing it as people bustled around the town.

The library was one of the oldest buildings around, a gray bundle of granite built decades ago. To get there, Tick always took a shortcut between the fire station and the drugstore, a thin alley the width of his shoulders. The stone walls that towered over him as he walked along the alley made him think of old medieval castles.

He had almost reached the end of the alley when a quick breeze whipped past his left ear, followed by an eerie, haunting moan that rose up behind him like the last call of a lonely ghost before heading back to its grave. Tick spun around, stumbling backward when he saw what was there.

A swirling, rippling cloud of gray smoke floated in the alley, surging and receding, billowing out then shrinking back again every two or three seconds. Like it was . . . *breathing*.

And then the smoke turned into a face.

The wispy smoke coalesced and hardened, forming into unmistakable facial features. Dark eyes under bushy gray eyebrows. A crooked nose with black, gaping holes for nostrils. Thin lips pulled back into a wicked grin, exposing an abyss of a mouth with no teeth. Wild, unkempt hair and beard.

Tick willed himself to move, but he could only stare in amazement at the impossible thing floating in front of him.

The moaning sound returned—a deep, low groan filled with grief and pain. It came from every direction, amplified by the narrow stone walls, growing louder and creepier. Tick felt goose bumps break out all over him, chills washing across his skin in waves.

"What . . . who are you?" he asked, amazed that he had found the courage to speak.

Instead of answering, the smoky face groaned louder, its eyes flaring wider.

Then it lunged toward Tick, who turned and ran for his life.

CHAPTER 6

THE LADY IN THE TREES

Tick shot out of the alley at a full run and slammed into a man walking past, both of them tumbling to the ground in a chaotic jumble of arms and legs.

"I'm sorry, I'm sorry!" Tick yelled, helping the man to his feet as he looked back at the alley, expecting the smoky apparition to appear. But nothing came out and the creepy sound had stopped completely.

"It's okay," the man replied as he brushed himself off. "What's the rush?"

Tick finally focused on the man he'd tackled and saw it was Mr. Wilkinson, the school custodian. "Oh, just going to the library. Sorry." Tick took three hesitant steps so he could see clearly down the alley. It was empty, no sign of a spooky ghost-face anywhere. "Well, gotta run. Don't want to waste any study time!"

Not waiting for an answer, Tick took off for the old library building, wondering if somehow Mr. Wilkinson had saved him from a terrible fate.

Five minutes later, Tick stood doubled over in the lobby of the library, hands on his knees, gasping like each breath might be his last. Even though the thing in the alley had disappeared and not chased him, Tick had run as hard as he could until he was safe inside the musty-smelling entryway of the old building.

Maybe I am *imagining things,* he thought. *There's no way I just saw what I think I saw.*

The librarian behind the desk gave him an evil stare as Tick caught his breath. If he'd been in a better mood he would've laughed at how she fulfilled every cliché in the book: hair up in a bun; glasses perched on the tip of her nose with a linked chain drooped around her neck; beady eyes that told small children they'd never reach adulthood if they didn't read thirty books a day. This librarian must be new; the rest of the staff knew him like a mother knew her own kids.

He spotted Ms. Sears over by the non-fiction section and quickly walked toward the computers, trying to avoid her; the last thing he needed right now was some nice chitchat about the weather.

She saw him anyway.

"Hi there, Tick," she called out to him, her beaming smile managing to calm his nerves a bit. Ms. Sears had gray, tightly curled hair that looked like a cleaning pad permanently glued atop her freckled head. "What are you up to today? Here to study up on your chess strategy? Or maybe look for a pen pal?"

Tick shook his head, trying to dislodge the heavy feeling that clung to his bones like an oily sludge. "Nah, I just wanted to poke around on the Internet. Got a little boring over at my house."

"Your dad didn't break out the karaoke set again, did he? If so, I hope all your windows were closed." She gave him a wink.

"No, I think he finally figured out he sounds like a wounded goat when he sings." He knew his voice sounded tight and he hoped Ms. Sears didn't notice. So many questions bounced around inside his head he felt like he'd need surgery to relieve the swelling.

"Oh, Tick, you better hope I don't tell your father you just said that," she replied. "By the way, I hear you're no match for him in that silly football video game."

Tick forced a laugh. "How in the world did you know that?"

"Small town, kiddo. Small town."

"Yeah . . . guess so." An awkward silence followed, and he shrugged his shoulders. "Well, I better get to a computer."

"Have fun. Let me know if you need any help." She turned and pushed her book cart down another aisle.

Relieved, Tick jogged to the long row of computer desks and found an empty one, glad to sit down and rest. As he pulled out his library card, he nervously glanced around, though he had no idea what he was looking for. *Getting a little paranoid, aren't you?* he chided himself. *There has to be a perfectly reasonable explanation for all of this. Something.*

He slid the card into the electronic reader, then typed his password when the prompt appeared on the screen. A few seconds later a window opened for him, connecting him to the Internet. Peeking around the library stacks like a top-level CIA agent searching for spies, Tick pulled out the two mystery letters and unfolded them, pressing them flat on the desk next to the keyboard.

He read through them both again, even though he already knew the first thing he wanted to try on the Internet search engine. He hoped other people had received similar letters and were talking about them in blogs or message boards. Holding his breath, wishing like crazy he'd find something useful, Tick typed "M.G." and clicked SEARCH. An instant later, the computer screen told him how many hits: 2,333,117.

Great.

Web sites about MG Cars, Madagascar, Magnesium, MG Financial Group were listed, but nothing that gave any kind of hint about who had sent the two letters. He tried other phrases: "frightening things"; "despicably deadly"; "forty-nine days plus five tomorrows."

Nothing useful popped up.

Discouraged, he sat back and stared at the screen. He'd been afraid to admit how much he really wanted there to be others like him. He didn't want to be alone in this crazy stuff. The first letter had been addressed to "Dear Master Atticus," but the wording of the message made Tick think more than one letter had been sent out, a plea for help from anyone willing to give it.

Well, maybe he'd have to be the first one to put some clues out there for other people to find.

Rejuvenated by the thought, he typed in the address for the Pen Pal site, then logged into his own section and personal profile. He briefly described the situation, listed some of the key phrases from both letters, then asked if anyone out there had received something similar. He clicked SUBMIT and sat back in the chair again, folding his arms. Hopefully, if anyone else in the world searched for the same things as he'd just done, they would somehow get linked up with his Pen Pal information and e-mail him.

It was a start.

The snow had started up again, big fluffy flakes swirling in the wind. Tick pulled his red-and-black scarf up around his ears and mouth as he left the library and headed for home. He walked in the opposite direction from where he'd come earlier, perfectly willing to take the long way around in order to avoid the haunted alleyway. He shivered, not sure if it was from the cold weather or the memory of the spooky smoke-ghost.

He walked all the way around the downtown area, doing his best to stay in the most public of places. The sky had melted into a dull gray, flakes of white dancing around him like a shaken snow globe. *Maybe that's where I am,* he thought. *I've been sucked from the real world and placed in some alien's giant coffee table knick-knack.*

A shot of relief splashed through his nerves when he finally made it to the small section of forest that lined the road to his neighborhood. All he wanted was to go home and warm up, maybe play his dad in Football 3000 . . .

From the corner of his eye, Tick saw something move in the trees just to the left of the road. Something huge, like a moose or a bear. He turned and looked more intently, curious. Though he lived in a small town, big animals rarely ventured into the woods this close to his neighborhood. Just a few feet away from him, a shadow loomed behind a thick tree frosted with snow, its owner obviously trying to hide from him. *Animals don't hide,* Tick thought, warning alarms clanging in his mind as he readied himself to run.

But then the thing stepped out from behind the tree and Tick's feet froze to the ground.

Despite its enormous size and odd appearance, it wasn't an "it" at all.

It was a person. A lady.

And she was eight feet tall.

CHAPTER
7

MOTHBALL

The sight of a giant, skinny woman coming out of the forest didn't help Tick's anxiety much after his experiences with the freaky thing in his bedroom and the ghost-face in the alley. He yelped and started to run down the street toward his home, only making it two steps before he tripped over a chunk of ice that had fallen off the back of someone's tire well. His face slammed into the fresh snow, which was, to his relief, powdery and soft.

By the time he scrambled up from the ground, the enormous woman was beside him, helping him to his feet instead of ripping out his throat. Her face fell into a frown, as though saddened to see him so afraid. Her expression somehow made Tick feel guilty for running away so quickly.

"'Ello," she said, her voice husky and thick with a strange accent. "Pardon me looks. Been a bit of tough journey, it has." She stepped back, towering over Tick. Her eyes were anxious and hesitant and the way she fiddled with her huge hands made him think of Kayla when she was nervous. The gesture made the giant lady seem so . . . *innocent*, and Tick relaxed, feeling oddly at ease.

She had thick black hair that cascaded across her shoulders like a shawl, her face square and homely with bright blue eyes. Her gray clothes were wet and worn, hanging on her impossibly thin body like droopy sheets on a wooden laundry rack. The poor woman looked miserable in the cold, and the slight hunch to her shoulders only added to the effect. But then she swept away that impression with a huge smile, revealing an enormous set of yellow teeth.

Tick knew he was staring, but he couldn't look away. "You're . . . huge," he said before he could stop himself.

The woman flinched, her smile faltering just a bit. "I'm a bit lanky, I'll admit it," she said. "No reason for the little man to poke fun, now is it?"

"No . . . I didn't mean it that way," he stammered. "It's just . . . you're so *tall*."

"Yeah, methinks we established that."

"And . . ."

"Lanky. Come to an understanding now, have we?" She pointed down at him. "The little man is short and ugly. Mothball is tall and lanky."

Tick wasn't sure he'd heard her right. "Mothball?"

The woman shrugged her bony shoulders. "It's me name. A bit unfortunate, I'll admit it. Me dad didn't have much time to think when I popped out me mum's belly, what with all the nasty Bugaboo soldiers tryin' to break in and all. Fared better than me twin sis, I did. Like to see you go through life with a name like Toejam."

Tick had the strangest urge to laugh. There was something incredibly likable about this giant of a person. "Buga-*what* soldiers? Where are you from?"

"Born in the Fifth, I was, but lived in the Eleventh for a season. Ruddy rotten time that turned out to be. Nothin' but midgets stepping on me toes and punching me knees. Not fun, I can promise ya that. At least I met me friend Rutger there."

Every word that flew out of the woman's mouth only confused Tick even more. As hard as it was to believe the sheer size of the lady standing in front of him, the conversation was just as bizarre.

"The Fifth?" he asked. "What's that, an address? Where is it? Where's the Eleventh?"

Mothball put her gigantic hands on her hips. "By

my count, you've done asked me several questions in a row, little man, and none time to answer them. Me brain may be bigger than yers, but you're workin' it a bit much, don't ya think?"

"Okay, then," Tick said. "Just answer one."

"Ain't it in the Prime where they say 'Patience is a virtue'? Looks like you missed out on that bit of clever advice."

Tick laughed despite the craziness of it all. "Mothball, I'm more confused every time you speak. How about you just tell me whatever you want, and I'll shut up and listen." He rubbed his neck, which hurt from looking up at her so much. His scarf was crusted in snow.

"Now that's more like it, though I must admit I don't know what to say now." Mothball folded her arms, her face scrunching up into a serious frown as she stared down at Tick. "No harm in tellin' that you're from the Prime, I reckon, and that I'm from the Fifth, and me friend Rutger's from the Eleventh I told you about just now. Wee little gent, old Rutger—looks a little like a ball of bread dough, he does. The poor bloke is short as a field swine and twice as fat. You'll be meetin' him, too, ya know, right directly if he's about his business."

"Wait," Tick said, forgetting his promise to be quiet, at which Mothball rolled her eyes. "You sound like you know who I am. This is somehow related to the letters I got in the mail, isn't it?"

"What else, little man? Did ya ever see an eight-foot woman *before* you got the notes from the Master?"

"Mast—" Tick paused, his mind churning like the snowflakes that swirled around his body. This giant woman had obviously come to talk to him specifically, for a purpose, and yet he'd learned nothing. "Look, Mothball, maybe you could explain everything, from the beginning?"

She shook her head vigorously. "Can't do that, little man. Can't do that at'all."

"Then why did you come here? Why did you step out of the woods to talk to me?"

"To rub ya a little, give ya a bit of confidence, ya know. Me boss sent me. Sendin' me all over the place, he is, just to help where I can."

"Help with what?"

"Not sure to be quite frank. I know I can't talk about the messages, and I can't tell you anything about the Master or the Barrier Wand or the Realities or the Kyoopy or the Chi'karda or anythin' else to do with 'em." She held out a finger as she said each of the strange items as though she'd been given a list beforehand. "Other than that, feel free to ask your questions, since I have no idea anymore what to talk to ya about."

Tick rubbed his eyes, frustrated. He tried his best to memorize each of the odd words Mothball had said, burning them into his mind for later analysis. "Miss

Mothball, it's official. This is the craziest conversation I've ever had."

"Sorry, little man. Truly I am." She kicked the snow at her feet, making a huge divot. "'Simportant you figure things out for yourself. It won't work otherwise. But, er, maybe you've seen something, er, *strange* since you got those letters?"

Tick's interest perked up considerably. "Yeah, I have. Just a couple of hours ago I saw this smoky, wispy thing that formed into a face and made a freaky sound. Can you tell me about that?"

Mothball's face lit up despite the scary subject matter of his question. "Ah! Tingle Wraiths! That's what you've seen, I'd bet me left shoe. Scary fellas, them. Now *that* I can talk about."

"You know what they are? Where they come from?"

"I ruddy well should! They almost killed me friend Rutger just last winter. 'Ere, did you get a little tingle down your spine when the Death Siren started? Ya know that's where they get the name from." She paused. "Ya know, *tingle*. Down your spine. Tingle Wraith. Get it?"

"Yeah . . . I get it." If she noticed his sarcasm, she didn't show it. "But what are they?"

"That awful sound you 'eard is the Death Siren and it only gets louder and louder, I'm afraid. They can't move more than a few feet or so once their face is formed, but there's no need as long as you can hear that terrible cry of theirs. Thirty seconds, once it starts—that's all you've got."

"What do you mean?"

Mothball's brow furrowed as she wagged a finger at him. "If any man, woman, or child hears the Death Siren for thirty seconds straight, their brain turns right to mush. Nasty death, that. Seen it happen to an old bloke once. His body flopped around like a chicken with its ruddy noggin lopped off. The poor wife finally let 'im out of 'is misery. Bludgeoned him over the head with a teapot, she did."

"You're serious?"

"Do I look like the kind of person who'd make funnies about an old woman knocking 'er own sweet husband over the head with a teapot?"

"Well . . . no, I guess."

"Sad, it was." She stared at an empty spot past Tick's shoulder for a few seconds, then looked him in the eyes. "You'll be all right. S'long as you can run, they'll never catch you. Just avoid 'em if you can."

"Don't worry, I will."

A long pause followed, and Tick began to panic that Mothball would leave without telling him anything else. "So . . . what do I do? What are the messages *for*? Who is M.G.? What's supposed to happen on the day he talked about in the first clue?" The questions poured out, even though he knew what her answer would be before she said it.

"Sorry, can't speak about it. Master's orders."

Tick wanted to scream. "Well, then I guess there's not much more for us to talk about, is there?"

"Not much, you thought right there, little man."

Tick shivered, staring absently at the world of white surrounding them. "O . . . kay. So, what do we do now?"

"Best be on me way, then." Mothball bowed her head, as if she felt just as awkward as he did. A few seconds later she snapped her fingers and looked up. "Ah, me brain must've shut off there for a moment. I forgot something." She pulled out a small writing pad and a pencil from her pocket. "What's yer name—if you don't mind me asking?"

Her question surprised Tick. "You don't know? How did you find me if—"

"Just be needin' to verify, I do." She held her pencil at the ready, waiting for his answer.

"Atticus Higginbottom. But everyone calls me Tick."

She scanned the pad with the tip of her pencil. "Ah, there you are." She wrote a big checkmark where the pencil had stopped, then reached into a different pocket and pulled out a crumpled yellow envelope. She held it out for Tick. "'Ere ya go, little man. Congrats to ya on makin' a very wise and brave choice not to burn the Master's first letter. Now this should keep you occupied for a spell."

Nothing was written on the front of the envelope, but Tick took it, knowing it had to be the second clue. He didn't know why he felt so surprised. M.G. never said *all* the messages would come through the mail. But it did seem odd to receive two on the same day. Maybe M.G. was sending another kind of message altogether: *Never assume anything, expect the unexpected.*

He folded the envelope and put it in his pocket, anxious to go home and read it. "Thanks. I guess I won't bother asking you any questions about it."

"Shapin' up right nicely, you are." Mothball smiled. "Very well, until next time, then. Best of luck to you and yours and all that."

Tick felt an overwhelming feeling that if she left, he'd never understand anything that was going on. He desperately wanted her to stay, to talk, to help. But having just met her, he didn't know what to do or say. "You really have to go?" he asked, like a small child begging Grandma to stay just a little while longer.

Mothball's face softened into the nicest, kindest expression Tick had ever seen. "'Fraid so, little man. Got others to visit, ya know. Quite weary on me legs, it is, but not much choice in the matter. You'll do well— me bones tell me as much."

"Will I ever see you again?"

"I hopes ya do, Master Tick. I certainly hopes ya do."

And with that, the tall woman turned and walked back into the thick copse of trees, her large shoulders sending an avalanche of snow off the limbs where she brushed them.

Tick stared for a while, half-expecting to see a magic poof of smoke or the fiery blastoff of an alien spaceship, but nothing happened. Mothball had simply vanished into the trees.

His life had turned completely crazy and for some reason it made him more excited than he'd felt in a very long time.

He set off for home with a smile on his face.

Mothball waited until the boy went around a bend in the snow-covered road before she stepped out from behind the thick tree where she'd been hiding. She shook her head, bewildered by the exuberance and innocence of youth. He was a fine one, this Atticus Higginbottom, and though she knew she wasn't supposed to do it, she'd settled on the one she'd be rooting for in this whole mess.

She walked the half-mile to the designated spot that lay deeper in the forest. No one in these parts probably remembered that this place had once been a burial ground, its wooden grave markers long since decayed and crumbled to dust.

Poor deadies, she thought. *No one comin' to pay respects and such.*

She triggered the nanolocator signal for Master George, then waited for her boss to work his navigation skills. Funny little man, he was. A *good* man, really. As nervous as a midge bug caught in a toad paddy, but a kind and gentle soul when you dug down deep. Why, he'd saved her life, he did, and she owed him for it.

Several long moments passed. Mothball fidgeted back and forth on her feet, wondering if the restless man had messed up a thingamajig or whatchamacallit on the Barrier Wand. He was a very *precise* old chap, and usually responded in a matter of seconds, especially when expecting the nanolocator signal, as he should be now. Mothball had been right on schedule.

A small deer bounced along nearby, leaving delicate little footprints in the thick layer of snow. To Mothball's delight, it stopped to examine the unusually tall visitor. She was so used to scaring creatures away, it felt nice for a change to see something not turn and take flight.

"Watch out for the little man, won't you?" she said, glad no one was around to see her talking to a deer. "Tough times ahead, he's got. Could use a friend like you."

The animal didn't respond, and Mothball laughed.

A few seconds later, she felt the familiar tickle at the back of her neck. As she *winked* away from the forest, vanishing in an instant, she couldn't help but wonder what the deer would think of such a sight.

CHAPTER
8

A VERY IMPORTANT DATE

Tick tore open the envelope from Mothball the second he'd left the odd woman's line of vision. He had to pull his gloves off to do it, and the cold bit into them with tiny frozen pinpricks. With no surprise, he pulled out a single piece of cardstock that looked exactly like the others. His fingers growing stiff in the frigid air, he read the single paragraph.

```
    At the appropriate time, you must
say the magic words with your eyes
closed. If you can't speak and close
your eyes at the same time, you
belong in a hospital. As for what
```

```
the magic words are, I can't tell you
and I never will. Examine the first
letter carefully and you will work
them out.
```

He read it again three times, then stuffed the letter and the envelope into his coat pocket. Shivering as he put his gloves back on, he couldn't help but feel a mixture of excitement and wariness.

Magic words? Eyes closed? What is this, Oz?

Things were getting just plain weird. Pulling his scarf tighter, Tick rubbed his arms, trudging through the snow toward home.

He got to his house just in time for dinner, which he wolfed down like a kid determined to eat all the Halloween candy before a sibling stole it. He barely heard the conversation around the table and excused himself after stuffing the last three bites' worth of spaghetti into his mouth all at once.

He leapt up the stairs to his room, determined to finally put some major thought into figuring out the clues. Something about seeing an eight-foot-tall woman appear out of the woods on a snowy day made everything seem *real*. Though he had no idea about the whys or hows or whats, he was now committed to the game.

Tick unfolded the original letter and both clues and put them on his desk, pointing his lamp to shine directly on their stark black words. He reread the first letter from M.G., which seemed to be mostly an introduction to set things up. The most recent message said the first letter would reveal "magic words" he'd need to say on a special day, but he'd get to that later. One thing at a time.

The first clue obviously told him the date of that special day—the day when he'd have to have solved the ultimate puzzle spelled out by the coming clues. He focused on the paragraph, reading it several times.

> Mark your calendar. One week from the day before the day after the yesterday that comes three weeks before six months from six weeks from now minus forty-nine days plus five tomorrows and a next week, it will happen. A day that could very well change the course of your life as you know it.
>
> I must say, I hope to see you there.

As he read through it, he tried to visualize in his mind the stated time periods, adding and subtracting as he went. But by the time he got to the end, the words always jumbled up and fell apart inside his thoughts. He realized he needed to treat it like a math problem, solving it in sections until everything could be added together.

He pulled out a pencil and drew parentheses around phrases that were easy to identify as a stand-alone period of time. Then he assigned letters to them to help him solve them in the most logical order. All the while, he knew he must be the biggest dork this side of the Pacific Ocean, but he didn't care. He was just starting to have fun.

He first attempted to figure out the clue from beginning to end, adding and subtracting time with each new phrase as it came in order. But he kept hitting a snag because of the words "before" and "six weeks from now" in the middle of the paragraph. The phrases seemed to split the timeline into two pieces and he realized he needed to work around them, not from first word to last word.

After a half hour and lots of erasing and starting over, he copied the phrases and their assigned letters to a different sheet of paper. Then, using the Seattle Seahawks calendar that hung next to his bed (which also had a one page, year-at-a-glance section for this year and the next), he penciled in the dates as he figured them out. When he finished, he leaned back in his chair and took a look:

Beginning Date: Today, November 26.

A. 6 weeks from now = January 7

B. 6 months from A = July 7

C. the day before the day after the yesterday that comes 3 weeks before B = 3 weeks plus 1 day before B = 22 days before B = June 15

D. 1 week from C = June 22

E. D minus 49 days = May 4

F. E plus 5 tomorrows and a next week = E plus 12 days = <u>May 16</u>

He went over his math again to make sure he'd done it right, and was just about to put the calendar away, quite satisfied with himself, when he realized he'd missed the easiest and most important part of the clue. The beginning date.

You idiot, he thought.

Whoever M.G. was, he or she would have no way of knowing when people received the cryptic letters, much less when they would test out the first clue to figure out the all-important date. Tick reread one of the lines from the first letter:

```
Beginning today (the fifteenth of
November), I am sending out a sequence
of special messages . . .
```

November the fifteenth. Even before officially starting the messages, M.G. had provided the mystery's first hint: the start date needed to solve Clue Number One.

Tick quickly went through the calendar again, calculating three times what the date should be based on the new starting date, erasing and rewriting. Finally, confident that he'd solved it, his paper showed a different result:

May 6

At first, he worried that the results were only *ten* days apart when the beginning dates had been off by *eleven*, but after looking at the calendar three times, he determined it had to do with June only having thirty days.

May sixth. The all-important date. Just over five months from now.

Tick wrote the date in big letters on the bottom of the first clue, then ripped out the one-page calendar and stapled it to the back of the cardstock. He examined the second clue for a while, which really did nothing but refer him to the first letter he'd received as a code or something to figure out the "magic words." After an hour of staring at the typed message, his brain exhausted, he gave up. He folded everything up together and stuck the stack in his desk drawer.

For the rest of the evening, Tick couldn't quit thinking about the first clue. According to the stranger known as M.G., something very important was to happen on May sixth of the next year.

But what?

Much later that night, after playing Scrabble with his mom and Lisa (Tick's best word: galaxy, 34 points on a double-word score), eating two-thirds of a bag of Doritos while watching *SportsCenter* with his dad (swearing on his life he'd never eat another chip—a promise he knew wouldn't last past tomorrow), analyzing the clues for a while (still no luck with the magic words), then reading for an hour in bed (the latest seven-inch-thick fantasy novel he'd checked out from the library), Tick finally went to sleep.

In the middle of the night, ripping him from a dream in which he'd just received the very prestigious Best Chess Player in the World trophy, crowds chanting his name and cheering wildly, Tick heard the *sounds* again: the metallic whirring, the scraping, the patter of tiny footsteps. All coming from inside the closet, where the door was closed.

Something bumped against the door.

Tick sat up, suddenly very, very awake.

CHAPTER
9

THE GNAT RAT

Tick's first instinct was to run and get his dad again, the creepy chills of the night he'd first heard the noises returning in full force. But he steeled himself, resolving not to go running off like a baby again until he knew it was all for real. Whatever was moving around in his closet couldn't be very big, and it had to have a reasonable explanation. Maybe it was just a squirrel that had chewed a hole through the wall—too small for them to have noticed that night when he and his dad had searched the room.

What about the mechanical fan sound? he thought. He told himself that maybe the little squirrel had accidentally eaten his dad's electric shaver, but then realized he was probably one step away from the mental hospital talking to himself like this, and telling jokes at that. *Just go check it out,* he told himself sternly.

He reached up to his headboard, keeping his eyes riveted on the closet, and flicked on the lamp. The warm glow banished the dark shadows, illuminating fully the door with its many posters and sports banners taped haphazardly across it. Encouraged and braver with the light on, Tick swung his legs around and stood up from his bed, hoping the closet door didn't burst open when he did so. Nothing moved. The sound had completely stopped.

Maybe I just imagined it. I haven't heard it since it woke me up.

Think it all he wanted, he couldn't convince himself. A slice of fear cut through his heart, making it pound even harder, sending a pulse of heat through his veins. His hands were sweaty and his shoulders and back tingled, making him remember what Mothball had said about the smoke-ghost he'd seen in the alley. The Tingle Wraith. But its sound had been totally different, and Tick didn't really expect to see one in his closet.

No, this was something different, if anything at all.

He crept over to the door with ginger steps, staring at the thin sliver of space between the floor and the bottom of the door. If anything shot out from that crack, Tick knew he'd die of a heart attack on the spot.

He stopped a couple of feet away and paused, clenching and unclenching his fists.

Just open it, you sissy.

He reached forward and twisted the handle, knowing his dad had done the exact same thing just over a week ago, remembering that there had been nothing there then.

He pulled the door open and stepped back.

Something very odd rested on top of a pile of dirty clothes.

Something Tick had never seen before in his life.

⌇

Edgar Higginbottom was a light sleeper, which he hated. Anything and everything woke him up. Cars outside, dogs barking, a child crying. When his kids had been babies, Edgar had woken up the instant any of them fussed. Often he'd lain there, wishing against all hope that Lorena would somehow hear and offer to take a turn checking on them or feeding them. But he always got up after a few seconds, feeling guilty for being so selfish after all his wife had gone through to bring those kids into the world in the first place.

This time, though, it had been a sudden light that snapped him awake, followed by the slight creak of someone walking in the house. He pushed himself up onto one elbow and looked at the door to his room, which stood slightly ajar. Judging from the angle of the shadows caused by the light, and the direction from which the sound had come, he guessed Tick had gotten out of bed for some reason.

What's he doing up at—Edgar looked at his clock—*three in the morning?*

He flopped back down onto his side, then rolled his big body onto his back, rubbing his eyes and yawning as he stared at the ceiling. Then, with a grunt, he threw off the covers and sat up on the edge of the bed, searching for his slippers with his toes.

He found them, put them on, and stood up.

⁓

Tick's mind seemed to split into two factions as he stared at the object. One side wanted him to run because anything that magically appeared in a closet had to be bad. The other side wanted to investigate because the thing looked completely harmless. The latter won the battle, his curiosity once again victorious over common sense.

He stepped closer and dropped to his knees, leaning forward.

It was a strange metal contraption, about a foot long, five or six inches wide, and maybe eight or nine inches tall. Its shiny gray surface had no blemishes, sparkling and clean, with round, gear-looking things attached to the side. A thin handle was attached to the top of the box and a small snout-like nose and a sinuous metallic tail were attached to either end. Along the bottom edges a series of ten evenly spaced rods poked out from the box and curved toward the floor, ending in a flat piece of metal about the size of a quarter. The first thought that popped into Tick's mind was the thing looked like a stainless steel accordion, ready to march away.

But it didn't move or make a sound.

Tick noticed some writing on the side of the box, shadowed by the light coming from the room. He shifted his position closer and squinted his eyes. It took a few seconds, but he finally made out what it said:

GNAT RAT
Manufactured by Chu Industries

What in the world . . .

Tick thought of Mr. Chu, his science teacher, but he obviously had nothing to do with this. Tick would know if his favorite instructor had his own company or was affiliated with one. It had to be a coincidence.

But . . .

His mind was blank, churning to come up with an explanation for the weird thing sitting in his closet. It had to be related to the letters from M.G., the Tingle

Wraith, and Mothball, but how or why . . . ? No clue.

And what in the world is a Gnat Rat? He reached out a finger and brushed the back of the smooth gray metal box.

The thing jumped.

Tick gasped and fell backward, even though the Gnat Rat had barely moved—an inch at most—before coming to rest again. A slight buzzing came from it like the distant sound of his mom's oven timer from downstairs. Whatever the thing was, it had just turned on or powered up.

A mechanized clicking sound sprung up and the ten pairs of metal legs started moving back and forth, slowly marching the Gnat Rat off the pile of clothes and out of the closet, toward Tick. His eyes wide and focused on the toy-like thing coming at him, Tick stood up, unsure what to do. It seemed totally harmless, a cheap robot you could buy at any discount store.

But then he remembered it slamming into his door when he'd closed it from the hallway that night. He thought about its name: Gnat Rat. And finally, he thought about how it had somehow *disappeared* and come back, magically. All of these things led to one conclusion.

A Gnat Rat is bad.

Tick was about to bolt away when he heard a loud click like the sound of a gun being cocked. He looked

in shock at the ominous toy. A small door slowly swung open on the Rat's back side.

Then little *things* started flying out of it.

~~~

Light or no light, a son suffering from insomnia or not, Edgar couldn't ignore the call of nature. He finished washing his hands in the bathroom, flicked off the light, and stepped back into his bedroom. Trying his best to be quiet so Lorena could sleep— though he probably could've danced around the room with cymbals on his knees and blowing on a trumpet and she would've remained dead to the world—Edgar walked through the room and into the hallway.

Sure enough, it was Tick's room with a light on, and an odd mechanical hum echoed out his door and down the hall. *Did he get some new gizmo I don't know about?*

Edgar had taken only one step forward when he heard the boy scream.

~~~

Tick shrieked as dozens of winged, buzzing little drones flew out of the Gnat Rat in a torrent like a pack of raving mad hornets. Without exception they came directly at him, swarming around his body before he could react, attacking, biting, *stinging*.

Tick swatted at them, slapping and hitting his own body, dancing and kicking, yelling for help. Pinpricks of pain stabbed every inch of his skin, under his clothes, in his hair; the mechanical gnats were hungry and Tick must've looked awfully delicious. Panic shot through him in a rush of adrenaline, his mind shutting down, offering no ideas on what he should do.

He heard his bedroom door slam against the wall.

"Atticus!" his dad yelled.

But Tick couldn't look at him. He'd squeezed his eyes closed, scared the gnats would blind him. They were relentless, attacking him over and over again, their sharp stingers finding fresh spots to hurt him with a frightening ease. Overwhelmed by pain and fear, he fell to the ground.

He felt his dad gripping his arms, dragging him across the floor and out of his room. Down the hall, into the bathroom. He heard the rush of water in the bathtub.

Dad, he thought, wanting to warn him, but afraid to open his mouth. *They'll eat you alive, too.*

It hurt too much to cry. Tick felt like he'd been taken to an acupuncture school and the overanxious students had given up on the little needles and decided to use knives instead. His whole world had turned into one big ouch. He'd never felt so hopeless.

His dad heaved Tick off the floor and plopped him

into the tub, splashing the cold water all over his paja-mas, his skin, his hair. Though his whole body felt racked with pain, Tick sensed the gnats leaving him in hordes even before he'd landed in the shallow pool of water.

They're machines, he thought distantly. *They run on electricity. The water would kill them.*

An angry buzz filled the bathroom, but Tick couldn't bring himself to open his eyes. He heard a towel whipping through the air. His dad must be trying to chase the gnats away and out of the room. Horror filled Tick's stomach as he realized the vicious gnats might be going for his sisters, his mom.

"Dad!" he yelled with a slur, his mouth swollen. "Kayla! Lisa! Mom!"

And then he passed out.

⌐◡

"What were they?" the doctor asked. "Where did they come from?"

Edgar didn't feel like talking. Even if he did, he had no answer for the man.

They stood in a curtained-off section of the emer-gency room, surrounded by the sounds of medical machines beeping, the murmur of voices, the squeak of gurneys rolling along the hallway; a child cried in the distance. Everything smelled of ammonia and disinfec-tant. It was all extremely depressing.

Edgar stared down at his son lying on the bed, eyes closed. Every inch of the boy's body looked red and puffy, pockmarked with hundreds of black dots. Lorena and Lisa cried in the corner, clutching little Kayla in a three-way hug. Edgar felt certain his heart had broken into two pieces and was slowly sinking to his stomach.

Tick had always been a lucky kid. Edgar liked to joke that Tick had been born clutching a rabbit's foot. When Tick had been only five years old, the family had taken a shopping trip to Spokane and Tick had darted for the middle of a busy road, already two steps past the curb before Edgar even noticed. Even as Edgar had sprinted to save his boy, he watched in utter horror as a huge truck, blaring its horn and screeching its brakes, seemingly ran right over Tick. Edgar would never forget the scream that erupted from his own throat at that moment, an alien sound that still haunted his dreams sometimes.

But when the truck passed, Tick stood there in the street, untouched, his hair not so much as ruffled. It had been nothing short of a miracle.

Then, a few years later, the family had gone to the coast for a summer trip, enjoying a rare hot and sunny day on the Washington beach. Tick, showing off his newly discovered body-surfing talent, had been swept away by a sudden and enormous wave, sucking him out to sea. The current pulled the poor boy from the soft sands directly into an area of jagged, vicious rocks nearby. Edgar and Lorena barely had time to register the shock and terror of what was happening before they saw Tick standing on a jutting shoulder of stone, waving with a huge smile on his face.

Or the time he fell off the big waterslide tower at Water World Park, only to land on a pile of slip 'n slide tubes left there by a family eating lunch.

The stories went on and on. They never talked about it; Edgar was afraid to jinx the whole thing, and he had no idea if Tick even realized anything out of the ordinary was happening. Kids rarely do—life is life, and they know nothing different until much later.

But despite all that he'd seen of Tick's narrow escapes, Edgar couldn't help but feel the panic rising in his chest. Had the boy's streak of luck finally run out? Would he survive this—

"What *happened*?" the doctor repeated.

"I don't know," Edgar mumbled. "A bunch of bugs, or bees, or gnats, or something attacked him. I threw him in the bathtub, shooed the things away with a towel. They stayed in a tight pack, and when I opened a window, they flew right out."

The doctor looked at Edgar, his expression full of doubt and concern, eyebrows raised. "*You* shooed them away?"

"Yes, I did." Edgar knew the man's concern before he said it.

"But you—"

"I know, Doctor, I know." He paused. "I didn't get stung. Not once."

CHAPTER 10

THE TEMPTATION OF THE FLAMES

Tick could think of a million things he'd rather do than get stung all over his body by mechanical gnats that popped out of a demon lunch box with legs. It was a long list and included being dropped in a boiling vat of vinegar and having his toenails removed with hot pincers. Two days after the attack, he'd returned home from the hospital feeling and looking much better, but the experience remained vivid in his mind, playing itself out over and over again. Without any doubt, he knew the Gnat Rat and its stinging bugs had been the single worst thing that had ever happened to him. And that included the time Billy "The Goat" Cooper had almost broken Tick's arm in front of the girls' locker room.

Despite the lingering horror he felt, Tick was madly curious to know where the Gnat Rat had come from. And where it had gone. The boxy contraption must have disappeared right after releasing the bugs because his dad said he never saw it and saw no signs of a nest or a hole anywhere in the walls or floorboard. The Rat would've been impossible to miss since Tick had collapsed right next to it in his room. The thing had simply vanished—or run away to whatever magical hole it lived in. Either way, Tick knew he could never look at the world in the same way again, and the knowledge made him feel sick, fascinated, and scared, all at the same time.

The doctors had probed him over and over, not bothering to hide their suspicion that some serious child abuse had occurred. But they found dozens of stingers, just like the ones that came from a normal yellow jacket common to the area. That finding, coupled with the obvious fact that Edgar and Lorena Higginbottom were perhaps the two nicest people to ever live in Deer Park, and quite possibly the world, quickly dissolved the distrust of the doctors toward the parents.

Though they said no fewer than a hundred times how impossible it seemed that the bees targeted Tick and no one else, let alone the fact that bees rarely attacked during the middle of winter, the doctors eventually let the matter drop and sent Tick home.

I must have some seriously sweet blood, Tick thought, picking at the bandages covering his arms.

The only thing more baffling than the lone victim and the Gnat Rat disappearing was how quickly Tick healed. He almost felt disappointed he wouldn't miss more than a couple of days of school. Almost.

Now, lying in bed, staring at the ceiling late the next Tuesday night, he couldn't sleep. More than ever before in his life, Tick felt terribly *afraid*. His life was at risk, and for what?

He'd put on a show for his family, acting brave and cracking jokes, but he knew he did it more for himself than anyone else. He didn't want to accept the horror of what he'd experienced, didn't want to accept the potential for worse things to come. But the fear crashed down on him after dinner and he'd never felt so hopeless.

Sighing, he sat up in bed and retrieved the letter and clues from his desk drawer, staring at them for a long moment. As he did, he felt the last ounce of bravery drain from his spirit. Quietly, he crept from his room and took the letters downstairs to the living room.

It was the only room in the house with a fireplace.

~

Twenty minutes later, the gas-log fire had heated the entire room, its blower wafting warm and comforting air across Tick's face as he sat directly in front of it, staring at the licking flames. The rest of his family had long since fallen asleep, and he had been extra, extra careful not to wake his freakishly light-sleeping dad. This was Tick's moment of truth and he needed to be alone.

He gripped the first letter tightly in his right hand, clenching a fist around the wrinkled cardstock. He didn't know how it worked, but he trusted the instruction told to him by the mystery-person, M.G. If ever he wanted it to stop, just burn the letter and everything would "cease and desist." Tick had no doubt it was true, just as he had no doubt that Gnat Rats, Tingle Wraiths, and an eight-foot-tall woman named Mothball really and truly existed.

Burn the letter, stop the madness.

The thought had run through his mind a thousand times since he'd first come to consciousness after the brutal gnat attack. Only two clues in—ten to go— and he wanted to quit. *Desperately* wanted to quit. How could he keep going, when things worse than the Gnat Rat might attack him? How could he, Atticus Higginbottom, a kid with a pretty decent brain but the body of a thirteen year old, fight the forces that some unknown enemy threw at him? How could he do it?

He sat up, crossing his legs under him, facing the fire. He thought about the tremendous ease of simply throwing the letter into the fire not two feet in front of him, of watching it crinkle and shrivel into a crispy ball of black flakes, of returning his life back to normal. He could do it and be done. Forever.

And then it hit him—an odd feeling that started somewhere deep down in his stomach and swelled into his chest, spreading through his fingers and toes.

The first letter said many lives were at stake. Whether that meant ten or ten thousand, Tick didn't know. Neither did he have any idea how twelve clues, written to him in cryptic messages from some stranger, had anything to do with saving people's lives. But could he really risk that? Could Tick really be a coward and throw this challenge to the flames, when so much might be on the line? When so many people's lives were on the line?

Even if it were just *one* person?

What if that one person was Kayla and her life was in the hands of someone else? The thought gripped Tick's heart, squeezed it hard. He pictured Kayla's big-toothed smile, her cute look of concentration when she played on the computer, her giggle fits when Tick tickled her under her arms. Tick's eyes rimmed with tears. The thought of anything bad happening to his little sister made him feel a sadness that was heavy and bleak.

In that moment, in the darkness of deepest night,

sitting in the warmth of a flickering fire and thinking about things far beyond what any kid should have to contemplate, Tick made his decision, committing to himself that he would never waver from it, no matter what.

In that moment, he answered the question posed to him by the one known as M.G.

Will you have the courage to choose the difficult path?

"Yes," Tick whispered to the flames. "The answer is yes."

He folded up the letter and turned his back on the fire.

In a place very far from the home of Atticus Higginbottom, Master George awoke with a start. Exactly what had jolted him from sleep, he wasn't sure, but it didn't make him very happy. He rather liked the act of blissful slumber and believed very strongly in the old adage about beauty sleep. (Though he knew if Mothball or Rutger were around they'd say something persnickety about him needing to sleep for the next forty years to gain a single ounce of beauty.)

He looked down at his toes, poking out from his red crocheted socks like little mice searching for food. He'd pulled his blanket up too far, exposing his feet, and wondered if the chill of the night had awakened him.

No, he thought. *I don't feel cold. This was something much more. Something* shook *me.*

And then he shot up into a sitting position, any remnant of sleep completely quashed. He threw the covers off, put on his velvet slippers, and shuffled to the next room where all kinds of buzzing machinery and humming trinkets blinked and clinked and chirped. A large computer screen took up the entire left wall. Several hundred names were listed in alphabetical order, their letters glowing green, a variety of symbols and colors to the right of each name.

One of the names had a flashing purple checkmark next to it, which made Master George gasp and sit down in his specially-ordered, magnetically adjustable, ergonomically sophisticated swivel chair. He spun in three complete circles, moving himself with the tips of his toes, almost as though he were dancing. And then he laughed. He laughed loud and long and hard, his heart bursting with pride and joy.

After many disappointments, someone had finally made a Pick, one so powerful it had shaken the very foundation of the Command Center. *The ramifications could be enormous,* he thought, giddy and still chuckling.

And then, to his utter and complete astonishment, defying every sense of rational thought in his bones, two more purple checkmarks appeared on the screen, almost at the same time.

Three? So close together? Impossible!

He stood up, rocketing the chair backward with the backs of his knees, squinting to make sure it hadn't been a trick of his eyes. There they were—three purple marks.

While dancing an old Irish jig he'd learned from his great-grandpapa, Master George went in search of his tabby cat, Muffintops. He found her snoozing behind the milk cupboard in the kitchen and yanked her into his arms, hugging her fiercely.

"Dearest Muffintops," he said, petting her. "We must celebrate right away with some peppermint tea and biscuits!" He set her down and began rummaging through his pots and pans to find a clean teapot. Once he'd set some water on the stove, he straightened and put his hands on his hips, staring down at his whiskered friend.

"My goodness gracious me," he said. "Three Picks within a few minutes of each other? I daresay we have a lot of work to do."

Upstairs in his room, Tick was wide awake, despite the late hour.

He studied the first letter from M.G. until the sky

outside faded from black to bruised purple and the first traces of dawn cast a pallid glow outside his window. The wind had picked up, the infamous branch that used to haunt his dreams as a kid taking up its age-long duty, scraping the side of the house with its creepy claws of leafless wood. But Tick kept reading, searching, *thinking*.

The magic words.

He didn't know what they were, why he needed them, or what would happen on May sixth when he was supposed to say them, but he knew they were vital and he had to figure them out. And the first letter supposedly told him everything necessary to do just that.

Nothing came to him. He searched the sentences, the paragraphs, the words for clues. He tried rearranging letters, looked for words that were perhaps spelled vertically, sought the word "magic" to see if it lay hidden anywhere. Nothing.

He remembered the famous riddle from *Lord of the Rings* where the entrance to the Mines of Moria said "Speak friend, and enter." It had literally meant for the person to *speak* the word "friend" in the Elven language and the doors would open. But nothing like that seemed to jump out at Tick as he sought for clues.

Figuring out the date of the special day from the first clue had been a piece of cake compared to this, and he grew frustrated. He also felt the effects of staying up all night and a sudden surge of fatigue pressed his head down to the pillow, pulled his eyelids closed.

When his mom poked her head in to wake him up for school, he begged for one more day, knowing she'd have a hard time arguing with a kid who'd been eaten alive just a few days earlier.

After his mom tucked him back into bed and patted his head like a sick three year old, Tick pondered the pledge he'd made by the fireplace the night before—to keep going, to fight the fear, to solve the puzzle. No matter what.

I'm either really, really brave or really, really stupid.

Finally, despite the light of sunrise streaming through his window, he fell asleep.

PART
2

THE JOURNAL

CHAPTER
11

OLD AND DUSTY

That Friday, completely healed and caught up on the work he'd missed at school, Tick sat in his science class, trying to pay attention to Mr. Chu as he talked about the vast mysteries that still awaited discovery in the field of physics. Usually, Tick enjoyed this class more than most, but he couldn't get his mind off the second clue, frustrated that he wasn't able to crack the code of the first letter.

"Mr. Higginbottom?" Mr. Chu asked.

Tick's attention whipped back to the real world, and he stared at his teacher, suddenly panicked because he had no clue why Mr. Chu had said his name. "Sorry, what was the question?"

"I didn't ask you a question," his teacher answered, folding his arms. "I was just wondering why you're staring out the window like there's a parade out there. Am I boring you?" He raised his eyebrows.

"No, I was just . . . pondering the physics of the tetherball outside."

Several snickers broke out in the room, though Tick knew it wasn't in appreciation for his joke. Some of the kids in his class didn't even listen to what he said anymore; they automatically laughed at him whenever he spoke because they assumed the others would think they were cool for poking fun at the nerdy Stinkbottom with the Barf Scarf. The laughter didn't faze Tick in the least; in his mind, those people had ceased to exist a long time ago.

"Well," Mr. Chu said. "Maybe you'd like to come up to the board and give us a diagram of what you're thinking about?" Tick knew the man had to give him a hard time every now and then or it would be overwhelmingly obvious that he favored the smart kid with the red-and-black scarf.

"No, sir," Tick replied. "Haven't figured it out yet."

"Let me know when you do. And in the meantime, grace me with your attention."

Tick nodded and resettled himself in his seat, looking toward the front of the classroom. Someone behind him threw a wad of paper at his head; he ignored it as it ricocheted and fell to the floor. Mr. Chu continued his lecture, but faltered a few minutes later when someone grumbled about how boring science was.

"Oh, really?" Mr. Chu asked, his tone almost sarcastic. "Don't you realize all this stuff leads to things that are much, much more fascinating? We need to build a solid foundation so you can have a lot of fun later."

He only received blank stares in answer.

"I mean it! Here's an example. How many of you have heard of quantum physics?"

Along with a few others, Tick raised his hand. He'd once watched a really cool show on the Discovery Channel with his dad about the subject. Both of them had agreed afterward that quantum physics must have been something *Star Trek* fans invented so they'd have another topic to discuss instead of debating the average number of times Mr. Spock visited the toilet every day.

"Who'd like to take a stab and tell us what it's about?" Mr. Chu asked.

Trying to make up for his earlier daydreaming, Tick was the only one who offered. Mr. Chu nodded toward him.

"It's about the really, really small stuff—stuff smaller than atoms even—and they have a lot of properties that don't seem to follow the same rules as normal physics."

"Wow, you're smart, SpongeBob," someone whispered from the back. He thought it was Billy the Goat, but couldn't be sure. Tick ignored him.

"Such as?" Mr. Chu prodded, either not hearing the smart-aleck remark or disregarding it.

"Well, I don't remember a whole lot of the show I saw on T.V., but the thing that really seemed cool was they've basically proven that something can literally be in two or more places at once."

"Very good, Tick, that's part of it." Mr. Chu paced back and forth in front of the students, hands clasped behind his back, trying his best to fit the mold of Very Smart Professor. "We can't get into it very much in this class, but I think many of you will be excited to learn about it as you study more advanced classes in high school. My favorite aspect of the Q.P., as we used to call it in my peer study groups, is the fact they've also proven you can affect the *location* of an object simply by observing it. In other words, how you study it changes the outcome, which means there must be more than one outcome occurring simultaneously. Does that make sense?"

Tick nodded, fascinated, wishing they could drop the easy stuff and dig deeper into this subject. He didn't bother to look around the room, knowing that the rest of his classmates would once again return nothing but blank stares.

"Basically," Mr. Chu continued, "it means alternate versions of the present could exist at any moment, and that your actions, your observations, your *choices* can determine which of those you see. In other words, we're living in one of maybe a million different versions of the universe. Some people call it the multiverse." He folded his arms and shook his head slightly while staring at the floor, a small smile on his face, as if recalling a fond memory. "Nothing in all my studies has ever fascinated me as much as quantum physics."

He paused, looking around the room, and his face drooped into a scowl of disappointment like a kid who'd just told his parents he'd seen a dragonfly, only to get back a "Who cares? Go wash your hands for dinner" in return.

"Uh . . . anyway, I guess that's enough on that subject. The bell's about to ring. Don't forget your monthly research report is due tomorrow."

Tick gathered his things and put them in his backpack, not worried about the assignment; his had been done since before the Gnat Rat attack.

Mr. Chu came up to him and put a hand on his shoulder. "Tick, you should think about studying quantum physics in more detail when you get a chance. It's right up your alley. Pretty crazy world we live in, don't you think?"

"Tell me about it," Tick muttered. "Hey, Mr. Chu?"

"Yes?"

"Does your family . . . I mean . . . have you ever heard of a company called Chu Industries?"

Mr. Chu's face wrinkled into a look of confusion. "No, never heard of it before. But there are a lot of Chus in the world. Why?"

"Oh . . . nothing. Just an ad I saw somewhere. Made me wonder if you had anything to do with it."

"I wish. Sounds like it could've made me rich."

"Yeah, maybe. Well, see ya tomorrow." Tick swung his backpack over his shoulder and walked to his next class.

That night, Tick decided he needed a better way to organize the letters and clues he'd received from M.G. and Mothball, especially knowing that because of his decision not to burn the first letter, more and more would be coming.

He went down to the basement and rummaged through a couple of boxes labeled with his name and last year's date. Every year or two, Lorena Higginbottom insisted on a full top-to-bottom cleaning of the entire house, and her number one rule was that if you hadn't used something in more than a year, it needed to be thrown away or put into storage. These boxes were the result of last spring's mine sweep through Tick's closet.

He remembered he'd been given a journal for Christmas two or three years ago from his Grandma Mary. He'd vowed to write in it every day, chronicling the many adventures of the genius from Jackson Middle School, but the night he'd sat down to complete his first official entry, he hadn't been able to think of one thing that sounded interesting. He had managed to write his name on the front cover before he'd put it aside, hoping Grandma Mary would never find out. She'd have been devastated if she knew what had happened to her gift.

But he'd never forgotten how cool his name looked on the cover, and the journal would be the perfect thing for him now. Tick's life was no longer boring or uninteresting.

He found the journal lying beneath a stack of Hardy Boys books. Tick had read each of them several times before they'd made way for bigger and better novels. He pulled the journal out and stared at the cover. It had a marble-brown hardcover, its edges purposely worn and slightly burnt to make it look like the old record-book of an international explorer on the high seas. The pages inside were slightly yellowed for an aged appearance, lined from top to bottom, just waiting for him to record his thoughts and notes and scribbles.

It was perfect.

In the center of the front cover was a three-inch wide rectangle of burnt orange where he'd written his name a couple of years ago. Using the permanent black marker he'd brought downstairs with him, he added a few more words to the title. Finished, he held the journal up and took a prideful look:

TICK HIGGINBOTTOM'S JOURNAL OF CURIOUS LETTERS

He then took out the glue from his mom's scrapbooking case and pasted the first letter from M.G. onto the first page of the journal, centering it as best he could. He left a few blank pages for notes and calculations, then glued in the first clue, along with his solution and the ripped-out calendar with the special date of May sixth circled. Finally, he attached the second clue. He made sure everything was dry, then closed the book.

Satisfied with his efforts, and glad to have everything he needed in one portable book, he took his journal and went back upstairs.

The next day, almost as though the mysterious M.G. knew Tick was organized and ready to go, the third clue came in the mail.

CHAPTER 12

THE VOICE OF M.G.

It was Saturday, and just as he had done a couple of weeks earlier, Tick spied on the mailbox, waiting for the mailman to show up. The day was clear and crisp, the sun almost blinding as it reflected off the snow still covering the ground. Tick sipped hot chocolate and watched countless little drops of water fall from the trees in the yard as clinging icicles dripped away the last remnants of their lives. His mom and dad had gone Christmas shopping, Lisa was upstairs playing house with Kayla, and the soft melody of Bing Crosby crooning "White Christmas" echoed through the house. Tick didn't know if life could be any better.

The truck finally rumbled up to his house around

noon, and Tick didn't bother looking to see if there was any sign of a yellow envelope. He had his boots and coat on and was out the door before the mailman had even left for the next house. By the time the truck drove off, Tick had already pulled out the stack of letters.

Sitting right on top was a crumpled yellow envelope with the same messy handwriting, postmarked from South Africa. Other than a strange lump in one corner, the rest of the envelope was flimsy and flat. Intrigued, a shiver of excitement rattling his nerves, Tick sprinted back to the house and up to his room in no time, where the *Journal of Curious Letters* lay resting on his bed.

He ripped open the envelope and peered inside, seeing nothing at first. He billowed it out, turning it upside down and shaking it until a little, flashy square fell out and tumbled off the bed. Tick picked it up off the floor. It was a tiny cassette tape, the kind his dad used when he made everyone talk about themselves for a tape to send to Grandma and Grandpa in Georgia. (A couple of years ago, his dad had finally switched to a video camera, but he still occasionally used the tape recorder, too.)

Nothing had been written on the tape label, but it didn't take a rocket scientist to figure out what M.G. intended the recipients of this clue to do. It took Tick ten minutes to dig out his dad's little tape machine, hidden behind some socket wrenches in his dad's infamous "junk drawer." Tick could hardly contain himself as he went back to his room, locked the door, popped in the tape, and pushed PLAY.

He heard a few seconds of scratchy background noise, then a loud clank. Tick, pencil in hand, planned to transcribe every word into his journal, but once the message started, he could only listen, fascinated.

A man spoke, his voice quirky and heavy with a British accent. Not like Mothball's accent; no, this man's voice sounded much more sophisticated and tight, like the head butler at an English manor who has just realized his entire staff is stricken with the flu on the night of the big Christmas party to which hundreds of very important people are invited.

Well, one mystery had been solved: M.G. was a man.

When the short message ended, Tick laughed out loud, then rewound it to listen again. Then he quickly fast forwarded through the rest of the tape to make sure there were no other messages. On the fourth time, he wrote every single word into his journal:

Say the magic words when the day arrives,
then hit the ground below you ten times, as
hard as you can, with a very specific object.
It's a bit of a quandary because I can't tell
you what the object is. Let's just say, I hope

your soul is stronger than mine because there
are no exceptions to this requirement. Also,
the object must be the opposite of wrong but
not correct.

Whew, glad to have that bit done. I really
need to use the lavatory before I . . . oh,
sorry, . . . meant to turn the recorder off.
Where is that confounded button . . . ? Ah!
There we are—
     Click.

Tick hit the STOP button, shaking his head at how
crazy this M.G. guy seemed. Ever since he'd mentioned
peppermint sticks and sweetened milk in the first letter, Tick had sensed a subtle sense of humor in the
man, a contrast to the message of doom that seemed to
be laced throughout the clues and warnings. He wondered if he'd ever get to meet M.G. He'd already begun
to feel a sense of trust toward him.

Tick stared at his own handwriting, rereading the
words, committing them to memory. Something in the
back of his mind told him this one was simple, an itch
he couldn't quite scratch. The mystery lay in figuring
out what the object must be. Once he knew that, it
seemed pretty obvious what he needed to do: hit the
ground ten times after saying the magic words.

Tick decided it really came down to two phrases:

Let's just say, I hope your soul is stronger
than mine

and

the object must be the opposite of wrong but
not correct

Thinking, Tick flipped to a blank page in the
journal to see if jotting down notes could whip up his
brain functions into a frenzy. Staring at the empty
lines on the page made him suddenly remember that
he'd never written down the odd words Mothball
had said that day by the woods when she'd been list-
ing the things she wasn't allowed to mention. Mad
at himself for not doing it sooner, Tick squeezed his
eyes shut and searched the darkness of his vision, hoping bright neon words would jump out and remind
him of what she'd said. One or two did almost immediately, and after a few minutes he'd remembered
four and wrote them in a list on the left side of the
page.

The Master
The Barrier Wand
The Realities
The Kyoopy

There'd been another weird word that he couldn't quite recall. Nothing else came to him, and he realized his eyes were getting droopy, his brain nice and ready for an afternoon nap. Wanting to check his e-mail—and needing some fresh, cold air to wake him up—he threw his new journal into his backpack and headed off for the library, telling Lisa he'd be back in a couple of hours.

"Tick, don't you ever take that scarf off?" Ms. Sears asked, stopping Tick before he could make it to the library computers. He'd spent some time studying his *Journal of Curious Letters*, as well as finishing up the last bit of homework for the weekend, and wanted to check his e-mail account, though he'd yet to receive anything since leaving the hint phrases on the Pen Pal site.

"I guess my neck gets cold pretty easily," he said, shrugging while he faked a shiver. Of course Ms. Sears knew about his birthmark, but he wanted to avoid a lecture on not being ashamed of who you are. "Any cool books come in lately?"

Her brow furrowed as she thought, making her entire weave of hair shift like a jittery land mass triggered by an earthquake. "There's a new one by Savage, but I think he's too scary for you," she said, trying to hold back a smile.

Tick rolled his eyes. "I'll take my chances."

"Okay, but if you have nightmares, tell your mom that I warned you." She smiled. "I'll hold it up at the counter for you."

"Thanks, Ms. Sears." He inched toward the computers, and she got the message.

"Okay, then," she said. "Have fun."

He nodded, then sat down at a computer as soon as she walked away. His mind still spun, the clues of M.G. bouncing around his brain like renegade alphabet soup. He knew several things for sure, and he also knew what he still needed to figure out. For some reason, on May sixth he needed to close his eyes, say some magic words that he didn't know, and hit the ground ten times with an object still left to be determined. Piece of cake.

After logging into his e-mail Web site, he hesitated a second before hitting the INBOX button. He'd checked his e-mail almost every day for weeks, and he was always disappointed to find nothing there. *But what are the odds?* he thought. Who knew if anyone else out there had received anything, much less went searching the Internet for others. But Tick felt like he'd explode if he didn't find someone with whom to swap ideas and thoughts.

He clicked the mouse.

The INBOX page only took a couple of seconds to load and a subject line written all in capital letters caught his eye the instant it appeared. His breath caught in his throat. He stood up in excitement, his chair tipping backward to the ground with a ringing metallic clang. He noticed a few scowls from the other library patrons as he righted the chair and sat down, the skin of his face on fire. Once settled, he looked at the screen again, hoping his eyes hadn't been lying to his brain.

But there it was, in black capital letters, bold against the white background:

From: SOFIA PACINI
Subject: MESSAGES FROM M.G.

CHAPTER
13

TALKING TO SOFIA

As he opened the e-mail, Tick's heart pounded so much he felt like he was trying to breathe underwater. He could hardly believe it; to receive an e-mail from another person experiencing the same mysteries as he was would validate everything once and for all—even more than meeting Mothball or being attacked by the Gnat Rat.

Forcing his eyes to slow down and take in each word, Tick read the e-mail.

Dear Atticus Higginbottom,

I'll write to you in English, since I know you must be a typical American who can only speak

Americanese, and my English is, well, brilliant.
My name is Sofia Pacini and I live in the pretty
Alps in the country of Italy. Do you know where
Italy is? Probably not. You're too busy studying
the Big Mac and the Spider-Man and not world
geography. Maybe you can learn from Sofia
and be smart. I'm just teasing you, so please
don't cry. :)

I saw your post on the Pen Pal Web site and almost
swallowed my shoe. No, I didn't have a shoe in
my mouth, it just sounds like something a funny
Americanese boy would say.

Tick paused, trying to hold in a laugh since he'd
already embarrassed himself enough in front of the
library crowd. But this Italian girl . . . *was she for real?*
He continued reading.

I got a letter from a person named M.G. in
November. You too? At first I laughed and thought
it was my friend Tony, but the letter came from
Alaska, so I don't know. Then more came, and I
met a really tall lady called Mothball. Did you meet
her? She's like a walking tree with clothes, but I
like her.

So what do you think? Is this for real? What will
happen on the day? Did you figure everything out?
Find anyone else? Write me back.

Your new friend,
Sofia

P.S. You have a weird name, btw.

Tick hated when the e-mail ended, wishing she'd
written him pages and pages of what she thought
and felt and if she'd figured out the magic words or
anything else. He clicked the REPLY TO SENDER
button.

Dear Sofia,

He paused, wondering what in the world he should
write to her. The chilling thought hit him that maybe
he shouldn't trust her. Maybe she was on the side of
whoever or whatever had sent the Tingle Wraith and
Gnat Rat. Maybe she was a spy, ready to feed him
information leading him away from the solution, not
toward it.

That's just a chance I'll have to take, he thought.
Shrugging the worry away, he began typing his message.

I know I have a weird name. Everyone calls me Tick,
so you can, too.

Sounds like we're in the same boat. I've received
three clues now, one of them on a tape. How about
you? I met Mothball, too. She gave me the second
clue. Maybe we can help each other?

He almost started telling her the things he'd figured
out and which ones had him stumped, but decided to
wait to see if she would write him back. One more e-mail
from her ought to help him know for sure if she was okay.
After thinking for a minute, he finished his letter.

I wonder how many others like us are out there.
I hope someone else writes me. Let me know if
anyone writes to you, OK?

Have you seen anything like a ghost made out of
smoke that turns into a grandpa face? What about
a Gnat Rat? That thing put me in the hospital, but
I'm OK now. How old are you? I'm thirteen, and I
live in Washington, though you already know that
because I guess you saw my Pen Pal account.

You're from Italy? That's way awesome. I wish we
could meet and talk face to face about this stuff.

I'm keeping all my notes in a book called Tick
Higginbottom's Journal of Curious Letters. Pretty
cool, huh?

Talk to you later,
Tick

He clicked SEND, knowing Sofia probably wouldn't
read the e-mail until tomorrow because it was already
past bedtime in Italy. His initial excitement tempered
by the thought that he wouldn't hear back from Sofia
for at least a day, he logged off the computer and
grabbed his backpack.

On his way out, Ms. Sears reminded him of the
book she had held for him and he checked it out just
to be nice. With everything going on in his life, reading a new book suddenly seemed dull in comparison.
Tick shook his head; he never would've thought he'd
say *that*.

The book tucked safely in his backpack next to his
journal, Tick exited the library and headed home.

Halfway there, he figured out the answer to the
third clue.

It came to him when he tripped over a big stick in
the middle of the sidewalk. As he rubbed his knee while

sitting on the cold ground, he looked at the soles of his shoes, which were caked with chunky black sludge. He wondered where they'd gotten so dirty and had just had the thought that it must've been from the mud caused by the melting snow when both of the important phrases from the third clue seemed to solve themselves simultaneously, several words flashing across his mind's eye in a rush of understanding.

Opposite of wrong but not correct.

Opposite of wrong but not the word *correct. The word* right!

Soul is stronger than mine.

Sole *is stronger than mine.*

Sole *of his shoe.*

Sole *of his* right *shoe.*

Not bothering to get up from the sidewalk, Tick whipped out his journal and turned to the page where he'd written the words from the audio tape. He'd misunderstood when M.G. said he hoped Tick's soul was stronger than his. The real word was *sole*, not soul, meaning M.G. hoped the sole of his shoe was strong enough to protect his foot, his *right* foot, as he hit the ground with it ten times.

Tick scribbled his thoughts down then stood up, his blood surging through his veins. Though he still felt so clueless it was ridiculous, he'd taken another small step. On May sixth, Tick needed to say magic words that he didn't know then stomp the ground with his right foot ten times.

As he ran the rest of the way home, he couldn't help but marvel at how completely stupid that sounded.

Three days passed with no reply from Sofia, and though he'd never met her, Tick felt worried sick that something terrible had happened to her. Or that maybe she'd given up and burned the letter from M.G., surrendering once and for all. Tick could barely think of anything else, losing his focus in school; he actually got a B on a test, shocking his English teacher beyond words. Every morning and night he checked his e-mail at home, and he swung by the library every chance he got.

When an entire week had passed in silence, his heart felt completely ill and he didn't know what else to do but give up on her.

The Thursday before Christmas vacation started, he walked home from school, his head down, staring at his feet through the falling snow. They'd had a couple of weeks' break from the white stuff, but it had come back with a fury the night before and hadn't let up. Tick didn't complain, of course, he loved the heavy snow. But he couldn't cheer up, feeling sad about Sofia and the lack of any more clues from his mysterious stranger.

He was just passing the patch of woods where he'd met Mothball when something caught his eye on the other side of the road. A wooden sign had been hastily nailed to a sharpened stick and hammered into the ground. Some words were painted on it in messy blue paint, the letters dripping like blood. He couldn't tell what most of the sign said from his position, but two of the words stood out like a pair of leprechauns in a hamster cage.

Atticus Higginbottom

CHAPTER
14

SHOES AND MITTENS

Tick ran over to the sign, squinting his eyes through the swirling snow to read the smaller words underneath his name. His brow crinkled in confusion. He read the sign over again, almost expecting the words to change the second time. Just when he thought he was used to how bizarre his life had become, he received a message that seemed to make no sense.

Atticus Higginbottom
Meet me when night is a backwards dim
Don't look for a her 'cause I am a him
The steps of your porch will do just fine
But don't bring snakes, spiders, or swine

For you I have important news
In return I ask for children's shoes
One more thing, or see me spittin'
Be sure to bring two nice soft mittens

If Tick had woken up that morning and guessed one thousand things a special sign made just for him might have said, a request for children's shoes and mittens would not have made the list. Not knowing what else to do, and not real keen on anyone else seeing the sign, he yanked it up out of the ground and carried it home with him, trying to sort out the message. There didn't really seem to be too many clues in the poem, just a request to meet on the steps of his porch.

Meet me when night is a backwards dim

Tick figured that one out almost instantly. "Dim" spelled backward was "mid," which meant the stranger wanted him to be waiting on his porch at midnight—presumably tonight. The now familiar shiver of excitement tickled Tick's spine as he looked at his watch and saw he still had almost seven hours to wait.

Bummer, he thought. It was going to be a long evening.

At dinner that night, Tick sat with his whole family eating meatloaf, the one thing in the universe his mom cooked that disgusted him like fried toenails. If given the choice, it would've been a tough decision between the two. He absolutely hated, despised, and loathed meatloaf. Yuck.

He forced down a bite or two, then did his best to smash the gray-green blobs of meat into a little ball so it looked like he'd eaten more than he really had. Kayla devoured hers, though she put just as much on the floor as she did in her mouth.

"What's the latest at school?" Dad asked, reaching for the bowl of mashed potatoes.

"Not much. I'm doing okay." Tick realized he'd let his mind get too occupied lately, spending less time with his family. He resolved to do better. They were, after all, just about the only friends he had in the world, besides Mr. Chu.

And Mothball, he thought. *And Sofia. Maybe.*

"Just okay?" Lisa said. "What? Did Einstein Junior get a bad grade or something?"

"Oh, please," his mom said through a snicker as though the idea was the funniest thing that had ever been spoken aloud.

"Well . . . I did get a B on my last English test."

Dead silence settled around the table like he'd just announced he was an alien and was about to have a baby because on Mars the men were the ones who got pregnant. Even Kayla had dropped her wad of meatloaf, staring at him with blank eyes.

"What?" Tick asked, knowing very well what the answer would be.

"Son," his dad said, "you haven't gotten a B on anything since I've known you. And I've known you since the day you were born."

"Yeah," Lisa agreed. "I think the world has stopped spinning."

Tick shrugged, scooping up a mouthful of green beans. "Ah, it's nothing. Maybe I had bad gas that day."

Kayla laughed out loud, then yelled in a sing-songy voice, "Tick had tooty-buns! Tick had tooty-buns!"

That broke everyone up, and dinner continued like normal.

"Anything happen lately with your Pen Pal account?" Mom asked.

Tick almost choked on his potatoes, for a split second worried that somehow his mom had logged into his account and seen the e-mail from Sofia. But then he realized he was just being a worrywart, her question totally innocent. He'd been doing the Pen Pal thing for a couple of years, still having never really connected with anyone for more than a few letters here and there. No one had ever seemed interesting enough for him to want to stay in touch—or maybe it was the other way around.

"Not really. I got an e-mail from some girl in Italy, but she seems kind of psycho."

"Psycho?" Dad asked. "Why, what did she say?"

"She called me an Americanese boy and asked me a million dumb questions."

Mom tsked. "Last time I checked, not speaking English well and being curious did not make someone a psycho. Give her a chance. Maybe she likes chess."

"Maybe she's cute," Lisa added. "You could marry her and join the mafia."

"Sweetheart," Dad said. "I don't think everyone from Italy is in the mob."

"Yeah, it's probably only like half," Tick said. He expected Lisa to laugh at his joke, but was disappointed to see she thought he'd been serious.

"Really?" she asked.

"It was a joke, sis."

"Oh. Yeah, I knew that."

"Well, anyway," Dad said, moving on. "I think this weekend we should all go see a movie, go bowling or something. Who's in?"

By habit, everyone around the table raised their hand. Kayla shrieked as she waved both arms in the air.

"All right, plan on it. Everyone meet right here at noon on Saturday."

For some reason, right at that moment, the thought hit Tick that he should tell his dad about everything.

Keeping the secret was eating away at his insides and now with nothing but silence from Sofia, the feeling was getting worse, not better. Just thinking about telling someone seemed to take a thirty-pound dumbbell off his shoulders.

Next time Mom's out shopping, he thought, *I'll tell him. Maybe he can help me figure everything out. If he believes me.*

Tick put his dishes away, then watched some ridiculous game show on TV with his family. The whole time, he thought of one thing and one thing only.

Midnight.

It was time for bed, but Tick wanted to check his e-mail one more time. He felt obsessed, checking it constantly in hopes that Sofia would finally write him back.

He sipped a cup of hot chocolate as he logged into the computer in the living room, almost spilling his drink when he saw Sofia's name in the INBOX. He put his cup down and leaned forward, clicking on her e-mail.

Dear Tick,

Someone needs to teach you how to answer a stinking question. I asked you many and all you did was write back asking me more. If I lived in the USA, I would smack your head with a pogo stick. I am a good, smart Italian girl, and so I will actually answer your questions.

First, I have to tell you that I had a very hard week. Something is chasing me, and I'm very scared. I almost burned the letter five times. Well, not really. When a Pacini makes a decision, a Pacini never goes back. I made my choice, and I'll stick to it like butter on a peanut, or whatever you crazy Americans say.

Anyway, I will now answer your questions.

I have four clues now. I got the last one last night. Maybe you did, too. It's about dead people, which doesn't sound good.

We should definitely help each other.

Saw the ghost thing, but not the rat thing. Don't want to talk about it.

I'm twelve years old, almost thirteen.

I like your journal idea. I made one, too. Hope it's okay to steal your name. Mine is called Sofia Pacini's Journal of Curious Letters. I even used English to make it seem like yours.

I joke a lot, and if we meet you will think I'm crazy.
Last summer I beat up seventeen boys. Glad we can
be friends.

Ciao (that's Italiano, smart boy)
Sofia

He'd just finished reading the e-mail when his
dad told him to log off and go up to bed. Grumbling,
he obeyed, hating that he'd have to wait until tomorrow to write Sofia back. He thought about sneaking
downstairs after his parents were asleep, but he knew
Edgar "Light Sleeper" Higginbottom would catch him
as soon as he heard the buzz of the computer fan. It was
going to be hard enough to tiptoe through the house
and open the door to the front porch at midnight without waking him.

He brushed his teeth and said good night to everyone, then got into bed, his lamp on for reading. He
decided to take a break from the fantasy novel he had
been reading and pulled out the book by Savage, flipping to Chapter One.

Twenty minutes later, he did the worst thing he
could possibly do.

He fell asleep.

CHAPTER
15

LITTLE BALL OF BREAD DOUGH

Tick snapped awake a half-hour after midnight. His alarm clock glowed with evil red numbers, as if they wanted to make sure he knew his mistake was unforgivable.

Jumping out of bed with a groan, he ran to his window and looked outside for any sign of the supposed visitor. He couldn't see the entire porch from his angle, but the steps were visible in the bright moonlight that poked through a break in the clouds. No one was there, and Tick felt his heart sink.

I'm such an idiot!

Maybe he'd messed the whole thing up and lost the trust of M.G. He didn't know who'd painted the sign, but he had no doubt it was related to the M.G. mystery, and he even suspected it was Mothball or maybe her friend Rutger. She'd said he might come visit him. Sofia mentioned in her e-mail that she'd received the fourth clue, but Tick hadn't seen his yet. What if the midnight meeting was supposed to provide it?

Hardly able to stand the frustration and worry, Tick put on some warm clothes, determined to go outside and search for his visitor.

Stepping only on quiet spots in the house, avoiding the most obvious creaks and groans he knew from years of experience, he crept down the stairs and to the front door. After quietly slipping into his coat and boots, then wrapping his scarf tightly around his neck, he very carefully unlocked the deadbolt, then turned the handle. Knowing if he opened the door slowly, it would let out a creak that would wake the dead, he jerked it open in one quick motion, preventing almost any sound at all.

His heart pounding, he stepped out into the bitterly cold night, quietly shutting the door behind him.

After searching the whole yard and finding nothing, he sat on the front porch and put his head into his cupped hands, squeezing his eyes shut in anger at himself. How could he have been so stupid? He should never have lain down to read—everyone knew that was the number one way in the world to make yourself fall asleep. He blew out an exasperated sigh as he leaned back and folded his arms, looking up at the sky. Dark, churning clouds, their edges softly illuminated by the moon hiding behind them, seemed to move across the sky at an unnatural pace like something from a horror movie in fast forward.

Tick shivered, and he knew it wasn't the cold alone that caused it.

He leaned forward to stand up when something hit him on his right temple, followed by the soft clatter of a rock tumbling down the steps. He looked just in time to see a pebble the size of a walnut come to a rest a few feet away.

Belatedly, he said, "Ow" as he looked around to discover where the rock had come from. Nothing stirred in the darkness, the only sound a slight breeze whispering through the leafless trees in the front yard and sighing over the snow-covered bushes lining the front of the house. He thought one bush may have moved more than the others, and he was just about to investigate when another rock hit him, this time in the right shoulder. Sure enough, the rock came from the suspected bush, the powdery layer of snow almost completely knocked off.

"Who's over there?" he asked, surprised he didn't

feel more scared. "Quit throwing rocks like a baby and come out."

The bush rustled again, then a small figure stepped out from behind the branches. It was impossible to make out details in the scant light, but the person looked like a little kid, maybe six or seven years old, bundled up in layers and layers of clothes. He or she resembled nothing so much as a big round ball with little bumps for arms and legs and a head.

"Who are you?" Tick asked, standing up and stepping closer. "Are you the one who left me the note on the sign?"

The little person walked toward him, waddling like an overweight duck. A shaft of moonlight broke through the clouds just as the visitor reached a spot a few feet in front of Tick, revealing in vivid detail what he'd thought was a child.

It was a man. A very short and very fat man.

He was dressed all in black—black sweat pants and sweatshirt, black tennis shoes, black coat, black hat pulled over his ears. Tick's dad had once made a joke that sweat suits were made for people to exercise in, but the only people who seemed to wear them were fat people like himself.

Knowing all too well what it felt like to be made fun of, Tick always tried never to do it to anyone else. As the strange little round man walked up to him, Tick promised himself he would do his best to refrain from all known fat jokes.

"I'm *large*, okay?" the man said, though he barely came to Tick's waist. His voice was normal with no accent or strange pitch. Tick didn't know why that surprised him so much, but then he realized he'd been expecting the guy to sound like one of the Munchkins from *The Wizard of Oz.*

So much for not judging others on their looks.

The short man continued, "And I must be the dumbest fat guy you'll ever meet, because I wore all black to camouflage myself in a place that is covered in *snow.*"

Tick stared, with no idea how to respond.

"My name is Rutger," the stranger said, holding a hand up toward Tick. "My hand might be the size of your big toe, but don't be scared to shake it. Nice to meet you."

Tick reached down and clasped Rutger's hand, shaking it very gently.

"What's that?" Rutger asked. "Feels like I'm grabbing a floppy fish. You think I'm made of porcelain or something? Shake my hand if you're gonna shake my hand!"

Tick gripped harder and shook, completely amazed by this new person. He finally spoke back. "Sorry. I'm just a little surprised. I didn't know . . ."

"What? That I'd look like a shrunken Sumo wrestler? Come on, let's sit and talk awhile. This weight is killer on my tiny legs." Rutger didn't wait for a response, walking over to the porch steps and taking a seat on the bottom step. Even then, his feet barely touched the ground in front of him.

Tick smiled, finally feeling at ease, and joined Rutger on the steps. "So, you're friends with Mothball, right?"

Rutger slapped his round belly. "You betcha I am! That tall stack of sticks is the best friend a man can have, even if she *is* three times my size. Well, up and down, anyway, if you know what I mean." He raised his hand vertically, as if guessing the height of something. "Ah, Mothball's a funny one if you get her going. Word to the wise though. Don't ever ask her about the day she and her twin sis were born unless you have about seven days with nothing else to do but sit and listen."

Tick grinned. "I'll remember that. Why'd you throw those rocks at me?"

"Why were you late?"

"I . . . uh, good point. Slept in."

Rutger looked at Tick intently, searching for something. "Looks like you forgot your assignment, too."

"I did? What—" Then Tick remembered the poem and what it had asked for. He'd meant to scrounge around in the basement to find some old shoes and mittens. "Oh, never mind—you're right, I forgot. Sorry."

Rutger slapped Tick on the shoulder. "It's okay, I can wait."

"Huh? You mean . . ."

"That's right, big fella. Come back with what I asked for and maybe I'll talk."

Tick paused before responding, hopeful that Rutger would wink and say he'd only been kidding. "You're . . . serious?"

Rutger leaned closer like a giant rubber ball rolling forward. "I've been to more places in the last two weeks than you've seen in your whole life, boy. My shoes are just about ready to call it a day and walk off my feet— no pun intended, though that was a pretty good one. And my hands—cold, young man, *cold.*"

"You mean, the shoes and mittens are for *you?*"

"Who else, boy? Do you think I'd be traipsing around the Realities with a little child stuck to my hip? Of course they're for me!" His voice had risen considerably, and Tick worried his dad would hear.

"Don't talk so loud. You'll wake the whole neighborhood."

Rutger answered in an exaggerated whisper. "You won't hear another peep from me until I'm holding a nice new pair of shoes and a warm-as-muffins pair of mittens." He nodded curtly and folded his arms.

Tick stood up. "I'll go—but what did you mean when you said the *Realities*?"

"Oh, come on, boy. It's all about the kyoopy—science, Chi'karda, Barrier Wands!"

Tick stared, wondering if anyone in history had ever answered a question as poorly as Rutger just had. "What are you talking about?"

Rutger put two fingers together and swiped them across his lips, the age-old sign for zipping one's mouth shut.

"Fine," Tick muttered. "Be back in a minute."

He walked up the porch steps and opened the front door. Just before he stepped into the house, Tick heard Rutger say something creepy.

"Good. Because when you get back, we need to talk about dead people."

CHAPTER
16

NOWHERE IN BETWEEN

Tick wasted five minutes searching for the box in the basement where his old clothes were stored—the ones his mom couldn't bear to part with. He finally spotted it and pulled almost everything out before he found a pile of shoes of varying sizes. He chose three pairs that seemed the closest to Rutger's size, then rummaged through everything else again, searching for mittens or gloves. He found nothing.

He walked back upstairs, still doing his best to keep quiet, and dove into the closet holding all of their winter clothing. He finally came across a pair of yellow mittens his grandma in Georgia had knitted out of yarn a long time ago. They'd been his once, but Kayla had been wearing them ever since she destroyed her own pair in the fireplace. Tick tried not to laugh at the thought that they should fit Rutger just perfectly.

I can't believe I have a Hobbit in my own front yard.

Holding in a snicker, he went outside.

"Oh, those will do just fine. Just fine! Thank you." Rutger hurriedly pulled on the mittens, then replaced his worn shoes with a pair of sneakers that Tick must've grown out of very quickly because they still looked relatively new.

"Glad to be of service," Tick said, settling on the step beside his new friend. He shivered from the cold and tightened his scarf around his neck. "Now I think you had a lot to tell me? What was that about dead people?"

The little man rubbed his newly wrapped hands together and leaned against the step behind him. "Ah, yes, dead people. There's a phrase that Mas—" He caught himself before saying anything else, looking at Tick with guilt written all over his face.

"What?" Tick asked.

"Oh, nothing . . . nothing. I was just going to say that there's something a good friend of mine always says: 'Nothing in this world better reflects the difference between life and death than the power of choice.' Says that all the time, my friend does."

"What does that have to do with me?"

Rutger looked at him intently. "What's your name, son?"

"Atticus Higginbottom. Or Tick."

"Yes, that's right." Rutger pulled out a notepad and pencil from his pocket, then started scanning it, much like Mothball had done. "There you are, and there we go." He wrote a checkmark next to Tick's name, then put the pad and pencil back into his pocket. When he pulled his hand out, this time he was holding a yellow envelope. "I believe you've been expecting this."

"The fourth clue?"

"You got it."

He handed the envelope to Tick, who immediately ripped it open then pulled out the cardstock containing the next message from M.G. Before he could read it, Rutger placed a pudgy hand on top of the clue.

"Remember what I said about dead people, young man."

"What exactly *did* you say?"

"Well, nothing really, now that you mention it. Wasn't supposed to say much, anyhow. It's for you to figure out."

"You've really cleared things up for me, Rutger, thank you."

The round man's eyes narrowed. "Do I sense a hint of sarcasm?"

Tick laughed. "Not just a hint." He pulled the message out from under Rutger's hand. "May I please read this now?"

Rutger waved a hand. "Read to your heart's delight."

Squinting to see in the patchy moonlight, Tick did just that.

> The place is for you to determine
> and can be in your hometown. I only
> ask that the name of the place begin
> with a letter coming _after_ A and
> _before_ Z but nowhere in between. You
> are allowed to have people there with
> you, as many as you like, as long as
> they are dead by the time you say the
> magic words. But, by the Wand, make
> sure that _you_ are not dead, of course.
> That would truly throw a wrinkle into
> our plans.

Tick looked over at Rutger. "I can bring people with me, as long as they're dead before I say the magic words? That doesn't make any sense."

The short man smiled and shrugged his shoulders. "Hey, I didn't write the clues."

"And how can a letter come after A, before Z, but

nowhere in between? Wouldn't that exclude all twenty-six letters?"

"Who am I, Sherlicken Holmestotter? You figure it out, kid." He rubbed his arms and shoulders with his mittened hands.

"Sherlicken who? Do you mean Sherlock Holmes?"

Rutger gave him a blank stare. "No, I mean Sherlicken Holmestotter, the greatest detective who ever lived."

Tick didn't know what to think of that answer. "So are you going to tell me anything worthwhile or not?"

"I'm leaning toward the *not*, actually."

"Boy, you and Mothball sure are a lot of help. Why didn't M.G. just send me letters in the mail like he did with the other stuff?" Tick shivered again, and realized his warm clothes and scarf weren't enough to block out the freezing cold.

"Nice to meet you, too." Rutger looked down at the ground, no small feat with his huge belly. "I guess you didn't want me to come, did you?"

"Hey, I was just kidding." Tick tried to keep from laughing as he reached out and patted the man's shoulder. Maybe it was the guy's size, but Tick felt like he was consoling a little kid. "I'm glad we met. I just wish you could tell me a little more about what's going on."

"Trust me, I'm dying to tell everything, but that would defeat the whole point, now wouldn't it?"

Tick threw his hands up in frustration. "What *is* the point?"

Rutger grew serious. "I think you know, Tick. You've made a choice to pursue this endeavor, and no matter what, you must see it to the end. By the very act of making it to the special day, and solving the riddles of what will happen at that time, you will be properly prepared for . . ." He paused, fidgeting with the buttons on his coat.

"For what?"

"I can't tell you."

"What a surprise." Tick wanted to be angry, but instead felt torn between disappointment and eagerness to solve everything at once. He'd always been that way; he wanted to know things right then and now, which was probably one reason why he did so well in school. He often read ahead in his books, curiosity lighting the fire of his impatience, which only added to his status as Nerd-Boy of the Universe.

"I will say this," Rutger said. "I truly hope you make it, Tick. I want to see you when it all comes down to the boiling point." He turned his squat little body and looked Tick in the eye. "You'll be there, I'm sure of it."

"I'll try."

Rutger snorted. "*Try* is for dingbats with no heart. You will *do*, young man, *do*."

"Who are you—Yoda?"

"Huh?"

"Never mind."

Rutger stood up with a loud groan, seeming to barely rise in height even though he had his legs straight under him. "Well, must be off to the wild blue yonder. Feels like I haven't eaten in three weeks." He patted his stomach. "Boy, I sure do enjoy a lovely meal now and then." He cleared his throat loudly, as if trying to give a hint.

"Where are you from, anyway?" Tick asked, trying his best to avoid any subject that dealt with the man's weight.

"I, young man, am from the Eleventh—the finest place you could ever visit."

"The Eleventh?"

"Things developed a little differently there, if you know what I mean."

"No, I don't know what you mean."

"Oh. Yes. Well, someday you will."

Tick sighed. "What were those words you said earlier? Kyoopy, Barrier Wands, chika-something?"

Rutger only raised his eyebrows in reply.

"Let me guess, you can't tell me."

"That's my boy, getting smarter by the minute." Rutger stretched and let out a big yawn. "Well, it was very nice to meet you, Tick. I expected someone a little more generous with treats and goodies, but what can you do?"

Tick rolled his eyes. "Do you want something—"

"No, no, maybe *next* time you can be a good host," Rutger replied with no subtlety. "You go on inside and stuff yourself with turkey and beans while little old Rutger walks his long journey home. At least I have new shoes, I guess."

Little? Tick thought, but wisely didn't say. "Oh, hang on a minute. You're a pathetic actor." He slipped inside the house and grabbed some bread, a bag of cookies, and a couple of bananas, throwing them all into a grocery bag, trying his best to be quiet. He forced himself to take extra precautions with every trip through the front door. He didn't need his dad waking up to find him giving out free food to a weird little fat guy in the middle of the night.

When he handed the bag to Rutger, the man beamed with joy. "Oh, thank you seven times over, my good man! Thank you, indeed!"

Tick smiled. "You're welcome. When will I see you again?"

Rutger started down the sidewalk, looking over his shoulder as best he could. "Many tomorrows, I expect, many tomorrows. Good-bye, Master Atticus!"

"Bye." Tick waved, feeling a pang of sadness as he watched Rutger set off down the road.

Edgar watched from the upstairs window in the hallway, his emotions torn between fascination at the miniature fat man that seemed to have struck up a friendship with his son, and his sadness that Tick was involved in something very strange and had failed to tell his own father about it. He and Tick had always had a special bond, sharing anything and everything. Had things changed so much? Had his boy grown up, leaving his poor father behind to wallow in ignorance?

It all made sense now. Tick had been acting so bizarre lately and the reasons behind it could very well change the way Edgar viewed the world in which he lived. As he'd watched the two speak together on the steps of the porch, he'd readied himself to run outside at the first sign of danger. But the man seemed to be a friend, and Edgar decided to wait a while before he confronted Tick about it.

He told himself he didn't know why he wanted to wait, but his heart knew the truth. Deep inside, he hoped his son would decide to tell him on his own what was going on. Edgar could hold out just a little bit longer—maybe a day or two—watching his son's every move.

Down below, Tick waved as his short friend disappeared down the dark road.

Quickly, Edgar turned and went back to his room.

CHAPTER 17

SMOKY BATHROOM

The next day was Friday, the last day of school for two weeks, and Tick thought it would never end. Having enjoyed a grand total of four hours of sleep the night before, he nodded off in class constantly, waking with an unpleasant string of drool on his chin more than once. Mr. Chu was the only teacher who gave him a hard time about it, but Tick survived.

Finally, the last bell of the day rang.

Tick was at his locker, the excitement of the coming vacation days perking him up a bit, when disaster struck in the form of a tap on his shoulder. He turned to see Billy "The Goat" Cooper sneering at him with arms folded, his goons gathered behind his massive body.

Just wait it out, Tick, just wait it out.

"Well, looky here," Billy said, his voice the sound of marbles being crushed in a vice. "Looks like Ticky Stinkbottom and his pet Barf Scarf are excited to go home and wait for Santy Claus. Whatcha getting this year, Atticus? A new teddy bear?"

"Yes," Tick said, stone faced, knowing it would throw the Goat off track.

Billy faltered, surely having expected Tick to adamantly say no or try to walk away. "Well, then . . . I hope . . . it smells bad."

Tick really wanted to say something sarcastic—*It's a teddy bear, not a Billy the Goat doll*—but his common sense won out. "It probably will, with my luck," he said instead.

"Yeah, it will. Just like your feet." Billy snorted out a laugh, and his cronies joined in.

Tick couldn't believe how idiotic this guy was, but held his face still and said nothing.

"Here's an early Christmas present for you, Ticky Stinkbottom," Billy said, and his cronies' forced laughter ended abruptly. "Stay in your locker for three minutes, instead of the usual ten. Then, go into the bathroom and stick your head in a toilet. Do that and we won't bother you until we get back from Christmas break. Deal?"

Tick felt his stomach drop because he knew Billy

would send a spy to make sure he did what he'd been ordered to do. "With my hair wet, I might catch a cold on the way home."

Billy reached out and slammed Tick up against the locker, sending a metallic clang echoing down the hallway. "Then I guess it's a good thing we don't have school for two weeks, now isn't it?" He let go and stood back. "Come on, guys, let's go."

As they walked off, Tick lowered his head and stepped into his locker, closing the door behind him.

A few minutes later, he stood alone in the boys' bathroom, staring at his distorted image in a moldy, warped mirror. He pulled down his scarf with two fingers and examined his birthmark, which looked just as ugly as ever. He felt himself sliding into that state of depression he'd visited so often before he had resolved to quit letting the bullies rule his life.

But then he thought of Mothball and Rutger, the letters and clues, and the way they all made him feel *important*. He snapped out of the gloom and doom, and smiled at himself in the mirror.

Forget those morons. I'm not sticking my head in the toilet, spy or no spy.

A moving smudge suddenly appeared on the reflection of his face, like black moss growing across the mirror. Startled, Tick reached out and touched it with his finger, but only felt the cool hardness of the glass. In a matter of seconds, the entire mirror was dark, blacking out everything. Tick took a step back, a shot of panic shooting through him.

The blackness grew, enveloping the wall and the sink, moving outward in all directions. It took on substance, puffing out like black cotton, devouring the entire bathroom wall. Tick spun to see that all the walls and the ceiling were covered now, dark smoke everywhere. The room looked like the result of a five-alarm fire, but Tick couldn't see flames and felt no urge to cough.

Then, with a great whooshing sound, every bit of the strange smoky substance rushed to the exit of the bathroom in streaks of wispy darkness, coalescing there into a big ball of black smoke. Tick's heart stuttered to a stop as he realized what hovered between him and the exit.

A Tingle Wraith.

Tick moved to run, but stopped instantly. He had nowhere to go. The Wraith completely blocked the one and only exit out of the bathroom, its dark smoke already forming into the same ancient, bearded face he'd seen in the alley a few weeks ago. Mothball's words about the creature came back to him, sending a sickening lurch through his body.

If any man, woman, or child hears the Death Siren for thirty seconds straight, their brain turns right to mush. Nasty death, that.

Tick turned to look for another way out. A tiny window let some daylight in, but other than that, there were only stalls and urinals. He ran to the thin slat of a window and grabbed the metal crank bar to open the window. He twisted the bar clockwise and a horrible screech of metal on metal boomed through the room as the glass slowly tilted outward.

Somewhere in the back of his mind, he knew the Wraith would start its deathly cry soon. He looked over his shoulder and saw the mouth forming into a wide, black abyss.

Tick quickened his pace, cranking the window as hard as he could. It jammed when it reached the half-way point. He pushed and pulled but the lever wouldn't budge. He beat against the glass with both fists, but ended up with bruised knuckles, leaving the dirty glass unbroken. Desperate, he tried to squeeze through the window anyway, pushing one arm through. It didn't take long to see it was hopeless. The crack was too thin.

He ran to the stalls, jumping up on one of the toilets to see if he could lift a ceiling tile and climb up. But it was too far above his head.

And then he heard it, the worst sound to ever beat

his eardrums, a cacophony of nightmarish wails. The sound of dying men on a battlefield. The sound of a mom screaming for a lost child. The sound of criminals at the gallows, waiting to drop into their nooses. All mixed together into one horribly terrifying hum.

The Death Siren.

Thirty seconds.

As the Wraith's cry increased in volume with every passing second, Tick squirmed his way onto the top of the stall siding, balancing as it creaked and groaned below him. He held on with one hand and reached up with the other, stretching to see if he could touch the tiles. His fingertip brushed it, but that was all.

Frantic, he jumped back down to the floor and ran out of the stall, spinning in a wide circle, looking for ideas, for a way out.

The Death Siren rose in pitch and volume, growing more horrible by the second. Tick covered his ears with both hands, hoping to quell the noise, but the stifled groan he heard was worse. Spookier. Creepier. He knew it was almost over, that he only had a few more breaths until his brain turned to mush from the loud, haunting cry.

He looked directly at the Tingle Wraith. As he stared at its wispy black face, long and old and sad, its mouth bellowing out the terrible sound, Tick realized he had only one choice.

He dropped his hands from his ears, closed his eyes, and ran straight toward the smoky ghost.

Tick held both arms out in front of him, stiffening them like a battering ram, and charged. He crossed the floor in two seconds, his clenched fists the first thing to make contact. Not knowing what to expect, and his mind half insane knowing the thirty seconds were almost up, Tick threw himself forward with every bit of strength in his legs and feet.

A cold, biting tingle enveloped his hands and arms and then his whole body as he ran straight through the black smoke of the Wraith. The Death Siren took on a different pitch—lower, gloomy. Tick felt like he'd dived into a pool of arctic water, everything muffled and frigid and dark.

But then he was through the Wraith's body, slamming into the wall on the other side. His mind sliding into shock, Tick flung open the bathroom door and threw his body out into the hallway, banging the door shut behind him.

Silence filled the school, but he could still hear a muted ringing in his ears, like the tolling of death bells.

CHAPTER
18

EDGAR THE WISE

Tick crouched on the floor of the hallway, panting for several minutes, exhausted and unable to move another inch. He kept looking at the crack under the bathroom door, sure the Tingle Wraith would follow him, but nothing came out. Mothball had told him the Wraiths couldn't move very much once they were positioned and formed. Their weapon was the Death Siren.

He finally stood, his nerves and heart settling back to normalcy, filled with relief. Tick felt sure the creature had gone away. Shaking his head as he remembered the horrible feeling of running *through* the Wraith, he set off for home, knowing what he had to do.

It was time to have a little chat with Dad.

The next few hours seemed to take days. Tick did his best to act normal: showering to wash away the icky feel of the Tingle Wraith, joking around with Mom and Lisa, playing with Kayla, reading. When his dad finally came home from work, Tick wanted to take him up to his room right that minute and spill the whole story. He couldn't do this alone anymore. He needed support, and Sofia was just too far away.

But Tick had to wait even longer because after dinner, Dad challenged Tick to a game of Scrabble, which he usually loved, but tonight seemed to drag on longer than ever before. To liven things up, he put down the word "kyoopy," at which his dad had a fit, demanding a challenge. Tick held in a snicker as he lost the challenge and had to remove the word, losing his turn. He still won by forty-three points.

Finally, as they were cleaning up the game, Tick managed to casually ask his dad to come up to his room for a minute.

"What's going on, son?" his dad asked, sitting on Tick's bed, one leg folded up under the other. "You've been acting a little strange lately."

Tick paused, running through the decision one last time in his head. This was it, no turning back. He couldn't tell his dad about everything tonight and then say he was kidding tomorrow.

All or nothing, now or never.

He chose *all* and *now*.

"Dad, there's a good reason I've been acting so crazy." Tick leaned down and pulled his *Journal of Curious Letters* from underneath the bed where he'd stowed it away that morning. "Remember that letter I got a few weeks ago? The one from Alaska?"

"Yeah. Let me guess—it wasn't from a nice Pen Pal buddy?"

"No, it was from a stranger, saying he was going to send me a bunch of clues in hopes I could figure out something important that could end up saving a bunch of people." He paused, expecting his dad to say something, but he only got a blank look, ready to hear more. "I thought it was a joke at first, but then weird things started happening—like the Gnat Rat—and I started receiving the clues and I've met some very interesting people and I believe it's true, Dad. I *know* it's true."

Tick expected a laugh, a chastisement, a lecture on not playing make-believe when you're thirteen years old. But his heart lifted at his dad's next words.

"Tell me everything, from the beginning."

And Tick did.

It took thirty minutes, and Tick showed his dad every page and note of his journal, hiding nothing, repeating every word he could remember of his conversations with Mothball and Rutger. He told it all, and when he finished, he felt like three loads of concrete had been lifted from his chest.

His dad held the journal in his hands, staring at the front cover for a long minute. Tick waited anxiously, hoping with all his heart that his dad would believe him and offer help.

"Tick, you're my son, and I love you more than anything in this world. This family is the only thing in the universe I give a crying hoot about and I'd do anything for any one of you guys. But I need some time to digest this, okay?"

Tick nodded.

"I'm going to take your journal. I'm going to study it tonight. And I'm going to think long and hard about everything you've told me. Tomorrow night, we'll meet again right here in this very spot. And if anything weird or dangerous happens, you find me, you call me, whatever you have to do. Deal?"

"Deal. Just let me copy down the fourth clue so I can work on it while you have my book."

When he was finished, the two hugged, his dad left the room, and Tick fell asleep with no problem at all.

The next night, Tick sat at his desk in the soft golden glow of his lamp, studying the fourth clue he'd scribbled on a piece of paper, waiting for his dad to come. Something about this riddle made him think it wasn't as hard as it first seemed, and he read it again, thinking carefully about each word.

The place is for you to determine and can be in your hometown. I only ask that the name of the place begin with a letter coming <u>after</u> A and <u>before</u> Z but nowhere in between. You are allowed to have people there with you, as many as you like, as long as they are dead by the time you say the magic words. But, by the Wand, make sure that <u>you</u> are not dead, of course. That would truly throw a wrinkle into our plans.

Tick closed his eyes and thought.

It really came down to two hints: the letter the place begins with and the thing about dead people. The word that kept popping into his mind when he thought about the latter was *cemetery*. It matched the clue perfectly—a lot of people would be there and they'd all be dead. The way M.G. worded it made it sound like Tick would have to kill people or something, but he obviously didn't mean that, it was just a clever twist of language. The place where he was supposed to go on May sixth had to be a cemetery.

And yet, what about the letter it begins with? *After* A and *before* Z, but nowhere in between . . .

"Son?"

Tick snapped back to reality and turned to see his dad standing in the doorway. "Hi, Dad." He stood from his desk chair and went over to sit on the bed, in the same position as last night. A surge of anxiety swelled in his chest, hope and fear battling over his emotions as he awaited the verdict.

His dad joined him, a somber look on his face, his eyes staring at the *Journal of Curious Letters* gripped in both of his hands. "Tick, I've read through this a million times and thought about it all day." He finally looked at his son.

"And you think I'm psycho." Tick was amazed that at the same time he could both want and not want his dad to tell him what he thought of everything.

"No, not at all. I believe it. All of it."

Tick couldn't suppress the huge grin that shot across his face. "Really?"

His dad nodded. "There's something I didn't tell you last night. I, uh, saw you talking to the little man you called Rutger. I saw for myself he was real. And the whole thing about those gnats. I can't get that out of my mind. Then there's the letter from Alaska. I know you don't know anyone up there." He shook his head. "It's a lot of evidence, son. A lot."

"So you—"

His dad held up a hand, cutting off Tick. "But that's not why I'm convinced."

"It's not?"

"No." His dad leaned forward and put his elbows on his knees. "Tick, I've known you for thirteen years, and I can't think of a time when you've ever lied to me. You're too smart to lie, too good of a person. I trust you, and as I looked into your eyes as you told me this crazy story, I knew it was true. Now, I wanted some time to think about it and such, but I knew."

Tick wanted to say something cheesy and profound, but all that came out was, "Cool."

His dad laughed. "Yeah, cool. I can feel it deep down that this is important and that you were chosen to help because you're a special kid. There's always been something almost magical about you, Tick, and I think I knew that someday your life would take a turn for the unique. We've never really talked about it, but I've always felt like you had a guardian angel or some kind of special gift. These letters and clues and all this weird stuff has to be related somehow."

Tick didn't really know what his dad was talking about, and didn't care—he was too excited about finally having someone nearby who knew what was going on. "So you'll help me figure it out?"

"Now, maybe I can help a little here and there with the riddles but"—he pointed a finger at Tick—"you better believe I'm going to be the toughest bodyguard anyone's ever had. All this dangerous stuff scares me too, you know?" He reached out and gave his patented bear hug, then leaned back. "So where do we go from here?"

Tick shrugged. "I guess we just keep getting the clues and hope we can figure everything out by May sixth."

His dad scratched his chin, deep in thought. "Yeah . . ." He seemed doubtful or troubled.

"What?"

"I was thinking maybe this M.G. guy expects you to be a little more proactive. You know, dig a little deeper to find out what's going on."

"Dad, I can tell you're thinking really hard 'cause it looks like you might bust a vein."

His dad ignored the joke. "You have two weeks off from school for Christmas, right?"

"Right."

"And I have plenty of vacation time . . ." He paused. "But what would we do about your mom? I don't want her involved in this. She'd worry herself to the deathbed quicker than she can make a batch of peanut-butter cookies."

"Dad, what are you talking about?"

His dad's eyes focused on Tick. "I think we should do a little investigating."

"Investigating?"

"Yeah." He reached out and squeezed Tick's shoulder. "In Alaska."

By the next evening, Edgar had it all arranged, in no small part due to his clever and cunning mind, he kept telling himself. After using the Internet to discover that Macadamia, Alaska, was only three hours' drive from where his Aunt Mabel lived in Anchorage, everything fell into place. Edgar hadn't seen his aunt in years, and his mother had told him awhile back that Mabel's health wasn't doing so well. She'd stayed in Alaska even after her fisherman husband died over a decade ago, insisting that her failing heart, hemorrhoids, and severely bunion-infested feet would make a move impossible.

The plan was set, the tickets purchased, the rental car reserved.

In ten days, just after Christmas, Edgar and Tick would fly to Anchorage, Alaska, for a three-day visit with Aunt Mabel.

Lorena had grilled Edgar on how crazy it sounded to go on vacation on such short notice, but Edgar played it cool, claiming he'd been thinking about his aunt ever since Tick had gotten the letter from Alaska. And the winter break gave them the perfect opportunity.

He also used the excuse that because the tickets were expensive, only two people could afford to go. Plus Tick had been a baby the last time he had seen his great-aunt, so he didn't know her at all. Kayla was too young to appreciate the trip, and Lorena and Lisa seemed more than pleased to not have to go to a bitterly cold land of ice and snow in the middle of winter when the sun would only peek above the horizon for a couple of hours a day. Finally, Edgar pulled out all the stops, asking Lorena if she really was in the mood to hear Mabel tell her the fifty top things she'd done wrong in her life.

Lorena kissed Edgar and told him to have a good time.

When Edgar told the news to his aunt over the phone, she almost blew up his left eardrum with her shrieks of excitement. Of course, she soon settled down and told him to be sure and bring lots of warm clothes, to remember his toothbrush, to have earmuffs for baby Atticus, and about one hundred other pieces of advice.

All in all, the plan fell into place quite nicely.

Edgar only hoped that once they got to Alaska, Mabel would quit talking long enough to allow them to investigate the town of Macadamia.

Someone had sent that first letter.

And Edgar meant to find out who.

CHAPTER
19

AN ODD CHRISTMAS PRESENT

Tick had felt so relieved that his dad believed his story and wanted to help, the whole Alaska expedition didn't really hit him until the next day when his dad told him he'd bought airline tickets. His dad seemed to think they could find out who mailed the original letter and get more information from him or her. Tick thought a trip to Alaska seemed plenty exciting all by itself, and he could barely stand having to wait ten more days.

Every day of Christmas vacation, Tick and Sofia exchanged e-mails, finally getting into a consistent groove of answering questions and learning more about each other. Tick could tell Sofia was feisty and confident—not someone to mess with unless you wanted a nice kick to the shin, or worse. She was also very smart, and Tick rarely noticed a language barrier. He felt like they were similar in many ways and he found himself liking her very much. They even played chess online, though it took almost a week to finish one game because of the time difference.

Sofia was the first to figure out the last piece of the fourth clue—the first letter of the special place. At first, Tick worried they were violating some rule by helping each other with the clues, but Sofia pointed out that none of the letters said they couldn't. In her opinion, the guy in charge should be impressed they'd had the initiative to seek out others and collaborate.

Tick felt dumb when Sofia told him the answer.

```
    I only ask that the name of the
place begin with a letter coming
after A and before Z but nowhere in
between.
```

Tick already suspected the clue pointed them to a cemetery, but it was Sofia who explained that cemetery began with a "C," a letter that was certainly after A and before Z in the alphabet. *Also, the letter was nowhere to be found in the word "between."* That's what the sentence had meant, which now seemed painfully obvious to Tick.

They wondered about *which* cemetery to go to, since any decent-sized town had more than one. But the wording of the clue made it clear that the particular place they went to didn't matter, as long as it was a cemetery. Sofia would choose one in her hometown at the appointed time, and Tick would do likewise.

Of course, both of them recognized how strange it was that they had to go to a graveyard but that it didn't matter which one. But everything about the whole mess was odd, so they were getting used to it.

Tick was really happy to have found Sofia; for the first time in a long while he felt like he had a friend. Yeah, she lived in Italy and liked to beat up boys, but beggars couldn't be choosers. He couldn't wait to get the next clue and talk to her about it.

On Christmas Day, he got his wish.

It had been a perfect couple of days. Snow fell in billions of soft, fluffy flakes, blanketing the yard and the house in pure white, covering up the dirt and grime that had begun to show up after a couple of weeks without a fresh snowstorm. The classic songs of Bing Crosby and Frank Sinatra floated through the house like warm air from the fire. Tick's mom went all out in the kitchen, cooking up everything from honey-baked ham to stuffed bell peppers, cheesy potatoes to fruit salad, chocolate-covered peanut butter balls to her famous Christmas cookies, which were full of coconut, butterscotch, pecans, walnuts, and several other yummy surprises.

Tick was stuffed and happy, remembering once again why the holiday season had always been his favorite time of year. And it only helped matters that he'd be heading to Alaska in a couple of days. Life was sweet.

After the hustle and buzz and laughter of Christmas morning, tattered wrapping paper lying about in big colorful piles, Tick sat back on the couch, staring at the new goodies he'd received: three video games, some new books, a couple of gift certificates, lots of candy. He usually felt a twinge of sadness once all the presents had been opened, knowing it would be 365 long days until the next Christmas. But today he felt none of that. He felt content and warm, excited and happy.

The mystery of M.G. and his Twelve Clues had brought a new light to Tick's life and, despite the dangers that came with the letters, he'd never felt more alive.

He looked up at the decorated tree, its dozens of white lights sparkling their reflection in the red metallic balls and silver tinsel. Something square and bulky tucked behind a large nutcracker ornament caught his attention. He'd looked at this seven-foot tree a thousand times in the last month, and he knew the thing buried in the branches hadn't been there before this morning.

Instantly alert, he looked around to see what his

family was doing. His mom had her nose in a book, his dad was in the kitchen, Lisa had earphones on listening to her new CDs, and Kayla played with her kitchen set, making pretend pancakes and eggs. Trying to look non-chalant, Tick got up from the couch and walked over to the tree, staring at the spot that had caught his eyes.

A box, wrapped in an odd paper with pictures of fairies and dwarves and dragons, was snuggled between two branches, held up by a string of lights. The words "From M.G." were clearly scrawled across the box in blue ink. Tick looked around one more time before he snatched the unopened present and stealthily placed it with his other things. Then, grabbing a big armful of stuff, including the mystery box, he headed upstairs to his room.

He sat on his bed and stared at the strange wrapping paper. The present itself was very light and he felt certain the next clue must lie inside. But who had put it there, and when? He ripped the paper off a plain white cardboard box. After flipping open the lid, Tick saw exactly what he'd expected.

The fifth clue. He pulled out the cardstock paper and read the message.

```
Everything will fail unless you
say the magic words exactly correct.
It behooves me to remind you that
```

```
I cannot tell you the words, nor
will I in the face of any amount of
undue pressure you may apply toward
me. Which, of course, would be quite
difficult for you to do since you
don't know who I am and since I live
in a place you cannot go.
      Best of luck, old chap.
```

Tick read the clue a couple more times, then glued the cardstock into his journal. He thought about the trick used in the fourth clue with the word *between*. Something similar could be happening here.

```
Everything will fail unless you
say the magic words exactly correct.
```

Say the magic words exactly correct. Could "exactly correct" be the magic words? Tick thought it would be really dumb if that were the answer; plus, he'd been told the first letter from M.G. would reveal the special words, not one of the later clues.

Tick closed the book, frustrated. This new message told him nothing he didn't already know, only that he had to say something specific when the day came, something *magic*. Other than that, M.G. just seemed to be rubbing it in that he wouldn't tell Tick what the words were—neener, neener, neener.

Disappointed, wondering if he was missing something obvious, and still baffled at how the present had gotten into his family's Christmas tree, Tick went downstairs and e-mailed Sofia about the fifth clue. Knowing she probably wouldn't respond for a while, he joined his dad in the kitchen, sharing the news as he started snacking on everything in sight.

Sofia wrote him back that night, which would have been early the next morning her time. His heart lifted when he saw her name in the INBOX and he quickly clicked on the message.

Dear Tick,

I got the Fifth Clue, too. Doesn't say much, does it? I think your idea that the magic words are "exactly correct" is just what you say. Stupid. No way, too easy.

I'm sure you're excited for the big trip to Alaska with your dad. You'll probably get lost and eaten by a polar bear. Your funeral will have the coffin closed because all that will be left is your right pinky

finger. Just kidding. I hope you escape alive.
I thought I saw a man spying on me yesterday. He
looked mean, but disappeared before I got a look.
Not good.

Have fun in Ice Land. Write me as soon as you
return.

Ciao,
Sofia

Tick reread the sentences about the man spying on
her. Sofia threw that in like she was telling him she'd
bought a new pair of socks. If some creepy-looking
dude was watching her, chances were he'd be coming
after Tick next. Unless someone was already spying
on Tick and he hadn't noticed? He felt the familiar
shiver of fear run up and down his spine, once again
reminded that this M.G. mystery business wasn't all
fun and games.

He wrote a quick note back to Sofia, telling her
to be careful and that he'd write her again the second
he got back from Alaska. He was just about to log off
when he heard the chime of his e-mail program. When
the new e-mail message popped up, Tick felt like an icy
fist had smashed his heart into pulp.

From: DEATH
Subject: (no subject)

His stomach turning sour, Tick clicked on the e-mail. It only had one line of text.

See you in Alaska.

CHAPTER
20

THE LAND OF ICE AND SNOW

Two days later, Tick and Edgar sat in their seats on the airplane, thirty thousand feet in the air, soda and stale pretzels making them look forward to a much better meal once they landed in Anchorage. Tick sat by the window, his dad's oversized body wedged into the aisle seat like a Macy's Thanksgiving Day Parade balloon stuffed into the back of a pickup truck. The steady roar of the plane's engines made Tick feel like his ears were stuffed with cotton.

The two of them had discussed the fifth clue and the strange e-mail from "Death" many times over, with no progress. Tick didn't know who was more determined to figure everything out—him or his dad.

They'd gotten much braver—or dumber—with every passing day, to the point they were willing to ignore an obvious and outright warning like the one received in the e-mail. They were going, and that was final.

"We need to keep a sharp lookout," his dad said through a mouthful of pretzels. "If either one of us sees something suspicious, yell it out quickly. When in doubt, run. And we need to stay in public as much as possible."

"Dad, I'd say you sound like a paranoid freak, but I agree one hundred percent." Tick took a sip of his drink. "I think I'm half excited and half scared to death."

"Hey, we're committed, right? There's no turning back now."

"Cheers." They clicked their plastic cups together.

In two hours, they'd be in Alaska.

Seven rows back, a tall man with black hair and razor-thin eyebrows crouched in his tiny seat as best he could, reading the ridiculous in-flight magazine, which was full of nothing but advertisements and stupid articles about places he'd never care to visit. This spying business was deathly boring, and he hated it. No action, no results, boring, boring, boring.

But all of that would change very soon. The Spy would become the Hunter.

His name was Frazier Gunn, and he'd worked more than twenty years for Mistress Jane. He despised the woman, *loathed* her, in fact. She was the cruelest, most selfish, despicable, horrifying creature he'd ever met, and yet, his devotion to her was absolute. An odd mixture of feelings, but that's how it had to be when you served someone who planned to take over the Realities. They needed a leader like her, ruthless and without conscience. He didn't have to like her—he only needed to *pretend* to like her.

Because someday he planned to replace her.

Of course, if he ever failed even one of his assigned missions, she'd feed him to the Croc Loch near the Lemon Fortress with no remorse. But he was safe for now and had been promised a great reward if he could unlock the secret behind the bizarre series of letters Master George had sent out to kids all over the world. He had only recently discovered the identities of several recipients, enabling him to further his investigation with stealth and caution. But finally, the time for intimidation and action was at hand.

It'd been a fun trick sending the "Death" e-mail to the boy named Atticus, quite clever in fact. It was the dumb kid's own fault for putting his information about the letters on the Internet for anyone to find. There'd been a slight risk that Atticus might've chickened out and not gone to Alaska, thereby ruining a chance to learn more for Mistress Jane, but Frazier couldn't resist the calculated threat.

He reached into his pocket to feel the reassuring lump of the special *thing* he'd brought along to perform the important task he planned. He couldn't wait to activate it; the devices they'd retrieved from the Fourth Reality were so much fun, futuristic and deadly. The spectacle would make all the hours of spying on the brats around the world worth every minute.

And if it didn't work, there was always Plan B. Or C. Or D.

Giving up on the magazine, Frazier Gunn leaned back and closed his eyes. The boy and his father couldn't very well disappear on an airplane, now could they?

Tick felt so relieved when he and his dad were finally in the rental car, bags safely stowed away in the trunk, heading down the frozen freeway to Aunt Mabel's house. Even though it was still mid-afternoon, the land around them had grown dark, the sun's brief journey above the horizon having ended an hour ago.

Tick held a map in his lap, navigating for his dad. Mabel lived on the outskirts of Anchorage in a small suburb that seemed pretty easy to find. Most of the way followed one main road that stretched endlessly before them, the faded yellow lines of the lane markers seeming to flash then disappear beneath the car.

"Well, Professor," Dad said. "Prepare yourself for Aunt Mabel. She's quite the character and full of more ideas on how to save your life than you'll probably care to hear. Just know that she means well and do a lot of nodding."

"I'm excited to meet her."

His dad laughed. "You should be, you should be. Trust me, if you want entertainment, we're going to the right place."

They'd eaten at a fast food restaurant before heading out from the airport, and Tick still had his soda, from which he took a big long swallow. "You think she'll mind when we go exploring out to Macadamia?"

"You can bet your life savings she'll mind, all right, but, oh well. We'll tell her we didn't want to waste such a good opportunity to see the sights of this beautiful land she calls home. That'll get her, I hope."

"When do you think we'll drive out there? Tomorrow morning?"

"Sounds good to me. That'll give us the whole evening with Mabel tonight, and breakfast tomorrow— she makes a mean plate of eggs, bacon, the works. Hopefully, we can figure some things out and return to her place tomorrow night."

"I just hope Macadamia isn't a dead end."

His dad reached over and patted Tick on the leg.

"No, we'll find something. It couldn't have been a ghost that sent that letter, now could it?"

"Judging by what I've seen lately? Maybe."

"Good point."

Tick studied the map. "Looks like you turn into her neighborhood up there to the right."

Edgar flipped on the blinker as he slowed the car.

~

A mile or so behind, Frazier Gunn pulled off the road and stopped, not wanting to take any chances of being spotted. He'd wait an hour or so, then find himself a discreet parking space where he could watch the house. The boy and his father would probably spend the night, saving their planned expedition to Macadamia for tomorrow.

Frazier wanted to see what they discovered there before he put his plan into action. Every little bit of information on what Master George was up to might help Mistress Jane's cause, and Frazier meant to find out everything he could. When the two adventurers drove back to Anchorage after their investigation, he'd implement the device that sat in his pocket, ready and hungry to get to work.

He grinned at the thought.

~

Tick and his dad stood in front of the door to Aunt Mabel's home, staring at the plastic flowered wreath that must've hung there for two or three decades— its every surface covered in dust. The house itself was a cold and weary pile of white bricks, but the warm light shining through colorful curtains in the windows made it seem like the coziest place on Earth. However, neither of the Higginbottoms moved to push the doorbell just yet.

"Well, here we are," Dad said. A thick layer of snow and ice covered the yard around them; it looked like a miserably frigid wasteland that hadn't seen the full sun in years.

"Here we are," Tick repeated, gripping his suitcase.

"Now, one last warning." Dad looked at his son. "Aunt Mabel is at least one hundred and fifty years old, she laughs like a hyena, and she smells like three tubes of freshly squeezed muscle ointment."

Tick grinned. "Good enough for me. I love ancient history and watching nature shows, and I don't mind the smell of peppermint."

His dad nodded. "That's the spirit. Let's do this thing." He reached out and pushed the doorbell button.

Three seconds later, Aunt Mabel pulled the door open.

CHAPTER
21

OLD, FUNNY, AND SMELLY

Little Edgar!" she yelled, a shriek that sounded like fighting cats. The intense smells of peppermint and homemade cooking wafted out of the house with the warm air, and Tick had to suppress a laugh.

Aunt Mabel looked as ancient as Tick's dad had indicated, her heavily wrinkled but thin face covered in at least three pounds of makeup, capped off by bright red lipstick covering a lot more than her lips, as if she'd been jumping rope when she applied it that morning. Her small body seemed too frail to support the loud burst of excited salutations that came from her lungs as she hugged both Edgar and Tick.

"So good to see you! So glad you made it safe!

About time you came to visit your poor old Auntie!"

Tick returned the hug, suddenly feeling very relieved and at home. She was family after all, and this trip obviously meant the world to an old widow who lived alone. Despite the icy cold weather, Tick felt warm inside and looked forward to getting to know his great-aunt Mabel— though he had to admit she did scare him a *little*.

"Well, come in, come in!" she said, her fake teeth sparkling as her face lit up like a giddy clown. "I need to sit these bones down—my bunions are inflamed like you wouldn't believe. Take off your coats and such— especially that hideous scarf, young man." She gestured to the side of the foyer where they put their coats and bags—Tick left his scarf on by habit, despite what she'd said—then Mabel led them into a small living room where a couple of couches covered in orange velvet beckoned for them to sit. A dusty lamp with beads hanging from the shade glowed a dull yellow from its stand on a chipped wooden end table. The entire house looked like it had been decorated with props from a really old TV show.

Once they were settled, Aunt Mabel brought in three steaming hot cups of herbal tea; it tasted like boiled cardboard but warmed Tick very quickly. He leaned back on the soft couch and put his foot up on his knee, eager to see Mabel in action.

"Well, land's sake, it's a delight to see you boys," she

started. "Living up here at the North Pole with nothing but seventeen quilts and a couple of icicles to keep you company makes a woman grow old quicker than she should. And let me tell you, when you were born before any of your neighbor's *grandparents*, you can forget having friends come over to play pinochle and watch reruns of *Andy Griffith*." Mabel paused, but only long enough to take in a huge gasping breath. "There's this boy that lives down the corner—mean as a snake, I tell you. He came over to shovel my driveway after the last storm, but he *didn't* put salt on the sidewalk to melt the ice. The nerve of that young troublemaker . . ."

After coming from the wintry air into a nice warm house, and after a long day of busy travel, Tick felt his eyelids dropping as Aunt Mabel continued to rant about each of her neighbors and their various faults and crimes. He tensed his muscles in an attempt to wake himself up.

". . . and Missus Johnson down the road—I'm pretty sure she's a *spy* for the Homeland Security International Espionage and Intelligence Spy Division. Always snooping, asking questions, you know. Just the other day, I was taking my garbage out to the road as she was walking by. Do you know what she said to me?"—Mabel didn't pause long enough for anyone to answer—"She had the nerve to ask me how my *health* was doing. I tell you right here and now I bet she wants to set up a sting operation from this house once I'm dead and gone, buried like a sack of dirty clothes in the town dump. And Mr. King up by the corner—did you know he has *thirteen* children? And every last one of them the spawn of the devil or my name isn't Mabel Ruth Gertrude Higginbottom Fredrickson."

And so it went for at least another twenty minutes, Tick finally having to pinch himself to stay awake. His dad seemed pleased as could be, smiling and nodding the entire time, throwing out a few "Hmms" and "Uh-huhs" every now and then. Finally, as though she'd exhausted her capacity to use her frail body's vocal cords, Mabel stopped talking and leaned back in her seat.

"Uh, wow," Dad mumbled, caught off guard that his aunt had actually quit yapping. "Sounds like your life is a lot more interesting than you let on, Aunt Mabel. We're sure glad we could come and visit you." He looked over at Tick, raising his eyebrows.

Tick straightened in his seat. "Yeah, I'm really excited I finally got to meet you." He raised his cup as if saluting, and immediately felt like an idiot.

"You boys aren't mocking me, are you?" Mabel asked, her eyes narrowing.

"No!" Tick and his dad said in unison.

"Good. Let's eat some supper." She squirmed in her seat, but couldn't move an inch. "Atticus, dear boy, be a gentleman and assist your elders." She held out a hand.

Tick jumped up and gently helped her stand, then escorted her into the cramped but cozy kitchen.

A wave of mouth-watering smells bombarded them when they entered, and Tick proceeded to eat the most scrumptious meal he'd had in a long time, which was saying a lot considering how good of a cook his mom was. There were freshly baked rolls soaked in butter, grilled chicken with lemon sauce, corn on the cob, mashed potatoes with chunks of garlic—all of it delicious.

Aunt Mabel talked the entire time they ate, covering every topic from her ingrown toenail to how she'd finally lost her last tooth to decay, but Tick barely heard her, enjoying three more helpings of the fantastic dinner.

Frazier crept up to the car of his prey, his eyes flickering to the house of the old woman. He'd watched their shadows leave the front room and head deeper into the house, probably to the kitchen for dinner. The thought made his stomach rumble and he resolved to bag this place and find something to eat as soon as he'd accomplished his task. Even expert spies like himself had to chow down every once in a while.

He crouched behind the left front tire, making sure the body of the car stayed between him and the house. He reached into his pocket and pulled out the special device—an oval-shaped metal container, about eight inches long and three inches wide, a seam wrapped around the middle. On one side of the seam, several buttons and dials poked out. Frazier looked at the familiar label on the other side—the label that marked items taken from the Fourth Reality:

Manufactured by Chu Industries

He split the little machine into two pieces along the seam, slipping the part with the controls back into his pocket. The other half, with its dozens of wires and clamps coiled inside like poisonous snakes ready to wreak havoc, didn't look nearly as menacing as it should, considering what Frazier knew it could do to something like a car. More precisely, what it would do, indirectly, to the people *inside* the car.

Frazier snickered, then reached underneath the tire well to place the Chu device as far and as deep as he could toward the engine. He pushed the small button in the middle and heard a hiss followed by a metallic clunk as the gadget reached out with tiny claws and adhered itself to the car. A spattering of tiny clicks rang out as the machine crawled its way to where it needed to go.

Smart little devices, these things. In a matter of moments, the beautiful but deadly trinket would find exactly what it needed.

Once in place, it only needed Frazier's signal to come alive.

⁓

Aunt Mabel must think I'm three years old, Tick thought.

It all started at bedtime. Mabel followed Tick into the bathroom and pulled a container of floss from a dusty cabinet. She yanked off a three-foot long piece and handed it to Tick.

"Now, catch every nook and cranny," she said as Tick started threading the minty string between his two front teeth. "You never can tell what nasty little monsters are having a nice meal of your gums."

Tick finished and threw the used floss into a small wastebasket, wishing Mabel would leave him alone. When she didn't move an inch, hovering behind him as he stared into the mirror, Tick reached over and grabbed his toothbrush and toothpaste. Warily glancing back at Mabel, he finally turned on the water and started brushing.

"Here, let me take a turn," Mabel said a few seconds later. To Tick's horror, she reached around his shoulder and grabbed the toothbrush from his hand

and began vigorously scrubbing his teeth, pushing his head down lower with her other hand. Tick never would've thought such an old and frail woman could have so much strength in her arms. "Gotta get those molars!" she yelled with enthusiasm.

Next came pajama time. Tick had brought a pair of flannel pants and a T-shirt to sleep in, but that was not good enough for Aunt Mabel. She went to the basement and dug through some boxes before returning with a musty old pair of long johns that were as red as her lipstick and looked like Santa's underwear. Tick begrudgingly put them on, heeding his dad's pleas that they do everything humanly possible to make the old woman happy so nothing jeopardized their trek the next day. He almost broke his promise when Mabel topped everything off by twisting a scratchy wool stocking cap onto his head. Instead, he forced a grin and followed her to the bed she'd prepared for him.

After tucking him in with no fewer than seven thick quilts, Mabel kissed him on the forehead and sang him a bedtime song, which sounded like a half-dead vulture warning its brothers that the chickenhawk he'd just eaten was poisonous. Tick closed his eyes, hoping that if Mabel thought he was asleep, he could avoid an encore. Satisfied, Aunt Mabel tiptoed out of the room—making sure before she closed the door that the night-light she'd plugged in worked properly.

Tick rolled over, wondering if his great-aunt would do the same routine with his dad. When he finally quit laughing at the image of Mabel brushing his dad's teeth, Tick fell asleep.

~~~~~

The next morning, after a wonderful meal of eggs, bacon, sausage, cheese biscuits, and freshly-squeezed orange juice, and after a long lecture on how important it was not to talk to strangers, especially those holding guns or missing any teeth, Tick and his dad were able to escape for a day of "exploring the wonders of Alaska." Aunt Mabel seemed exhausted from her efforts and couldn't hide the fact that she was almost relieved to get some rest from taking care of the boys.

After filling up the car with gas and junk food, Tick and his dad began their three-hour journey, the *Journal of Curious Letters* sitting on the seat between them.

Next stop: Macadamia, Alaska.

CHAPTER 22

GOING POSTAL

After driving down the straightest road Tick had ever seen—with nothing but huge piles of snow and ice on either side—they pulled into the small town of Macadamia right around noon. The first thing they did was stop at a gas station to fill up the car for the drive back so they wouldn't have to do it later. The cracked and frozen streets were deserted, with only a few cars parked along the main road in front of various dilapidated shops and dirty service centers.

"Well, I figure we have about six hours until we need to head back," Tick's dad said as he started the car again. "Or, if we don't discover anything today, we can always call Aunt Mabel and tell her we got stuck somewhere for the night and that we'll come back tomorrow. She won't want us taking any risks."

"Yeah," Tick said. "But she'll be spitting nails if I'm stranded at some nasty hotel without her there to brush my teeth for me."

His dad laughed. "You're a good sport, Professor. Now you know why your mom and Lisa were just fine letting the two of us come up here alone." He put the car into gear and drove away from the gas station. "The lady in the gas station said the post office was just up here on Main Street. That'll be our first stop."

Five minutes later, Tick followed his dad through the frosted glass door of the post office, loosening his scarf, not sure what to expect. But he did have an odd sensation in his stomach, knowing the original mysterious letter from M.G. had been mailed from this very building. It was almost like seeing the hospital room where you'd been born, or a house your ancestor had built. Despite how he felt, this was where any investigation would have to begin—he just hoped it didn't end here as well.

The place was boring, nothing but gray walls and gray floors and gray counters—the only thing breaking the monotony was a tiny faded Christmas tree in a corner with six or seven ornaments hanging from the sparse branches. No worker was in sight.

"Hello?" Dad called into the emptiness. A little bell sat on the main counter; he gave it a ring.

A few seconds later, an old man with bushy eyebrows and white stubble on his cheeks and chin appeared from the back, looking none too happy that he actually had to serve a customer. "What can I do for you?" he asked in a gruff voice before his feeble attempt at a smile.

"Uh, yes, we have a question for you." Dad stumbled on his words, as if not sure of himself now that the investigation had officially begun. "We received a letter—postmarked from this town—in the middle of last month. In November. And, we're, uh, trying to find the person who sent it to us, and, um, so here we are." He rubbed his eyes with both hands and groaned. "Tick, your turn."

"Oh. Yeah." Tick pulled the original envelope from his journal, where he'd stuck it between two pages, then placed it on the counter. "Here it is. Does this look familiar to you at all, or the handwriting?"

The man leaned forward and for some reason sniffed the envelope. "Doesn't mean a thing to me. Good day." He turned and took a step toward the back of the office.

Tick felt his heart sinking toward his stomach. His dad gave him a worried look, then quickly said to the man, "Wait! Does anyone else work here? Could we speak to them?"

The old man turned and gave them an evil glare. "This is a small town, you hear me? I retired a long time ago, until I was forced to come back last month because one of the workers decided he was a psycho and up and quit. Good riddance. If you want to talk to him, be my guest."

"What was his name?" Tick asked. "Where does he live?"

The formerly retired postal worker sighed. "Norbert Johnson. Lives north of here, the very last house on Main Street. Don't tell him I sent you."

The man left the room without another word or a good-bye.

⌒

They pulled up in their car at the dead end of Main Street, staring at a small house that seemed to huddle in the cold, miserable and heartbroken. Tick didn't know if it officially approached haunted-house status, but it was close—two stories, broken shutters hanging on for dear life, peeling white paint. A couple of dim lights shone through the windows like dying fires. Two wilted trees, looking as though they hadn't sprouted leaves in decades, stood like undernourished sentinels on either side of the short and broken driveway.

"Son," his dad said, "maybe this time you should do the talking."

"Dad, you're supposed to be the grown-up in this group."

"Well, that's why I'll provide the muscle and protect you from harm. You're the brains of this outfit; you do the talking." He winked at his son then climbed out of the car.

Tick grabbed his journal and followed him down the icy driveway, up the creaky wooden stairs of the snow-covered porch, then to the sad-looking front door, brown and sagging on its hinges. His dad knocked without hesitating.

A long moment passed with no answer or noise from inside. Tick shivered in the biting cold and rubbed his arms. His dad knocked again, then found a barely visible doorbell and pushed it, though it didn't work. Another half-minute went by without so much as a creak from the house.

Dad moaned. "Don't tell me we came all this way and the man we need to talk to is on vacation in sunny Florida."

Tick craned his neck to look at a window on the second floor. "There're lights on inside. Someone has to be home."

"I don't know—we always leave a light on when we go on vacation—scares the burglars away." He knocked again, half-heartedly. "Come on, let's go."

With slumped shoulders, they started down the

porch steps. They were halfway down the sidewalk when they heard a scraping sound from behind and above them, then a low, tired voice. "What do you folks a-want?"

Tick turned to see a disheveled, gray-haired man peeking out of an upstairs window, his eyes darting back and forth around the yard, looking for anything and everything.

"We're trying to find Norbert Johnson," Tick shouted up to the window. "We have some questions about a letter mailed from here."

The man muttered something unintelligible before letting out a little shriek. "Do . . . do you work for Master George or Mistress Jane?"

Tick and his dad exchanged a baffled look. "Master George . . ." Dad said under his breath, then looked back up toward the man at the window. "Never heard of either one of them, but my son got a letter from someone named M.G. Could be the same person, I guess."

The man paused, his squinty eyes scrutinizing the man and boy below him for signs of trouble. "Do you swear you've a-never heard of a woman named Mistress Jane in your life?"

"Never," Tick and his dad said in unison.

"You've a-never seen or worked for a lady dressed all in yellow who's as bald as Bigfoot is hairy?"

Tick couldn't believe how weird this whole conversation had become. "Never."

The man slammed his window shut without saying another word, leaving Tick to wonder if this Norbert guy really had gone bonkers like the old postal worker had suggested.

The front door popped open and Norbert stuck his head out, smoothing his thin gray hair. "Come on in," he said in a quick, tight voice, looking around the yard again. "I've got something for you."

———

Frazier had pulled to the side of the road two houses down from the one at the end of the street, curious as to what Tick and his dad would learn from the man who lived there. It seemed they merely wanted to discover if the postal workers knew who had mailed the letter they had received, but something about the whole thing seemed fishy.

With his spy equipment—conical sound trapper, thermo-magnetically heightened microphones, and molded earpieces—Frazier had heard every word exchanged in the post office and had found it quite interesting.

Norbert Johnson. The name didn't ring a bell, but Mistress Jane certainly didn't tell him about every person she came across in her travels. Maybe she'd interrogated Johnson about the whole affair. That would have been enough to drive any man crazy. The way Norbert had acted at his own house—all nervous and paranoid before finally letting the two strangers in—sure seemed to support the "crazy" theory.

Frazier picked up his eavesdropping gadget and pointed it at the house, then reinserted his earpieces. It took a few seconds to pinpoint the murmurs of the conversation before he locked it in place as best he could, settling back to have a listen. The first thing he heard made his eyes widen. It was the voice of the man named Norbert.

"Here you go. The big lady told me it's called the sixth clue."

CHAPTER
23

BONDING WITH NORBERT

Big lady?" Tick asked, holding the yellow envelope like his life depended on it. "Who gave this to you?"

They sat in a messy living room, not a single piece of furniture matching any of the others. *At least it's warm,* Tick thought. He and his dad sat on a frumpy couch that leaned toward the middle, facing Norbert on his rickety old chair, where he wrung his hands and rocked back and forth.

"Big ol' tall woman. Looked like ugly on a stick," Norbert answered in almost a whisper. "Just about scared me out of my pants, what with her a-coming out of the old graveyard behind my house."

The mention of a cemetery made Tick's ears perk

up. *It can't be a coincidence* . . . It must be related somehow to the fourth clue and where he was supposed to go on May sixth.

"Did she say anything else to you?" Dad asked. "Talk to you at all?"

"Not much." Norbert's fidgeting made Tick's head dizzy. "Told me some real smart kids would come a-looking for me, and I should give that there letter to 'em. Gave me several copies. Don't know about you fellas, but when an eight-foot monster lady tells me to do something, I'm gonna pretty much do it. So there you go."

Tick inserted his thumb under the flap and started ripping open the envelope as Norbert kept talking.

"Since that piece of parcel looked just like the ones from the British fella, and since I figured the British fella was an enemy of the Banana Lady, I reckoned I'd be a-doing a good task."

Tick stopped just before pulling out the white cardstock of the sixth clue. "British? Who was British?"

His dad leaned forward, a surprisingly difficult task that made the pitiful couch groan like a captured wolverine. "Mr. Johnson, I'm more confused than the Easter Bunny at a Christmas party. Could you please tell us everything you know about the letter we got from Alaska and who sent it? Maybe start from the beginning?"

"The Easter Bunny at a—" Tick began, a questioning smirk on his face.

"Quiet, son."

Norbert finally settled back in his chair and began his story, seemingly relieved that he'd been given direction on how to go about this conversation. Though Tick desperately wanted to read the next clue, he slipped it inside his journal and listened to the strange man from Alaska.

"I'd worked there at the post office in Macadamia for twenty-plus years, and I was just as happy as can be. Well, as happy as a single man in his fifties who smells a little like boiled cabbage can be." Tick involuntarily sniffed at this point, then tried to cover it up by scratching his nose. Norbert continued without noticing.

"Then *they* had to come along and ruin my life. It was a cold day in November—of course, every day is cold in November when you live up here, if you know what I mean. Anyway, first this busy little British gent named Master George, dressed all fancy-like, comes walking into my shop holding a box of letters that looked just like the one I gave you." He pointed at the journal in Tick's lap. "Goes off about how they need to get out right away, do-da, do-da."

Tick decided that last part was Norbert's way of saying "etcetera" and held in a laugh.

"I assured the fella I'd take care of it and he left. Wasn't a half-hour later when the scariest woman I've ever laid eyes upon came a-stomping in, dressed from head to toe in nothing but yellow. And she was bald—not a hair on her noggin to be found. Called herself Mistress Jane, and she was mean. I'm telling you, *mean*. You could feel it coming off her in waves." Norbert shivered.

"What did she want?" Dad asked.

"She was a-looking for Master George, which told me right away that the British gent must be a good guy, because Lemony Jane surely wasn't."

Tick felt like the final mystery of a great book had been revealed to him. The source of the letters suddenly had a name, a description. He was no longer a couple of initials and a blurred image. M.G. had become Master George. From England. And he was the good guy.

"She threatened me," Norbert continued. "She was cruel. And I couldn't get her out of my mind. Still can't. She's been in my dreams ever since, telling me she's gonna find out I lied to her."

"Lied to her?" Dad repeated.

"Yes, sir. Told her I'd never met anybody named Master George, and I hid the letters under the counter before she could see them. Flat out lied to her, and she told me bad things would happen if she ever found I'd a-done it. And done it, I did."

"So . . ." Tick started, "you quit your job because you were scared of her?"

Norbert looked down at his feet as if ashamed of

himself. "You got me all figured out, boy. Poor Norbert Johnson hasn't been the same since the day I met that golden devil. Quit my job, went on welfare, borrowed money. I been hiding in this house ever since. Only reason I met the tall lady who gave me the letters is because I heard a noise out in the backyard."

"I thought you said she came out of a graveyard," Dad said.

"She did. Like I said, back behind my house is an old, old cemetery. Got too old, I reckon, so they built another one closer to downtown."

"Mothball," Tick said quietly.

"Huh?" Norbert replied.

"Her name is Mothball. The lady who gave you this letter." Tick slipped it from his journal and held it in his hand.

Norbert looked perplexed. "Well what in the Sears-and-Roebuck kind of name is that?"

"She said her dad was in a hurry when he named her, something about soldiers trying to kidnap them."

Norbert did nothing but blink.

"Never mind." Tick turned to his dad. "Why in the world would she have given *him* the sixth clue?"

His dad furrowed his brow for a moment, deep in thought. "Well, maybe it's like I said—I think they wanted us to be proactive and seek out information, not just wait around to find it. Maybe they went back to all the towns they mailed the letters from and gave copies of the clues to the postal workers who would cooperate. They knew if we did some investigating, going to the source would be the most logical step."

Tick thought for a second. "Dad, I think you nailed it."

"I'm brilliant, my son. Brilliant." He winked.

Norbert cleared his throat. "Excuse me for interrupting, folks, but what in the name of Kermit the Frog are you guys a-talking about? You came here asking me questions, but it sounds like you know a lot more than I do."

Dad leaned over and patted Tick on the shoulder. "My boy here, the one who's receiving these letters, is trying to figure out the big mystery behind them. We think it was a test of sorts to see if we'd seek you out, which is why you were given the sixth clue to give to us."

Norbert nodded. "Ah. I see." He rolled his eyes and shrugged his shoulders.

"Look," Tick said. "Do you know anything else about Master George, Mistress Jane, Mothball, anything?"

Norbert shook his head in response.

"Well, then," Tick said. "I think we've got what we came for. Dad, maybe we should get going. I can read the clue while you drive." Tick tried his best to hint that he didn't feel very comfortable in Norbert's house.

"Just a minute." His dad looked at their host. "Mr. Johnson, you've done a great service for us and we'd like to return the favor. Is there, uh, anything we can do to help you, uh, get your nerve back and go back to work?"

Norbert didn't reply for a long time. Then, "I don't know. It's awfully kind of you to offer. I guess I'm just too scared that woman is gonna come back for me and string me up like a fresh catch of salmon."

"Well, let me tell you what I think," Dad said, holding up a finger. "I agree with you one hundred percent. I think this Mistress Jane person must be evil, because we wholeheartedly believe what M.G.—Master George—is doing must be a noble cause because he wants my son's help. And we've committed to that cause heart and soul, as you can tell."

"I reckon I can see that. What's your point?"

"Well, if this . . . yellow-dressed, bald, nasty woman made you quit your job, shun society, and hole up in a house all by yourself, then I think she's won a mighty victory over the world. She's beaten the great Norbert Johnson once and for all, and will move on to her next prey."

Tick liked seeing his dad try and help this poor man and decided to do his part. "Yeah, Norbert, you're doing exactly what she wanted you to do—give up and be miserable. Go back to work, show her you're the boss of your own life."

Norbert looked back and forth between Tick and his dad, his face a mask of uncertainty. "And if she does come back? What then?"

"Then by golly," Dad said, "stand up to her. Show her who's in charge."

"And call us," Tick chimed in. "By then, maybe we'll have figured everything out and know how to help you."

Norbert scratched his head. "Well, I don't know. I'm a-gonna have to think about this."

Dad smiled. "Listen, we'll exchange phone numbers and keep in touch, okay? How's that sound?"

Norbert didn't answer for a very long time, and Tick wondered if something was wrong. But then he saw moisture rimming on the bottom of the man's eyes and realized the guy was all choked up.

Finally, their new friend spoke. "I can't tell you how much it means to me that you folks care enough to give me your phone number. I just wished you a-lived up here in Alaska. I could use a friend."

"Well, hey," Dad said. "In this world, with the Internet and all that, we can keep in touch just fine."

And with that, their new friendship was sealed and Tick felt mighty proud of himself.

Frazier watched as Tick and his dad stepped out of the house, then shook hands and embraced their new little buddy. They said a few more sappy words, just like they had inside, and headed for their vehicle.

What is this, a soap opera? I might need a tissue for my weepy eyes.

He snickered at his own joke, then put the car into drive, ready to follow, the twilight of midday having long faded into the full darkness of late afternoon.

Frazier pulled out his half of the special device, fingered the big button in the middle of its shiny gray surface.

In just a few minutes, he thought. *Just a few minutes and the show begins.*

CHAPTER 24

PEDAL TO THE METAL

Norbert stared out his frosty window, watching the boy Tick and his father climb into their rental car, warm it up, then begin their long trek back to Anchorage. Norbert hadn't felt this good in weeks, like he was doing something *right*, finally taking a stand against the yellow witch who haunted his dreams. He couldn't explain it—the boy and his dad seemed to pulse with some invisible force, strong and magnetic. Norbert felt like a new person, as if powerful batteries had replaced his old junky ones, revved him up to face the world like he'd never done before.

The new year could bring a new life. He'd go back to work . . .

His thoughts petered out when he noticed another car pull out into the road just moments after Edgar had driven past it. The black Honda had been parked on the sidewalk, idling, and wasn't in front of a house, just a blank lot of snow-covered weeds and brush. Something about that didn't seem right. Not at all.

Then it hit Norbert.

The person in the black car was *following* his new friends. That couldn't be a good thing. *No sir, that couldn't be good one bit.*

The new Norbert acted before the old Norbert could talk himself out of it. He threw on some warm clothes, a wool cap, and his faded, weather-beaten shoes. He frantically searched for his keys, forgetting where he'd put them since his last venture to town. They weren't on his dresser, weren't on his kitchen counter—he couldn't find them anywhere. After five minutes of hunting, he was just about to give up when he saw them on the floor under the table; he grabbed them and turned toward the garage.

The doorbell rang, freezing his blood solid.

Trying to stay brave, he ran up the stairs to his usual spying window and took a peek. Relieved, he saw it was just a kid girl with a man who looked an awful lot like Master George—dressed in a fancy suit, shiny shoes, the works. But this guy stood a lot taller and had plenty of hair, shiny blond hair slicked back against his skull.

Must be another one of those smart kids looking for their letter.

He bolted back down the stairs, grabbed another copy of Mothball's golden envelopes (could that *really* be her name?) and tore open the door. He held out the letter and was just about to drop it into the girl's hand and close the door when he caught a glimpse of his visitor's car parked in the driveway. It was much nicer and . . . faster than his. An idea popped in his head.

"You folks lookin' for a clue from M.G.?" he asked.

The befuddled (Norbert's new favorite word) strangers nodded in unison.

"Someone's in a whole lot of trouble—friends of Mothball," he said, then shook the envelope in front of them. "This is the sixth clue. If you want it, you've gotta help me save them."

⁓

Driving slowly down Main Street, with a full tank of gas in the car, Edgar settled his bones for the long drive back to Aunt Mabel's. He looked over at Tick, who was just pulling the sixth clue from its envelope.

"Read it, boy!" he shouted cheerfully. "I can hardly wait. What a trip, huh? What a trip!" He felt so good they'd accomplished something—not just getting the next clue, but perhaps helping poor Norbert get his life back together. Though he'd dared not admit it, Edgar had been scared to death their trip to Alaska would prove a waste, thereby nullifying his value to Tick, who'd had the courage to tell him about everything.

Tick put the white piece of cardstock down in his lap. "Nah, let's just wait 'til we get back to Washington. What's the rush?" Tick let out a fake yawn and stretched.

"Professor, these windows *do* roll down, and I *am* strong enough to throw you out of one."

"Okay, okay, if you insist." Tick read the words out loud, holding the paper up so Edgar could glance at it and follow along as he drove.

```
Recite the magic words at exactly
seventeen minutes past the quarter
hour following the six-hour mark
before midnight plus one hundred and
sixty-six minutes minus seven
quarter-hours plus a minute times
seven, rounded to the nearest
half-hour plus three. Neither a second
before nor three seconds after.
    (Yes, I'm fully aware it will take
you a second or two to say the magic
words, but I'm talking about the
precise time you begin to say it. Quit
being so snooty.)
```

"Oh, boy," Edgar said. "Can't say my head's in the mood to figure that one out. Glad it's your problem."

Tick laid the clue down onto his lap, already scrutinizing its every word. "I'll have it figured out by the time we stop for you to use the bathroom and buy more Doritos." He opened up his journal and started jotting down thoughts and calculations from the clue.

"Very funny," Edgar replied, elbowing his son. "You know, I was so worried about that 'death' e-mail you got, but now I'm feeling pretty fat and happy."

"Better than skinny and sad, I guess," Tick said.

Edgar laughed. *What a great kid I have*, he thought. *What a great kid.*

Frazier waited until he and his prey were well out of town, cruising down the long and straight two-lane highway that headed back to Anchorage. He hated how short the days were this far north. It wouldn't be as fun to watch the coming mayhem in the darkness. He looked in his rearview mirror and saw some lights in the distance, but they seemed too far back for him to be worried. Once he engaged the device, it wouldn't take long to have his fun and be done with it.

He gripped the Chu controller in his palm, put the tip of his thumb on the button.

Then he pushed it.

Tick stared ahead at the long blank road, lost in thought about the sixth clue. The headlights revealed nothing but cracked asphalt and dirty piles of plowed ice, swallowed up in darkness on both sides. *There must not be a moon out,* he thought. Even the snow seemed black tonight.

"Uh-oh," his dad said in a worried whisper.

Tick looked over and saw the tight cowl of panic on his dad's face. He felt something shudder in his chest. "What?"

His dad had both hands gripped tightly on the steering wheel, trying to squeeze the inner lining out of it. "The wheel's frozen!" His legs moved up and down, alternately pumping the gas and brakes as the frightening, plastic-springy sound of the pedal filled the car.

"Dad, what's wrong?"

His dad kept yanking on the wheel, pushing on the brakes. "It's not responding—it's not doing anything. I can't *do* anything!"

"What do you—"

"Son, the car's out of control—it won't let me . . ." His voice faded as he tried everything again, his look of disbelief overcoming the panic. "What in the . . ."

Tick could only watch, bile building in his throat and stomach. Something was horribly wrong, and it had to have something to do with their new enemies. "You can't get it to stop?"

Dad looked over at him, exasperated. "Son, I can't do *anything!*"

In unison, they looked forward. The road remained straight for as far as they could see, but it ended in blackness. Anything could be hiding in the darkness, waiting for an out-of-control car to smash into it.

"The steering wheel won't move?" Tick asked, knowing the answer anyway.

His dad unsnapped his seatbelt, squirming in his chair to turn around.

"What are you doing?" Tick yelled.

Dad reached over and unbuckled Tick's belt as well. "Someone's got to us, kid. We've gotta get out of here."

From the backseat, Norbert stared at the two cars in front of him as they gained ground, knowing deep inside that something terrible was happening. He sensed frantic movement in Tick's car—dark shadows bobbing and jerking around—and saw the calm demeanor of the person sitting in the one following them, barely revealed by the headlights of the car in which Norbert sat. They were almost on the stranger.

"It's now or never," Norbert said, then tapped the

shoulder of the man driving. "Put the pedal to the metal, pal."

"Do whatever he says," the girl said to the driver like she was his mother.

~~~~~

Frazier laughed as he saw the man and the boy squirming inside their car, desperate for a way out of this little predicament. He looked down at his controller, trying to find the dial that would make the car ahead go even faster. He finally found it and turned it up just a little, loving every minute of this game.

When he finally glanced back up to the road, he yelped as a car zoomed past him on the left, then swerved to the right to cut him off. Overreacting, Frazier slammed on his brakes and twisted the steering wheel, shooting off the road with a horrible squeal of brakes before slamming into a massive snowbank.

His airbag exploded open, scorching his forearms and catapulting the Chu device into the backseat.

~~~~~

Tick felt like a sailor going down with a submarine. The front doors wouldn't open; some kind of permanent locking mechanism kept them sealed.

"What could possibly be doing this?" Dad yelled, struggling to lean his huge girth over the back of the seat to check the rear doors. From the click of the handle being yanked and released, Tick knew they were locked, too. His dad groaned as he dropped back into the driver's seat.

The car had inexplicably sped up just a few moments earlier, rocketing them faster and faster toward the unknown. The car remained on a straight path for now—the steep piles of snow on the roadside nudging the wheels back onto the road if they began to stray— but it couldn't last much longer. Tick knew if they hit a turn, they'd be in a whole heap of trouble.

Tick felt a block of ice in the pit of his stomach; they probably had only a minute or two before they'd crash. "We need to break a window!" he yelled.

"Right!" Dad replied. "Plant your back on the seat and kick the windshield with both feet on my signal, okay?"

Desperation swept away Tick's fear, clearing his mind. "Okay," he said as he got into position, tucking his journal down the seat of his pants as far as it would go.

When they were both ready, feet stuck up above them, coiled for the kick, Edgar grabbed Tick's hand. "On three—one . . . two . . . three!"

With synchronized screams, they both kicked the windshield with all their might.

It didn't budge.

Screaming his frustration into the frigid air, a plume of frozen vapor shooting from his mouth, Frazier Gunn tried to open the buckled back door. When it stubbornly refused, he leaned over to look through the window, searching for the Chu controller. He couldn't see a thing.

How could this have all fallen apart? How?

He shot a quick glance down the road to see the fading red glow of two cars' taillights. The device would be out of range in a matter of seconds and once that happened, he'd have no more power over the car's operations. It would continue to drive like a maniacal machine until it ran out of gas or smashed into something.

Of course, without being able to turn, the latter is *exactly* what would happen. Crash, boom, bang. The thought made him pause, then smile. Chances were, he'd still complete his task, one way or the other. Mistress Jane didn't need to know all the details.

Not caring anymore about the controller or his banged up car, Frazier turned and headed back toward town.

He needed to find a cemetery.

On Tick and his dad's fifth synchronized kick, a huge crack shot across the wide glass with the sound of breaking glaciers. Tick's heart leapt to his throat and the next kick seemed to have twice the power from his adrenaline rush. Several more cracks splintered through the windshield like an icy spider web. Tick was crouched too far down in the seat to see up ahead, but his mind assured him they were probably shooting toward a bend in the road with brutal speed. One way or another, it would all be over very soon.

"One more ought to do it!" his dad yelled, gasping in breaths. "One . . . two . . . THREE!"

Tick kicked with both legs again, and almost slipped to the floor of the car when his feet kept going, crashing through the windshield with the horrible clinking and crackling sound of shattered glass. Several tiny shards flew back into the car from the onrushing wind, but the bulk of the windshield, held together by a strong film of clear plastic, flew up into the air and tumbled away behind them.

"Come on!" Dad yelled, helping Tick back into a sitting position.

The air ripped at their hair and clothes, so cold that Tick's skin felt like frozen rubber. Squinting his eyes, he saw a big turn in the road a couple of miles directly ahead. He couldn't tell what waited there, be it a cliff or a field or a towering barn; he saw only darkness, a wall of black tar.

"We've gotta hurry!" his dad screamed over the wind. "Together now, come on!"

Summoning every last trace of courage left in his body, Tick followed his dad over the dashboard and through the gaping, wind-pummeled hole that led to the hood of the car.

~~~~

"There they are!" Norbert screamed, his voice squeaky with panic. "Pull up there, right to the front! If those guys jump, they're dead!"

"Hurry!" the girl yelled.

The blond, fancy-dressed driver obeyed without a word, gunning the engine until their vehicle pulled even with the out-of-control car. Just a few feet away, to Norbert's right, Tick and his dad had climbed halfway onto the hood of the car, the wind trying to rip them to pieces.

"Okay, get as close as you can," Norbert said, rolling down the window. "I wanna see every scratch on that there paint job!"

Once again, like a soldier following orders, the driver did as he was told.

~~~~

Tick couldn't believe his eyes. Out of nowhere, a car had appeared to their left, just a few feet away. His first thought was that whoever had caused this whole mess had pulled up to finish them off. But then the backseat window rolled down, and his heart lifted when he saw the ridiculous face of Norbert Johnson, who was somehow smiling and yelling and crying at the same time.

"Norbert's come to save you!" he screamed over the howling, rushing wind. "I'll pull you through the window!"

Tick's dad immediately scooted back into the car to gain solid footing, then grabbed Tick by both arms, yanking him over to his side and toward Norbert's open window. "You first!" he yelled.

With no time to lose, Tick carefully inched across the hood, gripping the metal with the tips of his icy cold fingers, his dad helping him along with a firm hold. The other car was literally a foot away from theirs, running side by side like insane drag racers. Before Tick knew it, Norbert had reached out and grabbed him, pulling him through the window and into his car. He groaned and grunted as he rolled past Norbert and fell onto the floor of the backseat, suddenly safe and warm, feeling the sharp corners of his journal poking him in his side.

He scrambled up and onto the seat, looking toward his dad with a sudden burst of terror. His dad had half-crawled onto the hood, gripping the edge of the door bar with one arm and reaching out for Norbert with the other. The look on his dad's face made Tick hurt inside. He had never seen anything close to the fear and panic and sheer horror that now masked his favorite person's normally cheerful and bright demeanor. The man looked as terrified as any kid would be, and it scared Tick.

"Get my dad!" he cried. "Please save my dad!"

But Norbert didn't need any further instruction. He was on his knees, leaning out the window, grabbing at the large man with both hands. Tick knew his dad had to weigh three times what he did, and it wouldn't be easy to pull him off the other car and into this one. Not able to breathe, he looked ahead.

The road curved sharply to the right, just a hundred feet from where they were.

"Hurry!" he yelled.

Norbert suddenly jerked back into the car, his arms gripped tightly, pulling on Tick's dad as best he could. Tick watched as his dad's hands, then arms, then head, then shoulders squeezed through the open window, Norbert screaming with the effort.

"I'm stuck!" Dad yelled. "My big fat tubby body is stuck!"

"No!" Tick yelled. He reached forward and grabbed his dad's shirt, yanking and pulling as hard as he could.

"You can do it, Dad. Suck in your breath!"

"Son, I . . . can't, I'm stuck!"

Norbert and Tick kept working, gripping and regripping, heaving and reheaving. Though he couldn't bear to look, Tick knew they only had precious seconds left until it was all over.

"Pull away from the other car and slow down!" Norbert yelled to the driver. "Don't you worry, Mr. Higginbottom. We won't let go of you. Keep your feet up!"

The driver veered to the left as he slowly applied the brakes, though it seemed like the worst roller coaster ride in history to Tick. His dad would be roadkill if he slipped out of the window.

"Don't let go of Big Bear," Dad whispered to Tick, actually breaking a smile. "Please, don't let go of me."

Tick couldn't talk, he just squeezed his grip even tighter.

Just as the car slowed to a snail's pace, they heard a horrendous screeching and metallic crunch as the other car slammed into something they couldn't see. A bright flash lit the night around them as a terrible explosion rocked the air.

Even when they finally came to a complete standstill, and cheers erupted from everyone, including his dad, Tick couldn't let go. He scrambled around

Norbert and hugged his dad's arms and shoulders and head like he hadn't seen him in ten years, bursting into tears. After a very long moment, his dad finally spoke up.

"Professor, do you think you could give me a push now? I'm, uh, kind of stuck."

CHAPTER
25

THE GIRL WITH BLACK HAIR

Frazier stood in the snow-swept graveyard, shivering and rubbing his hands together as he waited for Mistress Jane to wink him back to the Thirteenth Reality. He'd sent the nanolocator signal several minutes ago, but she often took her time about these things. She always wanted to make sure people knew the Mistress was in charge; she helped others at *her* convenience, not theirs.

A crunch in the snow behind him made Frazier spin around to see who had intruded on his waiting ground. He almost lost his lunch when he saw what stood there.

Where did she *come from? She must be—*

He didn't have time to finish his thought before the gigantic woman covered his nose and mouth with a foul-smelling piece of cloth, gripping it in place with her huge hand.

As he faded into blackness, he couldn't help but wonder if Mistress Jane would even miss him.

Tick, his journal now clasped in his right hand, stared in disbelief at what could've been his death.

Next to him, his dad shook his head, arms folded as he stared down into the gully. "Boy, I'm sure glad I paid ten bucks for insurance. The rental company can pay for that mess."

They stood with Norbert on the side of the road, watching the licking flames as the once out-of-control car burned. When it ran off the road, the car had shot off a steep embankment and crashed into a rocky ditch, crumpling into a mass of metal and broken glass, consumed by gasoline fire.

Despite the cold, Tick was still sweating from the intensity of their last-second escape. As soon as their rescue car had come to a stop and they'd managed to dislodge his dad, they'd run to this spot, unable to believe that if Norbert had shown up only a few seconds later, Tick and his dad might be buried somewhere in the wreckage below.

"Norbert, I don't know how we can ever—" Dad said.

The postal worker waved his hand like swatting at flies. "Not another word, Mr. Higginbottom, not another word. I just a-did what any good upstanding citizen would've done in the circumstances. You folks made me feel like myself again. That's thanks enough."

Tick finally broke his stare from the burning car and looked at Norbert. "How did you know we needed help? And who are those people in the car back there?" The driver and his daughter had not gotten out yet, probably still in shock over what they'd just seen. "Why would they want to save us?"

Norbert smiled, a barely noticeable crack in his still-panicked face. "Those are some good questions you're a-spouting out, boy, good questions indeed. I reckon they're in the same boat as you and your daddy, here. Back at the house, I'd just noticed a suspicious car pull onto the road to follow you folks when this fancy man and his little girl showed up, a-looking for the same stuff as you. Let's go talk to them." He gestured to the destroyed car. "Gazing down there won't fix a thing. What's done is done. Come on."

They walked back to the car and to the people who had saved their lives. The driver's side door popped open when they were still a few feet away; a tall, nicely dressed man stepped out, smoothing his greased blond hair back as he did so.

He bowed slightly as they approached, closing his eyes for a long second. "Good evening, sirs." His accent was thick, maybe German. "I apologize that we have not formally made acquaintance—if you'll excuse me."

Tick's dad had moved forward to shake the man's hand, but stepped back in surprise as the stranger hurriedly walked around the car and opened the passenger-side door, bowing in deference to the person inside. Baffled, Tick stared as a girl about his age got out of the car and waved at them. Even though they'd been a couple of feet apart during the few crazy seconds it took to save his dad, Tick had not gotten a good look at the girl until now, thanks to the car's headlights that were still shining brightly in the darkness.

She had an olive complexion and long dark hair framing her brown eyes and thin face. She was maybe an inch or two shorter than Tick and wore clothes that seemed like nothing special—he'd almost expected a princess the way her blond companion acted toward her.

"Hi there," she said, her gaze focused on Tick.

She also had an accent, but very subtle. "Hi," he answered. "Uh, thanks for saving us—to you and your . . . dad."

The girl laughed. "Oh, he's not my dad. He's my butler."

The man jerked his head stiffly in another bow. "It is a pleasure. My name is Fruppenschneiger, but you may call me Frupey."

It took every ounce of willpower for Tick not to laugh. *Frupey?*

His dad lumbered forward, his legs obviously sore from the car ordeal, and vigorously shook the hands of Frupey and the girl. "Thank you, thank you so much. I still can't believe how all this happened. Thank you for saving us."

Frupey answered in his formal voice. "It was our pleasure, so that Miss Pacini may receive the sixth clue."

Tick felt his stomach lift off from its normal position and lodge itself in his throat. "What?" he croaked. "Did you just say . . ." He looked at the dark-haired girl, who was smiling like she'd just been crowned Miss Universe.

"Hello, Americanese Boy," she said, holding her hand out. "It's about time we finally met face to face, huh?"

Tick couldn't believe it.

Sofia.

CHAPTER
26

TIME CONSTRAINTS

I t took only a few seconds for Tick and Sofia to break past the thin wall of awkwardness; they did, after all, know each other very well from their e-mail exchanges. They sat in the back of the car and talked nonstop during the drive back to Norbert's home. Tick's dad squeezed in the backseat next to them, butting in every now and then to ask a question or two.

Sofia had never given Tick a hint in her e-mails that she was from a wealthy family, and nothing about her screamed it out, either. She said she'd planned all along to surprise Tick in Alaska, figuring she might as well go along, too. The cost of the trip was no problem for her family, and as long as Frupey the Butler went with her, Sofia's parents pretty much let her do whatever she wanted.

"So how in the world did you get so rich?" Tick asked when they reached the town.

"My ancestors invented spaghetti."

Tick laughed, but cut it short when Sofia looked at him with a stone-dead face. "Wait . . . you're serious?"

Sofia finally let out a chuckle and slapped Tick on the shoulder. Hard. "No, but I got you good, didn't I? Actually, my grandfather would say his father *did* invent it, or at least made it perfect. Ever heard of Pacini Spaghetti?"

"Uh . . . no. Sorry."

Sofia huffed. "Americans. All you eat are hamburgers and French fries." She pinched all five fingers of her right hand together in a single point, shaking it with each word; it was just like something Tick had seen once in a mafia movie about an Italian mob boss. Sofia even made a small "uh" sound after her words sometimes, like "and-uh" and "French-uh."

"Hey, I eat spaghetti all the time," Tick argued. "With authentic Ragu Sauce."

"Authentic . . ." Sofia pursed her lips. "Then I guess you've *also* never heard of Pacini Sauce. What is this . . . Rag-oo? It sounds like some kind of disease."

"It tastes pretty good, but, I tell you what," Tick said, "you send me some of your stuff and I'll try it."

"Frupey!" she barked at her butler, driving the car.

"Yes, Miss Pacini?" he said, looking into the rearview mirror.

"Please send three cases of our noodles and sauce to these poor Americans."

"I'll do it the second we return, Miss."

"Thank you." She looked back at Tick. "He's such a good butler. You really should get one."

"Yeah, right," Tick said, sharing a laugh with his dad. "The only thing my family's invented is Edgar Stew, and trust me"—he lowered his voice into a pretend whisper—"it wouldn't sell."

"At least your mom's a good cook," his dad chimed in, ignoring Tick's insult. "I bet we could get rich off her if we knew how."

"What," Sofia teased, "does she make a good hamburger and French fry?"

"Do you really think that's all we eat?" Tick asked.

"Oh, sorry, I forgot. She makes a good hot dog, too?"

Even as they laughed, Tick couldn't get over the craziness of it all. Here he was, joking around with a girl from Italy in the back of a butler-driven car, in the state of Alaska, having just escaped from a runaway Oldsmobile.

His life had certainly changed forever.

Once they got back to Norbert's, Tick's dad called Aunt Mabel and told her they wouldn't be back until the next day, then he called the police and began the long process of dealing with the car accident. Frupey and Norbert scrounged around in the kitchen, trying to find food for everyone. *Car chases evidently make people hungry,* Tick thought as his own stomach rumbled.

Tick and Sofia sat together on the pitiful couch in the front room, discussing the latest clue they'd received. They had to use Sofia's copy because Tick's bit the bullet along with the rental car—he'd failed to slip it back into his journal during the frantic rush of excitement. The only light in the room came from a junky old lamp without a shade, its bare lightbulb blinding if you looked at it directly.

"Well, it's obviously just like the first clue," Tick said as Sofia scanned the words again. "Except this one tells us the time instead of the day."

"You Americans are so smart," she replied. "How did you ever figure *that* out?"

"Man, you sure are smart-alecky for a rich Italian girl."

"Girl?" she asked, her eyes narrowing. "Do I look like a little baby doll to you?"

Tick laughed. "I never would've guessed you'd actually be *scarier* in real life than in the e-mail."

Sofia elbowed him hard in the stomach. "Just

remember what I told you—I beat up seventeen boys last summer. No one messes with a Pacini."

"It's okay, I don't usually go around picking fights with gi—, I mean . . . young women . . . who own spaghetti companies."

"That's better, Americanese Boy. Now let's figure this out, huh?"

"Sounds good, Italian . . . ese . . . Woman." Tick didn't understand why she could call him *boy*, but he couldn't call her *girl*. He wanted to laugh again—for some odd reason, he felt really comfortable around her—but he didn't particularly want another jab to the stomach. He took the sixth clue from her instead and read through it again while she stared into space for a minute, thinking.

Recite the magic words at exactly
seventeen minutes past the quarter
hour following the six-hour mark
before midnight plus one hundred
and sixty-six minutes minus seven
quarter-hours plus a minute times
seven, rounded to the nearest
half-hour plus three. Neither a second
before nor three seconds after.

(Yes, I'm fully aware it will take
you a second or two to say the magic

```
words, but I'm talking about the
precise time you begin to say it. Quit
being so snooty.)
```

Once again, M.G.'s sense of humor leaked through the message, and Tick found himself eager to meet the man Norbert had already met. At least now they knew his real name.

Master George. *Sounds like something from Star Wars.*

"How long did it take you to figure out the first clue?" Tick asked.

"How long it take you?" Sofia responded. Every once in a while, she messed up her English, but for the most part, she knew it perfectly.

"Once I sat down to do it, maybe an hour."

"Then it took me *half* an hour."

"Yeah, right."

Sofia gave him an evil grin and raised her eyebrows. "Should we race on this one? Like a . . . Master George Olympics."

Tick had assumed they'd work together to solve it, but her idea suddenly sounded very fun. *If I was a nerd before, I've hit rock-bottom geek stature by now,* he thought.

"You're on," he said, ready for the challenge.

"I'm on what?" she asked. "Speak English, please."

Tick rolled his eyes. "Here, we'll put the clue on this little coffee table, where we can both see it, okay? Neither one of us are allowed to touch it. I'll run and get some paper and a pencil from Norbert so you can have something to write on." He stood up.

"What about you?" she asked.

Tick held his journal out. "I'll write in this—why didn't you bring yours?"

Sofia shrugged. "I got tired of carrying it around. Who needs it?" She tapped her head with a finger. "It's all stored up here anyway. So, what about a prize? What does the winner get?"

"Hmm, good question." Tick scratched his neck, faltering when he realized he wasn't wearing his scarf— he must've lost it in the wind after they busted the windshield.

"What's wrong?" Sofia asked.

"Huh? Oh, nothing." He paused. His scarf was gone, and Sofia hadn't said a thing about his birthmark— maybe he could actually survive without . . . no. He had an extra one at home, and deep down, Tick knew it would be around his neck when he returned to school.

"Tick," Sofia said, staring up at him, "did your brain freeze?"

"No, no . . . it's just . . . never mind." He snapped his fingers. "I've got it—the winner gets to visit the house of the loser next summer. But, uh, you have to pay for it either way because you're rich."

"Wow, what a deal."

"I'll be back in a sec with the stuff."

A couple of minutes later, pencils in hand, the race began.

⟶

Just as he'd done with the first clue, Tick jotted down the phrases from the sixth clue that seemed to go together logically. Once he'd done that, he assigned letters to them to indicate the order they should be calculated. It seemed easy now that he'd gone through the process before.

The biggest problem was determining which midnight the clue referred to—the one that *began* the day of May sixth or the one at the end of it? Then he realized whatever time he ended up with probably wouldn't be midnight, so it really didn't matter.

He nervously glanced over at Sofia, who was doing a lot more thinking than writing, tapping her pencil against her forehead, staring at the clue.

I'm way ahead of her, he thought, then continued his scribbles.

A couple of minutes later, the page in his journal looked like this:

Beginning Time: Midnight.

A. six-hour mark before midnight = 6:00 P.M.

B. quarter hour following A = 6:15 P.M.

C. seventeen minutes past B = 6:32 P.M.

D. C plus 166 minutes = 9:18 P.M.

E. D minus 7 quarter hours = 7:33 P.M.

F. E plus a minute times 7 = 7:40 P.M.

G. F rounded to nearest half-hour = 7:30 P.M.

H. G plus three half-hours = 9:00 P.M. on
   May 6

"Bingo!" he yelled, turning to say his time out loud. His words died somewhere in his throat when he saw Sofia looking at him with a smirk, holding up her paper with the answer scrawled across it:

$$9:00 \ P.M.$$

"Dang," Tick muttered. "But you didn't even take notes or anything!"

"I've got brains—I don't need notes."

Tick folded his arms. "I take it back—you're not a woman. You're a *girl*. And I hate spaghetti."

"I believe Americans call this a . . . sore loser, right?"

"Something like that."

Sofia put her hands behind her head and looked up

at the ceiling, letting out a big sigh, relishing her win. "I can't wait to visit your little house in Washington. Will your mother make me a hot dog?"

Tick snapped up the sixth clue from the table and stood up. "If you're lucky. And what makes you think our house is *little*, rich girl?"

Sofia lowered her arms to her lap and eyed Tick up and down. "I looked at your clothes and I said to myself, he must live in a little house." She winked, then punched Tick in the leg, hard.

"Ow!" he yelled, rubbing the spot. "What's that for?"

"To let you know I'm kidding."

Tick shook his head. "You are one weird kid."

"Ah, yes. That's the kettle calling the papa black."

Tick burst out laughing, falling back on the couch holding his stomach.

"What's so funny?"

"Well, for one thing, you said it backwards. And it's *pot*, not *papa*."

"Whatever. When I come to visit you, I will teach you Italian so we can talk like intelligent people."

"I think spaghetti is just about the only Italian word I need to know, thank you very much. That, and pizza."

Sofia tried to punch him again, but this time Tick was too fast; he jumped up and ran out of the room, the sounds of pursuit close behind. Luckily, dinner was ready in the kitchen—ramen noodles and peanut butter sandwiches.

～⌒

The next day, Tick's heart hurt when he had to say good-bye to Norbert, then Frupey and Sofia after they dropped him and his dad off at a car rental agency— the rich girl and her butler had a flight to catch. In just one day, they'd become like close family, and he hated to think he may never see them again. At least he knew he could expect an e-mail from Sofia, and he hoped she really would come visit him next summer.

Of course, by then, the magic day would have come and gone, and who knew what might change after that.

After another couple of fun-filled days being pampered by Aunt Mabel and having his life mapped out for him in detail, Tick and his dad headed back to Washington.

Once there, Tick began the longest three months of his life.

PART
3

THE MAGIC WORDS

CHAPTER
27

APRIL FOOL

Tick stared at his own reflection in the dark puddle of grimy water only inches away from his face, dismayed at how pitiful he looked. Like a scaredy-cat kid, eyes full of fear. Both ends of his scarf hung down, the flattened tips floating on the nasty sludge like dead fish. He winced when Billy "The Goat" Cooper yanked his arm behind him again, ratcheting it another notch higher along his back until the pain was almost unbearable.

Tick refused to say a word.

"Come on, Barf Scarf Man," the Goat growled, digging his knee into Tick's spine, wedging it below his twisted arm. "All you have to say is, 'Happy April Fool's Day. Please get me wet.' You can do it, you're a big boy."

Tick remained silent, despite the pain, despite the mounting humiliation as more school kids gathered around the scene. A few months ago, he would've given in and said the words, done as the Goat commanded. He would've let it end quickly and moved on. But not now. Never again.

Billy pushed Tick's face into the water, holding it there for several seconds. Tick remained calm, knowing he could hold his breath much longer than the Goat would dare keep him down. When he finally removed his hand from the back of Tick's head, Tick slowly raised himself out of the water, spit, then took a deep breath.

"Say it, boy!" Billy yelled, unable to hide the frustration in his voice. If he couldn't get Tick to obey, the tables would turn and *he'd* be the one suffering a humiliating defeat. "Say it or I'll wrap your sorry scarf around your head and dunk you 'til you quit breathing."

Tick felt a sudden surge of confidence and he spoke before he could stop himself. "Go ahead, Billy Boy. At least then I'd never have to look at your Frankenstein goat face again."

His spirits soared when the crowd around them laughed. A few kids clapped and whistled.

"Frankenstein goat face!" one kid called out. "Billy the Frankenstein Goat Face!"

This created more laughs, followed by murmurs

of conversation and shuffling of feet as people moved away, evidently having had enough.

"Leave him alone, Goat Face," a girl yelled over her shoulder.

Tick closed his eyes and took a gulp of air, knowing Billy would push him down at least one more time, would hold him under longer than ever before. But to his shock, he felt his arm released; the pressure of Billy's knee against his spine disappeared. As Tick's entire right side lit up with tingles and pressure from the blood rushing back to where it belonged, he scooted away from the pool of water and turned to sit on his rear end, staring up at Billy.

The Goat looked down on him with an odd expression. It wasn't anger or hate. He seemed . . . surprised.

"You're weird, man," Billy said. "I'm sick of you anyway. Go home and cuddle with your Barf Scarf." He kicked Tick's leg, then turned to walk away with his hoodlum friends.

Tick didn't totally understand the storm of emotions that swelled within him at that moment, but he surprised himself when he laughed out loud right before the tears came.

As Tick walked home, he put Billy out of his mind and thought of the long three months he'd just endured.

After the thrill and excitement, the life-threatening danger and escapades of Alaska, he'd expected to come home and barely rest, clue after clue and stranger after stranger showing up at his doorstep, delivering one adventure after another.

But nothing had happened. Nothing.

He and Sofia e-mailed back and forth, never failing to ask the other if they'd seen something or met someone. The answer was always a frustrated *NO!*

Where were the clues? What had happened to Mothball and Rutger? Did something get lost in the mail? Had they somehow proven themselves unworthy? Had the man in charge moved on to other, more deserving, kids? The questions poured out of their minds and into their e-mails, but no answer ever came back.

Tick was sick with discouragement.

All he could do was watch the snow pile up in his front yard all through January and February. The weathermen loved reminding their viewers that it had been the worst winter on record, revealing snow tallies in fancy charts with as much enthusiasm as if they were announcing the lottery winners. It was March before the snow finally started to melt, revealing patches of deadened grass that desperately longed for spring.

Tick hadn't missed a single day of school during

the three months, trying his best to keep focused while he worried about not hearing from Master George. But even competing in the Jackson County Chess Tournament in the middle of March hadn't been the same and Tick had placed fifth in his age bracket. His family seemed shocked that he'd lost the top spot, but his mind had been somewhere else, and the three-year winning streak ended with a dull thump instead of a big bang.

His dad constantly tried to cheer him up, encouraging him that something would come soon, but after a couple of months, even his dad seemed disheartened. Like a wounded snail limping to its next meal, Tick lived out each day hoping for a letter from Master George.

Tick did receive one exciting thing in the mail: a package of free spaghetti and sauce from Frupey the Butler. True to Sofia's word, it had tasted wonderful, and Tick knew he could never eat the cheap stuff again.

But even in the depths of the three-month doldrums, Tick and Sofia had never given up. They made a commitment to study their own journals every day, even if only for a few minutes, to keep their minds fresh, hoping something new might pop out and surprise them. They forced themselves to stay active in the game, even if the other side offered no help. And every day, no matter what, they sent an e-mail to each other.

Tick felt sure he'd hit rock bottom when he got home and checked his e-mail, clicking on a new one from Sofia.

Tick,

Hello from Italy.

Ciao.
Sofia

Tick groaned and wrote his own quick reply:

Sofia,

Howdy from America.

Later.
Tick

Depressed, Tick shut off the computer and slumped his way up the stairs to wait for dinner. A few minutes later, he fell asleep with the *Journal of Curious Letters* clasped in his arms like a teddy bear.

April sixth was a Saturday, and the sun seemed to melt away any remnants of clouds, beating down with a warmth that hadn't been felt in months. Tick made his usual trek to check the mail, basking in the golden light, his spirits lifted despite the circumstances. The sounds of trickling water came from everywhere as the massive amounts of snow increased their melting pace, disappearing by inches a day now. It wouldn't be long before hundreds of tulips stood like fancy-hat-wearing soldiers all over the yard, the result of painstaking pre-winter planting by his mom over the years.

Even Tick, not exactly a flower expert, enjoyed his mom's ridiculous amount of tulips every spring.

As he made his way down the steaming sidewalk, Tick took a deep breath, loving the strong smells of the forest that returned with the melting snow. The scents of moist dirt and bark and rotting leaves that had lain beneath the white stuff all winter filled his nostrils, and he felt better than he had in months. Spring tended to do that to people.

His good mood was short-lived, though. When he saw that the mailman hadn't brought anything from Master George, he slipped right back into poor-little-Tick mode and went back inside the house.

Later that afternoon, Tick sat at the desk in his bedroom, working on the math homework he'd been too depressed to finish the day before. He'd opened up his window, grateful that he was able to do so without freezing to death; the winter had seemed to last for ten years. He was just finishing up his last problem when he heard the phone ring, followed by the sound of footsteps coming up the stairs and down the hall toward his room.

"Tick, it's your girlfriend."

He turned to see his sister Lisa at the door, holding out the phone.

"What?"

"Phone's for you. It's a girl."

Tick's first thought was that it must be Sofia—who else would call him? He jumped up from his desk and walked over to grab the phone. At the last second, Lisa put it behind her back, smirking at Tick.

"Wow, you seem awfully excited," she said, eyebrows raised. "Are we having a little love affair that we haven't shared with Sis?"

"Give it—it's probably my, uh, science project partner."

Lisa chuckled. "You're gullible, kid—it's actually a man." She handed him the phone and left.

Tick closed the door and sat on his bed, putting the receiver to his ear. "Hello?"

At first, all he could hear was static and the sounds

of . . . beeping . . . or some kind of machinery in the background. Then came a loud clonk, followed by a soft boink and then a rolling series of metal clicks, like someone cranking up a thick chain into a holding wheel. Finally, surprising him, he heard the distinct *meow* of a cat.

"Hello?" he repeated. "Anybody there?"

From the other end came a rattling sound as the person picked the phone back up. A voice spoke through the scratchy static, a man with the one accent Tick could identify—British. "Is this . . . let me see . . . ah, yes, is this Mister Atticus Higginbottom?"

"Yes . . . this is Atticus."

"Uh, dear sir, you were supposed to be walking about today. I mean, er—it's a nice day to go for a walk, don't you think? Simply smashing, really, from what I hear." The man coughed. Tick heard the cat meow again, followed by some muffled words as the stranger covered up his end with his hand. "In a *minute*, Muffintops. Patience, dear feline!"

"Sir, do I know you?"

"No, no, no, not yet, anyway. But we certainly have some common acquaintances, if you get my meaning. In fact, I'm on instruction from them, old chap."

"On . . . instruction?"

"Yes, yes, quite right. They need you to go for a *walk*, good man. Asked me to call you."

"A walk? Where?"

"The usual, I suppose. What's a young master like yourself sitting inside all day for anyhow? Got a bit of the flu, do you?"

"No, I was just . . ." But the stranger had a point. Tick should be outside on the first beautiful day of the year so far.

"Well, off you go. Not a moment to waste."

"But . . . where am I supposed to go? Who—"

"Cheers, old boy. Only a month to go—I mean, er, a month or two, yes, that's right."

"Wait," Tick urged.

The phone clicked and went silent.

CHAPTER 28

A MEETING IN THE WOODS

Tick told his mom he had to go to the library, then headed out the door. Though he didn't need a jacket, he'd instinctively put on his scarf, which began to scratch and make him too warm before he'd made it past the driveway.

Stupid scarf. He loosened it, but he couldn't bring himself to take it off.

The cloudless sky was like a deep blue blanket draped across the world, not a blemish in sight. As much as Tick loved the winter and snow, even he had to admit it was about time for some warm weather.

As he left his neighborhood and started down the

road that led through the woods to town, Tick thought about the phone call he'd received. Every instinct in his mind told him it had to be Master George—in fact, he realized he'd heard the voice once before. On the tape of the third clue.

Wow, he thought. *I just spoke with Master George.* Master George!

Tick felt a shiver of excitement and a sudden bounce lifted his steps. After three grueling months, things seemed to be rolling again. He just hoped he had chosen the right direction to take a walk, though he couldn't think of another way that could possibly be classified as "the usual."

He was almost to the spot where he'd seen the wooden sign with Rutger's silly poem scrawled across it when he felt something hit him in the right shoulder. A rock rattled across the pavement, and Tick looked into the woods across the street. The last time someone had thrown a rock at him—

Another one flew out of the trees, missing him badly.

"Rutger, is that you?" Tick said, cupping his hands around his mouth to amplify his voice.

No reply came, but a few seconds later another rock shot out, this time smacking him in the forehead. "Ow!" he yelled. "Do you really have to do that?"

"Yes!" a male voice said from within the thick trees.

Grinning, Tick crossed the street and stepped into the forest.

~~~~~~

It didn't take long to find them. Rutger, his stomach sucked in as far as it would go—which wasn't much— hid behind a tall, thin tree with no branches, his body jutting out on both sides. Mothball, on the other hand, was trying her best to squat behind a short, leafy bush, her head poking at least two feet above its top, her eyes closed as if that would somehow make her invisible.

It was one of the most ridiculous things Tick had ever seen.

"Uh, you guys really stink at hide-and-seek," he said. Both of them stepped out from their hiding places, faking disgust.

They looked the same as the first time he'd met them. Rutger, incredibly short and round as a bowling ball, still wore his black clothes and the shoes and mittens Tick had given him months ago, though it seemed too warm for the outfit. Mothball had different clothes on, but they were still gray and hung on her eight-foot-tall frame like flags with no wind. The forest floor was mushy and wet and water dripped on them from the branches above.

"'Ello, little sir," the giant woman said, a huge smile crossing her wide face.

"Looks like you're a lot smarter than we thought," the tiny Rutger added—well, tiny in terms of height. If anything, he looked even *fatter* than the last time Tick had seen him. "But . . . I don't suppose you brought any *food*?"

"Man, am I glad to see you guys again," Tick said, ignoring Rutger's plea for something to eat. "What took you so long?"

"'Tis all part of the plan, it is," Mothball said in her thick accent, folding her huge arms together. "Master George—he's a smart old chap—reckoned he'd take a long wait and see who stuck it out. You know, weed out the ninnies with no patience."

"Last time you guys wouldn't tell me M.G.'s name," Tick said.

Rutger reached out and lightly slapped Tick on the leg. "Well, you figured it out yourself, now didn't you? Wouldn't it seem silly for us to not say his name when you already know what it is? Good job, old boy, good job!"

Tick knew he probably had little time available to him and wished he'd sat down to organize all of his questions before going out. He had a million things he wanted to ask, but his mind felt like soup in a blender. "So . . . how many kids like me are left? How many are still getting the clues?"

Rutger stared up at the sky as he slowly counted on his fingers. When he got to ten, he quit and looked at Tick. "Can't tell you."

"Thanks."

Mothball shifted her large body and leaned back against a tree. "Master George sends his regrets on the bit of trouble you had in the northern parts. Never meant that to happen, he didn't."

Tick squinted his eyes in confusion. "Wait a minute, what do you mean by that?" He couldn't put his finger on it, but something about her statement struck him as odd.

Rutger cleared his throat, trying to take the attention away from Mothball, whose face suddenly revealed she'd said something she wasn't supposed to.

"All my good friend means," Rutger said, "is that we never expected our, uh, enemy to catch up with you so quickly. Don't worry, though, we've, uh, taken care of the problem for now." He rolled his eyes and turned around, whistling.

"Didn't help matters much there, now did ya, my short friend?" Mothball muttered.

A swarm of confusion buzzed inside Tick's head, and he felt like the answer was somewhere right in the middle if he could just get to it. "But . . . what about the Gnat Rat thing, and the Tingle Wraith? You make it sound like—"

"Come on, now," Mothball said, straightening back to her full height. "Time's a-wasting, little sir. Got a lot to talk about, we do."

"But—"

"Mister Higginbottom!" Rutger interjected, spinning his wide body around to look at Tick once again. "I immediately demand you cease these questions, uh, immediately!"

Mothball snorted. "You just said *immediately* two times in the same sentence, you lug. Methinks he gets the point without you blowin' a lung and all."

Rutger fidgeted back and forth on his short legs, as if he'd only spouted off to save themselves from getting deeper into trouble. "Just trying to . . . teach the young master some patience and, uh, other . . . things like patience."

"You two are without a doubt the strangest people I've ever met," Tick said.

"Try living with a million Rutgers in one city," Mothball said. "That'll give you weak knees." She paused, then laughed. "Quite literally, actually, if the little folks are in the punching mood."

"Very funny, Flagpole," Rutger said.

"Thanks much, Bread Dough," she countered.

Tick thought it was fun watching the two friends argue, but he was hoping for answers. "Did you guys get me out here for a reason or what? And what's up with the phone call from Master George?"

"Been sittin' here all ruddy day, we 'ave," Mothball said. "'Ad to spur you a bit, burn your bottoms to get a move on."

"Couldn't you have just knocked on my door?"

"What, and get the detectives called in? Spend the rest of me life in a Reality Prime zoo?"

Tick held up a hand. "Whoa, time out—what does that mean?"

"What?" Mothball asked, looking at her finger-nails as though considering a manicure.

"What's 'Reality Prime'?" His mind spun, the word *reality* jarring something in his brain.

Mothball looked over at Rutger, shrugging her bony shoulders. "Methinks the little sir's gotten hit over the head, he has. Did *you* 'ear me say that?"

"Say what?" Rutger asked, his face a mask of exaggerated innocence.

"I've already forgotten."

Tick groaned as loud as he could. "I'm not an idiot, guys."

Rutger reached up and grabbed Tick by the arm. "We know, kid, we know. So quit acting like one. We'll tell you what you need to know when you're ready, not a second before."

"So what, I can't ask questions?"

"Bet yer best buttons you can—ask away," Mothball

said. "Just don't complain like a Rutger when we say mum's the word."

"Now wait just one minute . . ." Rutger said, letting go of Tick and pointing a finger at Mothball.

"I get it, I get it," Tick said before Rutger could continue. He thought about the list of words in his journal he'd heard from these two, framing questions inside his mind. "Okay, what's a kyoopy? Can you answer that?"

Mothball and Rutger exchanged a long look, signifying to Tick that this was no longer a black-and-white issue—which would be to his advantage. "Come on," he urged. "As long as you don't tell me how to figure out the clues, what does it matter if I know a little bit about what's behind all this?"

"Fair enough, methinks," Mothball said. "Master George does seem a bit more willing to let on. I mean, he called you on the telly, didn't he?" She gestured toward Rutger. "Go on, little man, tell him 'bout the kyoopy."

Rutger scowled. "Do I look like Hans Schtiggenschlubberheimer to you?"

"Hans *who*?" Mothball and Tick asked in unison.

Rutger looked like someone had just asked him what gravity was. "Excuse me? Hans Schtiggenschlubberheimer? The man who started the Scientific Revolution in the Fourth Reality? If it weren't for him, Reginald Chu would never have—" He stopped, looking uncertainly at Tick. "This is impossible, not knowing what we can and can't say in front of you. Blast it all, I can't wait until the special day gets here."

Of course, right then Tick thought of his teacher, Mr. Chu, just as he had when he saw "Chu Industries" on the Gnat Rat. But just like before, he didn't think it could have anything to do with his science instructor— it had to be a coincidence. "Who is Reginald Chu?" he asked. "And what kind of awful name is *Reginald*?"

"It's not a very fortunate name," Rutger agreed. "Downright stinky if you ask me. Fits the man, though, considering what he's done. Started out with good intentions, I'm sure, but he and his company have done awful, awful things."

"Well, what's he done? And what is the Fourth Reality? What are *any* of the realities? Are there other versions of the universe or something?"

Mothball sighed. "This is balderdash, really." She leaned over and put a hand on Tick's shoulder. "Rutger's spot on, he is. We just don't know what to talk about with you. Methinks Master George will explain everything— if you make it that far."

"Listen to me," Rutger said. "Focus your mind on the clues for now. Don't worry about all this other stuff. You can do it, and it will all be worth it—when the *day* comes. You'll be taken to a very important place."

Tick felt incredibly frustrated. "Fine, but at least . . . Can you just answer one question? Just one."

Rutger nodded.

"Can you tell me, in one sentence each, the definition of a kyoopy and the definition of a . . . a reality. No details, and I won't ask any more questions about it."

Rutger looked up at Mothball, who shrugged her shoulders. "Blimey, just do it. The poor lad's mind might explode if we don't."

"All right." Rutger took a deep breath. "Kyoopy is a nickname for the theory of science that explains the background of everything we're about." He paused. "And a Reality is a place, uh, or a *version* of a place, if you will, that comes about *because* of the kyoopy." He looked up at Mothball. "Wow, that was good."

Right at that very second, something clicked for Tick and he felt like an idiot for missing it before. "Wait a second . . . kyoopy. You mean . . . Q . . . P . . . right? Q.P.?"

Rutger looked confused. "Was I saying it wrong before? Yes, yes! Q.P."

"Looks like the little sir is on to something," Mothball said, a satisfied smile on her lips, but Tick's mind was in another world at that moment. Q.P. He'd heard that phrase before from Mr. Chu, and he couldn't wait to ask him about it again.

Kyoopy. Q.P.

Quantum physics.

"Now," Rutger said, clearing his throat, "could we *please* move on? I believe you'll be wanting the next clue."

CHAPTER
29

A BUNDLE OF CLUES

The air had grown cooler as the sun made its way across the sky and toward the horizon. The drip-drip-drip of the melting snow slowed considerably, and Tick shivered as he eagerly waited to see the next clue.

Mothball pulled out a familiar yellow envelope, though this one seemed thicker than the others, and a separate piece of white paper had been stapled to the upper left corner, its edges flapping loosely as she handled it. After a long look at Rutger, Mothball handed the package over to Tick, who snapped it out of her hand without meaning to look so anxious.

"Thanks," he said, fingering the note attached to the envelope. "What's this?"

"Flip it over and read it," Rutger answered. "Thought you could at least figure *that* out by yourself."

"Very funny," Tick muttered as he did what he was told, lifting the paper to read the few sentences typed on the back:

```
    Within you will find the next four
clues in the sequence, numbers 7, 8, 9,
and 10. Now, most certainly you will
read these and conclude to yourself
that I, your humble servant, have gone
batty because they don't seem like
clues at all. I will only say this:
EVERYTHING you receive is a clue.
```

Tick looked up at Mothball, then down at Rutger, whose folded arms were resting on his huge belly. "Four clues at once?"

"He's a bit hasty," Mothball said. "You see, has to be *twelve* clues, there does, and we've only got a short time to go, ya know."

"Why does there have to be twelve?"

"'Tis part of the riddle, Master Tick." She winked at him. "There you are, I've just given you my own bit of a clue. Quite clever, I am."

"Yeah," Rutger grumbled. "A regular Hans Schtig-genschlubberheimer."

Mothball snapped her fingers as her face brightened with recognition. "Ah, I remember that name now! Yeah, me dad taught my sis and me all about him, he did. That bloke invented the very first version of the Barrier Wand."

Rutger shushed Mothball. "Are you crazy? I thought we were done giving out secrets the boy doesn't need to know yet."

Mothball shrugged as she winked at Tick again. "It's got nothing to do with the clues, little man. Give the sir somethin' to think about, it will."

"Barrier Wand?" Tick had heard those words before from Mothball. "I won't even bother asking."

Rutger turned to Tick, rolling his eyes as he nodded toward Mothball, as if he were shrugging off the escapades of a little kid. "Solve the riddle of Master George, be where you're supposed to be on the special day, do what you're supposed to do, go where you're supposed to go—then you'll know very well what a Barrier Wand is, trust me."

"Sounds good . . . I guess." Tick couldn't wait to tear open the envelope of clues, but he also wanted to stand there all day and ask them questions. "Isn't there anything else you can tell me? Anything?"

"Done opened our mouths quite enough, we have," Mothball said. "Master George will probably step on his cat he's so nervous about it all."

"You mean . . . he can hear us? Do you have a microphone or something?"

Rutger laughed, a guffaw that echoed through the trees, like he'd just been told the funniest joke of the century. "You have much to learn, kid, much to learn."

Tick looked down with mixed confusion and anger. "What's so funny?"

Rutger stuttered his laugh to a stop, wiping his eyes with pudgy hands. "Oh, nothing, sorry. Nothing at all." He cleared his throat.

"Well, off we go, then," Mothball said. "Best of luck, Master Atticus."

"Yes, yes, indeed," Rutger added, reaching up to shake Tick's hand vigorously. "Please, don't take anything the wrong way. I'm a little funny in the head sometimes."

"Yeah," Tick said. "I noticed."

Rutger's face grew very serious. "Mothball and I . . . well, we're rooting for you, kid, a great deal. You'll make it, and we'll meet you again very soon. Okay?"

"It's in one month," Tick blurted before he knew what he was saying. "May sixth. I have to go to a cemetery and stomp my right foot on the ground, at nine o'clock at night, and say certain words and close my eyes. I just have to figure out *what* to say, and—"

Rutger held up a hand. "Sounds like you're on the

right track." He and Mothball exchanged a look, and there was no doubting the huge smiles of pride that spread across their faces.

So far, so good, Tick thought. *I just need to know the magic words.*

"We really must be going, now," Rutger said. "Good luck to you, and be strong."

He and Mothball folded their arms in unison, staring at Tick.

"Okay, see ya," he said, then paused, waiting for them to turn and go. They didn't move. "Aren't you leaving?"

"Better we wait for you to be off," Mothball said. "Just tryin' to be proper and all."

"Man, you guys are weird." Tick smiled then, hoping they knew they had become two of his favorite people on the planet. He felt the familiar pang of good-bye, then gave a simple wave. "See ya later, I guess. Will you be there if I . . . make it—whatever that means?"

"We'll be right there waitin' on ya, we will," Mothball said. "Be the grandest day of yer life, bet yer best buttons."

Tick nodded, wishing he could think of a way to extend the visit, but knowing it was time to go. "Right. Okay. Bye." He turned and walked away, heading back through the trees toward the road.

Tick ran all the way home, his sadness at saying good-bye to Mothball and Rutger quickly melting into anticipation of opening the next four clues.

He closed the door to his room and sat at his desk, wishing he could somehow transport Sofia from Italy so they could rip this thing open together. The thought made him want to kick himself for not asking Mothball and Rutger about their interactions with Sofia or any other kids. He wondered if Sofia had received this package yet. He'd have to e-mail her as soon as he was done taking a look.

He opened up the envelope and pulled out four pieces of cardstock, exactly the same as all the other clues. Each card had its own message typed in the middle of the page, with a number written in blue ink directly above it with a big circle around it, indicating its place in the sequence—seven through ten. Tick wondered about the significance of the order as he spread everything out on his desk in front of him, then read the first one, the seventh clue:

```
Go to the place you have chosen
wearing nothing but your underwear.
Oh, calm yourself, I'm only giving you
a bit of rubbish. Don't want you to
think I'm without a sense of humor.
No, quite the contrary—you must dress
```

```
warmly because you never know where
you'll end up.
```

Tick paused, thinking. The first line had made his stomach turn over before he realized Master George was just kidding around. That's all Tick needed was to go running across town in his undies to hang out at a graveyard in the middle of the night.

Nothing else about the clue seemed mysterious or riddle-like at all, giving weight to the little note that had been stapled to the front of the envelope. This one seemed like nothing more than a warning to dress warmly. But according to the attached note, *everything* was a clue, so it had to have some kind of hidden message.

Just when I think I'm getting the hang of it, he thought, shaking his head. He moved on to the next one, the eighth clue:

```
Eventually you will fail. I say
this because the vast majority of
those who receive these letters will
do so, utterly. For those extreme
few of you who may succeed, I will
conveniently explain away this clue
as a small typing error. For you, it
was meant to say, "Eventually you will
not fail."
```

Tick surprised himself by chuckling out loud. This Master George guy had quite the sense of humor and sounded like he was as quirky as an elf in Santa's workshop. Tick couldn't wait to meet him.

As for the clue itself, there was nothing to figure out, no mysteries—not even any advice this time. More and more, Tick was beginning to think he'd missed something important he was supposed to get from these messages.

He moved on to the ninth clue:

```
Ordinary kids would've given up
by now. I know what is haunting you,
what is chasing you, what is making
your life miserable. Cheer up, friend,
much worse lies ahead.
```

This one made Tick sit back in his chair and pause for a very long time. It was the shortest clue yet, but packed with so much. The kindness of Master George showing empathy for what Tick was going through and the terrible things he'd seen. The encouragement that Tick wasn't just an ordinary kid. The pride knowing he'd stood up and endured. And finally, the almost humorous warning that he'd only seen the beginning and "much worse" was still to come.

Tick felt like three starving warthogs had been

unleashed inside his brain, grunting and thrashing to find food. He wanted to know the truth, to know *every-thing*, so badly it made his head hurt, and he felt frustrated to no end. He'd just read the next *three* clues, and yet seemed no closer to discovering the magic words. If his family hadn't been downstairs, Tick would've screamed at the top of his lungs.

Almost reluctantly—almost—he read the final piece of paper from the envelope, the tenth clue:

Remember to bring two items with you, stowed carefully away in your pockets, while you say the magic words. Sadly, I must refrain from telling you what the items are. I can only say this: they must be impossible to pick up, no matter how strong you are, but small enough to fit in your pockets, since that is where they must be, on penalty of death (or at least a particularly nasty rash). I realize this riddle is very easy, but my cat just messed on the Peruvian rug in my parlor, so I haven't much time to think of a better one. Good day.

Messed on the Peruvian rug in his parlor? Tick was beginning to like Master George more and more every second.

And the man was right—this one was too easy. Tick got up from his desk, excited to e-mail Sofia. Then he would show all the new clues to his dad.

It took him ten minutes to finally persuade Kayla to quit playing her Winnie the Pooh computer game, and another couple minutes to clean the sticky spots off the keyboard from her fingers. She'd broken the no-food-at-the-computer rule and helped herself to a Popsicle while maneuvering Pooh and Piglet through the horrible dangers of the Hundred Acre Wood.

He finally logged in to his e-mail and opened up the INBOX, hoping that Sofia had sent him something as well. His hand froze in midair, hovering over the mouse like a cloud when he saw what waited for him.

An e-mail from someone named "shadowka2056."

The subject line said, "Master George is crazy."

CHAPTER
30

THE THIRD MUSKETEER

Tick clicked open the e-mail, his heart pounding.

Dude, what's up with all this stuff, man? I couldn't
believe it when I was finally non-stupid enough to
search the Internet to see if there were any others like
me. Can you believe all this is for real? Actually, I guess
I should ask first if you're still doing this whole mess.
For all I know you burned the letter a long time ago.

My name's Paul Rogers and I live in Florida.
Ever been here? I can see that you're from
Washington—man, we're like on opposite corners
of America. How cool is that?

I don't know what to say until I know more about
what you're up to. Have you gotten everything?
Have you met Mothball and Rutger? They kept
telling me I needed to go to one of the postmarked
places to get another clue. I said, what do I look
like, King Henry the Eighth? I ain't made of money,
dude. I finally talked the little fat man into giving
me the clue anyway. Looks like there's more than
one way to skin a cat in this game.

Anyway, I'm up to Number Ten, how about you? If
you don't have a clue what I'm talking about and
think I'm totally bonkers, go ahead and delete this
e-mail. Trust me, you don't wanna know.

Laters,
Paul

Tick, excited, immediately hit REPLY and typed
out his answer.

Dear Paul,

I'm really glad you wrote me. I'm totally still in it,
and I'm up to the tenth clue as well. Pretty easy
one, right? Hands. Our hands. You can't really
pick up your own hands, but they can fit in your

pockets nice and easy. It's about time we had one that was simple, huh?

I actually did go to Alaska—it was my dad's idea. We almost got killed, but it wasn't too bad. We met a funny guy named Norbert who's met Master George! And he also met some crazy lady named Mistress Jane. From what Norbert said, I don't think I want to meet her.

There's another one of us—Sofia. She's from Italy and she was there, too. She didn't almost get killed though. But she did help save us.

Man, this e-mail sounds so stupid. By the way, you can call me Tick.

Have you figured out the magic words? I just don't get it—I've studied that first letter backward and forward and I don't see anything. I'm really hoping you know something I don't.

I don't really know what else to say. It's good to know there are at least three of us now. May 6th is coming soon.

Your new friend,
Tick

Feeling kind of dumb because he didn't say much worthwhile, but not knowing what else to do until he knew the guy better, Tick hit the SEND button, hoping Paul would reply quickly since he lived in the same country.

Tick then sent another e-mail to Sofia, telling her everything and asking her if she received the package of four clues.

On Monday, Tick sat in Mr. Chu's class, anxious for it to be over. Tick wanted to ask him about quantum physics, see if he could learn anything new that would give him a hint about what the "kyoopy" had to do with Master George. A warm sun beat on the windows, making the room hot and stuffy. Several kids had given up long ago, their heads making ridiculous jerking motions as they kept falling asleep and waking up.

Tick had yet to hear back from either the new kid Paul or Sofia. He must've checked his e-mail at least twenty times on Sunday, with no luck. He didn't get it—every time *he* got an e-mail, he responded in a second, excited to keep the conversation going. Oh, well.

The bell finally rang and the students filed out of the room, at least three of them bumping into Tick's desk and knocking off his things. Each time, he picked them up without a word and put them back on his desk. The bully stuff seemed so silly now compared to the other things he was dealing with that nothing bothered him anymore. He defiantly adjusted his scarf and waited for the classroom to empty.

"Tick?" Mr. Chu asked as he finished erasing the whiteboard. "Aren't you going to your next class?"

Tick stood up. "Yes, sir. I just wanted to know if you'd have any time after school to talk about . . . something."

"Sure," Mr. Chu replied, raising his eyebrows in concern. "Is anything—"

"No, no, nothing's wrong. I'm just wondering about a subject we talked a little about a while back and I want to know more about it."

"What is it?"

Tick paused, nervous that somehow saying the two words would reveal everything about Master George and his mysteries. "Quantum physics," he finally sputtered out, as if ashamed of the topic.

"Oh, really?" Mr. Chu's face brightened at the prospect of sharing information on his favorite science subject. "What's sparked your interest?"

"I don't know—just curious I guess."

"Well, okay, I'd be happy to talk about it. Come by after school, okay?"

"Okay. Thanks." Tick gathered his things and headed off to his next class.

~~~

Long after the last bell had rung, Tick and Mr. Chu sat at his desk, discussing the many theories—all of them confusing—of quantum physics. The stale smells of dried coffee and old books filled the air as Tick leaned forward, his elbows resting on top of several messy piles of papers that needed grading. Through the window over his teacher's shoulder, Tick could see the long shadows of late afternoon creeping across the parking lot, where only a few cars remained.

"It's basically the study of everything that's teensy tiny," Mr. Chu was saying. "Now that doesn't sound like a very technical term, but that's what it's all about. Forget about the atom—that thing's huge. We're talking about electrons and protons and neutrons. And stuff that's even smaller—quarks and gluons. Sound like fun?"

"Well . . . yeah, actually," Tick answered.

"The basic thing you need to know is that all the stuff you *think* you know about the laws of physics—like, what goes up must come down—goes right out the window when you get down to particles that small. It's been proven those rules don't apply. Everything is different. And did you know that light has properties of both waves *and* particles . . ."

Mr. Chu went on to talk for at least a half hour straight, telling Tick all the basics of quantum physics and the experiments scientists had done to establish theories. What it really sounded like, though, was all a fancy way to say no one had a clue how it worked or why it was different from the big world.

"... and so by *observing* an electron, you are actually *deciding* where it is, what position it's in, what speed it's moving. And another person could be doing an alternate experiment at the same time, observing the same electron, but in a totally different position. Now, this is getting on the fringe of what the real experts say, but some people think an electron and other particles can literally be in more than one place at once—an infinite number of places!"

Tick felt like he was a pretty smart kid, but some of Mr. Chu's words made as much sense to him as an opera sung in pig latin. But that last sentence really made him think. "Wait a minute," he said, stopping his teacher. "You keep talking about these little guys like they're in a different universe. But aren't those tiny things inside my body, inside this chair, inside this desk? Isn't the big world you talked about just a whole bunch of the little worlds?"

Mr. Chu clapped his hands. "Brilliant!"

"Huh?"

"You nailed it, Tick, exactly." Mr. Chu stood up

and paced around the room in excitement as he continued talking. "They're not really separate sciences—they have to be related because *one* is made of the *other*. An atom is a bunch of tiny particles, and you, my friend, are nothing but a bunch of atoms."

"Right."

"This is where all the crazy, crazy theories come in—the ones that are so fascinating. One theory is that time travel is possible because of quantum physics. I don't buy that one at all because I think time is too linear for time travel to work."

Tick's head hurt. "Are there any you do believe in?"

"I don't know if *believe* is the right word, but there are some I sure love to think about." He paused, then sat back down at his desk and leaned forward on his elbows, looking into Tick's eyes. "One theory says there are different versions of the world we live in—alternate realities. An infinite number of them. If it can happen on the teensy-tiny level, why not on the big fat level too? All it would take is some vast manipulation of all those little particles that make up the *big* particles. Who knows—there might be some force in the universe, some law we don't know about, that can control quantum physics and even create or destroy different versions of our own world."

Mr. Chu had talked nonstop without breathing and finally took a big gulp of air.

"Sounds like it'd make a sweet movie," Tick said, trying to act like a normal kid with simple interests. But the truth was his thoughts were spinning out of control. Different versions of the world! Though he couldn't quite piece it all together, he knew this might explain where Mothball and Rutger came from.

"Oh, trust me, it's been done," Mr. Chu replied. "Especially the time travel part of it—but nothing I've seen that I like yet." He yawned. "I've talked your poor ear off for long enough, big guy. If you're really serious about studying Q.P., you should get a book or two from the library. It's fun stuff, especially for nerds like you, I mean, me." He smiled as he stood up and held out his hand. "Nice talking to you, Tick. It's always great to have students who actually *care* about what they're learning."

"Yeah, thanks," Tick said as he stood to leave. "See you tomorrow." He slung his backpack onto his shoulder and headed for the door. At the last second before leaving, another teacher—Ms. Myers—poked her head in from the hallway.

"Reginald, do you have a moment?" she asked. "I need to talk about parent-teacher conferences."

"Sure," Mr. Chu replied. "Come on in. Tick, we'll see you later. Thanks for coming by."

Tick almost dropped his books at the word *Reginald*, the coolness of their entire conversation fading into a disturbing, eerie feeling in his stomach. He forced out a good-bye, then quickly exited into the hallway.

He couldn't believe it, but he knew he'd never heard his favorite teacher's first name before. *It was Reginald? His name was* Reginald *Chu?*

Tick suddenly felt very, very ill.

CHAPTER
31

PAUL'S LITTLE SECRET

Tick lay on his back, staring up at the ceiling of his room as the last rays of the sun faded from the day, casting a darkly golden glow to the air. His stomach felt like someone had jacked up an industrial hose and pumped in five tons of raw sewage.

Reginald Chu.

He had thought it was all just a coincidence, but that was before he'd learned Mr. Chu's first name. Rutger said the founder and owner of Chu Industries, the ones who manufactured the Gnat Rat and had done "awful, awful things," was a man named Reginald Chu. Could there really be two people with that name in the world, much less two who both loved science? And who had both crossed paths with a kid named Atticus Higginbottom?

No way.

But then . . . how could his favorite teacher be someone who owned a major company the world had never heard of? Tick had looked up Chu Industries several times on the Internet, only to find nothing. Of course, he hadn't looked up the *name* Reginald Chu yet.

He got up from bed and headed downstairs, hoping a search might reveal something. As he passed Kayla on the stairs, clutching no fewer than five dolls in her small arms, Tick thought about the things he and Mr. Chu had discussed after school. One thing popped in his mind that seemed the most obvious answer to this dilemma.

Time travel. Mr. Chu created this horribly powerful company in the future and sent things back in time to haunt his old students.

Tick almost laughed out loud—talk about hokey and ridiculous. Despite the crazy stuff he'd seen the last few months, it didn't make him think any more than before that time travel was possible. Even Mr. Chu said it was a dumb theory. *Of course, if he was a bad guy* . . .

But what about the idea of alternate versions of the universe? Maybe his teacher had an alter ego in another reality. Just as nuts, but for some reason not *quite* as nuts. Tick shook his head, unable to believe he was actually having this conversation with himself.

He logged onto the Internet, then did a search for the name "Reginald Chu."

Three hits.

One obscure reference to a presentation Mr. Chu did at Gonzaga University with some other teachers, and a couple of unrelated hits about a guy in China. That was it. Just for fun, Tick typed in Chu Industries again, with the same result.

Nothing.

Trying his best to move his mind on to brighter things, he logged into his e-mail. He almost jumped out of his chair with joy when he saw replies from both Sofia and the new guy in Florida.

He froze for a second, not knowing which one to open first.

He clicked on Sofia's.

Tick,

Wow, another kid! Why did it have to be another American? That's all I need, running around with two boys who do nothing but eat hot dogs and belch and talk about stupid American football.

Yeah, I figured out the riddle about hands, too. BEFORE I got your e-mail, just in case you're wondering.

Next time you write this Paul boy, make sure to put
my name in the address, too. That way we can all
talk together.

Time is running out! We need to figure out the
Magic Words!

Ciao,
Sofia

Oh, please, Tick thought. *She just has to make sure I
know she figured it out on her own.*

He was about to hit REPLY on instinct, but remembered the e-mail from Paul. Tick quickly closed the one
from Sofia and clicked on the other.

Tick,

Dude, are you serious about the whole Alaska
thing? Man, I need to hear that story from the
beginning. Try to do a better job of it next time—
I couldn't understand a single thing you said
about it. :)

I must be the dumbest person this side of the
Mississippi because I didn't get the hands thing at
first. Now it seems really obvious.

But that's okay. I'm one up on you, big time.

I figured out the magic words.

See ya later, Northern Dude.

Paul

P.S. No way I'm telling so don't ask. Rutger said I'm not allowed to. We can talk about anything else, but each person has to figure out the magic words for themselves. Good luck.

P.P.S. I'm fourteen years old, six feet tall (yes, six feet), African-American, and drop-dead handsome. I love to surf, I play the piano like freaking Mozart, and I currently have three girls who call me every day, but my mom always tells them I'm in the bathroom. Let me know a little about you, too. Later.

What!

Tick sat back, unable to believe his eyes. He couldn't care less about Paul's little introduction at the moment— the guy knew what the magic words were! It was finally right there for the taking, but he wouldn't—*couldn't*— share.

That stupid little Rutger . . .

Tick hit the REPLY button, then added Sofia's e-mail address right after Paul's. From now on, hopefully they could stay connected as a trio and make their way toward the special day together. After pausing to think about what he wanted to say, Tick started typing.

Paul (and Sofia),

Okay, this e-mail has both of your addresses on it, so be sure and do that from now on so we can keep in touch. Paul, this is Sofia. Sofia, this is Paul. I'll forward the different e-mails to everyone later. Sofia needs to know that Paul seems to think he's something special. :)

Paul, did you really figure out the magic words? Are you serious? You really can't tell us? I've looked at that first letter over and over and over and I can't find the answer! Sofia, Rutger told Paul we're allowed to share and help each other, BUT NOT ABOUT THE MAGIC WORDS.

(If I ever get my hands on that guy . . .)

Sofia and I will just have to start figuring out a way to get you to tell us anyway.

Tick went on to write a very long e-mail, telling the story of Alaska and a little about himself and Sofia. When he finally finished and turned off the computer, Tick's eyes hurt. He was just standing when his mom called everyone in for dinner.

Frazier Gunn sat in his little prison cell and brooded.

How had it come to this? He'd been having a dandy of a time in Alaska, pulling off his plan to take care of *two* of the bratty kids George was scheming with—and poof. Everything fell to pieces.

After being knocked out in the freezing cold cemetery, Frazier had awakened in this teeny little room, which was barred and chained with enough locks to hold the Great Houdini. The walls of his cell were made of metal, lines of rivets and bolts all over the place. He felt like a grenade locked in an old World War II ammunition box.

And he'd been here for over *three months*. His captor had obviously injected him with a shockpulse because his nanolocator was dead, not responding whenever he tried to send a signal to Mistress Jane. Plus, if it had been working, she would've winked him away a long time ago. Of course, that fate might be worse than his current one. The woman had a nasty temper and low tolerance for failure.

At least he had a comfortable bed in which to sleep. And delicious food slipped through a small slot on the bottom of the door three times a day without fail. He'd been given books to read and a small TV with a DVD player and lots of movies. Mostly about cats, oddly enough, but still, it was enough to keep him occupied for a while.

But three *months*. He felt his mind slipping into an abyss of insanity.

To make matters worse, the room *swayed*. Not very much and not very often, but he could feel it. It was like a gigantic robot trying to put her cute little metal box to bed. He kept telling himself it was all in his imagination, but it sure seemed real enough when he leaned over the toilet and threw up.

Frazier was a miserable, miserable man, and it only poured salt in his wounds that he didn't know *why* he was here, or who had captured him.

It had to have something to do with that nuisance of all nuisances, George. *Master* George. *Please. What kind of man has the audacity to refer to himself as Master anything?*

The sound of scraping metal jolted him from his moping. He looked up to see a small slot had slid open in the center of the main door, only a couple of inches tall and wide and about waist-high from the floor.

This is new. He stood and walked over to the opening, peeking through. He yelped and fell backward onto his bed when a cat's face suddenly appeared, baring its fangs and hissing.

"Who's there!" he yelled, his voice echoing off the walls with a hollow, creepy boom. He recovered his wits and righted himself, staring at the small open space. The cat had already disappeared, replaced by a mouth with an old ruddy pair of chapped lips.

"Hello in there?" the mouth spoke, the voice heavy with an English accent.

"Yeah, who is it?" Frazier grunted back at his captor, though he already knew who was behind the door.

"Quite sorry about the inconvenience," Master George said. "Won't be long now before we send you on your way."

"*Inconvenience?*" Frazier snarled. "That's what you call locking up a man for three months?"

"Come on, old chap. Can you blame us after what you did to those poor children?"

"Just following orders, old man." Frazier sniffed and folded his arms, pouting like a little kid. "I never meant any true harm. I was, uh, just playing around with the car to scare them. No big deal."

"I must say," George countered, "I disagree quite strongly with your assessment of the situation. Mistress Jane has gotten too dangerous. She's gone too far. I mustn't allow you to return to her until . . . we've taken care of something."

"Taken care of what?"

"Just one more month or so, my good man," George replied, ignoring the question. "Then we'll send you off to the Thirteenth where we won't have to worry about you coming back."

Intense alarms jangled in Frazier's head. What the old man had just said made no sense. Unless . . .

"What do you—"

His words died in the metallic echo of the small door sliding shut.

CHAPTER
32

SHATTERED GLASS

A week went by with Tick, Sofia, and Paul e-mailing each other almost every day. They talked about their lives, their families, their schools. Though Tick had never met Paul and had met Sofia only once, he felt like they'd all become great friends.

Tick and Sofia used every ounce of persuasive skills they possessed to convince Paul to tell them the magic words. On more than one occasion, Sofia even threatened bodily harm, never mind that she lived on another continent. But Paul stubbornly refused, not budging an inch. Finally, the other two gave up and reluctantly admitted he was right, anyway. Better to follow the rules in this whole mess than risk jeopardizing their chances of achieving the goal all together.

The goal. What *was* the goal? Yeah, they pretty much knew that on the special day they had to perform a silly ritual in a certain place—probably to show their ability to follow instructions and obey orders as much as to show they could solve the riddles of the clues. But then what would happen?

Tick felt strongly that if they did everything correctly, they would *travel* to another place. Somehow Mothball and Rutger were doing it. Somehow Master George was traipsing about the world to all kinds of strange places, mailing letters. Tick always felt a surge of excitement when he considered the possibilities of what may happen on the special day, only to have it come crashing down when he remembered he hadn't figured out the magic words.

After dinner one night, Tick sat at his desk, his *Journal of Curious Letters* open before him, while his dad lounged on the bed with his hands clasped behind his head. Tick had told him everything, but his dad hadn't been much help, falling back on his normal Dad capacity of offering encouragement and rally cries. Tick suspected his dad knew more than he let on, but that he felt much like Paul did—it was up to Tick to solve the puzzle.

"Go through your list again," his dad said. "Everything we know needs to happen on May sixth."

Tick groaned. "Dad, we've gone over this a million times."

"Then once more won't hurt. Come on, give it to me."

Tick flipped to the page where he'd accumulated his conclusions. "Okay, on May sixth, I need to be in a cemetery—any cemetery—with no one else there but all the dead people."

"That excludes me, unfortunately." His dad let out an exaggerated sigh. "I still don't know if I'm going to let you do this."

"Dad, it'll be fine. It's probably a good thing you won't be there, anyway—I'm sure I'll be abducted by aliens or something."

"Whoa, now *that's* a dream come true."

Tick rubbed his eyes, then kept reading. "I need to be dressed warmly, and at nine o'clock on the nose I need to say the magic words, with my eyes closed, then stomp on the ground with my right foot ten times—all while keeping both of my hands in my pockets."

"Is that it?"

"That's it."

His dad rolled into a sitting position on the bed with a loud grunt. "All that's pretty easy, don't you think?"

"Well . . . yeah, except for one tiny thing."

"The magic words."

Tick nodded. "The magic words. At this rate, Paul

will be the only one of the three of us who gets to . . . do whatever it is that's gonna happen."

His dad scratched his chin, doing his best Sherlock Holmes impression. "Son, it can't be that hard. I mean, all the other clues have been challenging and fun, but not really *hard*, you know what I mean?"

"Maybe this is Master George's last way of weeding out those who aren't willing to stick with it. Maybe I'm one of those last schmoes who ends up losing. The seventh clue said most people would fail."

"Listen to me," his dad said, unusually serious. "I don't care what happens, and I don't care who this Master George fancy lad from England is. You're not a *schmoe*, and you never will be. You hear me?"

"Yeah, but . . ." Tick's eyes suddenly teared up and his heart seemed to swell and grow warm, like his veins had brought in steaming hot soup instead of the usual blood. It hit him then that he was worried—no, scared—that he wasn't going to solve the riddle of the magic words. He'd analyzed the first letter from M.G. more times than he could count, and nothing had come to him.

His dad got up and knelt next to his son, pulling him into his arms. "I love you, kid. You mean more to me than you can ever know, and that's all that matters to me."

"Dad, no offense, but . . . I mean, I really appreciate all your help." He pulled back from the hug and looked at his dad. "I want this so bad. I know it sounds dumb, but I *want* this. I've never really done anything important before, and Master George said I might be able to save peoples' lives."

"Then by golly we'll figure it out, okay? Give me that jour—"

His words cut off when a thunderclap of broken glass shattered the silence, followed by the tinkle of falling shards and a loud thump on the floor. Dad fell onto his back with a yelp and Tick's hand went to his chest, clutching his shirt like an old woman shocked by the spectacle of kids skateboarding in a church parking lot.

Someone had wrapped a note around a rock and then thrown it through the window.

While his dad went for the rock, Tick ran to the window to see if he could get a look at who had thrown it. He just caught a glimpse of a figure leaving the front yard and disappearing into the thicker trees of the neighboring woods.

A very short, very fat, figure.

⟨⟩

Snickering, Rutger waddled along on his short legs through the dark trees and back to the main road. The thrill of throwing the rock had been a great boon to his

spirits, and he had enjoyed every second of it. Now he just had to get away before Tick caught him.

As he thought about it more while escaping, he realized that breaking one of the Higginbottoms' windows maybe hadn't been the smartest thing to do, or the nicest. But it sure was funny.

He crossed the road and entered the forest on the other side, trying to remember the best way back to the old abandoned graveyard. He could've stuck to the road for a while longer, but he was worried he'd be caught. As he paused behind an enormous bush—it had to be big to hide *him*—he heard Tick's voice from a distance.

"Did you really have to break my window, Rutger!" the kid yelled.

Rutger laughed, then set off again, feeling his way in the darkness.

Tick and his dad walked up and down the road a few times, trying to spot the eccentric little man, but he was nowhere in sight, the darkness too deep. A slight breeze picked up, making Tick shiver.

"I can't believe he broke my window," he said, but then he laughed.

"You think it's funny, huh?" Dad said.

"Actually . . . yeah. That guy's crazy."

"Well, young man," Dad said in his best attempt at a stern voice, "maybe you won't laugh so much when I tell you it's coming out of your allowance. Come on, let's go see what the note said."

⁓

Tick picked up the rock, which was about the size of his fist, and carefully pulled the pieces of tape off the white cardstock that had been wrapped around the hard, cold surface. When he finally got it off safe and sound, he turned it over to see that it was the next clue—number eleven—from Master George.

"Read it, read it," his dad urged.

Tick read it out loud as he devoured each word with his eyes.

> Given that the day is almost here, I will issue a final warning. If you succeed in this current endeavor, your life will be forever altered, becoming dangerous and frightful. If you do not, very bad things will happen to people you may never meet or know. The choice to continue is yours.

"Dang it," Tick said.

"What?"

"I was hoping he'd give us another hint on how to come up with the magic words. This isn't a clue." Tick waved the paper in the air, then dropped it on the desk next to his journal. "It's just a warning. No different from the stuff he said in the very first letter."

"But remember," his dad pointed out, "he said *everything* you receive is a clue."

"Yeah, well right now I'm kind of sick of it." Tick flopped onto his bed and rolled over toward the wall.

After a long pause, his dad spoke quietly. "Sleep on it, Professor. You'll feel better in the morning, I promise."

The floor creaked as his dad walked toward the hallway; then the light went off and he heard the soft thump of his dad gently closing the door.

Despite the tornado of thoughts churning inside his mind, Tick fell asleep.

Tick knows he's dreaming, but it's still creepy.

He's in the forest, moonlight breaking the darkness just enough to make the trees look like twisted old trolls, their limbs reaching out to grab him, choke him.

Leaves and snow swirl around his body like fairies on too much pixie dust. A huge tree looms at his back. Tick watches the leaves spinning in the air, mesmerized.

He jumps to catch one, and some unseen force holds him in the air . . .

And then the leaves turn into letters.

One by one the letters pass in front of Tick, glowing briefly, teasing him with their riddles, reminding him that he can't solve the biggest one of all. The first letter.

The first letter.

The first letter . . .

CHAPTER
33

THE FINAL CLUE

The last yellow envelope from Master George came
on the third of May, only three days before the Big
Day. Tick came home from school on a warm and rainy
afternoon to find it on his pillow, addressed to him and
postmarked from Brisbane, Australia.

Until then, he'd been in a foul mood, with good reason.

Two days earlier, Sofia had announced she was
pretty sure she'd solved the riddle of the magic words.
Positive, in fact. Tick knew he should be happy for her,
but instead felt jealous and angry. Especially since he
knew she couldn't tell him; in his mind it was like Paul
and Sofia had this secret about Tick and kept giggling
about it behind his back.

With each passing day May sixth grew closer and closer and Tick became more dejected, moping around like an old man searching for his lost soul in an Edgar Allan Poe story. He just didn't get it—he was smart. He'd always thought he was way smarter than anyone his own age, and many who were older. Yet for some reason he couldn't figure out those stupid magic words! Paul and Sofia did it, why couldn't he?

As Tick opened the last letter, hoping against hope it somehow held the final link to the magic words, he thought again about how odd it was that Master George traveled around the world to mail his messages. And how Mothball and Rutger got around the world so quickly. It had to be something magical, and Tick sure hoped he'd find out all about it in three days.

He pulled out the white cardstock. The last clue. Scared to death he'd finish it and be no better off than before, he almost reluctantly read its words:

```
Everything you need to determine
the magic words is in the first
letter. Quit struggling so much and
read them, won't you? Listen to the
words of Master George-they've been
there all along! This is the last
clue. I shall never see or speak to
```

```
you again. Unless I do. Good-bye, and
may the Realities have mercy on you.
```

Tick slumped down on his bed, groaning out loud. It seemed like the last few clues had been a complete . . .

Wait a minute.

He sat back up and put the paper in his lap, reading through the clue again. Had Master George made a mistake while typing it? The second sentence made no sense.

```
    Quit struggling so much and read
them, won't you?
```

Read *them*? Why would he say *them* when referring to the first letter he'd sent out? There'd been only one piece of paper in that original envelope, so why would he use the plural word *them* when telling Tick to read it? The first letter . . .

Tick stopped. He felt like the Earth had stopped spinning and the air had frozen around him in an invisible block of ice; his mind and spirit seemed to step out of his body and turn around to look at him, not believing he could've missed something so obvious.

The first letter.

He grabbed his journal, ripping it open to find

the clue that had first revealed he needed to discover magic words to say on May sixth. It had been the second clue, telling him that at the appointed time, he would need to say the words with his eyes closed. Master George couldn't tell him what the words were, but the last sentence told him how he could figure it out himself:

        Examine the first letter carefully
        and you will work them out.

Old M.G. had been purposefully tricky with his language to throw his readers off the trail. When Tick read that clue the first time, his mind had immediately interpreted it as referring to the very first letter he'd received in the mail from Master George. And once that had been set in his mind, he'd never even considered the possibility of a different meaning. But what the mysterious man really meant *was* something entirely different.

The first letter.

Not the first envelope. Not the first paper. Not the first message.

The first letter.

M.G. meant that Tick needed to literally examine the first *letter* of something. And only one possibility made sense. Even though some of the Twelve Clues had not seemed like clues at all, Master George had been very clear.

Everything is a clue.

His blood racing through his veins like he'd just done windsprints, setting his heart into a thumpity-thump that he could feel and hear in his ears, Tick went through his *Journal of Curious Letters* page by page, clue by clue. He kept a finger on the last page of the dusty old book, flipping back there after seeing each of the twelve riddles in turn, jotting down a letter, then going back again.

One by one, Tick wrote down the first letter of each clue, twelve letters in all. When he finished, he sat back and stared at the result, wanting to laugh and cry and scream at the same time.

MASTERGEORGE

CHAPTER
34

THE MIRACLE OF
SCREAMING

Tick took his journal downstairs with him, eager to e-mail Sofia and Paul and let them know he'd finally—*finally*—figured it out. He placed his precious book on the desk and quickly logged in and sent off the messages, his excitement building by the second. He couldn't wait until his dad got home from work so he could tell him, too.

It's all in place now, he thought. *Just three days and it's really going to happen!*

Of course, he didn't know what "it" was, but that was beside the point.

Tick stood up from the computer desk and stretched, suddenly happier than he'd been in weeks. He felt stupid for all the jealous feelings he'd had toward his new friends and the whole thing in general; he'd acted like a little baby, at least within his own mind.

But that was all in the past, now. *Three days.*

So bottled up with energy he could hardly stand it, he decided to run over to the library and hang out like he didn't have a care in the world. Maybe he'd check out a book and read it as a reward. He'd probably have just enough time to finish it before the Big Day came. He told his mom he'd be back in time for dinner and headed out the door.

Halfway to the library, the sun finally breaking through the storm clouds that had hung over the world all day, he realized he'd left his journal sitting on the computer desk back home and wondered if he should go back and put it away. *No, I won't be gone that long.* As he ran on, he hoped he didn't look as ridiculously happy as he felt.

⌒⌒

Kayla noticed the ugly old book sitting on the computer desk, wondering where it had come from. It looked like something from her favorite Disney cartoon. Maybe it was a book of pirate treasure maps! She was a very young girl, but she knew one thing for certain.

Pirate treasure maps equal fun.

She looked around to make sure no one was around,

then grabbed the book from the desk, pulling it down onto her lap as she sat on the floor. Words were written in a little box in the center of the cover, but she recognized the first one right away.

Tick.

Uh-oh, she thought. *He doesn't like me to mess with his things.*

Well, just a peek couldn't hurt, could it?

She opened the book up and flipped through the pages, seeing lots of pieces of paper that had been glued to the ones already there. No pirate maps though. Maybe this was an art project her brother had been putting together as a surprise for her, though it wasn't very pretty. All it had were a bunch of words that looked funny.

Kayla quickly grew bored, sad the book didn't have anything to do with pirates. She was flipping through it one last time when one of the pieces of paper slipped into the air like it had been shot out of a cannon and dropped to the floor in front of her. She picked it up and saw that this one had more words than any of the others—a *lot* more.

The glue must've cracked, letting the boring old paper escape.

Well, Kayla thought, *now I'm in a pickle.* Her mom wouldn't let her use glue without a grown-up around and if she asked for help, her mom might be mad that she'd broken Tick's book. Plus, she couldn't remember exactly where the piece of paper had been inside the book.

Maybe, just maybe, Tick wouldn't notice it was missing since so many other papers were glued throughout. And if she just stuck it somewhere or threw it away, he might find it and then he'd know for sure she'd been messing with his stuff.

Kayla put the book back on the desk, then clutched the loose paper in her hands. With devious eyes, she looked over at the fireplace, focusing on the little knob that started up the gas and flame.

It'd been awhile since she'd had fun with fire . . .

Tick walked down the road of his neighborhood, holding the nice, thick book he'd checked out at the library. The sun slowly fell toward the horizon, the first glowing fingers of twilight creeping through the trees. Tomorrow was Saturday and after months and months of thinking and solving and worrying and running, he couldn't wait to spend a couple of days relaxing.

On instinct, he checked the mailbox when he got to his house, even though he already knew his mom had gotten it earlier—hence the twelfth clue. Tick couldn't help but hope absolutely nothing else happened until

Monday night, the Big Day. He needed a break from all the stress.

Easy to say when you have it all figured out, he thought. He'd sure not enjoyed the three-month-long "break" he'd had after Christmas.

He walked down the driveway toward his front door.

⁓

Kayla knew she didn't have much time. The warm fire licked the air with an almost silent whooshing sound, reminding her of how much she loved watching things burn. Now that it was mostly warm outside, they never had the flames going, and if her mom walked in, there'd be a certain favorite doll that would get locked away for a whole week. She needed to hurry.

She threw the stupid piece of paper into the flames.

A wave of ugly black stuff, rimmed with a fiery line of glowing orange, traveled across the paper from both of the short sides as the whole thing slowly curled up into a ball. A little line of smoke escaped into the room, and in a few seconds, all that remained was a crispy sheet of ash.

"Kayla, what are you doing!"

She jumped at her brother's voice, letting out a little shriek as she turned around to see him standing right behind her. Without meaning to, her eyes immediately looked over at the book sitting on the computer desk.

Tick followed her gaze, then practically leaped over to grab the book. He flipped it open, his eyes showing he already knew what had happened. His face reddened, his hands began to shake. He almost dropped the book. Then a *tear* fell out of his right eye. Kayla didn't understand; why would such a dumb old—

Tick's shout, full of rage, cut off her thoughts. "Bad girl, Kayla! You're a very bad, bad, naughty, stupid, naughty girl!" Then he ran out of the room and out the front door, slamming it closed behind him.

Kayla bawled.

~~~~~

Tick ran.

Clutching the journal in both arms, he didn't know where he was going, or how long it would last, but all he could do was run, his loosened scarf flapping in the wind. His heart wanted to explode out of his chest, panic and anger and disappointment crushing his feelings like someone had injected a full-sized elephant into his bloodstream. It hurt, and tears flowed down his face as he pounded the pavement with his clumsy feet. He fell twice, only to get up and keep running.

How could Kayla have done something so *stupid!* Everything had just fallen into place, everything was perfect. But now the message had been sent. Tick didn't know how, but he *knew* it had been sent.

Burn the letter, stop the madness.

Tick had been cut off. Even though he'd figured out all the clues, and was ready to perform the silly ritual in three days—he'd been cut off. Somehow Master George would know the first letter had been burned, which meant he'd think Tick had given up and was out of the game.

After everything, after all that work and sweat and danger, it was all over.

Tick was in the forest now, still running, dodging trees and brush, tripping and getting back up again, ignoring the scratches. He sucked at the air around him, forcing it into his lungs so his heart wouldn't give up and die.

But then it finally became too much. He stopped, doubling over to take in huge, gulping breaths. Sunset had arrived and the woods had grown very dark, the trees standing as monuments of shadow all around him. When he finally caught his breath, he straightened and folded his arms around the *Journal of Curious Letters*.

There had to be a way to fix this. There had to be.

Tick knew that Master George somehow tracked what all of his subjects were doing. Tick didn't know what kind of magic or futuristic device accomplished the task, but he knew his actions had been monitored.

How else did Mothball and Rutger always know where and how to find him? Even in Alaska! Based on what Paul had said, they went *there* to give him a clue, not the other way around.

Surely Master George cared more about Tick's intent than the mistake of Kayla burning the letter. And Tick's intent was stronger than anything he had felt in his entire life. He wanted to see this through. He wanted to reach the end of the mystery.

He wanted it very, very badly.

Not sure if he'd finally flipped his lid once and for all, Tick screamed at the top of his lungs, belting out several words as loudly as his body could handle.

"MASTER GEORGE, I DIDN'T BURN THE LETTER!"

It hurt his throat and made him cough, but he shouted it a second time anyway.

Drawing in a deep breath through his torn throat, Tick concentrated. He had to do something. He had made his choice long ago to *not* burn the letter. That choice still had to mean something, didn't it? If only he had chosen to take his journal with him to the library instead of leaving it where Kayla could find it.

He felt a funny tickle growing in the pit of his stomach, a reserve of energy he hadn't known was there. A wave of warmth spread up from his stomach into his chest. The air in the woods stilled around him, as if the whole world hushed, waiting for him to make his move.

Tick gritted his teeth. He tapped into that quiet pool of energy, channeling the heat that filled his body and forcing it through his shredded voice box, yelling out for the third time:

"MASTER GEORGE! I . . . DID . . . NOT . . . BURN . . . THE . . . LETTER!"

The woods swallowed up his words, returning only silence. The fire in his belly flickered and then went out, leaving Tick feeling weak and shaky.

He waited, hoping he would see some kind of sign that Master George had heard him. Nothing.

Dejected, throat burning, and not knowing what else he could possibly do, not knowing if what he had done had changed anything at all, he headed for home.

⁓

Kayla sat in the middle of the living room, hosting a tea party for her three favorite dolls. Humming to herself, she passed out cups of steaming hot tea.

The front door swung open, followed by her very sad-looking brother. His clothes looked dirty, his hair was all messed up, and he was sweating.

What happened to him? she wondered. *He was supposed to be at the library.*

He came into the living room and knelt down

beside her, pulling her into a fiercely tight hug. Kayla thought Tick was acting really weird but she finally squeezed back, wondering if he was okay.

"I'm sorry, Kayla," he said. "I'm really, really sorry I yelled at you like that." He leaned back from her; his eyes were all wet. "You're a good girl, you know that? Come here." He hugged her again, then stood up and headed for the stairs, his head hung low, that strange-looking book with his name on the cover gripped in his right hand.

Halfway up the stairs, he leaned over the railing and repeated himself. "You're a good girl, Kayla. I'm sorry I yelled at you, okay? I know you didn't mean to mess up my book."

Kayla was confused. When had Tick yelled at her? Earlier, he'd been talking to his friends on the computer while she played with her dolls but he hadn't said anything to her. And she hadn't touched his book at all. How could she? He had taken it with him when he left for the library.

She and her dollies laughed at the silliness of boys and she poured herself another cup of invisible tea.

Tick flopped down on his bed with a groan. How could he know if screaming in the woods had done any good? Was he really going to have to agonize all weekend, waiting, then head to the cemetery on Monday night and hope for the best? Was it really all over?

With a heavy heart he opened up his *Journal of Curious Letters* to torture himself by studying the spot where Master George's first letter had once been glued, safe and sound. When the front cover flipped over and fell in his lap, Tick looked at something he couldn't understand. He stared for a very long time at the page before him, his mind shifting into overdrive trying to comprehend the message his eyes were frantically sending down the nerve wires to his brain. A message that was impossible.

The first letter was *there*, glued to the page like it had always been, not a burn mark or blemish to be found. It was there! How . . . ?

Master George—or *someone*—had just pulled off the coolest magic trick Tick had ever seen.

~~~

Kayla had just poured the last cup when she heard loud thumps from upstairs—was somebody *jumping* up there?—followed by happy screams of joy. It was Tick, and he sounded like he'd just received a personal letter from Santa Claus.

What a weirdo, she thought, taking a sip of her tea.

~~~

Far away, Master George sat upright in his ergonomic chair, staring at the flashing lights of his Command Center. He shook his head, feeling a bit dazed. He'd just been readying himself to . . . do something.

He couldn't remember what exactly.

He'd been thinking about . . . Atticus Higginbottom.

But why? It was as if a bubble in his brain had popped, taking the last few minutes of his life with it. It was downright maddening—he couldn't remember anything. Why was he even sitting in the chair? He only sat here when someone had made a Pick—or if someone had burned their letter. He shook his head. *Had* someone burned their letter? Had *Atticus* burned his letter?

He looked up at the computer screen, counting the purple check marks. No. Everyone was accounted for, the mark by Atticus's name glowing bright and steady. That was good. The special day was coming up quickly and Master George couldn't afford to lose a single member of the group. Especially not Atticus.

I really must be getting old.

Bewildered, he stood up, calling for Muffintops, and thinking how much he'd like a nice pot of peppermint tea.

CHAPTER
35

THE FINAL PREPARATION

By Sunday night, Tick had heard back from Paul and Sofia about the strange incident with the burned letter and its miraculous reappearance. They were as shocked and clueless as he was about how or why it happened. Paul wasn't shy about expressing his doubt that it had occurred at all. His theory was Tick had been so stressed out about the magic words that he'd experienced one whopper of a bizarre dream.

But Tick knew it was real. He'd even asked Kayla about it and she didn't remember anything about burning the letter. No, Tick knew something magical had happened. Something supernatural. Something miraculous. And he couldn't wait to ask Master George what it might mean.

He sat at the desk in his room, waiting for his dad. The lamp on the desk provided the only light, failing miserably to push back the gloom. They'd planned all weekend to meet at eight o'clock Sunday evening to discuss the Big Day, and to run through the clues one final time. Though they didn't really know what they were planning for, it seemed they'd have only one shot at this. Or rather, *Tick* would have only one shot. The clues had been very clear—he must go alone, unless his dad wanted to drop dead of a heart attack right before the special time.

Tick had just pulled out the *Journal of Curious Letters* when he heard a soft knock at the door. "Come in," he called out.

His dad opened the door and shut it behind him. "Twenty-five hours to go, kiddo."

Tick groaned. "I know. I've been dying for this day to come and now that it's here, I wish we had a week or two more. I'm scared to death."

"Well, at least you're honest." Dad came in and sat on the bed, ignoring the loud creak of the bedsprings, which sounded as if they were about to break. "Most kids would act all tough and say they weren't scared at all."

"Then most kids would be faking it."

His dad clapped his hands together. "Well, we won't have much time to talk tomorrow night before you go, so let's run through everything."

Tick wasn't ready for that yet. "Dad?"

"Yeah?"

"What if . . . whatever I do *takes* me somewhere? Something tells me it will. What if I'm gone a long time?"

His dad's face melted into a look of deep sadness, all droopy eyes and frowns. "Professor, trust me, I've been so worried about all this I can't sleep at night. How could any good father let his son go off to who-knows-where to do who-knows-what and for who-knows how long? *Especially* after the dangerous things we've been through." He paused, rubbing his hands together. "But what can I say—I'm nuts? It's hard to believe in all this—but I believe in *you*. I'm taking a huge leap of faith, but I'm gonna let you walk out of this house and down that road"—he pointed out the window—"and off to wherever or whatever it is you've been called to do. It's going to *kill* me, but I'm gonna do it. I'm either the best or the worst dad in history."

A long silence followed. Tick felt something stir within him, a new appreciation for his parents and what they went through worrying about their kids. It couldn't be easy. And now Tick was going to do the worst thing possible to his dad—make him let him go without having a clue what might happen to his only son.

"What about Mom?" Tick finally asked.

His dad looked up from the spot he'd been staring at on the floor. "Now *that* could be a battle."

"What are you going to do? She'd never let me go."

His dad laughed. "That's exactly why you're going to go tomorrow night, and leave the explaining-to-Mom bit to me. Once you're gone, I'll sit her down and spill the beans, every little morsel, from beginning to end. Your mom and I have loved each other for many years, son, and eventually she'll understand why you're doing this, and why you and I feel so strongly about it."

Tick snorted. "Yeah, sometime after she tries to kill you for letting me go."

His dad nodded. "You're probably right, there. Just try to not be gone *too* long and maybe I'll survive."

Tick suddenly had a horrible thought. "What if . . . what if I never—"

His dad held up a hand and shushed Tick loudly. "Stop. Stop, Atticus."

"But—"

"No!" He shook his head vigorously. "You're coming back to me, you hear? These people know what they're doing, and you *will* come back to me. And there won't be another word said about it, is that understood?"

Tick couldn't remember the last time his dad had looked so stern. "Yes, sir."

"Good. Now let's run through those clues."

~

It took a half hour, but they read through each and every one of the Twelve Clues, studying their words one last time to make sure they hadn't missed anything. But it all seemed to be there, straightforward and solved. Looking back, it had all been pretty easy in a way. The real test seemed to be the endurance and the bravery to keep going.

And, of course, figuring out the magic words, which seemed to be the most important piece of the puzzle. No matter what else he'd done, without those words to say, he felt sure everything would fail.

When they read the twelfth clue, they realized they'd perhaps missed something—a little phrase their mysterious friend had thrown in to verify they'd decoded the magic words correctly.

Listen to the words of Master George—they've been there all along!

And they really *had* been there. If Tick had just known to look at the first letter of the individual clues, he probably would've figured out "Master George" the second they'd learned the name from Norbert up in Alaska.

And so, after thoroughly examining the entire *Journal of Curious Letters* with his dad, Tick felt ready to go.

Tomorrow night, in the cemetery close to downtown, at nine o'clock, he'd show up, alone, in warm clothing, say the words "Master George" with his eyes closed, hands in pockets, then stomp the ground with his right foot ten times.

After that, who knew *what* might happen.

⁓

Tick went downstairs to check his e-mail before bed, realizing this might be the last chance he had to see if his friends had sent anything. It was already approaching early morning on Monday for Sofia because of the time difference, and Paul was probably already in bed.

What would happen to the others between their turns and his? If they were being taken somewhere, would they just wait around all day until he arrived? Was the staggered time difference on purpose—so Master George wouldn't have to do . . . whatever he was going to do to everyone all at once?

There I go again, Tick thought. Asking a billion questions even though he knew the answer was out of his reach for now. One more day. Twenty-four hours. Then, hopefully, he'd know everything at last.

He logged in to his e-mail and was excited to see messages from both Sofia and Paul. He opened Sofia's, who'd sent hers hours before Paul.

Tick and Paul,

Not much to say now, huh? Don't think Sofia Pacini is in love with two American boys, but I really hope I see you both tomorrow. I'm sure somehow they're going to bring us magically together. Right?

Good luck. I wish we knew what to expect.

Ciao,
Sofia

For some reason, Tick felt a pang of sadness in his heart, realizing the possibility he might never hear from Sofia again. What if something terrible happened tomorrow? What if only *some* of the people who performed the ritual made it to wherever they were going? Tick told himself to shut up and clicked on Paul's e-mail.

My little buddies,

Hot diggity dog, tomorrow's the day. Let's don't jinx anything.

Hope you're right about us meeting. If so, see ya tomorrow.

Out.
Paul

Tick hit REPLY TO ALL and typed a quick message, knowing his friends might not see it anyway.

Paul and Sofia,

Good luck tomorrow. See you soon. I hope.

Tick

He turned off the computer and stood up, looking over at the fireplace. He thought back to the two events that had happened in the last few months related to the pile of stacked brick, now cold and dark. First, the commitment he'd made to not burn the first letter, to stay in the game—made while kneeling before a fire that could've ended it all. And then the bizarre incident with Kayla and the letter—something that either proved miracles really did happen or Tick had serious mental issues.

With a swarm of butterflies in his belly, Tick finally turned out the lights and headed up the stairs to his room, ready for one last night before the Big Day he'd been preparing for since November.

It took him over two hours to fall asleep.

PART
4

THE
BARRIER
WAND

CHAPTER
36

AMONG THE DEAD

The next evening—Monday night, May sixth—Tick stood on the front porch with his dad, looking at his digital watch every ten seconds as the sun sank deeper and deeper behind the tree-hidden horizon. The last remnants of twilight turned the sky into an ugly black bruise, a few streaks of clouds looking like jagged scars. It had just turned seven-thirty, and the temperature couldn't possibly be any more perfect for a romp in the town cemetery. Warm, with a slight breeze bearing the strong scents of honeysuckle and pine.

"Are you ready for this?" Dad asked for the fifth time in the last half hour.

"I guess," Tick replied, tugging at the scarf around

his neck, in no mood to offer any smart-aleck response. He felt like he should have done more to prepare, but there was nothing he could think of to *do*. The only real instruction he'd been given in the Twelve Clues was to show up and do a couple of ridiculous cartoon actions.

He did have a backpack full of warm clothing, some granola bars and water, a flashlight, some matches, and—most important—his *Journal of Curious Letters*. He didn't know if he'd be stranded somewhere and suddenly realize he needed to search for clues he'd missed before. Or maybe he needed it to enter the realm of Master George—kind of like a ticket.

Tick was as ready as he possibly could be. He looked at his dad, who seemed ten times more nervous than Tick did, wringing his hands, rocking back and forth on his feet, sweat pouring off his face. "Dad, are you okay?"

"No." He didn't offer anything else.

"Well . . . there's nothing to worry about. I mean, it's not like I'm going off to war or something. Mothball and Rutger will probably *be* there in the cemetery waiting for me. I'll be fine."

"How do you know?" Dad asked, almost in a whisper.

"How do I know what?"

"That you're not going off to war?"

"I . . . I don't know." Tick couldn't *believe* how the minutes dragged by.

"*Many lives are at stake.* That's what the man said, right?"

His dad's voice shook, worrying Tick. But he had no idea what to say. "I promise I'll come back, Dad. No matter what, I promise to come back."

"I don't know what scares me more," Dad said. "Letting you run off on your adventure or knowing I have to somehow tell your mom tonight that you may not come back for a while. Can you imagine how much that woman's going to *worry*? I may be strung up on a pole when you return."

"Dad, how long have you guys been married?"

"Almost twenty years. Why?"

"Don't you think she trusts you?"

"Well . . . yeah. What are you, a psychologist now?"

Tick shrugged. "No, I just think Mom will understand, that's all. She's always taught me right from wrong, hasn't she? And to make sacrifices for other people—to *serve* other people. I'm just obeying orders, right?"

His dad shook his head in mock disbelief. "Professor, I can't *believe* you're only thirteen years old."

"Thirteen and a half."

His dad barked a laugh, then pulled Tick into a hug, squeezing him tight. "You better be off now, son. Don't want to take any chances of being late, now do you?"

"Nope." Tick returned the hug, trying to fight off tears.

"I love you, Atticus. I'm so proud of what you're doing." His dad pulled back, still holding Tick by both shoulders as he looked into his eyes. "You go and make the Higginbottom family proud, okay? You go out there and fight for what's right, and fight for those who need your help."

"I love you, too, Dad," Tick said, hating how simple and stupid it sounded, but feeling the truth of it in his heart. They hugged again, for a very long minute.

Finally, without any need for additional words, Tick turned from his dad, walked down the stairs of the porch, waved one last time, then headed for his destiny.

He only wished he knew what it was.

⁓

Yeah, right, Edgar thought as Tick disappeared down the dark road. *Like I'm going to let my only son run off to who-knows-what all alone.*

Edgar turned and hurried back inside where he grabbed the flashlight and binoculars he'd hidden in the closet. Though he really did believe in the whole Master George affair, he was also a father, and he couldn't just let Tick go on his adventure without a little . . . supervision. After all, the clues hadn't banned anyone from being *near* the cemetery, now had they?

"Honey, Tick and I are going for a walk!" he yelled upstairs.

"This late?" her muffled voice called from the bedroom. "Why?"

"Don't worry . . . I'll explain everything when we get back!" He groaned at the prospect.

Before she could reply, Edgar was out the front door and down the porch steps. He'd have to be quick if he wanted to keep up with Tick.

One thing, Edgar vowed as he walked down the driveway. *I see one suspicious thing and I'm ending this.*

⁓

By the time Tick reached the forest-lined road that led to town, the sun had made its last glimmer upon the world and gone to bed for the night. Now past eight o'clock, darkness settled on the town of Deer Park, Washington, and Tick felt himself shiver despite the warm and comfortable air.

He couldn't believe it was here. The Big Day. The Big *Night.*

As he walked down the lonely road, the constant buzz of the forest insects broken only occasionally by a passing car, he ran through everything he needed to do in his mind. Even though it seemed so simple, he knew he only had one shot at this and didn't want to mess everything up. Dual feelings of excitement and apprehension battled over his emotional state, making him nauseated and anxious for it to be over, one way or another.

He arrived at the town square and passed the fountain area, where the shooting display of water had been turned off for the night, and made his way down the small one-way lane that led to the old city cemetery. A few people walked about the square, but it mostly seemed vacant and silent, like a premonition that something very bad was about to happen to this quiet and unassuming town.

Quit freaking yourself out, Tick told himself. *Everything's going to be fine.*

The entrance to the Deer Park Cemetery was a simple stone archway, both sides connected to a cast-iron fence encircling the entire compound. There was no gate, as though those in charge figured if some psycho wanted to visit dead people in the middle of the night, more power to them. As for grave digging, that had gone out of style with Dr. Frankenstein a couple of hundred years ago.

Tick paused below the chipped granite of the arch and looked at his watch, clicking the little light button on the side to see the big digital numbers: 8:37. Just over twenty minutes to go.

The moon, almost full, finally slipped above the horizon, casting a pale radiance upon the hundreds of old-fashioned tombstones; they seemed to glow in the dark around the chiseled letters declaring the names and dates of the dead. Barely defined shadows littered the ground, like holes had opened up throughout the graveyard, zombies having escaped to wreak their nightly havoc.

Once again, Tick shivered. No doubt about it, this was plain creepy.

Hoping it didn't matter exactly *where* he stood when he performed his little song and dance as long as he was inside the cemetery, Tick stayed close to the entrance, near a tight pack of graves reserved for young children. Tick pulled out his flashlight and flicked it on, examining some of the names while he waited for the last few minutes to pass. Most of the names he didn't know, but he did recognize a few that had been much-publicized tragedies over the last few years. A car accident. Cancer.

Despite his youth, Tick knew there must be nothing in the world so bad as losing one of your kids. Like he'd just swallowed a bag of sand, it hit him then that if anything happened to him tonight, his mom would be devastated. His poor mom. Of course, she'd be so busy yelling at his dad for letting him go in the first place that maybe she wouldn't have the time or energy to hurt properly.

He turned off his flashlight and returned it to his

bag. He pulled out the jacket and gloves and put them on, not wanting to take any chances that the instructions to dress warmly had been anything but literal. He tightened his scarf and glanced at his watch. He could see the numbers perfectly in the moonlight.

Five minutes to go.

He put his backpack on the ground, then thought better of it, swinging it back onto his shoulders. If he were about to magically travel somewhere, much better to have everything . . . *attached*.

For the millionth time, he wondered which was stranger—the things he'd been through or the fact that he actually believed there was something *true* behind it all. That he wasn't crazy.

One minute to go.

Tick stared at his watch now, clicking the button that made it show the ticking seconds as well as the hour and minute. As the appointed time grew closer and closer, his heart picked up; sweat beaded all over his body; he felt himself on the verge of throwing up.

Ten seconds.

He quickly put his hands deep into the pockets of his jeans, counting down the last few seconds inside his mind.

Five . . . four . . . three . . . two . . . one . . .

Tick closed his eyes and shouted out the words, "MASTER GEORGE!" He stomped the ground below him ten times with his right foot and a quick and cold shiver of excitement went up and down his back.

Tick waited, holding his breath for a long minute. He finally opened his eyes and looked around, but saw that he stood in the exact same spot as when he began. Everything was the same. He waited longer still, hoping something would change around him. Several more minutes passed. Then a half hour. Then an hour. Then two. Desperate, he went through the entire ritual again.

Nothing happened.

Absolutely nothing.

CHAPTER
37

A FAMILIAR NAME

Knowing for a fact he'd never felt so depressed in all his life, Tick began the long walk back home. He wished he had a cell phone so he could prevent his dad from telling his mom about everything—now that it was all moot. Now that Tick had failed, and wouldn't be going anywhere after all. At least then he could enjoy the one saving grace of Mom not thinking her husband and only son had gone bonkers.

If the town had been quiet before, it now seemed completely devoid of any life whatsoever. Tick didn't see one person as he walked past the fountain area, and there wasn't a light to be seen anywhere. Even the street-lamps had been extinguished, or they'd burned out.

Only the moon shone its pale milky brilliance around the square, making everything look like a much bigger version of the graveyard he'd just left.

Dead and quiet. Full of shadows.

Tick picked up his pace.

When he left the town behind him and started down the long road leading to his house, the creepiness increased. He couldn't explain it, but Tick felt a constant chill in his bones, like something very big and very hungry watched him from the woods. He looked back and forth, scanning both sides of the road, but saw only the tall shadows of the trees, black on black. This time, Tick threw all reservations out the window and simply ran, resolving not to stop until he lay in his bed where he could cry himself to sleep.

As he jostled down the road, concentrating on his feet so he wouldn't trip, Tick had to consciously ignore the feeling that an enormous ghost was right behind him, ready to tap him on the shoulder. Goose bumps broke out all over his body, slick with sweat. He kept running.

He made it to his neighborhood and finally to his house, not slowing until he reached the porch. He stopped, bending over with his hands on his knees as he gulped in air to catch his breath. He didn't want to walk back inside panting like a chased dog. But then the feeling he'd had near the forest returned full force and he ran up the steps to the front door.

The handle rattled when he gripped it, but didn't turn. Locked. He glanced at his watch where he could barely see it was just past eleven o'clock. Tick stepped back, looking for the first time at all the windows on the bottom floor. He should've noticed before—everything was dark, not a single light was on in the house. Yes, it was late, but his dad was supposed to be telling a very long story to his mom, so surely his parents were still up. They would stay up and watch for him, wouldn't they?

Tick knew his dad kept a spare key to the house hidden in a fake rock placed behind the bushes. He walked back down the porch steps and searched for it, even getting down on his knees to feel around with his hands. But they came up empty, even after scouring the usual area several times.

He couldn't find the key anywhere.

Tick sat back on his heels. *What in the world?*

Frustrated, Tick gave up and walked back to the front door, where he reluctantly pushed the doorbell.

A long moment passed. No one answered. Not a sound came from within the house. Tick, getting more worried by the second, pushed the doorbell again.

Still no response.

Finally, in a panic, he pushed the bell over and over again, hearing the loud ring through the wood of the door. He stopped when he heard a booming shout;

it sounded like it came from one of the upstairs bed-
rooms. The shout was followed by a quick series of loud
thumps—someone running down the stairs. Then the
door jerked open, revealing a man Tick had never seen
before in his life.

"What do you want!" the stranger screamed at the
top of his lungs, spittle flying out of his mouth. The man
was pale and sickly, so thin he looked like he'd crumble
into a pile of sticks at any moment. His ruffled black
hair stood up in patches on his head, his face covered in
a scraggly beard. Dark, sleep-worn eyes stared at Tick,
full of fire and anger. "Who are *you*, you little brat?
What do you want?"

Tick felt a sick fear swell inside his stomach.
"I'm . . . I'm . . . Atticus Higginbottom. I . . . I live
here."

"*Live* here? What are you, one of those no-good
townies? Get out of here!" The man kicked out, missing Tick badly. "Get!" He slammed the door closed.

Tick, his world crashing down around him, turned
and ran, the darkness weighing on his shoulders like
black stone.

Edgar stood in the dark cemetery, his chest rising and
falling with heavy breaths. He'd searched everywhere—
behind every tombstone, tree, and bush in sight. He

didn't know how it could be possible, but what he'd seen from his hiding spot across the road must not have been a trick of his mind.

It had really happened.

What he'd seen had *really* happened.

Tick had disappeared. Like a Las Vegas magic show, Edgar's only son had vanished from sight. There one second, gone the next. No smoke, no sound, nothing.

His son had *disappeared*.

Panicked, Edgar started searching all over again, even though he knew it was useless. Deep down inside, he tried to convince himself Tick was okay, that they'd known something like this would happen. This was what they'd been preparing for all along! Edgar told himself that Tick was safe now, in some other world or realm, learning how he could help save the lives that were depending on him. Where had all the good feelings about this whole mess gone to? He and Tick had devoted themselves to this cause, believing in its purpose.

But it hadn't seemed real until the moment he'd seen his son vanish. And now Edgar didn't know if he could ever forgive himself for letting Tick go. If something happened to his boy . . .

Dejected, a sinking weight of despair filling his stomach, Edgar finally gave up and headed for home. He was about to have a very long night explaining things to his wife.

Tick didn't know what else to do—where else to go—except back to the cemetery. Something *must* have happened when he'd performed the ritual—something horrible. He'd messed it up somehow, sending him to the wrong place or time. He thought back to the crazy things Mr. Chu had told him about quantum physics. Where *was* he?

Once he left his neighborhood, he couldn't run another step. He slowed to a walk, breathing heavily, constantly looking behind to make sure no one was following him—especially the creepy man who'd answered the door at his house.

It was a weird feeling to suddenly feel like the only place you've ever lived is no longer yours, occupied instead by some monster of a man willing to kick a little kid. Tick had run the gamut of emotions in the last hour—excitement that the special day was here, disappointment when seemingly nothing had happened, dejection and despair, panic and fear that his home wasn't his home anymore. Now he just felt numb as he slowly made his way back to town. To the cemetery. It was the only place where he could hope to find some answers.

He tried to take in his surroundings as he walked, searching for signs that other things about his hometown were different than what he was used to. But the darkness was too great and all he saw were shadows hiding other shadows. He almost pulled out his flashlight, but thought better of it—who knew what lurked in this new nightmare. He wanted to remain as hidden as possible.

As he entered the town square for the third time that night, he realized the lack of lights couldn't be a coincidence—the place was a haven for nothing but ghosts and ghouls. Where was he? What had happened to this place that should feel so familiar but instead seemed so alien? His heart hurting, his body exhausted, Tick picked up the pace again and quickly ran across the waterless fountain area and down the small road until he reached the entrance to the cemetery.

He didn't know how he'd missed it before, but Tick saw that more than half of one side of the stone archway had crumbled and fallen to the ground into a pile of dusty rubble. Dozens of rods from the iron fence were missing or bent, looking like the mangled teeth of a horrific robot. The moon vanished entirely behind a large bank of clouds, casting everything into sinister shadows. The tombstones seemed bigger, less defined, leaning at odd angles.

Tick rubbed his hands over his arms, standing in the same place where he'd performed the magic-words-

and-foot-stomping ritual. He finally realized what he was feeling.

Terror. Absolute, shrill, make-your-hair-stand-on-end terror.

Out of the corner of his eye, he saw a light come on.

He sucked in a quick intake of air as he turned to see a small spotlight shining on a single tombstone, about thirty yards deeper into the cemetery grounds. Compared to the heavy darkness around him, it seemed like the sun itself had changed its mind and come back for a nighttime visit. Realizing he hadn't seen a spark of electricity since leaving for his house and returning, Tick felt like he was witnessing some kind of magic trick.

Curious, he walked toward the light, ignoring the fear constricting his chest.

He stepped around several large graves, almost tripping on a stone border around a particularly wide one. He kept his eyes riveted on the bright spot, scared it might be a trap, but not knowing where else to go. As he got closer, he saw that the light came from a large flashlight, sitting alone in front of a grave. He looked around the area, squinting his eyes to see if any monsters or zombies were hiding in the shadows, readying themselves to jump out and eat him.

The light hurt his vision, and he knew if someone was out there, he wouldn't be able to see them.

He focused on the brightly displayed tombstone, now close enough that he could read the etched words, dusty indentations on an old black-gray slab of granite.

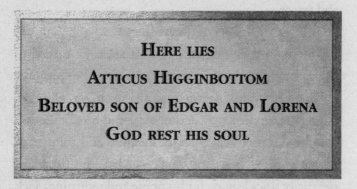

HERE LIES
ATTICUS HIGGINBOTTOM
BELOVED SON OF EDGAR AND LORENA
GOD REST HIS SOUL

Everything in his mind immediately vanished, all fear and thoughts washed away in the disbelief of what he saw before him. Tick fell to his knees, unable to take his eyes away from the words on the grave marker.

Tick looked at the dates.

According to the tombstone, he'd been dead for three years.

CHAPTER
38

SITTING DOWN

Before Tick could completely process the fact he was looking at his own grave, he heard a noise behind him. He twisted around, still on his knees, and for a split second thought he saw the reincarnation of Frankenstein's Monster. A scream formed in the back of Tick's throat. But it quickly fell mute when he realized the figure was someone very familiar, standing just a few feet away, towering over him.

Mothball.

Tick quickly stood up, relieved to see a familiar face, the questions flying out of his mouth before he had his feet under him. "Mothball, what's happening? Where am I? How did—"

The tall woman held up a hand. "Best the little sir keep quiet for a moment, let yer tall friend do the talkin' for a bit." She stepped forward and bent over to pick up her flashlight, grunting with the effort. "Not every day ya get to see yer own tombstone, now is it? Downright spooky, it is."

"Mothball, what's going on?" Tick felt tears forming in his eyes now that the initial shock of seeing his name on the granite slab had settled into a stark reality.

"What's going on?" Mothball repeated. "I'll tell ya what's going on. The little sir did it, he did. Solved Master George's riddles, made it quite nicely. Got lots of learnin' to do now, ya do. Hope yer mind's still got some empty spots."

Tick couldn't shake the sick feeling in his stomach. "Mothball, why does this grave have my name on it? Who's that crazy guy living in my house? Where is my family?" His voice broke on that last word, and he suddenly wondered if he really wanted to know the answer.

"One question at a time, if yer wantin' any answers." She pointed down at the tombstone. "There's a fine reason that there piece of rock has yer name on it." She paused. "Yer dead here, little sir. Dead as a mouse that's got no heart, you are. Smell worse than Rutger's feet I'd wager." She offered Tick a smile, but he was in no mood to laugh.

"What are you talking about? How can I be . . . dead? I'm standing here talking to you."

"I take it back, then. Yer *Alterant* is dead—that's what I meant." Mothball sighed and fidgeted, looking as uncomfortable as a vampire in a cathedral.

"An Alter-what? Mothball, *please* just tell me what's going on."

Mothball stepped closer to Tick, put one of her huge arms around his shoulder. Her flashlight was pointed at the ground, but it still illuminated her face enough to show creases of concern in her temples and brow, her eyes full of something indescribable—sorrow or compassion. "Perk yer ears, Master Tick, methinks I need to tell ya something."

Tick stared up at her, waiting. "What is it?"

"Life's a bit harder than you've ever known, it is. *Different*, too. When ya finally meet Master George, yer going to learn things that'd be a mighty bit hard for a grown-up to hear, much less a young'un like yourself. How it all works—the whys and hows and whatnot—better be leaving to me boss, I will. But I can tell ya one thing before we shove off." She paused, looking away from Tick into the darkness of the graveyard.

"Yeah?" Tick prodded.

"This . . . place. If things had been different for you, Tick—if different choices had been chosen, different paths taken—well, that really could be yer little self under this here pile of dirt. This version of the world is fragmented, as Master George calls it. It's weak, splintering, *fading*. All words I don't use much, I'll admit it. But we wanted ya to see it, to feel what it's like to see yer own self dead as a stump."

Tick shook his head. "But I don't get it, Mothball. Are you saying this is another version of our world? That I did something here that ended up with me dead?"

"No, no, no, you've got it all wrong. I'm not saying yer dead because of anything ya did directly—at least, not for sure. Probably never know, we will." She took her arm away, throwing it up in the air, frustrated. "Oh, this is rubbish—need to get a move on, we do."

"Wait!" Tick reached out and grabbed Mothball's shirt. "What about my family. Are they okay?"

Mothball knelt down on the ground, bringing her eyes level with Tick's. "They're right as rain, little sir. You don't have to worry about them at'all. See what I'm tryin' to tell ya is that the choices we make in this life can lead to things we'd never s'pect to have anything to do with us. Realities can be created and destroyed." She gestured with her head to Tick's tombstone. "That little feller might ruddy well be you for sure, he could. But ya just might have the power within yer beatin' heart to make sure it doesn't happen. That's what it's all about, really."

Some of Tick's anxiety and fear had vanished. Though he didn't have a clue what Mothball was talking about, he felt . . . *moved*, which made him feel very adult. "Mothball, when do I get to actually understand what it is you're talking about?"

Mothball smiled as she stood back on her feet. "Not much for speeches, I'll admit it. By the looks of it, you'd rather listen to a croakin' toad than hear me go on a bit. Righto, off we go." She moved away from the tombstone and walked deeper into the scattered graves of the cemetery, the beam of her flashlight bobbing up and down with each step.

Tick fell in line behind her, having to take two steps for every one of hers, adjusting his scarf and backpack as he went. "When you say 'off we go,' where exactly are we off-we-going *to*?"

"Ah, Master Tick," she said over her shoulder, "glad we got the bologna-and-cheese talk out the way, I am. Now's time for the fun part. Hope yer excited."

"I am, trust me. Anything to get away from this place."

Mothball laughed, a booming chuckle that seemed sure to wake up a few dead people. "Don't like the deadies, do ya? That'll change, it will. Most times it takes a place like this to go off winking, it does."

"Winking? What's that?"

"Find out soon enough, ya will. Ah, here we are." Mothball stopped, then turned around to face Tick. She shone her flashlight on a small patch of unmarked grass.

"Have a nice sit-down, we will." When Tick didn't move, she gestured for him to sit. "Right here, chop-chop."

"Why do we have to sit down?" Tick asked as he sat cross-legged in the exact spot where she'd shone the light.

Mothball sat across from him, folding up her huge legs underneath her. "No offense, lad, but methinks I've had enough of yer questions for now. Save them for Master George, and we'll all be a mite happier indeed."

Tick knew something amazing was about to happen, and his insides swelled with butterflies, like the last moment before a roller coaster shoots down its first gigantic hill. "Whatever you say, Mothball. I'll shut up."

"Now there's a line I'd wish old Rutger'd learn to say. That wee little fat man could talk the ears off a mammoth, he could."

Tick laughed, but didn't say anything, keeping his promise.

"All right, that about does it, I'd say," Mothball said to herself as she settled her body, growing still. "Just keep yourself nice and comfy there, lad, and good old Master George will wink us away any minute."

There was that word again. *Wink*. Tick almost asked about it, but kept quiet, nervously pulling on his scarf.

"Feel a little tingle on yer neck and back, you will," Mothball whispered. "Things'll change then, right quick. Try to keep yer pants on straight and don't go screamin' like a baby or you might just drown. Come to an understanding, have we?"

Tick nodded, his thrill of anticipation suddenly turning a little sour. *Drown?*

Before he could dwell on what she meant, he felt cold pinpricks along the back of his spine, a quick wave that he might not have noticed if he hadn't been waiting for it.

Then, as promised, everything changed.

In less time than it took to form a single conscious thought, Tick found himself thousands of miles from the graveyard. He sat in the same position as before, but now he was sitting inside a small raft, bobbing up and down in the middle of a dark and choppy sea of black water.

And it was raining.

Chapter 39

A Lot of Water

Nothing happened to mark their transportation from one place to another. No booming alarm, no bright flash of light, no movement of any kind. Tick and Mothball simply went from sitting across from each other on a small patch of grass in the middle of a cemetery to sitting across from each other on a raft in the middle of the ocean.

Heavy, cold rain fell from a sky Tick couldn't see, pelting his entire body, sluicing down the inward sides of the small boat and forming a standing pool of water. Mothball still had her flashlight fully ablaze; the light cast an eerie cone of radiance revealing countless pellets of rain and a small circle of angrily churning waters just a few feet from where they floated. The raft rocked back and forth, up and down, already making Tick's stomach ill.

Mothball shifted her body until she was on her knees, then shone the flashlight somewhere behind her. Tick leaned to his right to catch a glimpse of what she was looking at and saw a huge structure floating nearby, rigid and unmoved by the uneasy sea. He couldn't make out much as Mothball scanned the area with her light, but it appeared to be a building of some sort, a huge square made out of silvery metal walls, rivets and bolts scattered all over its slick and shiny surface. It seemed impossible that it could be a large boat or ship. It was just there, solid, like its foundation went all the way to the ocean bottom.

"Won't be but a moment!" Mothball yelled over her shoulder, working at something with her large arms and hands.

"Where are we?" Tick screamed back, several drops of heavy rain flying into his mouth, almost gagging him.

Mothball turned and looked at him, her hair and face soaked. "Middle of the ocean, we are!"

"Thanks a lot—figured that one out on my own!" Tick slicked his rain-soaked hair out of his eyes.

Instead of replying, Mothball set her right foot against the edge of the raft and pulled on something, grunting with the effort. After a second of hesitation, a bright light suddenly flared against the darkness of the storm, accompanied by the heavy groan of bending metal and the scrape of rusty hinges. Mothball had opened an enormous door of solid steel that led inside the boxy structure. Tick caught a glimpse of a long hallway lined with cables and wiring and thick ductwork.

"Made it, you did!" Mothball yelled into his ear as she grabbed him by the shoulders, helping him across the unstable raft and toward the opening. "You'll be speaking directly with Master George in a moment. Up ya go!" With a playful roar she picked Tick up and half-threw him through the open doorway.

He landed with a squishy flump, scrambling to stand up. Every inch of his body drenched, Tick rubbed at his arms, shivering from the uncomfortable, cold feeling of wearing wet clothes. His scarf drooped off his neck, soggy and seeming like it weighed a hundred pounds. He swung his backpack off his shoulders and placed it on the metal grid that made up the hallway floor.

Mothball crawled inside and closed the heavy door behind her. It slammed shut with a loud boom that rattled the entire structure. "Nasty business, that," she muttered as she climbed to her feet, stooping to avoid hitting her head on the low obstacles that ran along the ceiling. "Don't you worry, Master George is sure to have a roaring fire lit. Come on, now."

She started down the hallway and Tick followed,

barely able to contain his anticipation of meeting the man behind all the mystery.

Mothball rounded a corner and came upon a stout wooden door. Tick thought it seemed out of place inside a huge metal box floating on the ocean. She paused, then rapped three times with her large knuckles. "Got the last one, I did!" she yelled through the dark oak.

Muffled footsteps sounded from the other side, then the click of a latch. The door swung wide open and Tick's five senses almost crashed and burned trying to take in everything at once.

Beyond the open doorway was an enormous room that looked like it had been plucked out of an ancient king's castle and magically transported inside the metal building. Fancy, fluffy, *comfortable*-looking furniture sat atop lush carpets and rugs; the walls were covered in dark wooden bookshelves, complete with hundreds of leather-bound books; a massive brick fireplace cast a warm and flickering glow upon the whole room as the fire within it roared and crackled and spit. Several people were in the room, scattered amongst the plush furniture.

Tick recognized Sofia at once, sitting on an overstuffed chair next to the fire; when their eyes met, she stood and waved. Next to her was a couch where a tall, dark-skinned boy sat, grinning from ear to ear. That had to be Paul. An Asian boy sat next to him, short dark hair framing his angry, scrunched-up face. Tick thought he looked like he'd just been told he hadn't passed a single one of his classes at school. Rutger was there, too, his little round body perched atop a pile of cushions. He leaned back, clasping his stubby hands behind his head like he owned the place.

And finally, standing by the door, his hand still on the inside handle, was a man dressed in the fanciest suit Tick had ever seen, black and pinstriped, a long golden chain marking where his pocket watch hid for the moment. His face was puffy and red, like he'd just walked ten miles through a freezing wind. A round pair of glasses perched on his nose, making his dark eyes seem two times bigger than they were. His balding scalp was red and slightly flaky. Tick thought he looked a little odd and a little anxious, but somehow nice all the same.

"Master George?" he said, wincing when it came out more as a croaky whisper than anything else.

The man smiled, revealing slightly crooked teeth. "Indeed, my good man. Master George, at your service." He bowed his head and held out a hand, which Tick accepted and shook, his confidence and ease growing by the second.

"Nice to meet you," Tick said, remembering his manners.

"Likewise, boy, likewise." He stepped back and swept

his arm in a wide gesture, as if revealing the warm room as the grand prize on a game show. "Welcome to our first meeting with new members in more than twenty years."

"Members?" Tick asked.

"Why, yes, old chap—or, should I say, *young* chap?" Master George chuckled, then turned it into a cough when no one else laughed. "Ah, yes, well—welcome to your future, my dear boy. Welcome to the Realitant Headquarters."

Tick entered the room, knowing he would never, ever be the same.

CHAPTER
40

MASTER GEORGE

Have a sit-down," Master George said as he ushered Tick toward a chair between the fire and where Rutger rested on top of his pile of cushions. "The fire should dry your clothing in no time. We're simply delighted you could make it. We were beginning to worry a bit. The rest of these poor chaps had to listen to Rutger's interminable stories and recollections all day—quite a tasking thing to do, I assure you." He winked at Tick as he gestured for him to sit.

Tick sat down with a squish, looking over at Sofia. She waved again, then shrugged her shoulders as if to say, "What in the world have we gotten ourselves into?" Tick smiled back at her, wishing they could talk, but it seemed as though their host had a specific agenda and was eager to begin.

Master George stepped in front of the blazing fire, rubbing his hands together as he took in each person there with a lingering gaze. "We've got quite a lot to do in the next few hours, and more explaining than I daresay I look forward to. I haven't the faintest idea where to start." He pulled out a silk handkerchief and wiped his brow. "Look at that, would you? Already sweating and I've yet to say anything of importance."

"Maybe that's because you're standing in front of a *fire*," Rutger quipped, the simple effort of talking throwing his balance off. He tumbled off the pillows and flopped to the floor. "Ouch."

"'Tis going to be a long night, it is," Mothball muttered from where she stood in the back, arms folded.

"Rutger, *behave* yourself," Master George commanded, his face reddening for just a second before he replaced his irritation with a forced smile. "Now, let us begin, shall we? First things first—a quick go around the room for introductions." He motioned to Sofia. "Ladies first?"

"Okay," she said, seemingly pleased by the attention. She stood up and waved at everyone staring at her. "My name is Sofia Pacini, and I'm from Italy. I'm almost thirteen years old, and my family is famous for making spaghetti and several sauces. It's the best in the world, and if you haven't heard of us, you've got real problems." She looked at Master George. "Anything else?"

"Oh, no, that's very nice, thank you very much. Next?" He motioned with his eyes to the boy who must be Paul.

"Uh, yeah . . . do I really have to stand up?"

Master George said nothing, but shook his head.

"Great. My name is Paul Rogers, and I'm from the U.S. of A.—Florida to be exact. I've been chatting with Sofia and Tick on the Internet, so it's good to finally see you guys in person. I love surfing and playing the piano. I don't have a clue why I'm here, but I'm busting to find out. Oh, and I'm fourteen years old—way older than these kids." He pointed at Tick and Sofia.

"A delight, Paul, thank you. Mister Sato?" Master George nodded toward the Asian boy sitting next to Paul.

"I will say nothing," the boy answered in a curt voice, folding his arms for dramatic effect.

"Pardon me?" Master George asked, then exchanged looks with Mothball and Rutger. Something about his expression told Tick that Sato's actions weren't exactly a surprise.

"I trust no one," Sato replied. He looked around the room, pointing at each person in turn. "Not you, not you, not you, none of you. Until I know everything, I will say nothing." He nodded as if proud of himself for being such a jerk.

Tick glanced at Sofia, who made a pig face, pushing her nose up with her index finger and sticking out her tongue. Tick had to cover his mouth to keep from laughing out loud.

"Well," Master George struggled for words, "that's . . . splendid." He rubbed his hands together again. "I believe we all know my trusted friends Mothball and Rutger quite well by now, so Mister Higginbottom, please—tell us a bit about yourself before we begin our very long discussion."

Tick shifted in his seat. "Uh, yeah, I'm Atticus Higginbottom, but everyone calls me Tick. I'm from the east side of Washington state, I'm thirteen years old, I like science and chess"—he winced inside at how nerdy that made him sound—"and I'm excited to find out why we've been . . . brought here."

"Amen," Paul chimed in.

"You better talk fast," Sato said. "I want to know right now why you kidnapped me and brought me here."

"Kidnap?" Mothball asked, almost spitting. "What, left yer brain in Japan, 'ave you?"

"I only followed the instructions out of curiosity. Then you kidnapped me. I demand to be taken home."

What a jerk. He's going to ruin everything, Tick

thought. He looked at Sofia and rolled his eyes. She nodded, frowning in Sato's direction.

"Well, then," Master George said, his enthusiasm dampened. "Jolly good beginning this is."

"Just ignore the kid," Rutger said to Master George. He turned toward the disgruntled Japanese boy. "Sato, hear him out. If you don't like it, we'll send you right back where you came from. Now stick a sock in it."

Sato's face reddened, but he didn't say anything, huffing as he leaned back in his seat.

"And on that note," Master George said, trying his best to regain his composure, smiling broadly. "We shall begin. Rutger, would you please bring some victuals from the pantry? These good people must be famished."

Paul clapped loudly and whistled. Sofia, then Tick, joined him.

Master George waited until Rutger had scuttled out a side door. "Let me begin by saying how proud each of you should be of your accomplishment of simply being here today. I sent letters to hundreds of young people, and you four are the only ones who made it this far. Quite an accomplishment indeed. Especially considering the dreadful things I sent to test your mettle."

Tick perked up at this, remembering his conversation with Mothball and Rutger about how sorry Master

George had been about the Alaska incident, which made it seem like he *wasn't* as sorry about the other scary things that had happened—like the Gnat Rat and the Tingle Wraith. "You mean . . ." Tick began, but then stopped, wondering if he was out of line.

"Yes, Mister Higginbottom," Master George answered, seemingly not bothered by the interruption. "It was I, er, *we* who sent some of the things that must've scared you greatly. Objects like the Gnat Rat and Tingle Wraith are much easier to wink to and fro than humans, fortunately. But none of them could or would have hurt you beyond any easy repair, mind you. But the man in Alaska—the one sent by Mistress Jane—now that was an entirely different affair, I assure you. I do apologize for that bit of trouble."

"Wait a minute," Paul said. "Mothball here told me my brain would turn to mush if I heard the Tingle Wraith's Death Siren for more than thirty seconds."

"A slight exaggeration on her part," Master George answered with a look of chagrin. "Because of your still-developing brains, you would've recovered in no more than three or four weeks—albeit with a lingering headache and blurred vision. And a certain bodily odor we can't quite figure out . . ."

"*You* sent those awful things to attack us?" Sofia asked. "But why?"

"Yeah, man," Paul chimed in. "That's just not right."

"Finally," Sato said. "You people are starting to see why I am so angry."

"Why would you want to hurt us?" Tick asked, glaring at Master George, sudden confusion and hurt constricting his chest.

Paul's face looked like someone had just kicked him in both shins. "Dude, how can we trust you now?"

"Now please," Master George pleaded, holding up both hands in front of him. "We haven't even been about our business yet, and already we lose our focus!" His voice rose with every word. "Must I treat you like children? Are you no different from the hundreds who didn't make it nearly as far as you? If so, you may all leave this instant! If you can't handle a couple of cheap tricks like the Gnat Rat, then you've no place being here!"

Tick stared at Master George, surprised he could change from a nice old Englishman to an angry ogre so quickly. The others seemed as dead silent and awe-struck as he felt.

"This is no *game*," Master George continued, his face more flushed than before, though Tick would've thought it impossible. "Everything I've done was meant to bring to me the strongest, the bravest, the cleverest. I let no excuses lie on the table—none at all. If you couldn't persuade your mum and dad to let you come, then you'd be off. If you couldn't bring yourself to follow such silly instructions, then you'd be off. If you let a little thing like two days of horrendous bee stings bother you, then you'd be off. Now, you're here and I'm ready to begin instruction. Have I made a *mistake?*"

Master George shouted the last word, folding his arms and staring around the room, daring someone to respond. A full minute passed, the crackling fire the only sound in the room. Even Sato seemed impressed. Tick felt scared to swallow or breathe, afraid of how Master George would take it.

"All right, then," the Englishman finally said. "If from this point forward you'd be so kind as to act like the brave souls I meant to gather, we can move on." He paused, pretending to brush unseen dust off his suit jacket. "Now, you may be wondering why I sent letters only to young people such as yourself. Am I correct?"

No one said a word, afraid to rock the boat again.

"Come on, now," Master George said. "Only *children* would be afraid to speak up."

Everyone spoke at once at this remark, but Paul drowned out the others. "Never thought about it, actually. But now you mention it, that's a good question that I think I'd like to know the answer to very much. Uh, sir. Master." He cleared his throat. "Master George."

"Much better, much better. I knew you blokes from America were smart. Now—"

He was interrupted by a loud noise from the side.

Rutger shuffled through the door balancing two silver trays stacked with enormous plates of steaming hot food in his arms.

"Who's hungry?" he announced loudly. "I've prepared generous portions for everyone." Wonderful smells wafted across the room.

He started handing out plates and utensils, almost dropping the entire load with every step. "We've got roasted duck, thrice-baked potatoes, succulent legs of lamb with basil and—my favorite—roast beef. Plus a slice of cherry cheesecake." Panting, he put down a plate for himself then handed the last one to Tick. "Eat up!"

Tick needed no urging. After a quickly muttered thank you, he dug in as he balanced the plate on his lap. The food was tender and hot, juicy and rich. It may have been his hunger, but everything on the plate seemed the most delicious stuff he'd ever put in his mouth. By the sounds of smacking lips and slurping fingers from around the room, he wasn't alone in that regard.

"Well," Master George said, "I'm glad to see we still have our appetites. Now, if I may, I will continue our discussion. About the letters—the reason I wrote only to youngsters is because what you're about to hear would never be believed by a cantankerous old grownup. They're far too set in their ways, thinking they're all smart and such. No, I needed to bring in a new batch of recruits, and I knew they must be young and spry, ready to take on the world, as it were."

"Uh, Master George?" Rutger said through a large mouthful of food.

"Yes, Rutger?"

"Don't you think we should, uh, move on and tell them *why* they're here? Time's a wasting."

Master George snapped his fingers and waved his hands in the air. "Yes, yes, you're right, of course. Thank you, on we go." He folded his hands in front of him and looked down at the floor. "I shall now tell you everything, from beginning to end."

And so Master George began his story, the craziest, wackiest, most bizarre thing Tick had ever heard. And he loved every minute of it.

CHAPTER
41

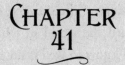

THE TALE OF THE REALITIES

What each of you considers the world in which you have always lived and breathed," Master George began, "is not exactly what you may think. It is in fact much, much more. Your world, the place where you were born, is what we call Reality Prime. It is the first and greatest version of the universe with which you are familiar. However, several decades ago, a group of scientists discovered great mysteries in the field of study we affectionately call the *kyoopy*."

Kyoopy! Tick thought. *The Q.P.! Quantum physics.*

"Now," Master George continued, "we haven't the time or need to explore the deep scientific mumbo-jumbo, but suffice it to say the scientists discovered that alternate versions of the universe exist in harmony and congruity with the world in which we grew up. The reality we all know so well is not alone—there are *other* Realities. Parallel universes that have evolved and developed differently from Reality Prime because of vastly significant events that literally broke them apart from ours."

"Master George," Paul interrupted. "I consider myself one smart dude, but this seems crazy."

Just let him talk, Tick thought as he took his last bite. He set the empty plate on the floor at his feet.

"Don't worry, Mister Rogers. Give me time, and all will become as clear as my mum's fine crystal."

"Sounds like a bunch of lies so far," Sato said, almost under his breath, but loud enough for everyone to hear.

Master George ignored him. "There is an energy force in the universe that binds and controls all the Realities, a greater force than any the laws of physics have ever attempted to define. This power is the lifeblood of the kyoopy, and only a handful of scientists even knows it exists. We call this power the Chi'karda, and everything we'll be about depends on it. Everything."

"What is it?" Tick asked, remembering that Mothball had once said the word to him.

"Rutger?" Master George asked. "What do I always say about the Chi'karda?"

Everyone turned to look at the short man, lounging on his pillows. "You always say, 'When it comes to individual destiny, there is no power greater in the universe than the conviction of the human soul to make a choice.'" He rolled his eyes as if he didn't want to be bothered anymore.

"Precisely," Master George said in a loud whisper, holding up his index finger. "Choice. Conviction. Determination. Belief. *That* is the true power within us, and its name is Chi'karda. It is the immeasurable force that controls what most scientists of the world do not yet understand. Quantum physics."

"So what does this . . . Chi'karda thing have to do with the alternate universes?" Sofia asked.

"It's what *creates* them, my dear girl," Master George answered. "It's happened throughout history, when choices have been made of such magnitude they literally shake the world and split apart the fabric of space and time, creating two worlds where there used to be only one, running parallel to each other within the complex intricacies of the kyoopy. What do you think causes earthquakes?"

"Wow," Paul breathed. "Serious?"

"Quite right, sir, quite right. The creation and destruction of alternate worlds through the power of the Chi'karda has been known to trigger great and terrible quakes. *Wow,* indeed. Allow me to give you an example that will explain it much better, so you can throw out the hard words and difficult phrases. Everyone, close your eyes, please." He motioned with his hands, urging Tick and the others to obey.

Tick closed his eyes.

"I want you to picture in your mind an enormous tree," Master George said. "Its trunk is ten feet wide, with twelve thick branches, er, branching off, breaking up into tinier and tinier limbs until they are barely measurable. Can you picture it?"

A scatter of mumbled yeses sounded across the room, even from Mothball and Rutger.

"The trunk of that tree is Reality Prime, the version of the world in which you were born and have lived your whole lives. The main branches of the tree are very established *alternate* Realities that have stood the test of time and survived, each one different from Reality Prime in significant ways. From there, the smaller and smaller branches are weak and crumbling Realities, *fragmented* Realities, most of them heading for the day when they will vanish altogether or be absorbed into another Reality. We had each of you visit one of those fragmented Realities before you came here, to give you a bit of understanding at what they can be like.

"The Realitants are a group of explorers devoted to charting and documenting the main branches of this tree for the sake of science and in hopes that one day we can better understand the makeup of the universe and how it works. And to, er, protect Reality Prime from potential, er, unforeseen dangers."

Master George cleared his throat loudly, and Tick's eyes flew open. Master George's hands gave the slightest twitch at his sides. "Until recently, we had fully charted twelve main Realities, and everything was going just splendid—there'd even been talk that perhaps some-day we'd discover the perfect Reality—a utopia if you will. But the reason you are here today is because quite the opposite has occurred. One of our own, a trai-tor like the world has never known, has discovered a Thirteenth Reality, and very bad things are about to happen. Very bad things indeed."

"I knew it," Sato grumbled.

"What's in the Thirteenth Reality?" Tick asked. "What's so bad about it?"

"Oh, Mister Higginbottom, it is quite a hard thing to talk about. With every other Reality, we've had mostly positive, fascinating experiences. For example, there's the Fifth Reality, home of our dearest Mothball. There, circumstances somehow led to a drastic change in the gene pool, where everyone became taller and stronger, evolving into a much different society than the one you know so well. Then, of course, there's the Eleventh, where Rutger was born. As you can see, they, er, had quite the, er, *opposite* effect in their Reality."

Everyone looked at Rutger, who patted his big belly as if it were his most prized possession.

Master George cleared his throat again and moved on quickly. "There's the Fourth, perhaps the most fascinating Reality of them all. Their world is much more advanced than ours, the technology revolution occurring much sooner there than it did in Reality Prime. Going there is much like traveling to the future—quite fascinating indeed. It's where I acquired the Gnat Rat and the Tingle Wraiths."

Tick's jaw dropped open.

The Gnat Rat. Manufactured by Chu Industries.

That explains it, he thought. *No wonder I couldn't find anything on them.* Mr. Chu couldn't have had anything to do with the company after all—it was in another Reality.

"But I haven't answered your question, have I?" Master George said, looking uncomfortable. "You most clearly asked me about the *Thirteenth* Reality, and here I am, doing everything in my power to avoid answering you."

"Well?" Sofia asked.

"What? Ah, yes, the question. The Thirteenth Reality. I'm afraid this new place is . . . quite extraordinary. You see, for the first time, a Reality has been discovered in which . . . oh, poppycock, this is difficult to say."

"Go ahead and say it," Mothball urged from the back. "These kids can take it, they can."

"Yes, yes, you're quite right, Mothball." Master George straightened his shoulders. "The Thirteenth Reality has a mutated and frightening version of the Chi'karda that simply chills my bones to think about. It is most certainly the source of every frightening myth, dangerous legend, or terrifying nightmare that has ever leaked into the stories and tales of the human race."

"A . . . *mutated* version of the Chi'karda?" Paul repeated. "What in the world does that mean?"

Master George's brow creased as he frowned. "Remember what Rutger told all of you about the sheer power of the Chi'karda? The Thirteenth has somehow turned that power of pure creation into something completely different. Something frightening."

"But why?" Paul pushed. "What does that *mean*?"

Master George's face paled. "It means that we have discovered a Reality that contains the closest thing to—oh, I hate to even utter the word—but it contains the closest thing to *magic* we have ever seen. And not the good kind of magic like in your storybooks. No, this is a very real, very *dark* power. And if it isn't contained, if it somehow escapes from the Thirteenth Reality, everything will be lost."

CHAPTER 42

THE DOOHICKEY

Magic?" Sofia said. "That sounds fun."

"You're talking, like, abracadabra and all that stuff?" Paul chimed in. "Wizards and broomsticks?"

"No, no, no, nothing of the sort," Master George replied, his face scrunched up in annoyance. "This is real—perfectly real—and it's all explained by the laws of science, particularly the kyoopy, quantum physics. It's all a matter of unique Chi'karda manipulation. In the Thirteenth Reality, though, it's been mutated into something far more powerful and horrific. And it can be controlled by someone who understands the nature of it."

"What can it do?" Tick asked.

"Well, it can make things fly, create horrible beasts,

the like. What all of you would consider magic, which is why I used the word—though any scientist would despise such ridiculous nomenclature. This is real, this is *science*. And while it's not unique to the Thirteenth, it is there that they've learned how to twist it, how to use it much more powerfully."

"What do you mean?" Paul asked. "The same power exists in other places?"

"Why, yes, of course. It's even here in Reality Prime— though thankfully not the dark and sinister version that exists in the Thirteenth. Ever heard of *luck*?"

Master George continued, excited, not bothering to wait for anyone to answer. "The Chi'karda is essentially the power of conviction, of belief, of strong choices. There have been instances where wonderful things have occurred, where the tiny world of quantum physics has fundamentally *changed* because of an overwhelming, powerful display of Chi'karda. Some call it a lucky break, good fortune, a windfall, a crazy coincidence. Oh, it's happened plenty, but in the Thirteenth, the Chi'karda has mutated into something hideous."

"Man," Paul said. "That is just plain awesome."

"*Awesome?*" Master George asked, his tone suggesting he felt exactly the opposite. "I assure you, there's nothing awesome about it once you know what Mistress Jane intends to do with this dark Chi'karda."

"Who is this Mistress Jane?" Sofia asked, glancing at

Tick then at Master George. "Norbert told us she went looking for you in Alaska. He said she threatened him."

Master George's face grew dark. "Mistress Jane is the most foul, despicable, wretched creature to ever walk the folds of the Realities. She was once one of us, someone who worked toward understanding and unity. But she betrayed us for hopes of glory and power. We have many spies in her camp, and we're certain she plans to annihilate the Reality system in its entirety. You have no idea the ramifications of her twisted plans."

"The tree," Rutger said through a yawn.

"Pardon me?" Master George replied.

"The tree, the tree! Use your analogy to explain what she wants to do."

"Ah, yes." Master George turned his attention back to the kids. "Imagine the tree for me again, if you will. One of the big branches we talked about—one of the main Realities that shoots off from the trunk of Reality Prime—is now under the control of Mistress Jane. Using the dark Chi'karda of the Thirteenth Reality, Mistress Jane plans to sever the other branches from the trunk, if you will, destroying them entirely. Then she can conquer Reality Prime and rule the known universe. If that happens, she'd be able to create her own twisted Realities at will, essentially recreating the tree for her own purposes."

If the other kids in the group were anything like

Tick, all Master George saw at that moment were wide-eyed stares. Tick had a feeling they underestimated the horrible intentions of Mistress Jane.

"Oh, poppycock, we're getting too deep into all of this," Master George complained as he paced back and forth in front of the fire. "All you need to know is there are different versions of the world we live in called Realities and all of them are important in their own way. Mistress Jane plans to use her newly discovered powers to destroy life as we know it. And we, the Realitants—and I mean *we*—must stop her."

"How?" Tick and Paul asked in unison.

Master George smiled. "Ah, yes, *how* indeed. It's time for the fun part, my good people. I have something to show you." He walked through a small door in the far corner of the room, reappearing a few seconds later. In his hand he held a long golden rod, at least three feet in length and several inches in diameter; it shone and sparkled in the firelight, polished to perfection. Up and down one entire side were a series of dials and knobs and switches, a small label below each one. Once he returned to his lecture spot, Master George held the rod high for everyone to see.

"This, my friends," he said proudly, "is a Barrier Wand."

Oohs and ahs sounded across the room.

"This instrument—and the Chi'karda Drive within

its inner chamber—is the single most important invention in the history of mankind. I say this without the slightest pause, *knowing* it's true. It is the *only* way a person can travel from one Reality to another. It harnesses and controls the power of the Chi'karda—manipulates it, bends it, wields it, shapes it."

Master George ran his hand down the length of the device. "*This* is how we control travel between the barriers of the Realities—what we call winking, because it literally happens in the blink of an eye. Without this Barrier Wand, and the few others like it, there would be no study of the Realities, no travel between them, no . . . Mistress Jane problem, actually. If we can remove her Barrier Wand from the Thirteenth Reality, she and her twisted powers will be trapped there for a very long time. Enough time for us to devise a more permanent solution to the problem."

"How does the Barrier Wand work?" Paul asked.

"Oh, yes, thank you for asking." Master George held the golden rod up so everyone could clearly see as he pointed out the controls running down the near side. "You simply adjust the doohickey here, then the thingamajig here, then the whatchamacallit here, and so forth and so on. It's simple really. Trust me—it *does* work. With this Wand, you can control the Chi'karda to such a degree that it will transport you between Realities."

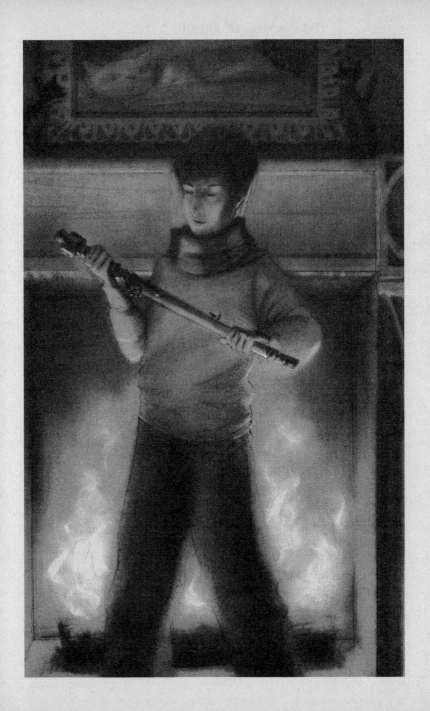

"Ooh, can I see it?" Sofia asked, her hands twitching with curiosity to hold the Wand.

"Of course. Come on up, all of you. Have a look!"

Tick shot out of his chair, grimacing at the coldness of his still-damp pants, and got to Master George first. He laughed out loud when he was close enough to read the labels on the instrument. "I thought you were joking."

"Joking about what?" Master George asked.

"The most important scientific discovery of all time, and the first dial is called the Doohickey?" Tick pointed to a neatly printed label on the Wand.

Sofia chuckled as she pointed at a small switch. "And there's the Thingamajig."

"That's for a very important reason, thank you very much," Master George said, momentarily pulling the Barrier Wand away from the kids. "It's so spying eyes can't figure out how it works. We've labeled them that way on purpose."

"Ingenious," Paul snickered.

Tick looked over at Sato, still sitting on the couch, arms folded in defiance. "Don't you want to see it?"

Sato stared at the floor. "Leave me alone."

Tick shrugged, then surprised himself when he let out a huge yawn. He glanced at his watch, surprised to see it was almost three o'clock in the morning.

Master George seemed to sense Tick's thoughts.

"It's grown very late indeed, my good associates. It's almost morning here. I think we should all be off to bed. We can finish our discussion tomorrow. There is still much to learn—and much to prepare for."

"Wait a minute—" Paul began.

"No, no, no," Master George said, waving his Wand like a great magician. "We must have fresh minds to continue. To bed it is—no arguments. No need to worry about the dirty plates; I'll be happy to clean up."

A hand grabbed Tick's shoulder and he turned to see Mothball.

"Come on," she said. "Off we go. I'll be showin' ya to yer sleepin' quarters. Methinks we could all use a good night's rest, I do. Come on."

She moved toward the side door. Tick, Sofia, and Paul fell in line behind her, grumbling like two-year-olds who didn't want to go to bed.

Sato didn't move a muscle.

"Looks like Mr. Happy will be sleeping on the couch," Paul whispered to Tick as they stepped through the door.

⌒◦

Sato fumed on the inside as he sat alone in the big room, the fire spitting, slowly fading to ashes. Master George hadn't so much as given him a glance, completely ignoring Sato's obvious distrust and unhappiness. They *all* ignored him for the most part, thinking they were so smart and so funny. *Better* than Sato.

Little did they know he'd listened intently to every single word that came out of the old man's mouth, storing them away inside his computer of a mind, learning every morsel. He had to know every piece of the puzzle if he hoped to accomplish what he'd planned to do from the very first day he'd received the letter from M.G.

He had to make things right. To quench the thirst for revenge that consumed him. To avenge the death of his family.

I need to stay sharp, he thought. *Befriend no one.* He couldn't trust anyone, precisely for the very reason his family died.

No, Sato would never make the same fatal mistake his parents had. And he'd never trust another person ever again.

Especially Master George.

CHAPTER
43

A BUMP IN THE NIGHT

Thanks are our digs?" Paul asked.

"I miss my mansion," Sofia moaned.

Tick agreed. Their "sleeping quarters" didn't look very inviting. They stood in a small rectangular room in which six cots had been set up, three along each of the longer walls. Folded gray and black blankets and pillows lay stacked on top of each cot. The only other furniture in the room was a desk and a three-drawer wooden dresser. The floor of the room was a flat metallic gray.

"Would you rather sleep out in the raft?" Rutger asked. "We can arrange it."

"Mister Tick," Mothball said, nudging him. "There's

some dry clothes in the chest of drawers there. Better be changin' out of yer soppies, ya should."

"Oh, thanks."

Tick walked over to the dresser as everyone else chose a cot and started spreading out their blankets. After a full minute of rummaging through the drawers, the only thing Tick found that was close to wearable was an enormous one-piece nightshirt. "This thing looks like a dress," he said to Mothball.

"If ya'd rather soak in yer wet undies all night, fine by me," she replied.

"Where's the bathroom?"

She nodded toward a short metal door. Sighing, Tick went and changed into his ridiculous pajamas.

Frazier Gunn had listened to the muffled murmurs of people talking all night. His captor had *guests,* apparently. Almost insane from the months of isolation, Frazier felt like chewing through the metal and killing every last one of them.

I'd need stronger teeth, he thought.

He knew he was going crazy, and he didn't care. He curled up on the floor like a dog and tried to go back to sleep.

Frazier longed to hear more clearly through the cold metal walls of his terrible prison. The only word he felt confident he'd understood in all these months was *Annika*. George had mentioned the name several times, and for some reason it resonated through the metal without being distorted beyond recognition.

Annika. An unusual name for sure. Frazier had only known one person in his life named Annika. She was one of Mistress Jane's closest servants and one of several people, including Frazier, who intensely competed for Jane's favor.

Was it a coincidence? Did George somehow know Annika? There'd always been rumors of spies in Jane's camp. Had Frazier discovered a gold nugget of information?

If only he could escape. If only he could warn Mistress Jane . . .

"Hey, looky!" Paul laughed when Tick walked out in his long nightshirt, which hung all the way to the floor. "If it's not Ebenezer Scrooge himself! Where's your stocking cap, Grandpa?"

"Very funny," Tick said as he walked to an empty cot and started setting up his bed.

"I think you look right handsome, I do," Mothball said.

"Uh-oh, looks like someone's got a crush," Paul said.

Sofia huffed as she settled under her blanket. "Paul,

you're almost as annoying in person as you were on the e-mail. Keep smarting off and you'll get a Pacini fist in the nose."

"Oh, come on, you know you love me." He leaned back against the wall with his hands clasped behind his head. "Man, this is the life—no chores, no one yelling at me to brush my teeth. I love living in the middle of the ocean."

"Ha!" Rutger barked from the doorway. "You'll be wishing for chores once we send you on your initiation mission."

Tick froze, his pillow still in his hands. "Initiation mission?"

Rutger nodded with a wicked smile. "You didn't think Master George was kidding about retrieving Mistress Jane's Barrier Wand, did you?"

"You can't possibly mean *we* have to do it," Sofia said.

"You'll find out tomorrow. Get some sleep."

"Oh, that'll be nice and easy after telling us something like that," Tick said, straightening his blankets and getting into bed.

"Dude," Paul yawned, "where in the world *are* we anyway?"

"That's an easy one," Mothball said. "Middle of the ocean, we are."

"But *where*? Which ocean?"

Mothball and Rutger exchanged a wary look. "Go on, you tell 'em," Mothball finally said.

"This is the headquarters of the Realitants, you see," Rutger began, "and there's a reason we're here. Master George has to do a lot of *winking*, a lot of working with the Chi'karda. And this is the one place in the world where it's the most concentrated, the easiest to penetrate and control. It's by far the strongest link between all of the Realities."

"But where *are* we?" Sofia insisted.

Rutger rocked back and forth on his feet. "You're going to laugh when I tell you."

"Blimey, just tell 'em, fat man," Mothball said, rolling her eyes.

"Yeah, tell us," Paul added.

Rutger folded his hands and rested them on his belly. "We're smack dab in the middle of the Bermuda Triangle."

⌒

Master George let out a long, blissful sigh as he stuck his sore feet into a tub full of salt and warm water. Muffintops jumped onto his lap, purring as she licked his hands.

"Hello there, little friend," he said, petting her soft fur. "Quite the day, we've had—busy, busy, busy. Never knew it would be so difficult explaining all the many things we know. Those poor little chaps. They've no idea what lies ahead of them. None at all."

Master George leaned back and closed his eyes, wiggling his toes in the hot water. "Dear Muffintops, can we really do it? Can we really send them to that dreadful place? There's a mighty good chance everything will fall to pieces, you know. They could be attacked or captured. I don't know if the Sound Slicers will be enough . . ."

The cat looked up at Master George, as if it wanted to answer but couldn't.

"Ah, yes, I know, I know. We've no choice really. Must let them *prove* themselves, mustn't we?" He paused, thinking about the three eager children and how different they were from the boy Sato. Of course, Master George had expected nothing different from the troubled son of his former friend.

Master George smiled. When he really thought about the potential of the four kids he had gathered together, he didn't know who he felt sorrier for in the coming days, weeks, and years.

His new batch of Realitants or Mistress Jane.

⟨⟩

"The Bermuda Triangle?" Paul asked, sounding like he'd just been told they were living inside an alien's big toe on Mars. "I feel like I'm in a bad made-for-TV movie."

Rutger answered. "For some reason this area by far has the biggest concentration of Chi'karda in the world. Something tremendous must've happened here a long,

long time ago, but we haven't been able to figure it out. There's certainly nothing recorded in the history books."

"Why's it such a big deal that there's more Chi'karda here than anywhere else?" Tick asked, stumbling only a little over the unfamiliar word.

"Why's it a big deal?" Rutger repeated, throwing up his arms like Tick had just asked him why he needed oxygen to breathe. "Do you have an unreasonable level of earwax, boy? Didn't you listen to a word Master George said tonight?"

"Hey, be nice," Sofia warned. "Unless you want a punch in the nose, too."

Rutger ignored her. "Everything having to do with the Realities revolves around the Chi'karda. Because it's so powerful here, it's the easiest place to *wink* to and from the other Realities. It's also the best place for Master George to monitor Chi'karda levels around the world. That's how he's watched all of you from day one so closely."

"How?" Paul asked.

"By using another invention from Chu Industries in the Fourth Reality. It's called a nanolocator."

"Sounds fancy," Sofia said. "Maybe Pacinis should make them."

"I assure, you, Miss Pacini, there's a big difference between making nanolocators and *spaghetti* sauce." Sofia leaned forward like she was ready to get out of bed and attack Rutger, but he held up his hands in reconciliation, then hurried to continue. "A nanolocator is basically a microscopic robot, but it's so tiny you can't see it with the naked eye. It crawls into your skin and sends various signals back here to the Command Center."

"What kind of signals?" Tick asked, shifting on his cot to get more comfortable. He wasn't sure he liked the idea of a tiny robot crawling under his skin.

"Signals that monitor your Chi'karda levels, your global position, your body temperature—all kinds of things. Our fearless leader had to have some way to keep tabs on you, don't you think? The nanolocators also told us where to send the Gnat Rats and Tingle Wraiths, which were programmed to find you and no one else."

"Ah, man, I feel so . . . violated," Paul said in a deadpan voice, then barked a laugh.

"How did he get it inside our bodies?" Tick asked.

"That's easy," Mothball said. "The little fella was on the first letter he sent you."

"Serious?" Paul asked.

"When each one of you opened the envelope and pulled out the letter, the nanolocator quickly sought a heat source—your hand—and slipped right between your skin cells." Rutger grinned. "Brilliant, don't you think?"

"Dude, that just seems *wrong*," Paul said, shaking his head.

"Oh, boo hoo," Rutger replied, rubbing his eyes in a mock cry. "How else were we supposed to know when or if you burned the first letter. Or when you made your Pick?"

"Pick?" all three kids asked at once.

"I'll take that one," Mothball said. "A Pick's what Master George calls a ruddy big decision. Your Chi'karda level spikes like a rocket shootin' off to space, it does. Showed up on his big monitor and let him know when yer were truly committed to the job he offered, when you really promised yourself there was no turning back. Smart old chap, don't you think?"

"Master George watched his big screen every day," Rutger said, "so he'd know when you made your Pick. Word is he just about suffocated his cat hugging the poor thing when you three made your Pick at almost the same time. That was uncanny."

Tick thought of that night he knelt in front of the fireplace and the decision he'd made to not burn the letter in his hand. He remembered the sensation of warmth that had spread throughout his whole body. *That was my Pick,* he realized. He'd felt that same sensation again later, when he screamed out in the dark woods and managed to somehow change reality. *Is that what using the Chi'karda feels like?* Tick shivered. It was a lot to think about.

"What are we in, anyway?" Paul asked, looking

above and around him. "Is this a boat or what?"

"No, it's a building, firmly rooted in the ocean floor far below us," Rutger said. "Master George used a little trick he learned from the Eighth Reality, where it's mostly ocean. They developed some amazing cabling technology that allows them to build entire cities on the ocean. We're perfectly safe and stable. You can barely feel the waves unless we have a real doozy of a storm."

Mothball yawned, a booming roar that made Tick jump. "Master George will have our hides, he will, if he finds out we kept you up so late. Come on, now, we need—"

"Wait," Tick interrupted her. "Just one more question, okay?"

"Be quick about it. Me bones hurt I'm so tired."

"What's the deal with cemeteries? Rutger said something once about the difference between life and death . . . I can't remember."

"It was another famous Master George quote," Rutger replied. " *Nothing in this world better reflects the difference between life and death than the power of choice.*' Chi'karda levels are very high in cemeteries. Master George says it has to do with the lingering effects of the life-changing choices those people made. One way or another, their choices led them to their fates, whether good or bad."

"And so we needed to go there because . . ." Tick

started but stopped, worried his answer would be wrong.

"So we could *wink* easier," Sofia said. "The stronger the levels of Chi'karda, the easier it is to travel between Realities."

"Exactly," Rutger agreed. "Not only can you travel between the barriers, you can travel between different locations of heavy Chi'karda spots within the *same* Reality. That's how Master George could wink you from your towns to this place. He simply honed in on your nanolocator signals and winked you away!"

"My head hurts," Paul groaned, falling onto his back as he rubbed his forehead.

"That's because you Americans aren't smart enough to get it," Sofia said. "I'll be happy to tutor you on everything tomorrow."

"Methinks I've had enough for one day," Mothball said. "Good night, all."

She and Rutger left the room, flicking off the light as they went.

A few more words were said after they'd left, but sheer exhaustion soon pulled the three of them into a deep sleep.

Something jolted Frazier out of his dreamless slumber.

He swatted at the dark air around him, scrambling

into a sitting position. What had it been? Was he—

He heard a loud thump against the wall by his cot. Then another, a clang of metal against metal that echoed throughout the small cell. Then another, this time *louder*.

What was that?

He scurried over to the light switch and flipped it on, squinting in the brightness. To his shock, a small dent, about three inches wide, bent the wall inward just above his bed. The bolts connecting the wall to the surrounding metal had loosened slightly, rattling as another big thump sounded. The wall bent even farther.

One final boom sounded through the room, and the entire piece of metal fell onto his bed, its bolts cracking like whips as they broke in half. Frazier stared past the hole in the wall, seeing the endless ocean in front of him, the first traces of dawn casting a purple glow over the deep waters. Then, inexplicably, a face appeared from below—someone he'd never seen before. It was a man with scraggly black hair and an unshaven face.

"Come on, Mister Gunn, we don't have much time!"

"What . . . who . . . what . . ." Frazier couldn't find any words after such a long time in confinement.

"Mistress Jane sent us to rescue you," the man yelled.

"Rescue me?" Frazier could hardly believe it.

"Yes!" the man replied. "And then we're going to destroy this place once and for all."

CHAPTER
44

ESCALATION OF PLANS

Tick woke to the awful smell of fish breath and an annoying scratchy feeling on his right cheek. From somewhere in the distance, he thought he heard a loud boom like an underground explosion. He opened his eyes to see two yellow orbs staring at him. It was a cat, pawing at his face to . . . wake him?

Tick sat up, accidentally knocking the cat to the floor. "Oh, sorry." The sleek feline hissed in annoyance, then padded over to Paul's cot to wake him as well.

That's one smart cat, Tick thought.

Sofia was already awake, rubbing her eyes and stretching. Tick looked at his watch to see only a few hours had passed since they went to bed. The thought made him twice as tired; all he wanted to do was go back to sleep.

But then the whole world seemed to go crazy at once.

Another boom, this time much louder, shook the building as it echoed off the walls. The door to the room flew open and banged against the wall, rebounding back and knocking Master George to the floor, who was wearing a bright red nightshirt even more ridiculous than the one Tick wore. He grunted and scrambled back to his feet.

"Good job, Muffintops, jolly good job!" Master George picked up his cat and petted its back. "You three, we must hurry! Our plans have been . . . escalated."

The others had slept in their clothes, but Tick still wore his horrible pajamas. As Paul and Sofia moved to follow Master George, Tick quickly went into the bathroom where he'd hung his clothes to finish drying. They were still damp, but he changed into them as fast as he could. He'd just pulled on his second shoe when someone pounded on the door.

"Mister Higginbottom!" came the muffled voice of Master George. "What part of 'we must hurry' did you not understand?"

"Sorry!" Tick called as he wrapped his scarf around his neck. He opened the door and followed the old man, who was already across the room. Another boom sounded, and Tick felt like he was in a bunker, taking heavy artillery from the enemy. He tried to fight the panic that surged up his chest and into his throat.

They gathered back in the main room with the fireplace. Sato sat in the exact same spot where they'd left him only a few hours before, though his puffy eyes showed he'd just woken up as well. Rutger and Mothball were there too; the tall woman had an enormous backpack perched on her shoulders.

Master George stood in front of the now-cold fireplace, holding the shiny Barrier Wand in both hands, his cat curled on the ground at his feet. "My friends, we are officially under siege."

"What're you talking about?" Sofia asked as another boom sounded in the building. "Is someone *bombing* us?"

"I'd hardly call them bombs, my good lady, but we haven't any more time to talk about it. Jane's power over the mutated Chi'karda must be growing if she has enough daring to attack us here. I must send you off on your mission immediately." He started adjusting the seven dials and switches of the Barrier Wand, his tongue pressed between his lips.

"Whoa, dude," Paul said. "I don't like the sound of this."

"We don't have time to argue," Rutger said from where he leaned against the door. "Master George and I will stay here and protect the Command Center as best we can; we have a few tricks up our sleeve that Mistress Jane doesn't know about. You four are going with Mothball to the Thirteenth Reality."

"The Thirteenth—" Tick started, his stomach falling into a pit of cold ice.

"Don't waste another moment of my time with complaints or questions!" Master George finished his flipping and turning of the Wand's controls and looked at the four recruits. "This attack on my home shows you the urgency of your mission. Follow Mothball's orders. She has weapons called Sound Slicers if you run into trouble. Please do me a favor and don't point them *at* each other. I'd rather you *not* return to me with your brains turned into runny oatmeal."

Sound Slicers? Tick wondered. He really wanted to voice a question, but the man in charge barely paused to breathe.

Master George held up a warning finger. "It is *imperative* you succeed in bringing back the Barrier Wand of Mistress Jane. We must seal her in the Thirteenth Reality forever. Or at least until we can properly prepare to fight against her evil magic hordes. If everything goes as planned, it should be quite, er, easy."

Tick didn't like the hesitancy in Master George's voice. He already felt like a rookie paratrooper about to be pushed out of the plane for the first time over a major battlefield, under heavy fire.

"Atticus, you enjoy chess, yes?" Master George said in a tight voice.

Tick couldn't think of a question that seemed more out of place. "Yeah."

"Good. Come here."

Tick moved closer to Master George, who put the Barrier Wand directly in front of his face. "It's been my experience that chess lovers are quite good at memorization. Am I correct?"

"Uh . . ."

"Excellent! Now look at each of the controls on the Barrier Wand and memorize their position. Exactly, now—there's no room for error, none at all."

"But—"

"Quickly!"

Tick swallowed the lump in his throat and did as he was told, scanning his eyes up and down the length of the golden Wand.

"Hurry, we only have a minute at most!" Master George said.

Pushing his panic away, Tick tried to freeze-frame the image of each dial, switch, and knob in his mind, storing it, *burning* it in his memory. He was still focusing on the bottom dial when Master George took it away and began switching everything again.

Master George spoke as he worked. "Mothball isn't . . . agreeable with Barrier Wands, so it'll be up to you, Atticus, to bring all of you back in case something happens to me."

Tick felt like someone had just poured acid down his throat.

"Mark your watches," Master George continued. "If I don't wink you back here in thirty hours—*precisely* thirty hours—that means that Rutger and I are in serious trouble. If that happens, Atticus, you will have to use Mistress Jane's Barrier Wand—which looks exactly like this one—in order to escape the Thirteenth Reality. Adjust it as I showed you, then hit this button on the top." He pointed at a perfect circle cut into the top of the cylinder. "It will wink you to one of our satellite locations where you will be safe from harm. Understand?"

Tick nodded, scratching his neck through his scarf, nervous and afraid like never before. Another explosion rocked the building, throwing everyone off balance; a brick fell from the mantle of the fireplace, a poof of dust billowing out. Master George almost dropped the Barrier Wand but caught it just in time.

Paul cleared his throat. "And how're we supposed to steal a Barrier Wand from the most evil woman in history, as you put it?"

"We have a spy named Annika in place. All you have to do is meet her and she will help you retrieve it."

"Is that all?" Sofia said.

"Listen to me," Master George said, all semblance

of his normal, cheery, quirky self gone. "You have all shown tremendous resolve and courage in making it to me, and I am proud as buttons to know you. But you must do this one last thing before officially becoming Realitants. Show me you can do this, and a life of adventure and intrigue awaits you, I promise. Do we have an understanding?"

The building rumbled again as Tick made eye contact with Sofia, then Paul. They looked as scared as he felt, which for some sick reason made him feel better.

"Let's do it," Paul said.

"Yeah," Sofia agreed. "Psycho Jane'll be sorry once I get my hands on her."

They both looked at Tick, waiting for his answer. "You know I'm in," he said.

"Splendid," Master George said. "Sato?"

Everyone looked over at the disgruntled boy on the couch. He stood up, trying to bring the scowl back to his face but failing; he was just as scared as everyone else. "I'm only going because I don't trust Master George and I want to make sure you three don't mess up." He walked over and joined the small group standing around the Barrier Wand.

"Sato," Master George said, in an unusually kind voice for someone who had just been insulted. "I know more about you than you understand, and I feel no anger. When you succeed in this mission, I hope to gain your trust, and may I daresay, to become your friend."

Sato said nothing in reply, looking at the floor.

A horrible sound of crunching metal came from the hallway where Tick had first entered the building, followed by another rocking explosion.

"Best be gettin' a move on, don't ya think?" Mothball said.

"Quite right you are, my dear friend!" Master George said, holding the Barrier Wand out in front of him, his arm rigid, so the golden rod stood upright in the middle of the group. "All of you, hands on the Wand! It'll be much easier if you're touching it!"

Mothball was first, wrapping her huge hand around the very top of the cylinder. One by one, the others followed her example, clasping the Wand in quick succession—Paul, Sofia, Tick. All eyes went to Sato, who turned and spat on the ground. Then, with all the enthusiasm of putting his hand into a cage full of rattlesnakes, he grabbed the lower edge of the Wand.

"I'm very sorry indeed we didn't have more time to talk," Master George said, his tone solemn. "I expected a few more hours at least, but we must move on, mustn't we? Remember the plan, and remember your courage. May the Realities smile upon you, and may we see each other again very soon."

Without waiting for a response, Master George pushed the golden button.

CHAPTER 45

THE THIRTEENTH REALITY

istress Jane sat on her throne, eyes closed, deep in thought as she waited for her next visitor. *What a life mine has become.* So many people hated and despised her, wished she were dead. But they simply did not understand. All of her cruelty and harsh rule had a purpose, and someday the Realities would know of her goodness.

All she wanted was to make life better.

What a poor existence the wretches of Reality Prime eked out from day to day. It was a marvel they continued on despite the drab bleakness of their lives—no power, no joy, no *color*. Jane would change all of that. The new and improved version of Chi'karda made every second a wonderful moment, and it must be shared. It must be *spread.* The Realitants had always talked about finding a utopian Reality someday, a paradise on Earth; Jane could make it happen.

She was so close to implementing her plan. One by one, she would fragment and destroy the branching Realities until only Prime and the Thirteenth remained. Then, with an army such as never before witnessed in all of history, she would take over Reality Prime, consuming it with the mutated Chi'karda. Only then could the universe be rebuilt, one world at a time, a better place for all.

In a million years, her name would still be remembered with love and worship.

She needed help, of course. She'd sent a letter to a very important person, setting up a meeting on May thirteenth—a meeting that represented the final and most important part of her plan. *Only one more week,* she thought. If Reginald Chu agreed to her terms at that meeting, nothing could stop her. Nothing. Especially not the pathetic and laughable Master George and his dwindling Realitants. Just hours earlier, she'd finally initiated the attack on his headquarters, an act for which she'd shown much patience, having wanted to do it for years.

One more week until the meeting with Chu. The final piece of the puzzle.

Jane opened her eyes. It was time to speak with Gunn.

Frazier felt sweat seeping into his eyebrows from his forehead, as if the skin itself were melting.

He stood before the huge wooden door with its iron bindings and handle, barely able to breathe as he waited for the horrible thing to open. He had failed, miserably, and there was no telling how Mistress Jane might react. Sometimes she was very merciful to her failures—allowing them to die with a quick snap of her odd abilities in this place. At other times, she displayed much less kindness. Jane had immense amounts of control over the mutated Chi'karda that existed in the Thirteenth, and she loved to . . . experiment.

A muted thump sounded from the other side of the door, followed by the odd sound of something *dissolving*, like the scratchy rush of poured sand or the amplified roar of a million termites devouring a house. A hole appeared in the middle of the door, expanding outward like a ripple in a pond, devouring the wood and iron of the door as it grew until the entrance to Jane's throne room was completely open.

Why can't she just open *the door*, Frazier thought to himself. *Always has to show off her twisted power.*

Frazier steeled himself, promising himself he would remain dignified as he met his fate. He knew he had only one chance to redeem his folly and perhaps to save his life. Smoothing his filthy shirt, he stepped forward into the gaudy and ridiculous throne room of Mistress Jane.

From top to bottom, side to side, the room was a complete sea of yellow.

Tapestries of yellow people on yellow horses in fields of yellow daisies. Yellow padded chairs on yellow rugs on top of yellow carpets. The walls, the couches, the paintings, the pillows, the servants' clothing, the lamps, the books—even the wood and bricks of the fireplace had been painted yellow. It made Frazier sick to his stomach, and reminded him once again that the woman he'd chosen to follow was completely insane.

But Frazier knew one day Jane would snap, and someone would need to replace her. *That's where I come in,* he thought. *If I can only survive this day.*

A buzzing sound from above made him look up to see two large insects flying down toward him.

Snooper bugs, he thought. *Could she be any more paranoid?*

The enormous winged creatures flew around him in a tight circle, their cellophane wings flapping in a blur, their elongated beaks snipping at his clothes and poking at his skin. Frazier winced, but kept still and silent, knowing the vicious things could get quite nasty if you didn't submit completely. Finally, after inflicting dozens of tiny wounds all over his body, the two Snoopers flew back to their nests. They didn't need to communicate anything further to Jane—if Frazier had been holding any poisons or weapons, he'd be dead.

"Come forward," a gruff voice said from the side. Frazier looked over to see a grotesquely fat man who looked like a hideous cross between a dwarf and a troll, hovering ten feet in the air, his plump legs dangling. His head, face, and chest were covered in dark, greasy hair, and he wore nothing but a wide skirt around his middle, proudly displaying his disgustingly bloated skin. "The Mistress will see you now." He held out a flabby arm, gesturing deep into the throne room. "Hurry. She is a busy woman."

Frazier shuddered and followed the guard's instructions, staring straight ahead. He didn't stop walking until he reached the Kneeling Pillow of Mistress Jane, where he did as countless others had done before him, dropping to his knees and kissing the ground before him. Then, daring to show some boldness, he leaned back on his legs and looked up at the preposterous throne.

It was black.

Mistress Jane had never explained to anyone why her throne was made from completely nondescript, heavy, black iron, nor had anyone ever dared ask. But Frazier thought it must be a symbol that her seat of power was so important, she wanted it to stand out among the world of yellow.

She sat on her black throne, dressed from head to toe

in the color she so dearly loved. She wore a hat embroidered with lace and daffodils that stretched a foot above her bald head. Her sparkling gown fit her body tightly, covering every inch from the middle of her neck to her shiny yellow heels. Horn-rimmed glasses sat atop her nose, her emerald eyes peering through like focused lasers.

Everything about this woman is just . . . weird, Frazier thought as he waited for her to say something.

"I don't know *why* we rescued you," Mistress Jane said, her voice taut with barely veiled anger. "We could just as easily have destroyed the complex of that *buffoon* Master George while you still sat inside, bawling your eyes out."

"Yes, Mistress Jane," Frazier replied. He knew better than to say anything else—yet.

"We finally had a hope of knowing George's plan once and for all—and you threw it down the drain in exchange for a little fun with your Chu Industries toy and a car. You better hope the attack on George takes care of any loose ends. SPEAK!" She belted this last word, causing several nearby servants to gasp.

Frazier stumbled on his words. "Mistress Jane . . . I n-never intended to k-kill them. I only meant to scare them enough to t-talk. I failed, and I'm sorry."

Jane stood up, her reddening face all the fiercer against the yellow background of her hat and dress. "They did not *die*, you blubbering sack of drool!"

Frazier couldn't hide his shock at hearing this. *How in the world did they escape before the car* . . .

He knew that now was not the time to wonder, now was the time for apologies and groveling. "I am very sorry, Mistress Jane."

"Listen to me well, Frazier Gunn," Jane said as she sat back down on her throne. "And let my servants put this on record. I give you one spoken sentence—one sentence only—to convince me why I should not send you to your death at the hands of the scallywag beasts. And not the nice ones that only take a week to digest their food."

Frazier closed his eyes, throwing all of his mental powers into quashing the rising panic and constructing a single sentence that could save his life. He had nothing. Nothing! But then a single word popped into his head, giving him an idea. It was desperate, but his only shot. Quickly, in his mind, he visualized each word of a sentence one by one, going over them several times. Finally, he opened his eyes and spoke.

"Master George has a spy in your presence, and I know who it is."

Jane's eyes screwed up into tight wrinkles, her brow creased. She folded her arms, studying Frazier for a long moment. "Nitwit!" she suddenly screamed, causing even more servants to gasp.

Frazier jumped, his heart sinking to the floor. "But—"

Before he could utter another word, a young girl dressed entirely in yellow zoomed through the air from the back of the room, stopping to hover directly in front of Frazier, facing Jane. No one had figured out how Jane used the mutated Chi'karda to enable flight, but seeing people flying always gave Frazier the creeps. It seemed so . . . unnatural.

"Yes, Mistress?" a high-pitched voice asked.

"Fetch me a banana sandwich." Jane leaned to the side, peering down at Frazier. "We have much to discuss, and I'm hungry. And make it quick!" She clapped her hands, a booming echo that shook the walls.

As the little servant flew off to obey Jane's orders, Frazier tried to regain his breath after that frantic moment when he'd thought for sure he'd be killed, all the while in disbelief that Jane could stoop so low as to rename a child *Nitwit*. Of course, the last one had been named Nincompoop, but had been disposed of once Jane got tired of yelling "Nincompoop!" every time she wanted something.

"Frazier!" Jane snapped.

"Y-y-yes, Mistress?" he stammered.

"Start talking."

Frazier told her about Annika.

It truly did happen in the blink of an eye, a quick tingle shooting down Tick's spine.

The instant Master George pushed the button on top of the Barrier Wand, the room of the Realitant headquarters vanished, replaced by thousands of massive trees covered in moss. Tick and the other recruits, along with Mothball, stood in a dark forest, hazy sunlight barely breaking through the thick canopy of branches to make small patches of gold on the earthy floor. The haunted sounds of exotic birds and insects filled the creepy woods, smells of roots and rotting leaves wafting through the air. Tick had the uneasy feeling that the forest wanted to eat him alive.

"Where are we?" Paul asked, though he must've known the answer.

"In the Thirteenth, we are. Deep in the Forest of Plague," Mothball whispered.

"Forest of *Plague?*" Sofia asked with a snort. "Lovely."

"A great battle was fought 'ere," Mothball said, slowly turning as she scanned the ancient trees, most of which were thick enough to make an entire house. Gnarled, twisted branches reached out as if trying to escape their masters. "Many moons ago, it was. Thousands died, their rottin' bodies creating a plague that was downright nasty. So I've 'eard, anyway. Must be true, seeing as there's quite a bit of Chi'karda here. Come on, follow me."

"Wait," Sato said, trying to sound stern but coming across as a grumpy jerk. "Tell us the plan before we take a step."

Tick rolled his eyes, but quickly so Sato couldn't see him do it. *Things are scary enough*, he thought. *Why does this guy have to make it worse?*

"The plan's quite simple, really," Mothball said, not acting bothered at all. "Right over yonder"—she pointed toward an ivy-covered copse of pine trees— "there's some right dandy Windbikes that we can take to meet Master George's spy, Annika. She's been settin' things up for months to get close to the Barrier Wand. We meet Annika, we get the Wand, we come back 'ere in thirty hours, and home we go."

"Sounds too easy," Sato said with a comical sneer.

"Sure it is, old chap, sure it is." Mothball turned and walked toward the pine trees. "Got a better idea, let me know. But best be right quick about it."

As Tick and the others followed their eight-foot-tall guide, Sato said from behind, "How do we know we can trust this spy? Maybe she works for Mistress Jane."

"Find out soon enough, we will," Mothball replied, not slowing at all.

"Quit your whining and come on," Sofia snapped.

Tick cringed, wishing his friend would ease up on the poor kid. Tick didn't like him either, but Sofia seemed way too harsh—who knew what Sato might do to retaliate.

Begrudgingly, Sato finally started walking. The sounds of footfalls crunching the thick undergrowth of the forest suddenly filled the air, echoing off the canopy of interwoven tree limbs.

Tick moved to catch up with Mothball, practically running to keep up with her pace. "I have a question."

"Go on and ask it, then." Mothball pushed an enormous branch out of the way that everyone else simply walked *under*.

"The alternate versions of ourselves in other worlds—does that mean there is one of me in every Reality?"

"That's usually the case, it is. We call 'em Alterants. Strange how all that works—even though the Realities can grow in vastly different ways from each other, there seems to be a definite pattern when it comes to the *people*."

"What do you mean?" Tick asked, stooping to avoid a huge chunk of moss that drooped over a thick limb like a giant beard.

"Even though a Reality may have different governments and cultures and climates and all that from another Reality, the general pedigree of people remains quite similar—downright spooky, it is." A huge bird cawed from overhead, followed by the squeal of a small animal.

"So in your Reality—the . . ."

"The Fifth, it is."

"Yeah, the Fifth. There's a really tall version of me there? My Alterant? And he's alive right now, with parents named Edgar and Lorena?"

"Chances are ya be right. Course, I've never met 'em, and never tried. Dangerous stuff, messin' with Alterants."

Sofia and Paul had been following closely and listening to every word while Sato hung back, only a couple of steps behind them. Though he acted indifferent to the conversation, Tick had a feeling Sato was intently paying attention.

"Why is it dangerous to mess with Alterants?" Sofia asked.

"Since I had dealings with Tick in Reality Prime," Mothball said, pausing a second to reassess her bearings. She changed directions slightly and headed down a shallow ravine scattered with boulders among the trees. "I didn't want to meet his Alterant in any of the other Realities. Not only could it make me go mad, it could lead to the little sir meetin' his taller self in my Reality. Disaster, that."

"Why?" Paul asked.

"If two Alterants meet and truly recognize each other for what and who they are, well, then only one of the poor blokes can survive. Still trying to figure out the why and how, we are, but one of them ceases to exist. Sometimes that causes a nasty chain reaction that can rattle the Realities to their bones. Bet yer best buttons some of the worst earthquakes and such you've had were because of Alterants seein' each other. Master George and the Realitants have worked their buns off to avoid such meetings, but Mistress Jane likes to bring Alterants together. She thinks it's funny. Mad, she is. Crazy as a brain-dead Bugaboo soldier."

That was the second time Tick had heard Mothball refer to Bugaboo soldiers, but he was too busy thinking about Alterants to ask any more questions.

"Whoa, man," Paul said. "This is some downright freaky stuff. You're telling me there's all these Pauls running around the universe? I better be a big-time surfer in one of them. And a world-class pianist in another."

"Face it," Sofia said with a smirk. "You're a no-talent bum in all of them, just like you are here. Or, there. Or, whatever."

Paul stuck out his tongue. "Sis, you're hilarious."

"Call me 'sis' again," Sofia challenged, raising her fist.

"Sis."

Sofia pulled back and punched Paul solidly on his upper arm with a loud thump.

"Ow!" he yelled, rubbing the spot. "That's no fair. I can't punch a *girl* back."

Tick laughed, and Mothball surprised everyone when she did, too.

"Glad my pain can give everyone a nice chuckle," Paul said, still wincing. "Tick, a word of advice. Don't mess with Italians."

"I learned that just from her e-mails. Whatever you do, don't rip on her spaghetti."

"Tick," Sofia said. "I like you. You're smart . . . for an American."

Sato completely ignored all of them, never breaking his stoic expression.

Before anyone could throw out another sarcastic remark, Mothball stopped next to a big pile of fallen branches and twigs. She turned toward the messy heap and took a deep breath. "'Ere we are." She bent over and yanked on a large branch, pulling it off the stack. "A little 'elp would be nice."

Tick grabbed a branch and everyone joined in, even Sato, who was mumbling something Tick couldn't understand.

Tick saw a glimmer of metal when he pulled off a prickly branch, his curiosity increasing his pace. Soon, they'd cleared the entire pile, and all of them stared at what they'd uncovered.

Three sleek and shiny motorcycles were lined up in a row, silver with sparkly metallic red paint. They were the coolest things Tick had ever seen, but there was one thing about them that seemed a little odd.

None of them had wheels.

CHAPTER 46

CHI'KARDA DRIVE

They're called Windbikes," Mothball said, gesturing with a wide sweep of her arm. "Quite fun, they are." Everything about the strange vehicles looked exactly like a normal bullet bike you'd see zooming down the freeway: a small windshield, silvery handlebars, shiny body with a big black leather seat. But the machine ended in a flat bottom instead of two round wheels.

"I hate to break it to you," Paul said, "but somebody, uh, stole the *tires*."

Mothball laughed, a booming roar that bounced off the overhanging branches. "You're a funny little man, you are, Paul."

"Are you telling us these things . . . fly?" Sofia asked.

"Well, I'd hope so, what with them not having wheels and all. Come on," she said while pulling the bike on the end away from the rest, pushing it across the ground. "There's three. One for me, and two for you kiddies to share. Methinks you'll be better off if ya go in pairs."

"Not me," Sato said. "I go alone."

"You'll go in a pair," Mothball said. "Or you'll sit 'ere and hug this tree all day." She stared down at Sato, daring him to argue. He said nothing in reply.

It was the first time Tick had seen Mothball use her size to intimidate someone. *I have a feeling this lady is a lot tougher than she acts.*

"Sweet biscuits!" Paul said as he grabbed hold of the next Windbike and dragged it a few feet away. "You're serious? This thing really *flies?* In the air?"

"Where else would it fly, Einstein?" Sofia said. "Underground?"

"You got me there, Miss Italy," Paul said, seeming to have grown accustomed to Sofia's smart mouth. "How does it work?"

Mothball sat down on her bike, her body taking up the entire seat that was meant for two. "You push this 'ere button, which turns it on, like so." She pressed a red button on the small dashboard under the handlebars. The Windbike came to life, humming like a big computer and not like a normal motorcycle at all. "Doesn't use gasoline. Takes hydrogen right out of the moisture in the air, it does, burns it right nicely. Come on, get on, now!"

"Who's going with who?" Tick asked.

"I'll go with you or Paul," Sofia said. "But not *him*." She nodded toward Sato, who scowled back at her.

"I don't want to go with you, either."

"Alrighty then," Paul said, clapping his hands. "Looks like it's me and Sofia on this one, Tick and Sato on that one." He pointed to the next bike in line.

Tick wanted to argue, but he didn't really want Sato any angrier than he already was. He looked to Sofia for help, but she only shrugged, not bothering to hide the smirk on her face. "Uh, great, okay."

Paul moved toward his bike and sat down right behind the handlebars, but Sofia would have none of it.

"I'm driving, tough guy," she said, pushing him backward as she squirmed her way in front of him.

Paul held his hands up in surrender as he scooted to the rear of the big seat. "You win, Miss Italy, you win." He looked over at Tick and mouthed the words, *"Help me."*

Sato pulled the last Windbike upright and pushed the button to turn it on as he swung his leg over and sat down in the driver's position. "Get on," he said, not bothering to look at Tick.

Tick felt like he'd rather pound his head against

the closest tree than get on the back of the humming machine. He hated how the mean kid from Japan was ruining everything.

Mothball must have noticed Tick's hesitation. "Come, now. Time's a wastin', it is."

"Yeah, sorry." Tick sighed as he sat behind Sato. The bottom edge of the Windbike had a railing with sticky pads for his feet. "Is this another invention from the Fourth Reality? Wait, let me guess—Chu Industries?"

"Nailed that one, you did," Mothball answered. "Chu rules a monopoly in the Fourth, he does—practically owns everything. Smuggled these bikes in a few months ago, we did, figuring they'd do right nicely for our little mission."

"What do we do now?" Sofia asked.

"Watch me very closely," Mothball said. She gripped the handlebars, then gently *lifted,* surprising everyone when the metal connecting her handgrips to the bike bent upward. As she did so, her Windbike rose several feet into the air with a slight surge in its humming sound; the top of her head almost bumped into a low-hanging branch.

"Cool!" Paul shouted.

Tick couldn't believe what he was seeing.

"Your hands control everything," Mothball said from above. "Push forward, go forward. The farther you push, the faster you go. Pull back and you slow down or stop, depending how hard ya do it. And ya go up or down by lifting and dropping the handgrips. Easy as breathin', it is."

Tick yelped and grabbed Sato's shirt as their bike suddenly leaped into the air and backward, then lurched forward and came to a sudden stop. A second later it shot forward again and flew around the closest tree, coming to a halt right above Sofia and Paul.

"It works," Sato said in a deadpan voice.

At the same time, all of them laughed. Even Sato broke into a smile for the first time since they'd met, looking back at Tick just as it turned back into a frown.

Tick had the strange feeling that maybe he was glad Sato had taken the pilot's seat after all, since he seemed to already have the hang of it. *I probably would've slammed us into the ground already, breaking all of our legs.*

Sofia tried it next, shooting straight upward until Paul's head slammed into the branch overhead.

"Ow, watch it!" he screamed. "I'm *tall*, remember!"

"Sorry," Sofia said through a snicker. Tick could see her push down and forward on the handlebars as the Windbike came down and flew around the same tree he and Sato had just circled. She came to a stop by pulling back with her hands, hovering right next to Tick.

"Told you it was easy, I did," Mothball said. She

revved her humming motorcycle. "Follow me!"

Her Windbike shot forward into the forest before she'd finished her sentence.

⁓

"You're sure of the meeting time and place?" Mistress Jane asked from her perch on the throne, glancing at her brightly yellow painted fingernails one by one.

"Absolutely," Frazier replied, trying his best to remain calm and professional, even though he knew how unpredictable his boss could be. He'd been put in charge of counter-spying on Annika since he'd returned and he had discovered some very interesting letters in the back of her closet. His relief at being right about her had far outweighed any fear he felt about damage she may have done. His hide had been saved and that was all that mattered.

"Tomorrow morning," he said, looking at the floor. "Dawn. Where the river meets the Forest of Plague. Annika will take the Barrier Wand from your throne room while you sleep, then deliver it to the Realitants."

"Why doesn't she just wink away with it herself? Why all the *drama?*" Jane said the last word with a low and sarcastic drawl.

Frazier swallowed despite his dry mouth. "She's under orders to keep her cover, stay infiltrated. Keep spying on you."

"Perhaps we should hide the Wand, end the plan this very minute." Jane lifted her hand and a small plate with a cup of steaming hot tea floated up from a nearby table and rested on her palm. She took a long and slurping drink.

"We could, Mistress, but then we might lose our chance to capture any Realitants who may have escaped George's Command Center before your attack. If Annika is not there with the Barrier Wand, they might suspect something and flee before we arrive."

"Frazier Gunn," Jane said with a sneer as she leaned forward in her throne, dropping the plate and cup onto the floor with a wet crash. She took off her lemon-decorated hat to reveal the shiny bald scalp underneath. Frazier shivered, knowing she did this only when she wanted to threaten someone. "This is your chance to redeem your pathetic failure of not bringing me those kids the *first* time I asked you to. If you fail me again . . ."

"You have nothing to worry about, Mistress. I'll have eyes on the Barrier Wand at all times and the army of fangen are ready to attack. Once the Realitants meet up with Annika, we'll charge in and take them all. They'll have nowhere to go."

"Are you sure the fangen are reliable? Last time I checked, they were still developing, still blind as bats."

Heat pulsed through Frazier's veins. "They're not at full strength, that's true. But they'll be plenty tough to take care of a few Realitants, I promise."

Jane paused a moment, staring him down as she considered his plan. "Fine, Frazier. But I want you personally to check and double check that the Chi'karda Drive in the Wand is disengaged before tonight. In fact, take the thing out altogether and give it to me so I can sleep with it under my pillow. Without it, they won't be able to wink away."

"And Master George's Wand? What if he tries to wink them back?"

Mistress Jane laughed as she placed the lemony hat back on her shiny head. "Oh, don't worry about him. He'll be far too *occupied* to do any rescuing." Her face flashed to red as she screamed, "Nitwit! Clean up this mess!"

By the time Mothball finally stopped next to an oak tree the size of a small building, Tick was desperate to throw up. After all the dodging and weaving through the maze of trees in the forest, his insides felt as if someone had shaken them like a maraca. When Sato pulled to a stop and lowered the Windbike to the mossy floor, Tick jumped off and ran over to a clump of bushes, where he spewed out every last morsel remaining in his stomach.

Paul made a wisecrack, but by the looks of his green

face, he didn't feel much better. Sofia and Sato seemed fine—as did Mothball—and Tick wondered if it was because they'd been driving.

Mothball removed her backpack and started pulling out all kinds of stuff. A tarp, some blankets, a little stove, packets of food.

"I thought we were in a hurry to meet our spy lady?" Paul asked, still walking off his nausea.

"What's that?" Mothball asked, concentrating on setting up the stove. "Oh, no, that be tomorrow morning when we meet Annika."

"Then why all the rush?" Sofia asked.

"Wanted to get far away from the deadies, I did." Mothball shivered. "The battleground where all those people died is downright spooky if ya ask me. Thought it best to be away a bit before we set up camp."

"So what do we do all night?" Paul asked as he leaned over Mothball's shoulder, not bothering to hide his interest in whatever she planned on cooking.

"Eat up, we will. Rutger prepared some right tasty dinners. Rest a bit, get some sleep. We'll be meetin' Annika just as the sun comes up, down by where the river that flows through Mistress Jane's fortress comes out and hits the Forest of Plague."

"How do we know for sure she'll be there?" Sato asked, still sitting on his Windbike. "Maybe she's turned on you."

"She'll be there, Mister Sato, no worries." Mothball ripped open a silvery pack of goop and poured it into a pot on her small stove. "One of our finest, Annika is."

"What if she's been captured?" Sato persisted.

"Then ya better be prayin' Master George survived his little battle and brings us back."

Tick sat down on a fallen log, unhappy that they had hurried to get here only to sit and wait for tomorrow. It was going to be a long night.

⁓

"Here you are, Mistress."

Frazier handed over the cylindrical pack of wires, nanochips, and instruments that made up the Chi'karda Drive, the heart and soul of her Barrier Wand.

Jane took the odd-looking package through her open bedroom door, examining it as though she suspected it wasn't the real thing. "You put the Wand back where it always rests for the night?"

"Yes, I did. The trap is set."

"I can't wait to find out why Annika has betrayed me," Jane said with a nasty smile. "How fun it will be to remind her why it's best to be on *my* side of things."

"Loads," Frazier muttered, almost forgetting himself. "The fangen are ready, Mistress, and are already moving into their hiding positions."

"That should be an interesting sight to watch—

them sniffing along, bumping into things." Jane pointed a finger through the crack of the door. "Remember, we need the Realitants alive. This is the perfect opportunity for me to learn what that weasel George is planning."

"Yes, Mistress Jane," Frazier said. "The fangen will be very . . . eager, but I'll do my best to restrain them."

The night was dark and cool, and Tick slept surprisingly well until Mothball shook him awake a couple of hours before dawn. He jumped at first, but his senses came back to him quickly.

"Time to be movin', it is," she whispered, then moved on to the next person.

They'd all slept on a wide blue tarp, each one of them given a single blanket to make it through the night. Tick had never felt *too* cold, and the soft undergrowth of the forest floor made for a nice mattress. All in all, he felt well rested once he got up and his blood started flowing.

After a quick breakfast of granola bars and apples, a unified hush settled on everyone as they helped Mothball pack up her things and stuff them into the backpack. The forest was mostly quiet, the occasional buzz of an insect or howl of an animal in the distance the only sounds.

Tick didn't know if he'd ever felt butterflies so intense as he did at that moment, waiting to hop back on his Windbike and fly off to meet Annika the spy. From what he'd heard about Mistress Jane, he doubted she would be very merciful if they blew the mission and got captured. What if Sato was right? What if this was all a trap? What if something went wrong? Tick tried not to think about his fears, putting his trust in Mothball and Master George.

"Everyone, gather 'round," Mothball said once she'd swung the backpack onto her shoulders. They moved together into a tight circle, intently awaiting instructions. "Just yonder there's a small break in the trees. Once there, we're going to fly up and over the roof of the forest to make it easy goin'. Just follow me, and we'll make our way to the meetin' point by the river. Once Annika comes with the Barrier Wand, we'll scuttle away right quick and head back for the old battleground in the forest. Got it?"

"Yeah," whispered Paul. "Sounds pretty easy to me."

"What do we do if something goes wrong?" Sato asked, seeming to show a little more interest in the group. "What is—how do you say?—our Plan B?"

"Yeah, what if this Annika lady doesn't get the Wand to us?" Paul asked.

Mothball paused. "Then we fly like the dickens back to the battleground to regroup."

"Why do I *not* feel assured this has all been thought out?" Sofia asked.

"Annika's been preppin' for months for this, she 'as," Mothball replied. "But if we don't get the ruddy Wand, won't matter much in the end. If we're to have any 'ope of defeatin' the Mistress, we need to trap her 'ere for a long time."

"Then let's do it," Paul said, holding his hand out, palm to the ground.

Tick got the idea and did the same, putting his hand on top of Paul's. Sofia followed suit, then Mothball. Everyone looked at Sato, whose face was hidden in the darkness. After a long pause, he finally gave in, placing his hand on top of the pile.

"Promise me," he said looking around the circle. "Promise me you people won't betray me."

His words surprised Tick, and by the shocked silence from his friends, he figured they were just as taken back.

"Promise me!" Sato yelled.

"Just who do you think—" Sofia began.

"No," Mothball said, cutting her off. "Sato 'ere had a bit of trouble in his past. Right deserving of his doubts, he is. Sato, I promise I won't be the one doin' any betray-ing. You can bet yer best buttons on that one."

"Me, neither," Paul quickly added. "Sato, we're in this together, man."

"Yeah," Tick agreed. "We're not going to betray you."

"And you?" Sato said to Sofia.

"I think you need an attitude—"

"Sofia!" Tick snapped, surprising himself.

She paused for a long time. "All right, all right. Sato, I promise I won't betray you, even though that sounds really lame. We're all a team, here. *Okay?*" She said the last word sarcastically, as if to preserve her dignity. "Can we quit holding hands now?"

"On three," Paul said, ignoring her. "On three, yell . . . *Go Realitants.*"

"Oh, come on," Sofia complained.

"Just do it," Paul replied. "Pump us up for some prime-time action and adventure. Ready?" He bobbed his hand up and down as he counted. "One . . . two . . . three . . . GO REALITANTS!" He threw everyone's hands up in the air as he shouted the last part with enthusiasm.

Tick and Mothball half-heartedly said the words with him, but Sato and Sofia didn't make a peep.

"Man, you guys are pathetic," Paul muttered.

"Let's just get on with it, Cheeseball," Sofia said. "Let's go get us a Barrier Wand."

And with that, they got on their bikes and flew toward the tops of the trees.

CHAPTER
47

ANNIKA'S TOSS

The dark sky had the slightest hint of purple as the Realitants shot out of the forest and skimmed along the canopy of trees, following Mothball in the lead. Tick knew he should be terrified, but he already felt completely confident in the workings of the Windbikes; they seemed invincible and effortless. The dark and puffy roof of the forest below them looked like a churning sea of storm clouds, making him feel higher in the sky than a few hundred feet. It was a little awkward holding on to Sato at first, but he enjoyed the rush of speed and the whipping wind.

For the first time in his life, he knew what it felt like to be Superman.

They traveled for a half hour before Mothball held up her hand to signal the others to slow down. The black purple of the sky had slowly brightened into a mixture of oranges and reds, streaks of fiery clouds scratched across it. Tick could see that the main forest ended a mile or so ahead, and almost swallowed his tongue when he saw what towered above the land beyond.

It was a massive fortress of stone and rock, still dark against the scant light of dawn. Dozens of towers and bridges dotted its skyline. It had to be the single largest structure Tick had ever seen—bigger by *far* than even the Seahawks' football stadium. It appeared that not only had Mistress Jane discovered a land full of something like magic, she'd set herself up in a castle fit for a king from any fantasy book in the library. Tick was in awe and had the sudden urge to explore the place.

The three Windbikes hovered next to each other, everyone in stunned silence as they gawked at the castle of Mistress Jane.

"Calls it the Lemon Fortress, she does," Mothball said. "Why that woman loves the color yellow so much is beyond me. Looney, she is."

"Are we sure they can't see us?" Paul asked.

"Not sure at'all. Come on, down we go. Got to be about our business." She pushed on her handlebars and flew toward the edge of the forest, the other two Windbikes right behind her.

They passed over the green cliff of the tightly packed trees and descended toward the ground, where a lush lawn of grass and wildflowers was sliced by the sinewy curve of a huge, sparkling blue river that spilled out from underneath the castle before finally disappearing into the forest. Not a person was in sight, and in a matter of seconds, the group had settled on the ground next to the deep, slowly moving waters, close enough to the trees to smell bark and pine.

"Where is Annika?" Sofia asked, not bothering to hide the frustration in her voice.

"Be along directly, she will," Mothball replied, but her face showed signs of worry as she stared at the Lemon Fortress with a creased brow.

From where they waited, they could see a cobble-stone path running along the river and up to a large double-doored entrance of the castle, just a few hundred feet away. Next to it, the river seemed to magically appear from nowhere, bubbling up from under the cold blocks of the castle's granite. At the moment, not a thing stirred anywhere except for the trickling river and the early-rising birds of the forest.

Tick was about to say something when Mothball shushed him, holding up a hand as she perked her ears, looking around for signs of mischief. At first, Tick couldn't hear anything, but then the faintest sound of giggling and high-pitched chatter came from everywhere at once, bouncing along the lawn in front of them and from the trees behind them.

"What *is* that?" Paul whispered.

The creepy cacophony of hoots and howls and wicked laughter grew louder.

"That can't be good," Sofia muttered, her eyes wide in her frightened face. "Mothball, what's going on?"

"Methinks we've been found out, I do," she answered, standing to get a better look at the Lemon Fortress. "Sounds like the fangen to me, and they be comin' fast. We may have to fight a bit after all. Don't worry, the lugs are still blind and clumsy so all ya'll need to do is move a lot and shoot 'em with these little gems."

She pulled out several dark-green cylinders from a side pocket on her backpack and passed one to each of the kids. They were thin and several inches long, one end tapering to a point. Tick took his and examined the shiny surface, noticing a small button toward the thicker end.

"What's this?" he asked.

"That there's the Sound Slicer," Mothball answered. "Point the narrowed bit at the beasties when they get close and push the button. Keep 'em off ya, it will."

"What does it—" Sofia began.

Before she could finish her question, the sound of wood scraping against stone echoed through the air.

Everyone turned in unison to see the wide double doors of the castle opening outward like the gaping jaws of a monster. The seam in the middle had barely grown a foot wide before a woman with long black hair shot out of it, dressed in a bright green dress, running with strained and frantic effort. In her right hand, she held a long golden rod.

The Barrier Wand.

"It's Annika!" Mothball roared as she jumped back onto her Windbike. "Quick! Fly to her—fly to her!"

She shot into the air and down the path of the river, toward the running woman, who kept looking behind her, terrified. She shouted something as she ran, but they were too far away to hear. As Tick scrambled onto the Windbike behind Sato, he saw tall, gangly figures pouring through the castle doors, more and more as the exit opened wider. He couldn't tell what the creatures were, but they seemed . . . *wrong* somehow. They were basically human in shape, but all comparisons ended there.

Sato shot through the air and pulled up beside Mothball as they drew closer to Annika. "What are those things?" he yelled.

The creatures' skin was a putrid hue of yellow, like they'd been infected with a horrible disease. Clumpy patches of hair sprang from their bodies in random places and they wore only scant, filthy clothing that looked like tattered sheets that barely covered their thick torsos. Their eyes were mere slits, burning red pupils peeping out like a glimpse of hot lava. And their mouths . . .

They were huge, full of pointy spikes of enormous teeth.

"Them's the fangen," Mothball shouted. "Nasty beasties, they are. But we can fight 'em off with a bit of effort."

Even as she spoke, the hackles and cries from the fangen grew louder. Tick looked around in horror as he saw more of the sickly creatures appearing from everywhere, out of ditches, over the crests of the surrounding hills, out of the forest. They came from all directions, some bounding along on all four of their skinny arms and legs, others running upright; still others had *things* sprouting off their backs, membranous extensions resembling dirty sails, tautly flapping in the wind. With horror, Tick realized they were wings.

"By the way," Mothball yelled, readying herself to dive for Annika. "Fangen can fly."

⌒⌒⌒

High above the grounds, safe in her room, Mistress Jane sat next to the open air of her window, listening with glee to the horrific sounds of her attacking army. Amazing what the power of this twisted and evil

Reality could create. This was her first practical use of the fangen. How wonderful.

But with so many against so few, it hardly seemed fair.

She looked down in her lap, where she cradled the Chi'karda Drive like a newborn baby. Without it, the pathetic band of Realitants could never use her Barrier Wand to escape. And she had already received word that Master George's Wand had been damaged beyond repair in the battle at the Bermuda Triangle. Good news, all around.

She did feel a little saddened by Annika's betrayal. Jane had trusted her with so many trivial and demeaning duties. What a pity she'd have to be done away with.

Mistress Jane screamed for something to eat. She had a show to enjoy before she sat down to strategize for her meeting with Reginald Chu in a few days.

Her plan to make the universe a better place had officially begun.

～⌒つ

Sofia had fallen far behind the other two Windbikes, too shocked by the sight of the onrushing creatures to push ahead any faster. She spun in a slow circle as she took it all in. The fangen were everywhere. The sight of the tall, awkward creatures, with their bony arms and legs attached to a thick, solid torso and their disgusting skin and patches of greasy hair, made her sick.

"Man, what are those things!" Paul shouted from behind her.

"Your long-lost cousins!" Sofia yelled back, knowing there couldn't possibly be a worst time to make a joke, but unable to stop herself.

"Hilarious—now hurry and catch up with Mothball!"

Sofia was about to push forward on the handlebars when something appeared right in front of them, shooting up from the ground.

One of the creatures, its enormous mouth baring fangs the size of small knives, hovered in midair, blocking their path. It looked hungry.

Sofia saw the wings for the first time, furled out behind the fangen like a horrific version of giant palm leaves.

From behind her, Paul suddenly screamed.

~~~~~~

The fangen moved twice as fast as Annika could run, and they were almost on top of her as Mothball dove toward the ground like a hawk on a field mouse. Her heart hurt at seeing the terror on her old friend's face as she ran, the fierceness in Annika's eyes enough to turn water to stone. Mothball leaned on the handlebars, willing the Windbike to move faster. She wasn't close enough to use a Sound Slicer, and even if she were, she couldn't use it; the thing would turn Annika's brain to jelly.

A fangen jumped on Annika's back, throwing her to the ground. Annika rolled, gripping the Barrier Wand with both hands and swinging wildly. She hit the creature in the face, a strange bark coming out of its mouth as it reared back in pain. Annika scrambled to her feet and kept running, the horde of fangen right on her tail. The clumsy things constantly stumbled over each other, but never lost ground due to sheer numbers.

Mothball was almost to Annika, screaming at her to keep running. Though Mothball was bigger than the usual rider of a Windbike—leaving no room for another passenger—she felt sure she could somehow lift Annika up and away from the monsters. Of course, the disgusting things could just leap into the air with their warped Chi'karda-melded wings, but she'd deal with one thing at a time.

About forty feet away, Mothball realized she was too late. Several fangen had caught up with Annika, flanking her to make sure she couldn't fight her way out again. Her eyes met Mothball's, and they seemed so full of fear that Mothball worried Annika might drop dead of it.

Determined to fight her way into the melee and

save Annika and the Wand or die trying, Mothball surged forward.

She was almost there when Annika threw the Barrier Wand into the air as hard as she could, the shiny rod glistening in the morning sun as it wind-milled end over end toward Mothball. An instant later, Annika disappeared under a mass of writhing yellow skin and claws.

Mothball reached out and caught the Wand with her right hand, screaming with fury at the beasts below her, knowing it was too late to save her friend.

Tick and Sato watched the entire ordeal play out from dozens of feet behind Mothball, flying in to help. Tick didn't know if he should cheer or cry when their tall friend caught the Barrier Wand in her hand.

He had time to do neither.

A pack of three flying fangen attacked their Windbike in a swarm of sharp claws and spiky fangs and flapping wings.

Paul screamed when the claws raked down his back, trying not to picture in his mind what it had done to his skin. On instinct, he gripped Sofia harder for support and kicked behind him with his right leg.

He felt a solid thump as his foot connected, followed by a hair-raising shriek that faded as the creature fell to the ground.

Sofia gunned the Windbike forward; it smashed into a flying fangen and sent it reeling to the side, hissing in frustration. Paul felt himself slipping backward and had to pull himself back onto the seat, all the while looking below them at the unbelievable sight. Everywhere he looked, more and more of the nightmarish creatures appeared, snapping at the air with their vicious fangs.

"Use the thing Mothball gave us!" Sofia yelled from up front, pulling it out of her pocket as she spoke.

"Sound Slicer," Paul whispered to himself as he grabbed his own.

Together, they aimed the little cylinders at the nearest pack of fangen and pushed the buttons. A low sound vibrated through the air, barely discernible but heavy, rattling Paul's bones as if he'd been standing next to tolling cathedral bells. Below them, the fangen suddenly plummeted toward the ground like they'd been hit with an invisible tidal wave.

"Whoa," Paul said.

In tandem, he and Sofia swept the area below them, firing the Sound Slicer at anything in sight. Hordes of fangen fell from the sky.

"Find Mothball!" Paul yelled in Sofia's ear.

Tick had never really been in a fight his entire life. He'd always walked away from them or taken the punishment or *avoided* them. But now he had no choice. With one hand clutching Sato's shirt, he punched and kicked with his other three limbs, thrashing wildly as he frantically tried to avoid the fangs and claws of the fangen.

Sato swerved back and forth with the Windbike, alternately accelerating and slamming on the brakes, popping up and down, trying his best to get away from their attackers. But for every one that fell away, two more seemed to show up.

Tick felt his elbow connect with something solid, heard an eerie yelp. His feet kicked away a fangen on each side of the bike at the same time. He punched another one square between the small slits of its eyes. More of the beasts swarmed in. Tick reached into his pocket and pulled out the cylinder he'd received from Mothball, only to have it knocked out of his hands, falling to the ground below.

He felt something sharp on his shoulder blade, turning around to see that one of the fangen had grabbed his scarf, pulling itself closer with jaws wide open. Tick had to let go of Sato with his other hand as he swung his elbow up and around as hard as he could, slamming it into the beast's neck. It screamed and fell away.

At that very moment, Tick's stomach shot up into his throat as the Windbike suddenly plummeted toward the ground. He just barely grabbed the edges of the seat, turning toward the front of the bike.

His heart skittered when he saw that Sato had *disappeared*.

He looked up just in time to see two fangen flying away, Sato firmly in the grasp of their claws.

CHAPTER 48

DOUBLE DOORS

Frazier Gunn watched the action from his perch high atop the walls of the Lemon Fortress. Seeing the swarms of fangen descend on the few Realitants—especially the big one who'd kidnapped him in the Alaskan cemetery—gave him a grim sense of satisfaction.

His place in Mistress Jane's hierarchy would surely skyrocket after this victory.

He saw the tall woman, grasping the useless Barrier Wand, dodging and weaving through hundreds of fangen as she tried to escape. He worried slightly she might break it—even though it couldn't be used without the Chi'karda Drive, the shell itself was a complex instrument in its own right that would take months to replace—but the army of creatures had direct orders to retrieve it safe and sound. Everything would be fine.

Surprised by a sudden yawn, Frazier decided he'd had enough; the fangen were already boring him. He turned around and went back into the castle proper, hoping Mistress Jane might call on him for congratulations very soon.

Tick knew Sato's fate was sealed if Tick couldn't gain control of the Windbike before it crashed into the ground below. The bike twisted and pitched back and forth as it fell, throwing his senses into complete chaos. He steeled himself, forcing his eyes and hands to focus on the leather seat, pulling himself toward the handlebars. Though he didn't dare look, he could *feel* the lawn and river rushing up to smash him to bits. He only had seconds to live unless he . . .

With one last grunt, he yanked himself upright and squeezed his legs on both sides of the bike's body. He quickly grabbed the handlebars and bent them toward the sky. With a lurch that almost made his stomach implode, the Windbike slowed to a halt then shot straight back up into the air. As dozens of fangen repositioned themselves to attack him again, Tick looked in the direction Sato had been taken. He could just see his flailing body, resisting the two creatures that'd whisked him away.

They were on a direct course for the top of the castle.

In the next instant, a million thoughts seemed to flow through Tick's mind, processing and reprocessing.

A few months ago, he'd made a very difficult decision. Even though his life had become frightening— just as Master George had promised it would—and even though he could've made it all go away with a simple toss of the first letter into the fire, he hadn't done it. Some courage he didn't know he'd had, some sense of duty and right he didn't know was so powerful, had swelled inside his heart and given him the conviction to make an extremely hard choice. He remembered thinking of his little sister Kayla, and what he might do if her life were at stake.

And now, truly for the first time in his existence, Tick had a chance to risk his own life to save another.

The question posed by Master George so long ago popped back into his mind.

Will you have the courage to choose the difficult path?

Tick screamed Sato's name and slammed the handlebars up and forward, bulleting the Windbike in a straight path toward the fangen. Toward Sato.

⟋⟍

Sofia continued to fly the Windbike as crazy as she dared, swerving and diving and skyrocketing upward in an attempt to evade the countless creatures coming after them. Her head hurt from the effort; her stomach begged her to stop.

Behind her, Paul continued to shoot as many fan-gen as he could with his Sound Slicer, defending her as she drove. He'd slipped and almost fallen several times, but she had no choice but to keep flying forward.

She caught a glimpse of Tick streaking past her on his Windbike.

Alone.

Where was—

Before she could finish her thought, one of the flying creatures slammed into them from the side, driving its head into the engine of the bike. Sofia lurched, barely hanging on as the body of the beast flipped under them and fell to the ground.

She felt Paul squirming behind her to right himself on the seat. "What was that thing *doing?*" he asked.

Unfortunately, they got their answer a second later.

With a loud sputter of electronic coughs, then a low whine that sounded like a baby elephant caught in a trap, the Windbike quit working. Completely.

This time, Sofia and Paul screamed in unison as they dropped toward the ground far below.

Tick had halved the distance to Sato and his captors in a matter of seconds. Even though they could fly, the fangen were no match for the Windbikes when it came to speed.

Tick leaned forward, keeping his eyes focused on his target.

He tried not to think of what would happen if they suddenly decided to drop Sato.

~

Mothball used the Barrier Wand like a staff, swinging it in wide arcs as she darted about on her Windbike, knocking the heads of the fangen, sometimes two or three at a time. She realized they'd be in a whole heap of mess if she broke the ruddy Wand, but Master George had always said the things were sturdy enough to withstand most punishment.

She'd just landed a particularly nice hit on a creature when she caught a flicker of dark movement to her right. She looked to see Paul and Sofia—and their bike—plummeting toward the ground.

She zoomed in that direction without an instant's hesitation.

~

Sofia's Windbike sputtered sporadically, humming to life with a jolt for the briefest of moments before dying again. Paul hugged Sofia tightly from behind, probably hoping she'd never bring it up again should they somehow survive.

But Sofia knew they'd be dead in seconds, and wondered what life as a Realitant might've been like. She thought she might have liked it.

Mothball didn't have time to think or ponder several options. Only one made sense, and she went for it, quickly stuffing the Barrier Wand through a belt loop with one hand while she steered with the other.

In a nosedive that made her eyes water, she rushed toward Sofia and Paul, who clung to their useless Windbike as it plummeted in a downward spiral. Their present course would smash them against a group of boulders clustered close to the river. Mothball intended to *change* that course.

At the last second before she caught up with the falling bike, Mothball swerved hard to the right then arrowed back in straight at Sofia and Paul, keeping pace with their rate of descent, knowing she only had one shot. As soon as she made contact, Mothball gunned her own Windbike, *pushing* the other one at an angle as it fell.

Toward the river.

What had been certain death was now a chance.

If the ruddy water was *deep* enough.

Tick flew up and over the stone parapet bordering the massive crown of the castle, then skimmed along the loose gravel covering the roof. The two fangen had touched down, folding their wings behind them; Sato was clutched between them, his head hanging low.

When they spotted Tick, the two fangen howled out a piercing cry, seeming to dare Tick to attempt a rescue. From both sides of the castle walls, more of the creatures charged in, hungry to join the fight.

Tick never slowed down.

"Sato!" he screamed. "Duck!"

The boy showed no signs he'd heard or even planned to do as he was told, but Tick knew he had no other choice. He leaned forward, trying to envision in his mind what he was about to do.

"Sato!" he screamed again, only thirty feet away. "Duck—NOW!"

To Tick's relief, Sato buckled his legs and fell toward the roof, catching his captors by surprise. Though they didn't let go, both fangen looked down at Sato, their attention diverted for an instant, their heads high enough to serve as a perfect target.

Tick yanked back and to the left on the handle-bars, leaning hard to the left as the Windbike spun, slowing as the back end swerved around and slammed into the upper bodies of the two fangen. Tick felt a jolt of pain as one of the creatures bit at his right leg before it toppled over. Both of the horrible creatures let go of Sato, stunned by the sudden impact.

Tick steadied the Windbike and lowered it all the way to the loose rocks of the roof. "Get on!" he yelled. Dozens of fangen were charging right for them.

Sato was bruised and battered, his face still pale with the terror of being captured, but he crawled to the bike and pulled himself onto the seat, Tick helping him the last few inches.

Out of the corners of his eyes, Tick saw a blur of yellowed skin and vicious claws. He felt an icy touch on his elbow. Before anything could take hold, Tick shot the Windbike up and away from the sea of disgusting monsters.

A storm of fangen took flight in pursuit.

Paul had absolutely no idea what happened.

His mind had been fading, shutting down into a blissful state of unconsciousness so he didn't have to feel the excruciating instant of pain when his body smacked into the ground. But everything changed in a sudden rush of intense cold and wetness.

Water engulfed him, filling his lungs as he instinctively sucked in air at the shock of impact. As he felt his feet slam into the river bottom—hard enough to almost break his legs—he sputtered and coughed, his instincts trying to prevent him from taking another breath and killing himself. The next instant, he felt a massive arm grab him around the chest and pull him through the water.

But not up—not toward air.

The arm pulled him to the *side*, skimming his body along the sandy river bottom.

Paul had one moment to wonder if he was dead before everything grew very dark.

Tick shot into the open air away from the castle, his blood freezing at the sight of countless fangen everywhere. The air was full of them, defying gravity as they flew with their pale, weak-looking wings. More crawled and ran across the grounds, an endless army of ants. Not knowing where to go or what to do, Tick frantically searched the sky and the ground for any glimpse of his friends.

A flash of red far below caught his eye. One of the Windbikes, in the *river*.

And no sign of anyone near it.

His heart sinking faster than he could ever fly, Tick slammed on the handlebars and catapulted toward the ground.

After swimming under the thick stone arch from which the slow-moving river exited the Lemon Fortress, Mothball kicked with all of her might toward the surface, dragging both Sofia and Paul in her arms. Desperate for air, she could only imagine how her two little friends were doing, if they still lived.

Her head broke through the surface with a loud splash; she sucked in the most refreshing breath of her life. Even as she did so, she pulled up with her arms, bringing Paul's and Sofia's faces above the water line.

Mothball's heart almost leaped out of her chest when both of the kids coughed and sputtered for air. With an inexplicable laugh, she dragged them to the side of the river where she helped them climb out and onto a wide stone walkway. Paul fell over, spitting and sucking, spitting and sucking. Sofia seemed better, taking in slow, deep breaths as she looked around, her eyes wide.

They stood next to the river in a long, dark tunnel that delved in one direction for what seemed like eternity, no end in sight. On the other side, the river disappeared under a thick stone wall, flowing outside the castle wall. Next to that stood the huge wooden doors they'd seen from the outside. They were still halfway open and letting in enough light to prevent them from being in complete darkness.

"This is where those creatures came from," Sofia whispered.

"Best be glad they're out there, now," Mothball muttered. She pulled the Barrier Wand out of the huge belt loop where she'd stuck it for safekeeping.

Paul had recovered enough to stand up, his chest still heaving as he fought to catch his breath. "What happened to Tick and Sato?"

As if in answer, they heard Tick shout from outside the doors. "Mothball!"

His Windbike had flown down from somewhere above; he hovered just outside, Sato on the back.

"Wait a minute," Paul said. "I thought Sato was driving the bike."

"Quick!" Mothball yelled, ignoring Paul. "Get in 'ere!"

She saw Tick obey immediately, shooting the Windbike through the narrow space between the half-open doors. Even as he did, Mothball grabbed the long ropes hanging on the inside of the huge slabs of wood that served as handles to pull them closed.

"Help me!" she yelled.

As the others moved to her side and pulled with her, Mothball looked outside. Just before the doors slammed shut with a loud boom, she saw the hideous sight of countless fangen charging directly for them.

CHAPTER 49

THE GOLDEN BUTTON

Mothball pulled an enormous plank of wood down into the slot that locked the double doors. "Won't hold 'em for long, bet yer best buttons." She looked at Tick, who'd parked the Windbike and now hugged his friends like they'd just won the Cricket tourney. "Save the celebratin' if you don't mind. Here." She held up the Barrier Wand, gesturing for him to take it.

"What?" Tick stammered. "Here? Now?"

"'Less you'd be wantin' to invite the fangen in first."

Tick frowned. "But I thought we had to get back to the battleground."

Something heavy slammed into the doors from the other side, followed by a thunder of heavy thumps and nerve-grinding scratches. The fangen wanted *in*.

"Only if we'd be wantin' Master George to grab us in a few hours," Mothball said. "No time for that now. It's up to you."

Without waiting for a response, she tossed the Wand in Tick's direction.

Tick caught the long golden rod with both hands, scared to death he'd drop it and break it. He hefted it in his hands, surprised at how light it felt.

"So . . . I just have to adjust the controls and poof— we're safe?" he asked Mothball.

"Be quick about it—and make no mistakes on the dials or we may end up in the wrong end of a beluga whale, we will. Once you're set, we all need to be touchin' it, then ya simply push the button."

A crashing thunk made them all jump. Tick saw the head of a huge axe embedded in the wood of the right door. With an ear-piercing squeal, the huge sliver of metal was yanked back out. A second later it landed again, throwing a shower of splinters all over the stone walkway. It disappeared and a red eye peeked through the rough slit, followed by a gurgly scream.

"Uh, Tick," Sofia said. "Maybe we should, I don't know, *hurry*?" She threw every ounce of sarcasm she could muster into the last word.

"Yeah, man," Paul agreed. "Giddyup."

"They're almost through . . ." Sato said, his voice taut.

"Okay," Tick whispered as he knelt down on the stone, holding the Barrier Wand in front of him delicately, like he held in his hands the most priceless artifact of the ancient Egyptians. "Here goes nothing."

More booms and cracks sounded from the doors. More cackles and deranged giggling. The left door started to buckle, like the fangen had just hit it with a huge battering ram.

"Take your time, Tick," Sofia muttered.

Tick ignored her, closing his eyes and bringing up the image of what Master George had shown him back at the Bermuda Triangle complex. He raised his mind's eye to look at the Doohickey, the uppermost control.

"Okay," he said, opening his eyes to focus on the real thing. While holding the rod with his left hand, he reached forward and turned the Doohickey three clicks to the right. He paused again, knowing it was better to get it right the first time instead of rushing and having to start all over again. He envisioned the Whatchamacallit, then the Thingamajig, slowly making the appropriate adjustments. He moved his attention to the next control down.

An ear-splitting crack made him yelp, looking up to see a huge seam had split the right door into almost two complete sections. Several yellowy arms squirmed through the opening, grasping and clawing to pull the pieces apart.

Tick, spurred into a fear-induced sense of focus, went back to work on the Barrier Wand.

⌒⌒

"The water ruined the ruddy Sound Slicers, no doubt," Mothball said as she ran forward to the doors, picking up a huge splinter of wood that had fallen inward onto the stone floor. She immediately got to work, whacking and stabbing any sign of the diseased yellow skin that squeezed through the large crack. With every shriek and scream of anger, she doubled her efforts.

Paul joined her, finding a smaller but sharper stick. Without a word to each other, they worked in tandem— Paul fighting the lower portion, Mothball the upper.

They only had to buy Tick a little more time.

⌒⌒

Sofia felt rooted to the ground, screaming inside with helplessness. Sato stood beside her, frantically looking around as if trying to find something to fight.

"What happened out there?" Sofia asked him.

Sato looked at her, his eyes drained of the hatred and mistrust he'd shown back at Master George's place. "He saved my life." Sato pointed at Tick.

"He did?"

Sato nodded.

"That's—" Sofia shrieked as something grabbed her ankle. She looked down to see a slick yellowed hand gripped around her, attached to one of the fangen, crawling out of the river. Behind it she saw another's head pop out of the water.

Before she could react, Sato kicked down with his foot, breaking the miserable thing's hand with a hideous crunch. It squealed and splashed back into the water, just as Sato got down on his knees and shot the other one with a muted *thump* from his Sound Slicer. The creature disappeared into the black water.

Sofia reached down and helped Sato back to his feet, then dragged him away from the river, seeing no signs of other creatures—for the moment.

The breaches in the doors were cracking wider, almost big enough for one of the monsters to squeeze through. A sickly arm reached inside, a glimmering silvery globe clutched in its hand. Sofia was about to shout a warning when Mothball whacked the thing's arm with her huge stick.

The tall woman turned around, her face on fire with rage, yelling at the others. "Run away from the door! All of you!"

Paul didn't argue, turning immediately to run down the dark tunnel. He grabbed Tick's arm as he passed, half dragging him along since Tick was still focused intently on the Barrier Wand.

"Come on!" Paul yelled. "We need to get out of their reach or they're going to fry us for dinner. Just a little farther in!"

Tick finally snapped his concentration and broke into a full run behind Paul. "I've almost got it," he said, panting. "Just one more dial."

The last word had barely crossed his lips when a horrible explosion of cracking wood boomed and echoed down the dark stone tunnel. The silver ball had been some kind of bomb.

The breach was complete.

⁓

Tick tried to ignore the noise of screaming and howling fangen pouring through the shattered doors behind them. Knowing he had no time left, he quit running and knelt down again, bringing the Barrier Wand up to his eye level. "Everyone come here!" he shouted. "Grab the Wand!"

He focused on the bottom dial—the Whattzit. He turned it to the correct position, then glanced over the other six controls, verifying each of them one last time. The other Realitants had gathered around him, leaning over to grasp the Wand in different locations, being careful not to cover up or bump the dials and switches.

The nightmarish sounds of the onrushing fangen grew louder. Sato used his free hand to shoot with his Sound Slicer, keeping some of them at bay, but Tick knew it was only a matter of time.

"Everyone ready?" Tick shouted over the cackles and war cries of the fangen and the teeth-jolting thumps of Sato's lone weapon.

"Do it!" Mothball answered for everyone. "Be quick about it!"

Unable to prevent a smile from spreading across his face, Tick pushed the golden button on top of the Barrier Wand.

Nothing happened.

The haunting chorus of horrible sounds continued. Tick and the others were still trapped inside the Lemon Fortress.

Tick pushed the button again, then again, triggering his finger up and down several times.

Nothing.

"What's *wrong*, Tick?" Sofia yelled.

"Dude, hurry up!" Paul added.

Tick ignored them, studying the controls to see if he'd made a mistake. One by one, he quickly scanned them, matching their positions with the image burned inside his mind. Everything was right.

He pushed the button again, with the same result.

No, no, no, he thought. *Not after all we just went through. You will work. You will work!*

"Tick!" Sofia yelled, swatting him on the shoulders in panic.

Tick could hear the creatures coming, could feel them.

Focusing, funneling the surroundings out of his mind and heart, Tick gripped the Barrier Wand, staring at it like he could melt it with his eyes. *They'd come so far . . .*

He felt that strange reservoir of heat deep in his stomach bubbling to life. He'd tapped into it twice before and now he reached for it eagerly, letting the warmth flood through his entire body, filling him with certainty.

Tick shouted into the air, louder than he'd ever shouted anything in his whole life.

"YOU WILL *WORK* YOU STUPID PIECE OF HUNK-A-JUNK!"

He closed his eyes and pushed the button one last time.

Tick instantly felt a tingle shoot down his back and the world around him fell into dead silence.

CHAPTER 50

THE CALM AFTER THE STORM

What do you mean, it *worked?*"

Mistress Jane glared at Frazier Gunn, who knelt before her chair by the window, like a criminal begging for his life. Surprisingly, Jane felt more intrigued than angry about this new development. Maybe she would let Gunn live after all.

"I don't know how it happened, Mistress," Gunn grumbled, sweat covering his face. "The Realitants disappeared and took the Barrier Wand with them."

Jane reached over and lifted the Chi'karda Drive from where she'd placed it on the stone ledge of the windowsill. "*How,* exactly, could they do that when I'm holding the heart of the Wand in my hands?"

"George must've winked them out somehow." Gunn kept his eyes fixed on the floor.

"Impossible," Jane said immediately. "I have first-hand reports that George's Wand broke in half. Plus, *you're* the one who said their plan was to go back to the ancient Plague battlefield and get winked hours from now."

"Then how did—"

"SILENCE!" Jane had endured this stupid man for quite long enough. "Leave me. I don't want to see you for a very long time." She dismissed him with a wave of her hand.

"Yes, Mistress."

Jane watched him get to his feet and shuffle away, murmuring incessantly his thanks for her gracious decision to let him live. He was lucky—losing the Wand was a major loss; its parts and mechanisms were equally as important as the Chi'karda Drive itself—but she had much more important things flying through the recesses of her brilliant mind.

How had they done it? How had they manipulated the Chi'karda powerfully enough without the Drive? And in the heart of her personal fortress at that? Did it have something to do with the twisted version of the mysterious force that existed in the Thirteenth Reality? Jane tapped a sharp fingernail against her lips, thinking.

Did one of those bratty kids have some kind of special power over the Chi'karda? Many questions indeed.

The implications were vast, the possibilities endless.

Despite the setback, Mistress Jane smiled.

To any outside observer, it would have seemed as though Tick and his friends had just won the Super Bowl, the World Series, and the NBA Championship in one fell swoop. Having been through so much, and after having hundreds of creepy yellow fangen within inches of tearing them to pieces, winking away to complete safety seemed reason enough to jump up and down, screaming and hugging and cheering and then to start all over again.

"What took you so long!" Paul yelled, whacking Tick on the back with a huge smile on his face.

"I was trying to decide if I wanted to take you or leave you behind," Tick replied, grinning.

They celebrated inside a room very similar to the one they'd left in the Bermuda Triangle, though a much smaller version—a couple of couches, a chair, a cold brick fireplace. A single window was placed directly across from the fireplace, and it looked out upon a dry palette of colors—oranges, reds, browns.

Tick brought his giddiness back to reason and

walked over to get a better look at the view. Beyond their room was a huge drop-off that led to a brown strip of river far below. Sheer walls of striated rock rose up from the valley on all sides, stretching in all directions as far as Tick could see. *This* was the satellite location Master George had said he'd send them to?

It was a canyon. No, it was *the* canyon.

"Are we inside the Grand Canyon?" he asked to no one in particular.

"That we are," Mothball answered. "This big crack's brimming over with Chi'karda, it is."

"Then where are Master George and Rutger?" Sofia asked.

A fallen mood filled the room like a sluggish oil spill, and no one said a word.

⟨⟩

Master George worked furiously on his Barrier Wand, welding and wiring and hammering. He and Rutger had managed to repel the attack from Mistress Jane with an odd assortment of weapons, but not before the creatures had smashed his Wand in half with an axe. At least they'd missed severing the Chi'karda Drive.

Knowing his deadline to pull the Realitants out of the Thirteenth Reality was only a couple of hours away, he wiped the sweat off his brow and doubled his efforts.

"Master George!" Rutger yelled from the other room, followed by the quick series of heavy thumps that always marked the little man running on his short legs.

"What *is* it, Rutger?" Master George asked, annoyed. "Can't you see I'm under considerable duress?"

His friend stopped in the doorway, panting like he'd just run three miles. "Master George!"

"Speak, man, and be quick about it!"

"The nanolocators . . . Mothball, Tick . . . everyone— they winked to our station at the Canyon!"

His old friend's news made Master George regret the harshness of his words. "That's wonderful, Rutger! Wonderful, indeed!" He went back to work on the Wand, very encouraged indeed.

~~~

Three hours after Tick and the others arrived at the Grand Canyon—three long and boring but happy hours—Master George and Rutger suddenly appeared by the fireplace without any warning, disheveled and dirty, but faces beaming.

Tick didn't know how to react; he felt shocked, relieved, elated, confused. He jumped up from the couch, his emotions swirling from all the highs and lows he'd felt since he'd awakened that morning. Mistress Jane's Barrier Wand lay on the couch next to him and he picked it up, excited to show Master George, who was already talking a mile a minute.

"I can hardly believe my eyes, old chaps! You did it, you really did it, indeed! I couldn't be more delighted if Muffintops bore twelve kittens this very instant. Why, I—" He stopped, catching sight of the now-filthy and battered Wand in Tick's hands. "Master Atticus, I simply *knew* you were up to the task. Congratulations to all of you." He focused on the Wand, holding his hands out timidly. "May I, er, see it?"

Tick handed over the golden cylinder, glad to be rid of it.

As soon as Master George took it in his hands, he frowned, his brow crinkling in confusion. "Why, it's so . . . *light*. Has Mistress Jane altered the construction somehow?" He turned the Wand over and unscrewed the bottom until it popped off. He then held the now-open cylinder up to his eye like a telescope, closing his other eye as he examined its insides.

Master George dropped the Wand to his side, a look of complete bewilderment on his face.

"What's the matter?" Mothball asked. "Look like a mum what's lost her kiddies, ya do."

Master George looked at Tick, dark thunderclouds gathering in his eyes.

"What?" Tick asked, taking a step back.

"Have you taken any pieces out of this Wand?"

THE JOURNAL OF CURIOUS LETTERS

Master George asked, his tone accusatory.

"Huh?" Tick looked over at Sofia, then Paul. Both of them shrugged their shoulders. "No. I didn't even know you could open it up."

Master George looked like he didn't believe him. "Young man, you are telling me you used *this* Barrier Wand to wink yourself and these good people to this place?"

"Um . . . yes, sir," Tick stammered, worried he was in serious trouble.

Master George harrumphed and paced around the room, mumbling to himself, throwing his arms up in frustration as if he were in a great argument. He looked like a gorilla on a rampage.

"What in the name of Reality Prime's wrong with ya, Master George?" Mothball asked.

Master George stopped, turning sharply to face the group. "My dear fellow Realitants—because you are all most certainly full-fledged members now—you have all witnessed something that could very well change the Realities forever. Tick, my good man, have you ever had anything remarkable happen before in your life? Something quite . . . miraculous, if you will?"

"Why? What do you mean?" Tick thought of the incident with the letter from Master George that Kayla had burned, and its magical return as though it had never happened. But he didn't want to say anything about it, feeling suddenly very embarrassed and confused.

"I don't *know* what I mean, actually," Master George said. "But you've just done something that defies logic."

"What are you talking about?" Paul asked. "What did Tick do?"

Master George held up the Barrier Wand for everyone to look at. "This Wand is *missing* its Chi'karda Drive." He paused, waiting for a response, as if he'd just revealed a mystery recipe stolen from the Keebler elves, but only Mothball and Rutger reacted, exchanging a startled glance with each other before turning to stare at Tick.

"Good people, this thing is completely useless without the Drive. It cannot *work* without the Drive. Better off using a turnip to wink between Realities."

Tick was stunned, his mind on the cusp of realizing what had happened, but resisting its huge implications.

"Then how did Tick make it work?" Sofia asked.

"I have no idea! All I know is that the only way he could've winked here is by a deliberate control of Chi'karda the likes of which I've never seen in my life."

Master George walked over to Tick, put a hand on his shoulder.

"You, sir, are a walking enigma. This changes everything."

CHAPTER
51

HOMECOMING

The next day and a half were a complete blur for Tick. Mothball broke the news of Annika's death to Master George and Rutger, neither of whom bothered trying to hide their emotions, weeping like children on each others' shoulders. Not much was said after that, except that Annika's courage in sacrificing her life to steal the Barrier Wand would never be forgotten. Tick hadn't known her at all, but he still felt sad she was gone.

As for how Tick had winked them away to safety, no one understood what had happened, least of all Master George. He kept saying that the amount of conviction Tick had channeled, the sheer *energy* of his desire to wink himself and the others back to Reality

Prime should've killed him. It must've been such an unusual display of Chi'karda that the instruments back in the Triangle didn't know how to measure it or surely Rutger would've noticed an anomaly.

Eventually, everyone grew tired of so many questions without answers, and looked ahead to what came next.

Going home.

Master George said that even though Mistress Jane had kept her Chi'karda Drive, it was useless without the Wand casing. It would take her several months to build a new Barrier Wand capable of using its power. For now, she—and her newfound dark and twisted magic—were trapped within the Thirteenth Reality. The new Realitants' successful mission had bought them considerable time, time which Master George needed to repair his headquarters, plan for the future, and think about the potential meaning of Tick's unexplained ability.

As young as the Realitants were, with worried families, Master George thought it best that they return to their homes, explain their futures, and continue their studies—all until such time came that Master George needed them again.

And need them he would, he assured them over and over.

And so late that night, Tick, Sofia, Sato, and Paul stood in a circle by the roaring fire—Master George *loved* fires, even in the middle of the desert in summer—

with Master George and his two assistants, Mothball and Rutger. Everyone was silent, the reality of saying good-bye a heavy weight on their hearts.

As for Tick, he felt like his *soul* hurt. Though he'd only known these people a short time, the experiences they'd been through had solidified them as the very best friends he'd ever had. He felt excited to see his family, but dreaded the thought of going to bed tonight, alone in his room, not knowing how long it might be before he'd see any of the Realitants again. It took every ounce of will in his bones to keep from crying.

"Sato, my young friend," Master George said, finally breaking the somber silence. "I'd like to invite you to stay with us, to help us at the Triangle. These others have families to return to, but, er, well—I think you'd likely agree that joining us at headquarters may be in your best interest. Your, er, guardians will barely notice you're gone, I expect."

Tick looked at Sato, shocked. The quiet boy from Japan hadn't said much since their return from the Thirteenth Reality.

Sato looked up, trying to hide the relief on his face, but failing. "I will stay." He looked at Tick, then the others, as if he wanted desperately to say something. Instead, he folded his arms and looked away.

Tick's whole perception of Sato changed in that instant. *What mysteries are hidden inside that brain of his?*

"We'll be simply delighted to have your help," Master George said. "Now, then, it's almost time to wink everyone back to their homes. But first, I have something to give all of you." He reached into the folds of his suit and pulled out a handful of thin gold-link chains, a heavy pendant swinging from each one. "These will forever mark you as official and bonafide Realitants."

Tick stared at the shiny gold ornament as Master George placed the chain over his head like he'd just won an Olympic medal. Tick studied the object hanging on his chain, bringing it close to his eyes for a better look. It was a miniature replica of a Barrier Wand, dials and all, solid and heavy.

"Be sure and wear them under your shirts," Master George said as he stepped back in front of the group. "No need to go around advertising you're a member of the most important society in the world. Plenty of enemies about."

As Tick tucked the Wand pendant under his scarf and shirt, feeling the cold hardness warm up against his skin, Rutger began passing out small pieces of thick paper to each of the kids. "These are your official membership cards, so don't lose them."

Tick accepted his, a stiff brown card that simply said, "Atticus Higginbottom, Realitant Second Class."

"Whoa," Paul said. "No one will mess with us now.

· I'll just whip this puppy out and they'll run like scared dogs."

"Very funny, young man," Rutger said, folding his chubby arms. "You just be sure and hold on to your Wand pendant and that card—you've earned them both."

"Yes, indeed," Master George said. "And now, we must really let you be on your way. Atticus, your name begins with an A, so let's send you off first."

Tick's stomach leaped into his throat. "Um, okay." He stepped forward.

"Wait a second," Paul said. "We need a send-off to pump us up." He held his hand out to the middle of the circle.

Tick joined him, then Sato, then Rutger, and Mothball. Master George chuckled and put his hand out, too. Rolling her eyes, Sofia finally did as well.

"Go Realitants!" Paul yelled. He groaned at everyone else's half-hearted attempt. "You guys need more team spirit."

"Please tell me we don't have to do that every time," Sofia muttered.

"Yeah," Tick agreed. "I think I'm with Sofia on that."

Paul looked devastated. "She's corrupted you."

Tick shrugged. "It *is* kind of corny." He paused, grinning. "Dude."

Master George cleared his throat. "Time to be off. Atticus, step up here, please."

Tick did so, adjusting the tattered and soppy scarf that clung to his neck like a frightened ferret. Mothball began the good-byes.

"Best of luck, little sir," she said, leaning down to give him a quick hug. "Get a little older and I'll be bringin' ya a nice tall girlfriend from the Fifth, I will. Better than a short fat one from the Eleventh, don't ya think?" She winked and stepped back.

"See ya, big guy," Rutger said, reaching up to pat Tick on the elbow. "Sorry about all the rock-throwing."

Tick laughed. "No problem."

"Later, dude," Paul said next. "See ya on the e-mail."

"Definitely."

Tick turned to Sato, who reached out and shook Tick's hand.

"Thank you," Sato said. "Next time I will save *your* life."

"There's a good plan," Tick replied with a smile. He turned to face Sofia.

She looked at him, her eyes revealing that she was trying to think of a smart-aleck remark. She finally gave up and pulled Tick into a hug, squeezing tightly. "E-mail me," she said. *"Tonight."*

Tick awkwardly patted her on the back. "Remember our bet—you have to come visit me in America. And I want some more free spaghetti sauce, too."

"Count on it." She pulled away, not bothering to hide her tears.

Tick turned to face Master George again, relieved the good-byes were over.

"Master Atticus, my dear friend," the old man said, his ruddy face beaming with a smile. "Your family will be so proud of you, as well they should. Quite a puzzlement you've given us to figure out, I must say. Busy, busy we'll be."

Tick nodded, not knowing what to say.

"Very good, then." Master George held up the Barrier Wand, having already set the controls. "Put your hand on the Wand. There we are."

"Bye everybody," Tick said, closing his eyes, hurting inside.

Master George had one final thing to say, though, whispering in Tick's ear. "Atticus, never forget the inherent power of the Chi'karda. Never forget the power of your choices, for good or for ill. And most importantly, never forget your courage."

Before Tick could reply, he heard a click.

He felt the now-familiar tingle.

Then came the sounds of birds and wind.

Edgar Higginbottom sat on his favorite chair next to the window, staring at the floor, wringing his hands together as he wondered for the millionth time what had happened to Tick. *He's lucky*, Edgar kept telling himself. *All those times as a kid—something's protecting him. He'll be fine.*

But it had been almost four full days since the boy vanished, and the worry ate at Edgar's heart like a hideous disease. Lorena was no better; they could barely look at each other without bursting into tears. Even Lisa was worried.

And yet Edgar knew it had been the right thing to do. Somehow, some way, he *knew*. Atticus Higginbottom was out saving the world, and when he was done, he'd come back home, ready for a new game of Football 3000. But when—

Edgar heard someone shouting outside. A kid's voice. *Tick's* voice.

He looked up, his heart swelling to dangerous sizes when he saw Tick running down the street toward the house. For a second, Edgar couldn't move, couldn't breathe, practically choking as he tried to yell for his wife. *It was him. It was* really *him!*

"Lorena!" Edgar finally managed to scream, squirming to get his big body out of the chair. "Lorena! Tick's back! I *told* you he'd be back!" He found himself laughing, then crying, then laughing again as he ran for the front door.

Lorena thumped down the stairs, faster than he'd ever seen her move in his life. Kayla and Lisa bolted out of the kitchen, eyes wide in surprise.

"He's really here?" Lorena asked, her hand on her heart as if she didn't dare hope Edgar had been telling the truth.

"He's back, he's back!" Edgar yelled with delight as he ripped open the door and ran outside.

Tick ran into his dad's arms, then, almost knocking Edgar down. They hugged each other, then parted to bring Lorena and the girls into the group. In one big tangle of arms, the Higginbottom family hugged and laughed and jumped and generally made complete fools of themselves. The world had suddenly become a very bright and cheerful place to be.

Finally, Tick pulled away, looking at each of his family members in turn.

"I've had a crazy couple of days."

~~~~

Later that night, well after dark, Tick stood in the front yard under a sky thick with black clouds, not a star or moon in sight, thinking.

He thought about everything that had happened to him, but his thoughts kept returning to the bizarre incidents of the letter reappearing in his *Journal of Curious Letters* after Kayla had burned it, and how he'd made the Barrier Wand work even though Mistress Jane had broken it. Somehow, the two events were linked, but Tick couldn't begin to understand why or how. Did he have some kind of weird, freaky power? Or did Mistress Jane do something to the Realities, altering how the Chi'karda functioned?

Master George'll figure it out, Tick thought, trying to ignore how much it scared him.

He turned to walk back inside when the ground around him brightened, the slightest hint of a shadow at his feet. To the east, the full moon appeared, shining through a brief break in the clouds.

As if it were a sign, Atticus Higginbottom, Realitant Second Class, pulled out the Barrier Wand pendant from beneath his shirt and squeezed it in his fist.

EPILOGUE

THE THWARTED MEETING

Reginald Chu, the second best inventor and greatest businessman of all time, looked at his skinwatch again. He sat atop a park bench made from the new Plasticair material his company had created, growing more furious with every passing second. The person who'd asked to meet him here was *late*.

And no one was ever late for the founder, owner, and CEO of Chu Industries.

He reached into his pocket and pulled out the odd note that had been mailed to him several weeks ago, without any kind of return address or postmark. He unfolded the wrinkly paper and read through the handwritten message once again.

Dear Mister Chu,

You don't know me, but we must meet very soon. I know you are aware of the Realities, but that you have never had much interest in them because the Fourth is so much more advanced than the others. But I have a proposition for you that I am certain you will accept. I know of your love for power.

As a measure of my sincerity, I will come to your Reality. Meet me in Industry Park by the Lone Oak at noon on the thirteenth of May.

Your future partner,
Mistress Jane

Reginald crumpled the note up into a ball, squeezing it in his fist. The audacity of this woman. Commanding him to meet her like he was some errand-running schoolboy—and then having the nerve to not even show up? Who called themselves *Mistress* anyway?

He looked at his skinwatch one last time, then stood up. The lady was obviously not coming.

As he walked back toward his building, Reginald

threw the mysterious note into a roving Recycabot, angry about the time he'd wasted. There was much to be done, things he'd mapped out and set in motion long before he'd received a letter from today's no-show, Mistress Jane.

Reginald was a very busy man.

A Glossary of People, Places, and all Things Important

Alterant—Different versions of the same person who exist in different Realities. It is extremely dangerous for Alterants to meet each other.

Annika—A spy for the Realitants who spends many months slowly gaining Mistress Jane's trust.

Atticus Higginbottom—Also known as Tick, a thirteen-year-old resident of Deer Park, Washington. He is very smart and loves to play chess, and often suffers cruelty at the hands of bullies. He begins receiving very strange letters that lead him toward a dangerous destiny.

Barf Scarf—A red-and-black scarf that Tick wears at all times to hide the ugly birthmark on his neck.

Barrier Wand—The device used to wink people and things between Realities and between heavily concentrated places of Chi'karda within the *same* Reality. To transport humans, they must be in a place concentrated with Chi'karda (like a cemetery) and have a nanolocator that transmits their location to the Wand. It is useless without the Chi'karda Drive, which channels and magnifies the mysterious power.

Bermuda Triangle—For reasons unknown, this is the most concentrated area of Chi'karda in each Reality.

Billy "The Goat" Cooper—Tick's nemesis at Jackson Middle School.

Chi'karda—The mysterious force that controls quantum physics. It is the scientific embodiment of conviction and choice, which in reality rules the universe. Responsible for creating the different Realities.

Chi'karda Drive—The invention that revolutionized the universe, able to harness, magnify, and control

Chi'karda. It has long been believed that travel between Realities is impossible without it.

Chu Industries—The company that practically rules the Fourth Reality. Known for countless inventions and technologies—some that are helpful and useful, others that are malicious in nature.

Command Center—Master George's headquarters in the Bermuda Triangle where Chi'karda levels are monitored and to where his many nanolocators report various types of information.

Edgar Higginbottom—Tick's father. Though overweight and not exactly handsome, he is instantly loved by anyone who meets him. A very light sleeper.

Fangen—The sickening abomination of a creature created by Mistress Jane, utilizing the twisted and mutated version of Chi'karda found in the Thirteenth Reality. Formed from a variety of no less than twelve different animals, the fangen are bred to kill and ask questions later. They can also fly.

Fragmented—When a Reality begins losing Chi'karda levels on a vast scale and can no longer maintain itself as a major alternate version of the world, it will eventually fragment and disintegrate into nothing.

Frazier Gunn—A loyal servant of Mistress Jane, though he hopes to replace her one day.

Frupey—Nickname for Fruppenschneiger, Sofia's butler.

Gnat Rat—A malicious invention of Chu Industries from the Fourth Reality. Releases dozens of mechanical hornets that are programmed to attack a certain individual based on a nanolocator, DNA, or blood type.

Grand Canyon—A satellite location of the Realitants. Second only to the Bermuda Triangle in Chi'karda levels.

Hans Schtiggenschlubberheimer—The man who started the Scientific Revolution in the Fourth Reality in the early nineteen hundreds. In a matter of decades, he helped catapult the Fourth far beyond the other Realities in terms of technology.

Kayla Higginbottom—Tick's four-year-old sister. Loves to burn things and have tea parties.

Kyoopy—Nickname used by the Realitants for quantum physics.

Lisa Higginbottom—Tick's fifteen-year-old sister. Horrible on the piano.

Lorena Higginbottom—Tick's mother. Loves to cook, and could sleep through a raging tornado.

Mabel Ruth Gertrude Higginbottom Fredrickson— Edgar's aunt, long since widowed, who lives in Alaska. Hasn't seen any of her family members in years.

Master George—The current leader of the Realitants. Overwhelmed by the betrayal of Mistress Jane, he sets out to strengthen his forces, sending out a series of tests and riddles to help him find worthy candidates. Loves his cat, Muffintops.

Mistress Jane—A former Realitant and the biggest traitor the world has ever known. When she discovered the Thirteenth Reality and its twisted, mutated version of Chi'karda, she quickly realized the power she could have for herself and the potential for ruling the universe. Her plans are only beginning. Loves the color yellow and is bald.

Mothball—A Realitant from the Fifth Reality, she is fiercely loyal to Master George. Regrets her name, which was given to her without much forethought by her father. Realizes she fared better than her twin sister, Toejam.

Ms. Sears—Tick's favorite librarian. Has funny hair that looks like a cleaning pad.

Muffintops—Master George's cat. Can't speak English, but loves milk.

Multiverse—A term used by Reality Prime scientists to explain the theory that quantum physics has created multiple versions of the universe.

Nanolocator—A microscopic electronic device that can crawl into a person's skin and forever provide information on their whereabouts and Chi'karda levels, among other information.

Nitwit—The unfortunately named servant child of Mistress Jane. Like those before her, Nitwit has been given the ability to fly, based on a manipulation of Chi'karda. Replaced Jane's prior child servant, Nincompoop.

Norbert Johnson—A post office worker in Macadamia, Alaska. Is terrified of Mistress Jane based on only one encounter.

Paul Rogers—A thirteen-year-old Realitant recruit from Florida. Loves surfing and playing the piano.

Pick—Master George's nickname for a major decision in which a person's Chi'karda levels spike considerably. Some Picks have been known to create or destroy entire Realities.

Quantum Physics—The science that studies the physical world of the extremely small. Most scholars are baffled by its properties and at a loss to explain them. Theories abound. Only a few know the truth: that a completely different power rules this realm, which in turn rules the universe: Chi'karda.

Realitants—An organization sworn to discover and charter all known Realities. Founded in the 1970s by a group of scientists from the Fourth Reality, the early Realitants used Barrier Wands to recruit other quantum physicists from other Realities. Their focus changes when one of their best betrays them and they decide they must seek out not only people of science, but those who have the courage, intelligence, and strength—along with the innocence of youth—to fight in the coming months and years.

Realities—A separate and complete version of the world, of which there may be an infinite number. The most stable and strongest reality is called Reality Prime. So far, twelve major branches of Reality Prime have been discovered. Realities are created and destroyed by enormous fluctuations in Chi'karda levels.

Fourth—Much more technologically advanced than the other Realities, due to the remarkable vision and work of Hans Schtiggenschlubberheimer.

Fifth—Quirks in evolution led to a very tall human race.

Eighth—The world is covered in water due to much higher temperatures, caused by a star fusion anomaly triggered in another galaxy by an alien race.

Eleventh—Quirks in evolution and diet led to a short and robust human race.

Thirteenth—A mutated and very powerful version of Chi'karda exists here. It is a world full of magic and darkness.

Reginald Chu—Tick's science teacher who shares the same name as the person in the Fourth Reality who founded Chu Industries and turned it into a world-wide empire. They may be Alterants of each other.

Rutger—A Realitant from the Eleventh Reality, he is best friends with Mothball. Works as Master George's right-hand man in the Command Center. Loves to throw rocks at Tick.

Sato—A fourteen-year-old Realitant recruit from Japan. He has a dark secret that makes him very reluctant to ever trust another Realitant.

Shockpulse—An injection of highly concentrated electromagnetic nanobots that seek out and destroy the tiny components of a nanolocator, rendering it useless.

Snooper Bug—A hideous crossbreed of birds and insects created by the mutated power of the Chi'karda in the Thirteenth Reality. Can detect any known weapon or poison and can kill with one quick strike of its needle-nosed beak. Pet of Mistress Jane.

Sofia Pacini—A twelve-year-old Realitant recruit from Italy. From an extremely wealthy family, she is tougher than nails and has no problem displaying it.

Sound Slicer—A small device that shoots out a heavily concentrated force of sound waves, almost too low for the human ear to register but powerful enough to knock something senseless if caught in its direct path.

Tick—Nickname for Atticus Higginbottom.

Tingle Wraith—A collection of microscopic creatures from the Second Reality, called spilphens, that can form together into a cloud while rubbing against each other to make a horrible sound called the Death Siren. After thirty seconds, this sound does unpleasant things to a human, but has never been known to actually kill one. Chu Industries has developed a way to train and program the Wraiths to form into the shape of a creepy old man's face (for fright effect) and appear to a certain individual based on a nanolocator, DNA, or blood type.

Windbike—An invention of Chu Industries, this vehicle is a motorcycle that can fly, consuming hydrogen directly out of the air for its fuel. Based on an extremely complex gravity-manipulation theorem first proposed by Reginald Chu.

Winking—The act of traveling between or within Realities by use of a Barrier Wand. Causes a slight tingle to a person's shoulders and back.

DISCUSSION QUESTIONS

1. Tick meets many strange people while solving the Twelve Clues, like Mothball, the tall and lanky woman with an unfortunate name, and Rutger, the short fat man from the Eleventh Reality. At first, Tick is scared of them both but soon learns to like and trust them. What lessons can we learn from that?

2. After his first fright with the Gnat Rat, Tick is tempted to burn the first letter from Master George. After much deliberation, he makes the choice to continue on, knowing that some important cause must exist behind it all. What does this teach us about courage and sacrifice? Would you have burned the letter?

3. When Tick and his dad travel to Alaska to investigate the postmark of the first letter, they find that Norbert Johnson has retreated to his home, scared to death that Mistress Jane will return to seek vengeance. They help him confront his fear and return to society and to the job he loves. How do you think that applies to your own life?

4. Tick wears a scarf to hide the ugly red birthmark on his neck. Do you think that's necessary? Is there something about yourself that you hide from others? Should you?

5. We learn in the story that every choice a person makes can lead to drastic changes in other Realities. How can we relate that to the choices in our own lives, and to the enormous consequences we may experience?

6. Tick debates whether or not he should tell his parents about the letters and the clues, but decides to do so in the end. Why do you think it's important to trust our parents and confide in them, even about the really hard things?

7. We find out in the end that it was actually Master George who sent the many frightening dangers that

Tick encountered while investigating the clues. Master George tells Tick that he did so to test his courage and help him grow into the kind of person capable of working as a Realitant. How can this perspective help you face the many trials and tough times thrown at you in your own life?

CHAPTER
1

THE TWO FACES OF
REGINALD CHU

Reginald Chu, founder and CEO of Chu Industries, stood within his massive laboratory, studying the latest test results from the ten-story-tall Darkin Project as he awaited word on the abduction of his Alterant from Reality Prime. It amused him to know the science teacher would be brought to the same building in which he stood—a dangerous prospect at best, certain death at worst. Mixing with alternate versions of yourself from other Realities was like playing dentist with a cobra.

Which is why his employees had been given strict instructions to never bring the *other* Reginald Chu within five hundred feet of the *real* Reginald Chu (the one who mattered most in the universe anyway). The look-alike would be locked away in a maximum-security cell deep in the lower chambers of Chu Industries, ready to serve his dual purpose in being kidnapped.

Dual purpose. Reginald took a deep breath, inhaling the smells of electronics and burnt oil that assaulted his senses. He reflected on the plan he had set into motion once the information poured in from his network of spies in the other Realities. Most intriguing developments with massive potential consequences—especially the bit about the boy named Atticus Higginbottom.

If Reginald were not the most supreme example of rational intelligence ever embodied in a human being—and he most certainly *was*—he would have doubted the truth of what he'd heard and had verified by countless sources. It seemed impossible on the face of it—tales of magic and power, unspeakable ability in the manipulation of the most central force in the universe: Chi'karda.

But Reginald knew it could all be explained within the complex but perfectly understood realm of science. Still, the possibilities thrilled him. The boy had no idea what was at stake. He had something Reginald Chu wanted, and no predicament in the world could be more dangerous.

Reginald walked over to the airlift, which ascended along the surface of the tall project device, allowed his retina to be scanned, then pushed the button for the uppermost level. As the low whine of the hovervator kicked in, lifting him toward the false sky of the large chamber, he heard the slightest beep from his nanophone, nestled deep within the hollow of his ear.

"Yes?" he said in a sharp clip, annoyed at being disturbed even though he'd *told* Benson to contact him as soon as he returned.

"We have him." Benson's soft voice echoed in Reginald's mind as if spoken from a long-dead spirit.

"Good. Is he harmed? Did you raid his house and gather his . . . *things?*" The airlift came to a stop with a soft bump, and Reginald stepped onto the metal-grid catwalk encircling his grandest scientific experiment to date. From here, all he could see was the shiny golden surface of the enormous cylinder, dozens of feet wide, reflecting back a distorted image of his face that made him look monstrous.

"Everything went as planned. No blips."

Reginald pointed a finger in the air, even though he knew Benson couldn't see him. "Don't you dare bring that sorry excuse for a Chu near me—not even close. There's no guarantee which one of us would flip into the Nonex. I want him locked away—"

"Done," Benson interrupted.

Reginald frowned at his underling's tone and took note to watch him closely, in case his lapse in judgment developed into something more akin to insubordination.

"Bring his belongings to me and ready him for the Darkin injection."

"Yes, sir. Right away, sir." Reginald's nanophone detected a faint quiver in Benson's voice.

Aha, Reginald thought. Benson had realized his mistake and was trying to make up for it with exaggerated respect. *Stupid man.*

"As soon as we infect him," Reginald said, "we'll need to start preparing. You've checked and rechecked that they're all there?"

"Yes, sir. The three of them will be together for another two days. Then school starts after the weekend."

"You're *sure?*" Reginald didn't want to waste any more time away from his project than he must.

"I've seen them with my own eyes," Benson said, the slightest hint of condescension in his voice. "They'll have no reason to suspect anything. Your plan is flawless."

Reginald laughed, a curt chortle that ended abruptly. "You always know what to say, Benson. A diplomat among diplomats—one not ashamed to squeeze a man's throat until he sputters his last cough. A perfect combination."

"Thank you, sir."

"Call me when you're ready." Reginald blinked hard, ending the call.

Clasping his hands behind his back, Reginald paced the wide arc of the Darkin Project, his carnival-mirror reflection bobbing up and down in the polished, cold metal. He loved doing this, loved the feeling he got when the words that lay imprinted in large black letters on the other side appeared in his vision. He slowed for dramatic effect, reaching out his left hand to trace the first letter. A few more steps and he stopped, slowly turning toward the cylinder to look at the two words for the thousandth time—though the thrill of it was no less than the first glimpse had provided.

Two words, spanning the length of his outstretched arms. Two words, black on gold. Two words that would change the Realities forever.

Dark Infinity.

NOW AVAILABLE FROM ALADDIN

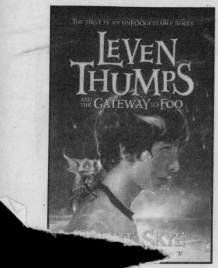

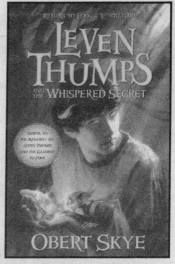

...Foo is in chaos, and only
Leven has the power to save it.

Leven and his friends travel across Foo to
restore Geth as the rightful king.

The war to unite Foo and Reality has
begun, and Leven is in for the adventure
of a lifetime.

Can Leven discover his new power before
the Dearth finds him?